Exodus

Volume II
The Orion War

by

Kali Altsoba

SECOND EDITION

About the Author

Kali Altsoba is the pen name used to publish future military fiction by the award winning military historian, Cathal J. Nolan. He is the author of multivolume works of international and military history. He received the top international award for military history in 2018, the *Gilder Lehrman Prize*, for his acclaimed *The Allure of Battle* (Oxford UP). His histories have been feature reviewed in academic and military journals, the *New York Times, Wall Street Journal*, and *The National*. He has given public lectures in Argentina, Britain, Canada, Israel, and all across the United States. Recent venues include the Chautauqua Institute, National World War II Museum, New York Historical Society, the U.S. Army Combined Arms Center at Ft. Leavenworth, the Ministry of Foreign Affairs (Kabul, Afghanistan), National Intelligence University, World Affairs Forum, and Center for Military and Diplomatic History. He has interviewed for or appeared on CBS Radio, Fox Radio, Radio Free Europe, Newstalk (Ireland), BBC *Mundo*, PBS and C-Span. He regularly consults on military historical research to the PBS series *NOVA*. He is featured on camera in the 2018 *NOVA* documentary on Dunkirk.

Author's Note (First Edition)

Some events in this series derive from real world acts of war, including war crimes and atrocities adapted from After Action reports, combat memoirs and eyewitness accounts. They come from widely varied armies, times and cultures, in dozens of wars across many centuries. The result is often grim and not for the fainthearted, cruel and pitiless, but true to the wide human experience of war waged over time. As dark as the tale becomes, as savage as some characters and combat depictions are, I hope my effort to root this series in a deeply human experience of the high politics of empire and the brutality of war will be rewarding to some readers.

Author's Note (Second Edition)

This book is reorganized, rewritten, and expanded. Three new chapters are added, along with character and situational development in all other chapters. The story develops earlier themes in the series, adds plot twists and enhanced character arcs that continue in follow on books. Combat depictions may echo real events drawn from veteran experience, but are all reset within a complex weave of character development and future war that is reshaping the history of the Thousand Worlds of Orion yet to come. There are numerous literary references woven into names, plot twists, characters, and dialogue. Some are explicit. Many are left implicit, as a kind of cultural "easter egg" for curious readers to discover and explore.

Contents

"If some god shall wreck me in the wine dark deep, even so I will endure. For already have I suffered full much, and much have I toiled in perils of waves and war."

Homer
The Odyssey

Toruń

The RIK landed on Genève months ago, falling out of the sky in waves of armtrak loaders and heavy troop carriers, protected by swarms of skycraft and low swooping drones. Now the flames of war lick at the outer defenses of Toruń, the place offworld tourists call the "Golden City of Wood." A quiet place for a large city, surrounded by vast, ancient forests, it's known to its more humble inhabitants as "Arbor City." Today, it is the last place of active resistance on all Genève, its garrison holding out around the great berm that surrounds the forest sanctuary. Everyone inside is waiting on the last, surging RIK assault on the berm. Waiting for the city to fall. Worse, waiting for catastrophic bombardment by fire that must raze wooden Toruń to ashen ruins, as the enemy has already razed the great forests of Northland to blackened stubs all around.

Toruń City resides a thousand klics inside its namesake woods. With access to abundant forest on Genève all towers are wooden, all its streets are laid down with beams of supercompressed timber. None of it was hewn in the deep northern forests. All building wood was brought north from permit cutting areas far beyond the old growth preserves, from Southland's vast tree farms. There's a tradeoff for cheap, renewable material. The structural height limit for wood buildings is thirty stories. No great towers rise in Toruń like they do in hairbrush rows in the Calmari twin capital of Lowestoft-on-Stamos; no ultrasteel and superconcrete monsters that literally scrape the top of the sky. The payoff is a wooden city with golden streets and gold and silver forest hues in every structure and sidewalk and street. And always and everywhere, a rich smell of deep forest under the urban bustle of Genève's only spaceport and large city.

Two lakes inside the walls, an ever wet northern climate to refill them, and vigilant and dutiful citizens ensure that Toruń has the water and the will to fight any fire that might break out. But the real city defense is not water and hoses or even its people. It's supercompressed wood that can hardly burn, and retardant microcoating. The fire tek system has worked for almost ten centuries, ensuring that a building might burn a rare time or two, but Toruń will not. At least not by accident. What the grim invader will do when he arrives is a different question.

To protect from wildfires a firebreak has circled Toruń down all the centuries. A wide perimeter and moat meets a final defense in a high earthen wall 100 meters tall and 300 meters thick, covered base to rampart by superhydrophobic concrete of immense compressive and armored strength. The berm wall sharply defined and limited city growth, but Toruń's tightknit community always liked it that way.

Toruń hasn't expanded upward or outward in the last 400 years. It may be the most contented place in all the Thousand Worlds of Orion. Or it was.

Already Toruń is shrouded in smoke and coated in ash. But not all of it came from fires set by the RIK. When enemy landers first fell on Southland, even before the RIK made the fast jump across open water to gain a toehold on the northern continent then break its Main Defense Line, General Amiya Constance did not wait for fire and war to burn a wicked path to Toruń. "Reinforce fire retardant on all towers, Firechief. I want roof sprayers and tanks as well as anti-skycraft guns on every rooftop. And soak all alleys and sidewalks with flameout, too."

"Soak, sir?"

"Triple the annual spray. Wait, belay that order. Use it all."

"All? Every ton of reserve?"

"Yes, chief. I want to wade in fire retardant. Hold nothing back. There's no point now."

"Yes general. I understand: soak Toruń until our people protest that they need waders."

"Exactly so, chief. But first send your crews and all your heavy equipment to the Berm Gate tomorrow morning. At first light. Everyone and everything that you can spare."

"May I ask why, general? Shouldn't we disperse them across the city and start soaking the streets and tower canyons as you want?"

"Not yet. First, we're going to start a fire."

"What?"

"Around the berm. I want you to burn the forest back at least another klic. We don't want to leave untreated wood so close for the enemy to use when he gets here, either for fuel or to build his siege huts and redoubts. And he *will* get here. When he does, I want clean fields-of-fire for wall gunners and berm defenders. We can't hit what we can't see. His field camo is at least as good as ours. Let's not allow our beloved old woods to give him any additional help."

"Yes general. A controlled burn around the entire city. *Hmmm* ... That's quite a fire you want, general."

"Then you better hop to it chief. The clock is running."

The interior city is quartered by smaller earthen walls, living growth on top and strong roots holding the soil in place. All Toruń smells of woody attars, moss, grass, sweet saps and musty woodland. Streets and short towers glow gold at night as amber lights reflect off deep grained ligneous streets and varnished buildings. "Golden City of Wood" isn't just a touristy slogan or illusion. It's the abiding visual reality and one of the deepest prides of all Genèvens.

A solitary road arrives hesitantly from the southeast. It's allowed to cross the outer moat, thence cut straight through the berm via a sternly guarded Gate. Four other forest roads form a semicircular route outside the city wall until they meet the first, joining just before the spot where the only moat bridge crosses under the berm as a single passage. The system is neat, well scaled, orderly and regular. Just like all prewar Genève. And its sturdy and proud freefolk.

Then war came and a tsunami of woeful refugees threatened to overflow the moat and berm as the defenders at the MDL gave way. The main body of KRA broke apart all along the coast, then tried but failed to reform at an improvised inner defense line. The remnants ran in broken bits to the edge of the forest zone, a lucky few managing to squeeze inside. Millions more civilians crowded along the forest roads, all leading to the Berm Gate and quiet Toruń.

The five rivers of refugees kept flowing until Toruń's population was swollen to three times its prewar size, with half again that number crowded outside the berm desperate to get in. So many fleeing soldiers and civilians asked for passage into the city that residents and local officials who at first welcomed and aided their country kinfolk panicked shamefully. It happened all at once, when a crowd gathered before Governance Hall demanding that Toruń be sealed off. The prewar mayor stood up before the sullen mob milling in the city's main square.

He's never been at war before, so he still sounds like a peacetime politician spinning the old tales, until he slips in a quick line about two Grün luxury liners that everyone knows were trapped in-system by the war and forced to ground. "Toruń is old and conservative but also modern and cosmopolitan. It's a haven for our artists, and for many of Orion's artists and writers, poets and teachers. There has always been room inside the berm for offworld Krevans and friendlies.

Our wonderful city is full of natural wonders and naturally wonderful people. And a haven even for a few unfriendly farfolk, for we are better than our enemies."

"*Booo!* There's no place here for Grünen! Expel all farfolk!"

He's startled, but recovers quickly and deflects blame. "To where? Into the forest? I would like nothing better than to kick out all those stranded from the tourist liners, but General Constance says they pose more danger wandering in the woods, where they would aid the advancing enemy."

"*Hissssss!* It's our city, *ours*. Not theirs. Not hers, either!"

"That issue is closed. By order of the garrison commander, not by me."

"*Shame, shame!*"

"A shame it is! But let me say this. Your city government still has some say over refugees. Toruńites always lived side-by-side in civic peace. Now a medieval siege is coming. Barbarians will be on the hills and in our woods, lobbing rockets, mortars and plasma over the berm. We have room in our hearts for our refugees but no more room in our streets or our homes." Well, that didn't take long. Sensing the ugly mood, he has already decided to go beyond expelling farfolk to blocking any more Genèvens from entering the city.

"Huzzah!" That's more like it. They cheer him now, knowing that he will cave to their cheers faster than to their threats. He's a hollow man, easily filled with frothy nothings, cheaply bought and turned by praise.

"As your mayor, I hereby order the Berm Gate closed. It's now barred to any more refugees."

"*Huzzah, huzzah!*"

"I do this because our beloved wooden city has reached full capacity." They smell his weakness. They want more.

"You're wrong! We're overstuffed already!"

"Kick them out! Kick them out!"

"You should've closed the Gate a week ago, two weeks ago!"

"I shall close it now. And I'll triple the guard."

"You lie! You're not the garrison commander."

"I'll use Toruń police."

"*Huzzah!*"

"I will stand guard myself, if I have to!"

"*Vive! Vive le maire!*"

He still can't let go of his prewar persona, or of politics. He has no idea how much Toruń and Genève have changed. How much change is coming to all the Thousand Worlds. Has he any shame at all? "Yet, let me say this. I'm closing the Gate today so that no more refugees enter Toruń. But we must never forget the kind, generous folk that we Toruńites are and will forever be."

He says it to a mob already forgetting who they once were. Satisfied with its easy victory, the mob turns back into a crowd, then breaks up into little clots of family or friends and disperses into the city. It has cheered him for giving up so quickly on what it wants, and now it starts to trickle home or back to work. It will reform and return tomorrow, or the next day. Always demanding more of him. For the mob has seen how easily this callow mayor gives in.

On the terrified refugees come, barred from entry or not. They arrive at the berm from all over Northland. A horde of gray ghosts gathers outside the city, hundreds of thousands, filling the wider firebreak General Constance made. They crowd against the berm, spill onto the bridge to press against and plead with young and embarrassed Gate guards. They're kids, in it way over their heads. "Please officer, a little water? I've not drunk in three days and my mouth is full of ash."

"Here, take my canteen."

"I need water too!"

"That was my last. Sorry."

"Mercy, a little mercy for my old mother. Won't you let her in?"

"I can't. I have my orders from..."

"What kind of orders are those to obey, to keep your own people out?"

"Please, please. I must get to Toruń market to buy *juhtúró* for my baby." It's a traditional quark dish made of ewe's milk. The guard the young mother bars from entry gives it to her own kids daily. She gave a wooden bowl of quark just this morning to her littlest one, who drank it greedily and asked for more.

"Sergeant, can we let this mother in? Just this one?"

"No. Stand your post. And stop talking to the refugees."

"What's going on here officers?"

"Nothing captain. It's all under control."

"Captain, are you a police captain? *You* can let us in!"

"Stand back! We have orders from the mayor."

"He's not *our* mayor!"

"Sergeant, no one gets past this line for any reason."

"Yes captain. Officers, do your jobs. Move these people back."

"You, yes you, mother. You must turn away. Go back."

"Go back where? There is no other place on all Genève."

"Go now! Troopers, push these people back."

Low flying Jabos stay away for awhile, distracted by Brusilov's fiery search for Madjenik in the southern forests. They're far more discouraged from direct attacks on the city by Toruń's bristle brush of anti-skycraft cannon, mounted on every tower roof and all along the berm wall. There is no angle of air attack that doesn't lead RIK skycraft into rising sheets of lethal energy. The guns fire curtain walls of *orange* and *green* plasma that unite on high to look like brilliant borealis over the city, even in daytime. Sheets of plasma shudder into hurtling skycraft, bringing the vulnerable Jabos crashing down to burn out as ploughing gouges in the ground, or smacking into the high trees of Toruń Woods. More bombers are lost to *starstreak* high velocity missiles that leap like mountain cats from the rooves of the tallest buildings, to claw surprised enemy pilots from the sky. Jabo pilots hate *starstreaks*, even more than sheet plasma.

"We have no missile like it, major general, sir."

"Who the fuck are you?"

"RIK liaison for skycraft support, sir."

"Tell me again what the problem is?"

"Our low attack Jabos and even the higher flying Raptors are vulnerable to their ground-to-air missiles, *shōshō*. Much more vulnerable than anticipated."

"Why? We're the Imperium. How can it be that they have better weapons?"

"Just this one. Well, I have to say their infantry's field camo is pretty good, too. We've had a helluva time picking off strays, ever since we broke their line."

"I know. I'm scouring this fucking forest with my infantry, looking for bandits under every bush and tree root."

"Back to the Jabos, sir. RSU has completed its analysis, *shōshō*. They say we haven't prepared proper skycraft because prewar we were too focused only on offensive operations."

"What? What kind of excuse is that?"

"Not an excuse, sir. Just an explanation. Rikugun weps designers were not told to make ready for this kind of long war at all, expecting nothing but swift victory, an endless advance on and above the ground. Never a city siege."

"Then we should have the firepower to blast through that godsdamn berm."

"Well sir, it looks like the designers not thinking too much about defense affected the way they thought about offense, too. Especially with our Jabos."

"What do you mean?"

"We maximized punching over counterpunching, firepower over armor. Our skycraft are all attack and almost no defense. One hit, even a glancing laser or plasma pulse, and they come tumbling down. So we've had to pull way back on bombing the berm wall, as you know."

"Well that's too bad for them. The designers. I want the name of the man in charge, of the Jabos especially. We're losing them by the hundreds. I want his head delivered to Pyotr."

"*Umm*, it was done already, *shōshō*."

"When?"

"Last week. I sent a squad to Daegu to pick him up. They crated the head, *hmmm*, he was bald by the way, and shipped it to Pyotr on Kestino."

"Was my name attached to the gift?"

"Of course, general. We knew you would want that."

"Well done. What's your name? I want you on my headquarters staff. You're a man who knows how to fight this fucking war."

When it's clear that RIK has no counter to the city's sheet plasma and *streaker* missile defenses it grounds all skycraft. Everyone on the berm wall and in the city knows that the hated dive bombers will be back. Hundreds, if not thousands, of them. But before that happens, the invaders try something else.

Kaigun ships are called in, to do a favor for Rikugun. The admirals are happy to comply, to show up the junior and rival service. But cruisers and Zerstörers fare little better. Great plasma tubes with "*bowels full of wrath and ready mounted*," spit indignation upward, above the blue Genèven sky into the first whispers of orbital space. It's a real deterrent. Several warships chance "flying the gap" over the city, to drop ice rounds and spray 'gougers' like those used over Southland. They score hits in the outer city, but pay a high price in broken armor plating, smashed engines and dead crew. After two days, the warships pull back, too.

"It's Rikugun's problem, not ours. Leave it to those ground hugging idiots to solve, but get my warships out of harms' way."

"What now, *shōshō*?"

"Wreck the city with our heavy artillery. I don't want to hear about their shields. Bring down those wooden towers they're so proud of in flames atop their heads. Then we'll go in on the ground. Fuck casualties."

One of his officers wonders. '*Does he mean civilians inside the city or out here among his own troops when he attacks?*' He means both.

"There'll be heavy casualties, sir."

"What of it? It's what Rikugun is for. My men are the scum of all the worlds, mere scum of the worlds. It's a wonder we can accomplish anything with them."

"Agreed, still…"

"I want blunt force trauma."

"This will slow things down, *shōshō.* It will wreck the city, too."

"What must be done, must be done. Start the drills, colonel. Practice them up. Get all brigades ready to assault the berm when I give the word. We'll go for three breaches at once. In the meantime, keep pounding them with my artillery."

It will be up to Rikugun's overwhelming ground forces to take Toruń in the old fashioned way. With brute force and raging murder, face-to-face with hand weapons and blood splattered on their combat weaves. They're on their way to the berm in huge numbers, encircling the city, settling down outside the ramparts.

Tramp, tramp, tramp.

Black boots pound the roads in unison.

Rat-a-tat-a-tat.

Snare drums call and mark the pace.

Tramp, tramp, tramp.

The RIK is snaking over Northland in long green columns. It's coming ever closer to Toruń Wood, driving all before it. The first scouts have reached the forest edge. Hear the drum call the grim battalions into staggered firing lines? Hear the sergeants bark out brutal orders?

"Oh my gods, no!"

"What are they doing?"

"Run! Run!"

Too late for that.

Listen to the soldiers shooting.

***

That same day, Raptors and Jabos strafe and bomb and burn out the five Old Forest Roads, setting Toruń Wood ablaze along with all the people trapped and pressed, crushed and panicking inside. With no way out. That's the day RIK Jabos start the "Great Fire of Toruń" that burns for a month, and smolders still.

"It's just as well to end it fast," whisper safe cynics and realists inside the city, sharing a rare private agreement among a surprising number of those safe inside.

One very fat man says it right out loud. "The Great Fire will melt five swollen glaciers of refugees flowing along the forest trails to just a trickle arriving at our berm and Gate. Once the dam holds, we can negotiate an end." He likes to use overly colorful metaphors in everyday speech. He thinks it marks him off from the common crowd as a man of refined wit and intellect. Afterward, he sits down and eats another mockmeat pie.

Skycraft pass overhead, heading back to base. The great fires move in from the roads into the deep woods. Tens of thousands of survivors stumble among the dead and dying along five charred paths. Most drop within a day or three, too burned or too dismayed to continue up the path that Zofia calls *Chemin des Mort.*

Only those at the top of the burned out funnels reach the berm, staggering out of ragged smog that covers all inside the city in layers of snowy ash and fine black soot. The soot settles over everything, like Harmattan dust. It's gritty. It's inescapable. Take a duster, wipe the black powder off the kitchen table, swipe away a dusky mix of what was just a few days ago a forest, animals and people. It won't make any difference. In half-an-hour you must do it again.

Red faced and dehydrated, many also badly burned, the last arrivals stand before guilty guards. They stare silently yet somehow plaintively from scorched and scarred faces with no eyebrow sentries left above haunted, unblinking eyes. A phalanx of gray ghosts assembles outside the city, rank upon rank pressing forward, huddling, whimpering, crying, dying. Pushing futilely on the backs of gray others locked outside by order of a mayor acting to placate fear of a mob that can't think beyond its fear. It has come to this at the Gate blocking access to Arbor City, the last free standing community and refuge on Genève.

After nine days of rising anger, General Amiya Constance, Toruń Garrison commander, has seen and heard enough. When Jabos return on the 10th day to hurl missiles and drop ball plasma on hapless civvies too crowded and crammed to escape another hard rain of death, when the Berm Gate *still* stays closed on mayoral order, Constance declares martial law. Army squads are sent to arrest the startled, protesting mayor and each and every councilor who voted to bar the Gate.

Another angry mob gathers to free its puppet mayor. It's rapidly dispersed by a scorching whiff of maser fire that General Constance orders sent low over the protestors' heads, with the next volley held ready to fire at chest and face height. A few civilian fools think she won't do it and rush the Toruń jail. They fall in smoking piles of astonishment and disbelief. The mob dissolves and runs.

Her first edict is "redouble the berm guard and clear the bridge and approach streets on this side of the Gate." Her second is to "raise the portcullis for two days, then one hour each day after that. Screen all applicants for entry. Refuse any who fail. Let in all the rest."

Over 200 civilians are crushed against the Gate or trampled the first time the portcullis goes up, before angry guards shoot down the most panicky offenders pushing too hard from behind, and regain control. Fast but orderly screening resumes as a surge of refugees squeezes through and over the bridge. Eager to get under the city's bombardment shield to escape the darting and diving Jabos that are growing ever more daring in their attacks, urged on by an angry *shōshō*.

As the Gate lifts each morning for just one hour, more pitiable supplicants are vetted. Any small suspicion, and some guard turns away a crying petitioner with a hard *thump*, warns off two more with a threatening wave of his maser pistol. Others pass through as quickly as they can, never once looking up or back. Wild rumors say that Krevan speaking infiltrators are trying to get into Toruń to burn the city down, that ethnic arsonists who speak Genèven dialects and know local places, foods and folkways, are sneaking into the city.

"Filthy traitors. Damn fifth columnists!" Maybe it's true, or maybe not. The Gate Guards take no chances. Anyone without Genèven ID is turned back, even if they speak Krevan with one of the local accents. No appeals. General Constance is absolute about the guards enforcing that.

The last to arrive are all badly burned, straining Toruń's medical resources. Food's not a problem though. Huge granaries along the export quays that served this agrarian world in better times heave with the spring harvest, even though the last collections of summer crops were left unclaimed with arrival of the Kaigun in orbit and the Rikugun ground assault. Too many youths were pulled from the summer harvest to don uniform and head out to die at the MDL.

Despite towering granaries and the luxury craft and tourism trades that built up over centuries, at its core Toruń is still an old fashioned garrison town. That history and tradition shows up in an unusual discipline that marks the families of garrison soldiers and the "jacks and jennies" of the local KRN flotilla. They're all 100% behind the general and her enforcement of martial law.

Support for the military government also comes from refugees with family ties to the local Silver or Gold Divisions. Military families organize as only they can do, helping the city police force keep order. Some rules are enforced with quick, rough justice in overcrowded lakeside refugee camps or down a darkened arboreal alley way. No more mobs of "Toruń firsters" dare show up outside Governance Hall. Hospitals and morgues instead see a fairly brisk trade in unexplained beatings that military police ignore.

The dock is off limit to all civvies. Even so, tens of thousands crowd below its high perimeter wall each day, hoping to beg or bribe a ride off this doomed and burning world. It's pointless, as no ships leave the docks anymore and haven't for months, with the Kaigun above. Civilian cargo craft and two Grün luxury liners are grounded, under strict navy control. Meanwhile, the last few KRN warships are secretly making ready for an all out suicide attack on the powerful Kaigun fleet in orbital patrol overhead. All seven little warships sport the KRN emblem on their prow, a teak roundel of a carved sunflower, under transparent armor.

The tops of all buildings are daubed with dark 'detector,' a chemical coating to warn of poison gases falling from the sky. The tallest bristle with multiple tubes of anti-skycraft guns, even though the "archie" won't make a difference by the end. Once the city's shields collapse, as they must under the hard bombing hitting them daily, once Jabos break though the smoke cover and overwhelm the berm defenses, the last defenders will fight to the death in a wooden city whose towers shall burn down around them.

Ash to ashes.

Dust to dust.

No phoenix rising.

Garrison families and a few others will find brief refuge in deep bunkers dug by KRA engineers beneath the lakes the last time Grünen were on Genève, and expanded for this new war. Their certain future is still to grieve lost fighters and dead family, then to be rousted and rounded up themselves by RIK ground troops as the burned down city is overrun.

Already, ashes of military dead are laid down in an ancient marble quarry tucked into a silent corner of the city. Over the entrance someone erected a laser cut stone: "*Their honored place shall never be with those cold and timid souls who knew neither victory nor defeat.*" No one remembers who said it or knows who etched it, but the bold words seem fitting and right.

***

KRA fighters from across Genève who crowd into Toruń never wanted this war, never wanted any of this. But they'll fight to the last if they must. They know that terrible things are happening all over Genève and on four other Krevan worlds invaded all at once in a stunning wave of orbital assaults that began the new war without warning, just a few months back.

Or is it six worlds invaded now? Seven? Eight? All 12 inhabited systems and 24 worlds of the United Planets of Krevo? It's only a matter of when, not if, war comes to them all. Wild rumors are everywhere, raising fear and despair about everything. They're getting hard to track, harder to confirm. And impossible to suppress. The military government tries and fails.

Sometimes the rumors sound good. Not so perfect as to be unbelievable. Just good enough and real enough to bring fresh hope to a known hopeless cause. A new one is doing the rounds today. It's *really* good. It's the best one yet. Is it an alchemist's tale slithering around Toruń's streets like the chemist's familiar, a whispering cat or serpent, transmuting into gold hope the hard leaden bars of the city's reality? Or is the latest exciting story another lying spread of quicksilver, oozing from superheated cinnabar? No one knows the truth of it, though everyone knows and tells and retells the story.

It's a rumor of swift counterstrokes by hidden Krevan fleets and armies. Best of all, it's a promise of imminent military intervention by righteous forces of the alliance Krevo had with the mighty Calmar Union in the last Orion War, and the one before that. The 'Auld Alliance.

"They'll soon be here to lift the siege! *Hurrah!*"

"This is a cruel trick by Pyotr, a tall tale to deceive and torment us."

"No, no! It's true, it's true! Why would anyone lie about it?"

Even the sensible wonder if it's a deliberate confusion of the quick to jig the dead. Does General Constance have any plan at all? Does Toruń dare hope to have a future? Surely not.

"No, it's *true!* The city will survive. The siege will be lifted by old allies."

"Rubbish! It's all a lie spread by our own commanders, trying to keep hope alive and our children still doing their military duty outside the berm. They should die with us in here instead."

"Arrest that man! He's spreading sedition against the military government!"

"Bah! Go ahead, arrest me! It's still a lie! We're all gonna die, even you!"

It's not that at all.

It's not a lie or a ruse.

It's just another rumor.

No one knows who started it or why, or when or how. They just know they can't take any more bloody rumors! Until the next one arrives.

A very fat one that got started in a KRA military canteen at first light one morning, spurred on by an excited orderly with real connections at HQ Coms. He whispered it to two mates over breakfast. "I know for sure it's true." He means the latest wild tale about an unfolding battle plan. A new hope. There are always rumors of battles and plans. What makes this time different is his connections. "My friend on Aral heard the War Council discuss it. It's *true*, I tell you!"

It is true. At least the part about an optical coded secret dispatch that arrived by bohr zone laser relay, addressed: '*General Constance. Eyes Only*.' It came from outside Genève system, from the capital of Yalto on Aral. It took hours at lightspeed to climb up to the outer Lagrange area and bohr zone in Aral system, then made an instant bohr or quantum jump of information to the outer Genève system, then took more slow hours moving only at lightspeed as a laser encoded message down to receivers in Toruń. By all known physics and interstellar communication standards, that's as fast as it gets anywhere. Or ever.

Even the Kaigun that now controls all Genève system space needs that vital interstellar relay to the rest of Orion, which is possible only through outer bohr relay stations. KRA Special Branch taps in to that weak link in the Grün coms blockade, right into the core *Rikugun Security Unit* feed. That's how Constance stays in contact with the Krevan central government on Aral, by piggybacking an undetected microstream of info onto the strong and constant RSU signal. It's a little bit like a sunbeam riding alongside a solar flare: fragile, erratic, interrupted, unreliable, intermittent. But if it gets through, it gets the job done. This one is boosted. It's so important Aral risks exposing its last link to Genève to get the vital message through.

RIK Fourth Army HQ duly intercepts the boosted message. RSU is a little surprised but not all that worried about the piggyback system it only just discovered. The war is all but over on Genève. Toruń *will* fall, sooner rather than later. What can a message or two achieve? Some final gesture? Still, Main HQ sets its senior cryptanalysis staff to the task of breaking the code. They're working at a fever pitch to decipher it, but it'll be a miracle if they succeed. It takes even General Constance half-a-day to read the code into Universal from the 'spooky' quantum info cloud it traveled in, and she uses the highest key there is and all computing power available. No way RSU can crack it in time. Or maybe ever.

The jubilant rumor monger knows all about the *Core Secret* link. Knows the message was boosted and therefore that it's real big stuff. He just doesn't have a clue what it really says and so he makes up all the rest. All that good stuff about rescue and reconstituting the 'Auld Alliance.

The dispatch is from the War Government in the capital of Yalto on Aral, still holding out planetside after the KRN lost a long and brutal naval fight for the system's asteroid belt, and KRA lost several ground fights on its ice moons. The excited soldier working on the inside at HQ Coms isn't wrong about that, even if his equally excitable friend got nowhere near the War Council's real message.

And yes, it does communicate a new action plan. But it says nothing about the 'Auld Alliance. The message is full of much grimmer news. Militarily, the war is lost. And worse, it reaffirms that politically Krevans are entirely on their own.

Just as General Constance deciphers the message and absorbs its import, Jan and Zofia and the survivors of Madjenik reach the botanical barrier between the Gold Oak Forest and the Toruń Wood ash lands. Even as they hurry across the flower field under an unnerving open sky, just as they see the gaunt dead trees and smell the ash zone, the general orders an assembly. All KRA not on active duty defending the berm perimeter or working archie on the rooftops, as well as all KRN jacks and jennies from Toruń Spaceport, are told to assemble.

"General Constance will speak to you and to the city, on a matter of great import. All military personnel not on berm or other essential duty will assemble outside in Governance Square at 0:400 hours tomorrow. That's an order."

'*Gods help me, and help us all. It's time to break this long silence and let all Toruń know what's coming. What we have to do. The terrible thing I must order, and the price to be paid.*'

Constance

General Amiya Constance is a real presence. Decades of command are etched in taut lines around her hazel eyes and in fine whisker-like indentations at the corners of her mouth. Her face is older, but almost absent the deeper creases of early middle age that a woman in her mid-eighties normally displays. Her just-starting-to-silver hair is worn in a traditional, low cropped style. Not even regular, prewar dispensation of a dilute civilian form of life lengthening 'suspensor,' these days restricted to combat medics, stops all fletchings of Time's Arrow.

Gold braid in willow and maple leaf clusters rests lightly on her high collar and low shoulder boards. Tendrils of silver filament wind down her sleeves. The effect gives her dress uniform a slightly organic and shimmering appearance, like silver vines climbing a strong oak. Her belt is a deep canary yellow, bright against the grainier uniform cloth that reminds of the cut of a Toruń oak table or a wheat field waving gently in a summer breeze, before the war.

She stands on a slightly raised dais to outline the War Government's plan to her fighters gathered below, huge vidscreens carrying her stern yet organic image on smoothly polished sides of tall wooden towers that frame and form the square. She broadcasts also across the city, into other towers crammed with civilians. With Toruń electronically sealed and the Berm Gate closed to all but military traffic, there's no fear of leaks to 'locust" besiegers squatting outside.

A crowd of 800,000 fighters and their families pack into the square and connecting streets. Another seventeen million civilians are watching indoors or underground in bombardment bunkers, or in packed lakeside camps. They're the last freefolk left on occupied Genève. Except for Madjenik Company, but neither the general nor anyone else in Toruń knows that Jan and Zofia and Madjenik are out there still, trekking slowly through ash toward the city.

Constance decides to pass out a little packet of hope where there's really none at all. She keeps darker thoughts to herself, hidden behind steel gray eyes and a stern, official tone. "Attention fighters of Genève! I will give operational details later, and only to those few who need to know, only to those who must see to execution of the War Government's plan that I am about to outline for you all. For the rest, listen closely. I shall say this only once."

Her tough words float out over the crowd not as a blast of war but as a slow and smoky smolder. Like a Southland shepherd's careful turf fire laid flat on the great plain, waiting for a load of friends and wood to come to rise into laughter and high orange flame. Even though no old friends are coming, the days of easy laughter are over on Genève, and only flame remains.

"All of us native to Toruń, those who came here under duress from across Genève, all Krevans everywhere share one great thing. We evince a powerful will to resist this great evil that comes uncaused and unbidden into our lives and homes. We rage against this new barbarism descending over free and peaceful planets, over our beautiful worlds of Brno and Katowice, Lwów, Aral, and our beloved Genève. And have no doubt, to all Krevan worlds before this war ends."

Murmurs of angry agreement rise above the square. She ignores them. She hasn't time for their anger. She must get them to agree to carry out the hard orders she will give them. "We all feel righteous fury that many millions already, and billions more to come, suffer unprovoked invasion, rapine and murder. That they are scattered from families and driven from their homes and farms for no fault or cause or sin of theirs or ours. We are peaceful folk. We do not deserve this fate."

More murmurs of sad agreement, melancholy mixed with defiance floating up from the square below. Listeners focus on a personal tragedy, moved by her passion and precision to pity of themselves and terror of their foes. Others move directly to fury. Then she comes to it. "Our last small warships will depart Genève, to join many more that will also leave other Krevan homeworlds. Under my authority as military governor, I decree that any and all larger civilian craft in Toruń Shipyard with bohr engines are now commandeered to this *Exodus* fleet."

That's just two more ships, unarmored liners. All the rest are too small, just in-system craft that can't make a bohr jump out. It's all she has to carry out her hard orders from Aral. '*It's nowhere near enough.*' The crowd is restless, unsure whether to cry or cheer. So most stay silent, thinking what the last ships' leaving means for them. For their families. To the city. Is this confirmation of an older rumor making the rounds, that the last warships protected by Toruń's city shield and batteries will make a suicide run against the Kaigun fleet orbiting above? Is the end truly so very close? There's a smatter of confused applause, mostly from sailors eager to get back into a fight from which they were chased to the surface by a vastly more powerful enemy, leaving friends behind. Soldiers and families feel only silent pity or sudden fear.

Constance thinks: '*Too many of us lack hard conviction after months of war. The worst of us are too weighed down by despair. I must firm the first, lift the second, and add a third portion of acceptance. But how to get them to agree?*'

"As of this moment, all KRN ships and KRA fighters in Toruń are under new orders. Fresh orders that just arrived from the War Government on Aral." The crowd leans forward as one, holds its breath as one, anticipating what's coming next. A decision about their lives and fate, made by strangers on a distant world.

"We are ordered to secure one of five sanctuaries inside the Calmar Union, to go there as best we can, then to hold it open to receive civilian refugees and as many of our armed forces as can escape the homeworlds and reach that old ally's space. Our friend in the 'Auld Alliance, but a silent neutral in this war."

A low moan as realization sets in, of what they feared and secretly already knew: no new alliance yet exists, no Calmari fleets or armies are coming to their aid. This is not the last war. There is no 'Auld Alliance this time. Even General Constance falters for a moment, but only inwardly. '*An old ally, yes. And a mighty power, unlike weak and defeated us. But an old ally and a power that remains blind to its own grave danger and thus neutral in this terrible new war.*'

"I repeat: we are leaving the homeworlds to find sanctuary in Calmari space, by order of the new War Government on Aral." The news is greeted by relief and disappointment, the latter greater than the former. The excited rumor monger is crestfallen. Someone pats him helpfully on the back. It doesn't help.

"So it's all a lie. I'm a fool! I believed my friend in Coms on Aral!"

"It's not a lie! Calmaris will give us aid and sanctuary. They're good people, mostly." It's a tough but wildly distressed young marine, his eyes glistening with moist hope and the residue of all his fears.

"Quiet! Listen to the general."

"Once there, we will protect the Aral government once it also moves into exile. Then we will guard and assist all Krevans who try to reach asylum in the five sanctuaries."

"The Calmari will surely give us weps, too, to defend ourselves."

"Maybe they'll still join with us, remake the 'Auld Alliance?"

"That's not what the general said, she said..."

"They *must* join us, else all this death and loss has been for *nothing*." It's another young marine. She's crying openly. A week ago she lost her best friend in combat. He was killed defending the westernmost berm wall.

"We're all alone, kid. Better get used to it." The chider is an older veteran from Silver Division. He was badly wounded on the first day of the war, burned all up one side by an Rikugun armtrak whose spandau's scored him with a near miss. Fresh, printed skin grafts poke out from under his utes, riding up his neck. They're still rough and pink and raw looking.

"Shut up all a ya, godsdamn it! The general's not done talking."

The crowd settles as Constance continues. "Our ships will cram in soldiers, sailors and marines, as many as each can carry. They'll dash past Kaigun heavy patrols in high orbit and any phantoms lurking at the Lagrange points. Then they'll tear out of system on fast quantum jumps, carrying free fighters on free ships who will ensure that our war goes on from exile."

In the city towers a cold civilian fear takes hold. '*Are they really going to leave us, undefended? The military means to run from Genève and leave us to the Grün occupation!*' The crowd of soldiers and sailors breaks into undisciplined chatter. It's only to be expected. Six months ago they were farmers or workers or students. Only a handful are lifers, professional military. And most of those are sailors in the long service prewar flotilla.

"We're running after all?"

"We're leaving Genève to the locusts?"

"Damn it, I won't go!" It's an angry, young soldier. The last of his squad, he retreated all the way from the MDL to Toruń. He's tired of running. A platoon mate who hobbled all the way alongside tries to calm him down. Another young soldier nearby shouts out his defiance, too. It provokes more yelling and debate.

"We're *not* running! I'll never run!"

"The general said we'll keep on fighting."

"With what? Where?"

"On the berm!"

"It'll soon be breached."

"We'll stand there anyway."

"The Calmaris aren't coming to help like we thought."

"They're abandoning us, the *bâtards*."

"No, no! We're going to go *there!* Who would've thought it?"

It's a plain jenny who shouts out her hope. She joined the KRN on her 20th birthday to see faraway places and meet queer farfolk. That was a year ago, and she still hasn't been offworld, She missed the opening fights for the system LPs and moons, before the last and smallest ships of the system flotilla were forced to ground under the protection of Toruń's shield and naval yard batteries.

"We're gonna get our people offworld and fight on for Krevo. *Huzzahh!*" That one's a brand new soldier yet to see combat, who thinks of war the way he read about it in old stories. Who understands nothing of the real war. That it's already lost. That death and defeat are straight ahead. He doesn't get what's going on. Or does he? Is that what the future holds for Genève's fighters, more combat and death in a long and bitter exile? The thought starts to creep into the crowd.

'*Better than the awful deaths coming soon outside the berm or after, in the burning streets of conquered Toruń.*' A pretty marine thinks it as she oddly mimes threading her tears onto a thin bracelet of fine brown hair a friend gave her as a forget-me-not. She has no pearls. Now that she's a soldier going to the fields of battle, she knows she never will.

Standing stern and silent on the podium General Constance lets all the low, gravelly grumbles move around the square. Let's them echo then subside. She lets news of defeat and retreat and abandonment sink all the way to the bottom before reaching down to teach them. "The War Government, the Aral garrison and last fleet in the capital system, will fight their way out soon. But not before every other Krevan world has sent its fighters to one of the five sanctuaries. Aral will hold to fix the enemy's fleets, to let the rest of us slip away to exile."

More murmuring, mostly in dissent. Some in confusion. She must speak over the low rumble, raising her voice to match its rise. "Aral has ordered us to form shuttle fleets from all available craft capable of making bohr. The KRA is under strict orders to limit fighting to rearguard and protective actions, as we are already doing along the berm here on Genève."

"Why? What's the point?" The solitary cry is so piercing it rises up to reach her on the podium. She looks down to the man who yelled it, straight in his eye. She answers him and all other doubters in the crowd.

"The plan is to send out *Exodus* fleets, to get as many of our people away as we can before the Kaigun shuts down all our space docks and blocks access to all egress via system LPs. The job of ground forces who stay behind will be to hold off RIK assaults until the *Exodus* ships leave."

The crowd is tense, wary and uncertain, especially when Constance utters the phrase "shuttle fleets" and speaks to them of mass evacuation. Like wiser civilians sheltering in the towers, they know that there just aren't enough ships. Not even a fraction of enough. "After that," Constance announces, "this beloved city *will* fall to the barbarian enemy who crowds now against the Gate."

The realization finally sinks in: they are to be divided into the saved and the abandoned, and soon to be conquered. Crying among scared civvies all around the edge of the square is drowned out by louder shouts of anger and defiance from the massed fighters crowded at its center.

"No retreat! Never!"

"We won't leave Genève!"

"This is madness!"

"We have to defend our homes."

"We won't leave! We won't!" Two buddies from school start a chant, defying their general and governor. "*Fight! Fight! Fight!*"

The crowd is confused, moving in two directions. At least as many fighters think of their families first, of a last chance to get a loved one offworld. Competing cries rise over the square, until one defeats the other.

"Long live Genève!"

"*Fight! Fight! Fight!*"

"*Vive* General Constance!"

"*Fight! Fight! Fight!*"

Tens of thousands of voices chant it now, pumping uniformed fists into the air to mark their fierce defiance. Staring down their general. Willing her to join them, to lead them all in a vulgar, gory last stand of exploding blood and bone, of death and vengeance. Lead them in a raging, final fight outside the berm. She stares back down at them. Unmoving. Not speaking. Waiting as little local arguments break out, get louder still, all across the packed square, a rumbling of disobedience and discontent underneath the ongoing, defiant chant.

A recent newlywed, now separated and lost, desperate to find and follow a leader, shouts out: "It's a good plan! It'll work."

"Whadda you know? You're just a dumb kid. You don't know squat about exile and evacuations and political shit."

"You shaddup, old man. I know as much as you!"

An older woman in KRA oak weaves has children sheltering under the lake, waiting for her to return this night. "What about our families?"

"They expect us to fight, not run."

"Do you have children? Do you want them to die by fire in Toruń?"

"Of course not! But dyin' is better than runnin' from locusts."

"I'm not go'in, neither."

"Godsdamn it, I'm gonna stay 'an fight!"

"We should trust the general."

"She knows more than we do."

"Ya trust her ta chuz who goes an' who stays, ev'n fur yur fam'ly?"

"I do, yes. She's got a good head and better heart."

"Yur a damn fool, den. Ya don't trust nobody in a *war!*"

Pushing.

Arguing.

Crying.

Shouting.

Cursing.

It's about to turn ugly down there in the packed and angry square. Constance waits until the hubbub subsides just a bit, then inserts herself into the lull. "Proud fighters and citizens of Genève, *I agree!*" She says it in a firming and commanding yet oddly calming voice. It's the voice of their general, born and bred to their world. They know it well. But now it's something more. The voice of a leader rising to meet her moment in history.

"It's better that we die fighting now than to live on as slaves. So know this. All my orders and the War Government will be obeyed. You *will* leave here when ordered to do so. Know also that I do not propose surrender. Neither does our new War Government on Aral. I say to you instead that we Genèvens, that all Krevans everywhere, shall fight on. We shall make peace no more, *forever!*"

A new and unified chant *thrums* through wooden echo canyons of Toruń's towers, vibrating along thick oak floors, thrilling everyone from small children to great grandparents. "*Krevo! Krevo! Krevo!*"

Little boys and girls think about their older siblings or parents in uniform at the berm and swell with pride. Old men and women remember their own youth, when they too wore silver or gold sheaves and stood a proud turn at guard. The throng roars out its approval, embraces this defiant general and the new War Government that at last rises to match its plans to their own stark resolve.

"*Krevo! Krevo! Krevo!*"

Constance is moved, yet she thinks: '*They don't understand. My people resist nihilism as the day resists night, losing each time yet always fighting back. Rising each day newly defiant in the face of the last defeat. Yet defeat is coming, as sure as night. Only this night may never see another dawn.*'

Their general's face is set and unmoving. She waits so long this time that the cheering finally subsides, surrenders to her more powerful silence. Then she gives it to them hard and straight. "Genève is cutoff. There's no time left to set up a fast shuttle service from here as there is still on those of our worlds as yet unoccupied, or like Aral holding onto one system LP bohr zone. Nor can we hope to board our families on the few ships remaining to us, small ships that may carry only a very few of us into exile, to one of the five neutral sanctuaries."

Silence.

Total silence.

A shroud of silence.

The silence of a tomb.

Except for low sobs. Mothers mostly, who weep to part from a loved child. A few daughters, too, standing in uniform beside mothers they will soon abandon.

"You shout that you want to fight. So do I. So do all loyal and true Genèvens and Krevans. But if you will fight tomorrow and forever you must do it from exile. We can't stay here and fight. We can't stay here and win. We can't stay and live."

They've always known it.

Hearing it from their general is different.

It makes it real. It makes it now. It makes it forever.

She's unrelenting, merciless with truth. "Most of you will not leave this place of ash and ruin. Most of you will stay and die here, with me. Yet some of you must leave. Some of you must accept to go into exile. Some of you must live so that Genève and Krevo shall not die."

They're starting to understand at last, taking in each heavy word, weighing it before setting it down to grasp the next. They think they know what and why, but not yet who or how or when.

"Only a handful of warships remain in Toruń. I can tell you now that until yesterday morning Captain Magda Aklyan and I worked on a last plan to make a suicide ramming attack on the Kaigun flotilla circling over our heads. That was before new orders arrived from Aral, from the War Government of all Krevo. Now Aral and I both order Captain Aklyan and her crews, and many of you, to drink a far more bitter cup of poison. You *will* leave Genève when ordered."

Audible dissent rises again, bursting out in angry confusion, in a toxic mix of fear and hope about those who must stay and who shall go. It's too much, being buffeted like this, staying or leaving, fighting on the berm or from exile, hoping to live or fated to die on Genève after all.

"We won't quit fighting!"

"We won't leave Toruń. You can't make us!"

"What'll happen when the enemy cross the berm, with so many in the city?"

"I won't leave my children."

"I won't abandon my city, not to the mad beast howling at the Gate. Never!"

"It's shameful to run. How can we leave even one old baba behind?" The last question is asked by a deeply shamed lad, who followed orders and marched away from a bitter old woman who threw insults and pebbles after him.

Constance understands them. She feels it too, more than anyone in the crowd below. This is her homeworld, too. She was born here. She will die here. '*It's not about leaving loved ones to a merciless enemy while they go into exile. It's about leaving at all. It's shame at running. It's about losing the war and abandoning everything these proud fighters and oath takers are still prepared to die for.*'

They glare up at her. '*Gods, I do love our people.*' She cuts them off, with an air of menace. "I know that few of you in those proud uniforms you wear want to leave. Some of you must, nonetheless. You *will* obey orders. I *will* decide who stays and who goes on the ships. There will be *no* appeal of my decisions. Full military discipline *will* apply to any and all who refuse orders."

The threat is clear and understood. They know this is a general who already ordered civilians shot at the Berm Gate. Yet now, she hits them even harder. "Know this thing, as well. All *Exodus* berths are reserved for military personnel only. No civilians. No families. No exceptions." That stops all grumbling cold. Truth is sinking in at long last, that some must go but most will stay and die. That for all, separation is coming and it will be forever.

"Realism is the need of this dark hour, so I'll speak to you only hard truth. I speak to serving military and civilians alike, as your general and your governor. I speak also as a Toruńite and Genèven. I say to you that *we cannot win this war.* Alone, we Krevans cannot defeat the Grün Imperium. We cannot even hold it at bay. It's too big, too powerful. They are too many and we are too few."

Silence is everywhere her voice carries. Although most adults already knew what she says is true, to hear their general say it still shakes them to the root. Quiet sobbing breaks out. Small children grow frightened by fear they see in a parent's eyes. Mothers think of the interrupted joys of their children's disrupted lives. Soldiers think of dead or lost comrades and comrades soon to die, of final partings made or yet to come. Secret lovers wonder if they'll ever embrace again.

"Yet, there is a way for Genève and Krevo to survive. And more." Her voice takes on the power of righteous confidence. Of justice delayed, yet promised and certain. Of vengeance laid down in cold plans, to be had some distant day in hot blood, when the *White Sails* return with cold eyed Ulysses at the head of the great warfleet and legions of allies at his side.

"We shall set aside all our petty differences and small grievances to unite around one policy, one word, one act: *resistance.* We shall make ready for war our children and our children's children. Arm them in body and in spirit. Stoke furnaces of rage in their bellies. Send them to howl red hatred at our enemy, to meet their gory hour as ours meets us today or on some near tomorrow."

"Genèvens, accept exile! But accept it for one reason only. To prolong this terrible war. To bring our hate and our cause to the consciousness of all other decent star nations. To fight on in exile until our old friends realize the deep and true nature of the Grün threat. Until they come to see the Imperium for the utter malignancy that it is, so that they return here with us to end it in fire and storm."

"On that day, when all free peoples unite with us, we'll start to beat these locusts from our doors. We'll scoop their feeble and broken winged bodies into great nets, bury vast hopper bands in long narrow graves we'll make them dig themselves to receive their own corpses."

No one speaks.

No one interrupts.

Few are crying now.

Defiance is rising in a million breasts. Hate filled and strong. Accepting that all life's fate is death, but defiant all the same. "We *will* stop this evil. We *will* take a full measure of revenge for the great injustice done to our peaceful lives and worlds. We *will* bring hard justice to those who did this callous thing to us. Who started this needless war. Who brought such malice down to our worlds."

"To that end, know that there are far greater sacrifices than death that I must ask of you. Fighters of Genève! Do not burn out in a hopeless last battle that must also destroy our beloved Arbor City. Do not accept that the enemy has put you in the death ground, forced you to choose only life or death. For there is a third way, a way to survival for Toruń and Krevo without forcing our surrender. A road not yet taken, an honorable path. *A way to continue the fight!*"

"When the time comes, and it is near, I shall ask most fighters gathered here today to march outside the berm with me, to fight and surely die defending our Arbor City. The enemy will cut 20 years, or 40, or 60 from each man or woman who falls with me outside the walls of Toruń. Laugh in his face, for he only cuts off one or two or three score years of fearing Death."

"I will ask of others a far harder duty and a much greater task. I ask you to leave Toruń to continue the long fight from exile. We who stay behind shall cut a path of fire for you away from Genève. We'll hold the enemy here by his throat as you depart. In return we ask that in years to come you remember with your courage and defiance those of us who stay behind. Above all, we ask that you remember us with your hate."

She pauses, chest heaving and voice cracking, but still strong and in control. Her image and her presence looming over the million fighters in the square below is overpowering. They would do anything for her at this moment. Anything. She's their voice and their soul. More than that, she's their general.

"It's not enough that you all do your best. Not enough to die for Toruń or Genève. Some of you must do much more. What's required. Your true duty. I understand that in our long history the hopeless cause has always been the only one worth dying for. I know that most of you are prepared for martyrdom. Yet, I prefer that some of you at least postpone it to a different day. You must leave burning Toruń behind so that you keep Genève alive. In long days and years of struggle yet to come, in fights that none of us can yet foresee, you will remember us who stay, by living. As we shall honor you who leave, with our deaths."

"Until then you must cleave to what is required above all things. You must live to fight on, until a day comes when you return arm-in-arm with all the other free peoples of Orion to liberate our graves. Water us on that day not with your tears but with the blood of our enemy. Only then may you rejoin us. Those who will die outside the berm or in the burning streets and towers of Toruń, fighting to the last so that you may keep our bright hate burning hot. Only then may you rejoin with all of us who stay, who refuse to lie with cold and timid souls who know neither victory nor defeat."

With that, she has them. They're with their general now, heart and soul and body. They hate as she hates. Vow red vengeance as she does. Stand determined to pay any price, bear any burden, suffer any sacrifice, go anywhere to continue the fight. This is the moment the war for Krevo ends and war for all Orion starts. Standing before their general in besieged and doomed Toruń, under her iron gaze they give her and give the war their assent. They commit to make murder and mayhem and bring vast destruction to the stars, tomorrow and forevermore.

They agree to sacrifice their children.

And their children's children, down the generations.

They consent to do what's necessary to wage this war.

Whatever is necessary, for as long as they shall live.

No one wearing green on the other side of the berm understands this yet. No one over there has any idea how the whole war will now change. Not simple RIK conscripts. Not arrogant General Brusilov or the cruel Jabo pilots. Not the fanatics of Purity or SAC death squads. Not the billions of weeping mothers yet to come.

No one on far off Kestino understands it, either. Not arrogant senior *shōshōs* already strutting conquerors' walks in Rikugun Main HQ, or cocky *taishōs* gliding through silvery halls of the Kaigun Fleet Office. Not the cold, gray men striding down long stone halls to work the torture dungeons under SAC HQ.

Not anyone inside the Jade Court either, already planning victory celebrations or jockeying for governorships of newly conquered worlds. Nor any of effete and pampered members of 'The Admitted' fawning over Pyotr yet stopped outside the gilded door of his private chambers in the Waldstätte Palast. Not even cruel Pyotr and Takeshi who together planned and started this war understand.

This fight is not over.

It’s far, far from over.

It’s only just beginning.

From now until forever,

it will be a whole new war.

Contact

Jan Wysocki crouches low in a half-meter of ash, waiting. Staring into the dark past the wizened trunks of burned out trees. Straining to see a shadow or a sign of Lt. Zofia Jablonski and the Forlorn Hope she's leading back, away from the Berm Gate. Back from the RIK main assault line that she nearly stumbled right into, scouting out front for Madjenik Company.

He's in a foul mood. Zofia is mad at him. The enemy is crowding the way in front of him, spread out in force and all around the berm that encircles the wooden city of Toruń. Above all, he has no idea what to do next.

Scared.

Stymied.

Stalemated.

He finally sees Zofia appear out of the night, at the head of 30 fighters of the Forlorn Hope he sent ahead of five heavy platoons spread out in attack echelon. He thought that his last order would likely kill her and them. So his breath catches in his throat to see her still alive. He holds steady as she moves in and crouches beside him, main weapon *humming* warm and low, pointed back to the enemy at the berm. She motions her fighters to take up spaced positions on either flank of the captain. She's at her very best in combat, showing all the skill that earned her the third spot from the top of her class at KRA Academy on her native Aral.

'*She's not even from Genève, yet she fits the company better than me.*' Only when they're all in position does she look at him, assessing him as professionally as if he was one of her troopers. It's a stern look, almost cold. Her jade eyes glare out from her darkened visor, demanding that he lead. Demanding that he finish the job he has no idea how to finish. Demanding that he be the man she wants and needs him to be. The man he knows he's not and thinks he will never be.

His mood worsens when his tac display acts up. It's already overfilled with *red* symbology marking off enemy armtraks, gun positions, and battalions of elite assault infantry. Now it suddenly flashes brilliant white and a startling blast of extremely loud static assaults his ears. He slams his hand against his helmet. "*Mita helvettia!* What the hell was *that?*"

Zofia felt it too. She's busy scanning her tactical screen display, trying to figure it out. The static stops crackling as their HUDs stabilize. In a nanosecond, everything in Jan's and Zofia's and Madjenik's world changes with a near instant dialogue flashing back-and-forth between intelligent machines. It's an *Identify Friend-or-Foe* (IFF) exchange between his HUD and...? '*Who? Who's out there?*'

Zofia is motioning at him excitedly with her right hand. Jan feels a rush of desperation, almost despair. '*Ahh gods, no!*' Jan thinks. '*Did the RIK just break into our company coms?*' It's not the Rikugun, not the enemy army whose link he thinks is now siting every one of his fighters on a target grid. Zofia and his HUD are both telling him that Toruń Central Command is calling.

"Only electronics so far, no voice," Zofia clarifies. "But it's a friendly call, captain. The first contact with HQ we've had in months." In another instant, TCC restores his right to full data access. A tiny orange scroll appears in a corner of his visor confirming that his command link is receiving updates, and far above the company and battalion levels for which Jan's code is preapproved.

Jan seems frozen in place.

He doesn't move or reply to the IFF.

He makes no response to the data whir.

He says nothing, he does nothing.

He's as motionless as glass.

He just crouches low, watching all the new, dancing lights on the interior of his helmet. Zofia urges him silently, willing him to pull himself together. '*Damn it captain, you have to snap out of this funk! We're back in contact with TCC. This is good news. Come on, get a grip!*'

She decides to stick to the book, confirming out loud what he's figured out already, without her. "Madjenik HUDs are now in range of TCC code bursts from friendly relays atop the berm. It's TCC contact sir, at last."

The KRA fell back on this primitive system after all its orbital milsats were taken out by Kaigun Zerstörers, its surface towers knocked down by RIK Jabos and its subsurface stations gouged out by orbital targeting. All other military nebs as well as the GovNeb and memex emergency backup were immediately jammed tight by orbital hacking satellites. All knocked out within two days, before the ground campaign. It made the ground attack almost easy for the enemy.

That's why there was no command relay in range 'till now, when short range ground stations picked up Madjenik's HUD link. Toruń is the last KRA base and free town standing. Its military relay the only one on Genève still broadcasting, searching for lonely survivors in the ash lands, but without really expecting to find any. TCC is just as surprised as Madjenik to make contact.

Zofia says it out loud again, trying to break through Jan's disturbing silence. "It's TCC linking up. Captain, you need to reply."

He snarls back: "I know. Now be quiet, lieutenant! I'm thinking."

Jan checks that his tactical package is ready and thinks a *send all* order. It's instantly executed by his command link in response to a quantum dot injected in his right cornea back when he made captain, long before the war. Back when he had already quit on his future. Long before he ever met Zofia.

In milliseconds Madjenik's weapons data, tactical and march history for the past three months, current personnel and unit information integrates with TCC. Headquarters' AI link auto returns a complete divisional portrait and grid layout of the city, and declassified diagrams of all city and berm defenses. Less than a minute later a clear, silent message flashes three times on Jan's and Zofia's viewscreens and all company HUDs: '*Welcome home, Madjenik.*'

Jan's integrated, long range tac display shows vastly greater detail, beyond what Zofia's HUD picked up on its own and shared as she crept up to the RIK line outside the berm: a basic and terrifying count of enemy units, and gunpits and strongpoints and armtraks, that she relayed to him before he ordered her back. The berm displays as a narrow *yellow* band. Above its ring a pastel *blue* miasma rises, a haze of aggregate information on 40,000+ sky cannon defending the city from the berm top and from upper balconies and roof tops of its highest towers.

There are too many friendlies in place around the berm and in the city for his HUD viewscreen to identify each one individually. Most are too far away in any case. So his limited HUD quite smartly marks the whole city in a fuzzy *blue* dome, an azure fog representing a gaggle of friendlies stretching beyond his visor's distance gauge. He knows that even more guns, and companies and battalions of *blue* KRA defenders continues all around the berm far side, protecting the western city well past where his glowing HUD symbology can follow.

'They have to be stretched dangerously thin. Yet they're concentrated targets, too, if the Jabos ever get through our archie and come down low and fast. Surprised it didn't happen yet.' He's right. He has a real good eye for these things. Strategic, not just tactical. Better than he realizes. General Staff level, actually.

Toruń's defenses are indeed worn down after three months of fighting. The end of the siege is drawing nigh as the enemy gathers for a final assault directly against the berm. '*What a bloody day and violent end that will be!*'

He switches to midrange tac view and instantly a bad thought comes fast and unbidden. '*Helvetti! This is going to be real hard.*'

"Lieutenant, what do you think?"

"I think we're in for a hell of a fight, captain."

"At least they don't yet know that we're out here."

"Agreed. If they did they would have swarmed us already."

Masses of enemy units show in both their HUDs in classic threat color. The nearest *red* markers look like they're positioned with the sole intent of stopping Madjenik getting to the Berm Gate. That's not true, of course. It just seems that way. In fact, they all face west, toward the berm, unaware that Madjenik is poised in stealth and deep ash to their rear, in the east.

Multiple *red* threats of varying shape and hue parallel the curving berm at 700 meters out. *Blue* symbols glow in parallel rows along its low rim: squares, rectangles, triangles and odder shapes representing hardened gunpits and varying unit types from entrenched infantry to combat engineers, to special assault squads armed with heavy maser and ball lightning cannon. Scattered at roughly even distances among the combat troops are *green* triage medic units.

"Most of our units are sharply reduced in fighting power. You see?"

"Yeah," Zofia replies. "Way down from barracks complement."

"Madjenik's not the only company to have fought hard these past months."

"For sure. There's been hard fighting here, lots of casualties in the garrison."

A line of *blue* hexagons confirms it, showing nearly all friendly units at half strength or less. The garrison is so badly reduced it's leaving thinned spaces in its perimeter to concentrate counterattack forces at critical points, to defend against breakthroughs and maintain a small fighting reserve to plug any gaps.

"If not for the berm and the archie, they would've been overrun long ago."

"One day, Krevans will sing ballads about the Siege in the Forest."

"Yeah sure, if any of us are left alive to bow the tune."

The strength of the defense is a strong double crescent around the Gate, slow curving with the rotation of the berm. It's a series of entrenched works half-a-klic deep and 1.5 klics long. The redoubt is studded with heavy cannon and support rapidos. A third of the way down either flank of the thick *blue* line on their HUDs heavy gun battery rectangles jut out at 45° angles."

"That's where General Constance is hiding her largest guns, backed right into the berm wall."

"I concur. Confirmed."

"She fears the locusts will try to roll up her weakened line on the ragged and exposed short flanks of the Gate. Yes, especially on the right flank. Over there."

"She must think they won't try to blast a hole somewhere else through the berm. Just look where all her heavy batteries are. She's all-in around the Gate."

"It's because she knows they can't bull their way through anywhere else. See? On the three month tac history scroll. Yes, there and there, and again."

"Right. They already tried that gambit, and lost a lot of men."

"She's positioned as well as can be, but she was forced to thin everywhere else to hold the Gate."

"Wait! What's that? They look like big hidden redoubts, built into the wall."

"You're right, lieutenant! It only looks like she's put every big gun she has right behind or above or beside the Gate. Her heaviest concentrations are really at either end of the central position, supporting the wider flanks just before they hinge around the curve of the berm."

"They're hidden bastions. They've got full enfilade on any Gate assault. Very clever! The *bâtards* may still force their way into the city, but it'll be a slaughter when they try."

"I bet those heavies haven't fired yet. She's saving them as a surprise for the big, direct RIK assault. Or do you think, maybe for something even bigger?"

"Who the hell knows. I just got here. You're the one in charge, aren't you?" Jan find's it oddly comforting to hear the old tone of borderline insubordination creeping back into Zofia's voice and speech. It has been a long time since he's heard it warble at him. Since he's heard her sound so, well, sarcastic and friendly.

"Either way, they've got a hard and nasty fight going on here. Everyone's dug in deep and tight."

"Well, maybe we can help our side a little," Zofia chirps, seemingly immune to the astonishing odds against that idea and Madjenik. "So, what's your plan?"

Jan doesn't answer. He's focusing on a midrange tac view projecting three klics of curving berm wall, showing the structure as taller and thicker than in his long range tac display. The berm's soft *yellow* mass again curves into gentle nothingness at either edge of his viewscreen. In this view, however, the Gate is off center but much more precisely indicated at 1.8572 klics due north, showing as a *black* upended rectangle inside *double yellow* frames.

"See that? That's the main kill zone and the last line of defense."

He notes six *blue* octagons showing heavy plasma cannon in close camo, embedded two-thirds up the superhydrophobic concretized berm wall, either side of the Gate. They're positioned to create intersecting, presited and deadly fields-of-fire. Any RIK main assault that tries to rush the Gate with mere blunt force will be in for a truly nasty shock. He worries about the big guns' survival.

'Once they give away concealed position by firing even once, there'll be no moving them or saving them.'

It's as if Zofia reads his mind. "Once they start, those guns must keep firing until the tubes overheat or counterbatteries knock them out and kill the crews."

“Well, that’s someone else’s problem. The good general’s. Not mine.”

Jan directs the command link to open up to sergeants, including five former privates he brevet promoted back in the southern forests. He had the company tek guys jump their HUDs up to the officer link in Pilsudski Wood, after losing most of his NCOs and all officers but Zofia, on the first day at the MDL. Squad orders are traditionally issued in the KRA by sergeants, over a low level tac link that officers could override and far too often did.

Not in Madjenik. Not anymore. Jan knows it’s far better to issue plain orders then leave the squads and NCOs alone. The new sergeants have proved his trust in them is well placed. So he brings them all onboard his thinking now. Like most smart company commanders he relies on NCOs for nearly everything. Especially the sergeants. The last originals are filling in for dead lieutenants. Five of the sergeants are only acting, with four wearing stripes less than two months.

Ten surviving corporals or just acting corporals bumped up from private or specialist lead the company squads, in place of all the dead or missing sergeants. Madjenik has suffered over 60% casualties since the MDL, but much higher rates than that among its junior officers and NCOs. The good news is that all the new NCOs trained in the toughest school there is. Not base camp or officer candidate courses but real combat. Where you learn to kill by killing, to fight by fighting, to lead by leading. Where the penalty for the smallest error, and sometimes even for success, is maiming and violent death of the people who trust you and follow you.

“Damn good fighters, all of them, the NCOs. You and I wouldn’t have made it to Toruń without them.”

“You got that right, captain.”

“Now I need them to help us get through the Berm Gate.”

“They’re all on your link, captain.”

‘*But fight against all that, guarding the Gate? How?*’

“OK folks, I need to hear what our options are. Speak freely.”

***

Jan is still thinking over the NCO's opinions when a flash message urgently lights up his visor. It's TCC tapping into his emergency luminal com link, asking if his tactical situation permits voice coms. Auditory only, no visual. He approves the upgraded connection.

A mature, authoritative woman's voice is inside his helmet. "General Amiya Constance here. Greetings, Captain Wysocki. Well done getting your company to Toruń from the far southeast and into assault position across from my Gate."

"Thank you, sir. Glad to be here, ready to assist." He chides himself: '*Really? Did you just say to a general with hundreds of thousands of troops in Toruń that you're glad to be stuck outside her berm, and you're some kinda relief?*'

"Well yes, captain, I suppose I'm glad that you're out there in support."

"I hope we can help, sir." Again he chides: '*Shit! That was even worse.*' Jan sees Zofia roll her eyes all the way up the night sky, the deep black full of Orion's stars with no canopy left overhead.

He hears a throaty laugh inside his helmet. "I'd rather talk about how we're going to help *you*. Let's get Madjenik through Toruń's blocked front door."

"I'd love to hear how, general. Honestly, I can't see any way myself."

"Well, I was holding something back to surprise our RIK enemy when he finally tries a direct rush for the Gate, but things change."

"You mean the hidden bastion guns, sir?"

"You have a good eye, captain. But no, I must save them for an even bloodier morning that's coming soon. I have a different surprise for you."

"I'm all ears, general."

"You've led Madjenik this far, so here's what we'll do. We're going to blow a big hole in the enemy's line right in front of the Gate, then you're going to bull rush him while we do the same on our side. Can you do your part in that, captain?"

"Yes sir."

"My engineers will push a big plasma mine under the center of the enemy line. Then our Gate guns will churn the site into an abattoir, before Madjenik rushes any survivors from the east while a garrison assault team charges from the west."

"Hit them from both sides at once, yes sir."

"You'll meet in the middle."

"Count on it, sir."

"Attack in a single, blunt wedge. There's no time or space for fine maneuvers. Success relies on speed, surprise, and all due force you can muster. Get across the crater the mine will make as fast as you can."

"We'll attack with all due speed sir, straight ahead. No deviations."

"Fire everything you have while still in combat glide mode. We'll do the same over here. Hold nothing back, or there'll be no tomorrow."

Jan likes this basic plan, which the general code names Operation *Trigon.* It's crude but elegantly simple in its design and brutality. Not some clever rapier thrust pulled from a tactical manual. It's closer to a street mugging with a meat cleaver.

He likes her next order a helluva lot less. "They won't see you coming, and they'll still be dazed from the mine and the barrage. Pause for nothing and no one. That means you must leave behind anyone who falls behind, for whatever reason. There's nothing to be done about that. Leave your dead and wounded."

"Sir?"

"*No stopping.* That's an order."

"Yes sir." He agrees with her in the abstract, but whatever she orders him do, there's no way he's leaving anyone behind. He did that once, back at the MDL.

Not again.

Never again.

Orders or not.

"A heavy sortie from our side will attack simultaneously with your charge. So tell your people to watch their damn IFFs! Let's not have friendly fire casualties when you meet my fighters in the middle of the blast zone the mine will make."

"I'll triple check all HUDs and verbally double warn everyone to expect to run right into friendlies somewhere in the middle of the fighting zone, after we leave the crater far side."

"Good, see that you do."

When blood's hot it's not enough for officers to rely on battle tek like coms and HUDs and IFFs. Fighters in action don't always see what's right in front of them, flashing on their viewscreens in bright *blue* and vivid *red.*

It takes more than hard tek to fight.

A battle is not a peacetime war game.

It takes quick wits and training to survive.

They need to be *told* what to do, and why.

Designated *Relief One*, a thousand volunteers from the Toruń reserve, mostly burly firefighters reassigned to the berm after soaking the city with retardant, will rush out to meet Madjenik on the near side of the crater, to guide and escort the 'Lost Company' home. To bring Wysocki's Wreckers to safety behind the berm. At least for awhile. Until the wall is breached, Toruń falls, and everybody dies.

"I can only spare a thousand. The rest must hold positions along the berm in case my counterpart sees this as an opportunity to attack the city perimeter elsewhere. We're stretched thin already. I must keep my people ready at the archie tubes, in the event our RIK friends decide to send down a wing of Jabos because we've lowered the front shield to let you in."

"I understand, sir. A thousand will be more than enough sir, with me leading 300 hard charging Wreckers from the other side." As soon as he says it he realizes it came out all wrong.

"Confidence is good. So I'll read that remark as your high regard for the proven fighting abilities of your fine company. As for your own judgment and leadership, let's both wait and see how that works out."

"The company, sir. Yes, that's what I meant. They're the best." He swallows hard and decides to just stop talking. The general's curtness suggests the same course of action. '*Gods, she's intimidating! But it was just a slip of the tongue. Why is she ragging so hard on me over it? What does she want from me?*'

His resentment surprises him. It's not how he usually responds to criticism, instead assuming that he must deserve it. Nor does he know that Constance is mapping his every word. That she *does* have plans for him. Immense plans. If he survives the fight that coming at the crater she'll make outside the Berm Gate.

"My engineers will have the mine ready in six hours from now, UST." That's three hours after military midnight, or four and a leftover bit past midnight in local Toruń time. "We'll launch the attack as dawn is breaking, as Genève's sun rises in the face of our enemy and he turns to find you stabbing his back from the east."

"We'll be ready, sir. Knives out."

"Rest until then, captain. You've done your duty, so far. There's nothing more you can do until morning. That's when we'll find out whether of not 'The Ghost' can fight. Move to assault position 30 minutes in advance. Wait for my order."

"Roger that, sir." He can't believe she just called him 'The Ghost.' He thought only RIK propagandists did that, over their military nebs.

"Good luck, captain. I trust I'll see you, Lieutenant Jablonski, and the rest of Madjenik inside Toruń in a few hours. Constance out."

***

"Everyone back 200 meters and rig for silence. Jablonski, get them under camo sheets 600 meters back from the rear of the RIK siege line."

"You heard the captain," Zofia whispers down the company audio channel. "Displace, camo up, and settle down. Then get some shuteye. Big day tomorrow."

Madjenik disperses in near total silence. '*They're all much better soldiers than they used to be.*' Jan thinks it as he watches each echeloned platoon move back in good order and disciplined quiet. '*Except maybe me.*'

No one in RIK Main HQ or on the berm line knows or even suspects that Madjenik is where it is. No one is looking for any threat at all to its perimeter siege lines approaching from the east, from out of the ash lands that used to be thick and green Toruń Wood. RIK thinks that the only things behind it are dead bandits and burned out trees. It's supremely confident, thinking it has killed both.

The last resistance on Genève is surrounded and locked inside Toruń. So confident is the local RIK combat brigade commander of this he posts no pickets behind his siege trench. The first lethal contact from the east will be a total surprise when Jan's attack wedge arrives.

Madjenik burrows down into a soft gray blanket of ash, under individual camo sheets. It will wait out the night, its last in the ash zone come what may on the morrow. Last to arrive where Jan waits with impatient concern is Zofia, trailing even the grim Forlorn Hope he ordered to do a final duty as the rearguard. He thanks and disbands the ad hoc unit, redeploying its 30 veteran fighters evenly across the Able-through-Easy combat platoons. Six to each. There'll be no reserve this time. Madjenik is going all-in, as a solid wedge. Just as his general ordered. It makes Jan uneasy, goes against all his instincts. '*But orders are orders.*'

TCC sends the final details of *Trigon* at 8:00 UST, with two hours to go to military midnight and three more after that until the mine blows. Already, the autumn sun has set over the western foothills, indifferent to where it passes over mountains let alone its place on human clocks. Utterly uncaring about what will happen below when its first stabbing light returns to Genève.

After consulting in whispers with Zofia and flashing final orders to the NCOs, Jan tries to get some sleep. It doesn't work. In his febrile tossing and worry he half remembers an ancient apocalyptic vision. '*Thence will come a fiery deluge, regions of sorrow and doleful shades and torture without end, where peace can never dwell and hope never comes.*'

Or something like that. He knows he might be mixing up two texts. He does that. Sometimes he curses that his mother insisted on giving him a private, classical education on top of his regular schoolwork. He curses more that he never tried to master it, so that verses elude him now when he tries to recall them. Still, he knows enough to recognize it means torture and Hellfire will soon rain down around the Berm Gate. '*That's for sure, once the general starts her barrage. Who'll be damned and who'll be saved then is beyond my or anyone's control.*'

He can't sleep. There are too many contingencies swirling in his head. He sits up and glances over at Zofia. She's deep asleep, curled around herself like a contented house cat. Or she's feigning it, dealing in silent privacy with her own personal angst and her own looming mortality in a near hopeless combat assault. He lies down again. '*I have to try to sleep.*'

Few fighters sleep during the longest, and likely the last, night of their lives. Some are overexcited to be this close to Toruń at last, after so much suffering in the southeast and on their forest trek. Others are curious about what the general and their captain plan, and how "we're all gonna get through the berm tomorrow!" Most think on missing lovers, lost friends, or about their own prewar lives, so dimly remembered they sigh and sway in the mind and dark, as gray and dead as ash zone trees. Still, it feels real good to rest legs, close both eyes, and maybe nod off for a few minutes now and then. To be anywhere but where they are.

Jan still can't sleep at all, so he relieves the first watch. "I'll take it from here. Get some rest." Two minutes later he looks to his left and sees that Zofia has taken up sentry about 50 meters away. She nods to him, then turns her head to scan. '*So, she wasn't asleep at all. Of course she wasn't.*'

Fighters curl in fetal balls or stretch lengthwise under full spectrum light-and-sound camo. Modified RIK *huff-duff* sensor blockers hum softly, audible at all only because they're at full power this close to the enemy. The wounded got the last of the water, but here and there a prone fighter sucks at her canteen, hoping for a final dreg. Tomorrow they'll slake a lifetime's thirst with deep, cold draughts from the clear reservoirs of Toruń. Or they'll drink nevermore.

Jan checks the tiny chronometer in the top left corner of his HUD. Local time shows in *green* beneath an *orange* UST clock. Either way, the mine blows at dawn. Never has he felt such foreboding and threat from an approaching day. In all the histories of all the wars, alertness flags to a natural low just before first light. Shock and disorienting effects of the mine explosion will be maximized, even though most of the enemy are surely on combat meds to counter stress. If Madjenik is lucky, quite a few will also be dull witted from too much drink or doing illegal robusto the night before. It's another good reason to attack at dawn.

Using an industrial laser hauled from Toruń Shipyard, combat engineers bored out the mine shaft and blast chamber two weeks earlier, readying for the big perimeter ground fight General Constance intends to lead herself to distract RIK sky and ground forces from departure of the *Exodus* ships. Now the mine won't be used in the last battle outside the berm after all.

"Instead, we'll help a lost company break in to the city." She's talking to her closest and most reliable aide-de-camp, Lt. Dylan Byers. "What do you say to that, lieutenant?"

"Frankly?" He's always frank with the general, since she insists on it, but still feels military protocol demands that he ask permission. "I don't see it as the wisest use of our last resources. It makes much more sense to stick to the original plan."

"You really think so?"

"No, actually I don't."

"I thought not. I know you Lt. Byers."

"It's just that..."

"Stop holding back. Speak your mind."

"Well then sir, I think you're exactly right. In a fight that's already lost, this seems the right choice. It's just the right thing to do. Those are *our* folk out there."

"Agreed, on all scores but one. This fight, this war, is neither lost nor over."

"It's not?"

"We still have the *Exodus* ships."

"Well yes, but only if we can get them offworld. All the captains have to do then is to somehow get small warships out of the system with every Kaigun asset available blocking the way or in full chase."

"You don't think they can do it?"

"I think it will be hardest thing any of us will try. Whether we're staying to die, like you, speaking frankly, sir, or leaving on *Exodus*. Getting past those heavy orbital patrols and then bohring out of the system? I don't see it. I'm not KRN, sir, but I can't see how to do it."

"Thank you for your candor, lieutenant."

"General Constance, sir. I didn't mean to offend. I only meant…"

"I gave you permission to speak freely. No offense is warranted."

"I'm glad of it, sir."

"Resume your post."

***

As Madjenik rests, engineers in sound baffle suits pack the cavity with a plasma bomb. Main guns on the high berm are told to wait three minutes after the detonation before shooting everything they have at pointblank ranges. The delay should catch milling enemy out in the open, inside an "absolute fire zone" 500 meters wide and deep. More guns will saturate an even wider killing field on either side of the crater in a barrage lasting seven minutes, keeping heads down and return fire suppressed until Madjenik makes its madcap dash.

Jan's orders are to mass at 2:30 UST. Madjenik must then advance in stealth to attack position, just 200 meters from the RIK line directly east of the Berm Gate. It will wait precisely 10 minutes after the mine detonates, timing its mad charge to the end of the saturation barrage. When the guns stop, Jan will release all Madjenik to crash the rear of the enemy's position. Then the race will start. Madjenik vs. Death, one chasing the other into a killing corridor, a gauntlet of hellfire through which Madjenik must run to live.

'*It's the best we can do,*' he concludes after reviewing the general's plan over and over. '*And a helluva sight better than any plan I had, which was none.*' He's glad someone else is now making the hard calls. Especially so capable and senior an officer as General Constance, the highest ranking KRA still alive on Genève.

Still, he decides to add a tactical wrinkle of his own. Madjenik will still bull rush the mine gap, but not in a single wedge as the general ordered. It'll form five platoon wedges moving in echelon, a semi disconnected larger wedge that he'll personally lead from the apex. '*What can the general do to me for disobeying her orders? I'll not likely survive the attack in any case. Very few, if any, of us will.*'

He thinks up the variant while looking up into a streaking, cold sunset, upon hearing familiar honking and watching several hundred snow geese passing high overhead in five companion 'Vs' that form a larger 'Vic'. They're leaving for the equator, thence to Southland for the long winter, oblivious to all the human ballyhoo below. '*Or really annoyed about all the noise we're making.*'

Jan hears a distant dog bark. He's always liked dogs, but he's never had one of his own. Didn't think he would be a good master to a dog. '*It's somewhere in the enemy camp. I hope it stays there. There'll be enough death today without my having to knife an innocent dog that wanders out here and barks out our position.*'

With nothing else to do but pace and watch and think, he notices that the air smells of burned metals and yellow clay as well as cold wet ash. Also of burned and rotting animal and human flesh. The burned meat smell he sets aside by thinking of it as some elk or deer trapped in a sudden gust of forest flames, not a charred countryman or woman or child struggling to reach the Gate yet falling short, to be roasted inside-out by compact microwaves from a heavy spandau.

Not so easily can he push away from his clogged and protesting nostrils the sweetly sick odor of weeks old putrefaction that is all around. Already, hidden bits of corpses that litter the forest floor on the outer margin of a battlefield are shifting from first decomp by aerobic bacteria to all out rotting by anaerobic species. By the trillions, the creatures are feeding on corpse tissues, fermenting sugars in forgotten livers and kidneys and fouled brains and bowels, releasing gas byproducts: ammonia, hydrogen sulphide, methane. The gases bloat corpses until they vent noisily from every orifice. Or inflate cavities, until they burst out a ruptured abdomen to rise above the forgotten battlefield and blend with the winds.

He looks down warily, worried that he'll see a fatty lump of discolored and indeterminate flesh he only noticed because it brushed his boot with a little *clink.* He realizes it was once an arm and hand. It's swollen but small. Perhaps a girl's or a woman's? Certainly it once was a fleeing refugee's.

Dark veins that once carried blood and oxygen down the foreshortened arm are filled now with anaerobic bacteria, fast converting the last hemoglobin into sulfhaemoglobin. The newer molecules in dead and settled blood give shriveling skin a marbled, greenish-black look. On two fingers slippage is so advanced that sheets of skin loosened and fell away, exposing pale thin bones. There are black blisters up-and-down the severed arm and on the back of what was indeed a young mother's hand. It's still wearing a wedding ring that cuts deeply into a finger that's blue-and-fat with death around the gold.

'*When alive, this hand may have held an infant to a suckling breast.*' He looks away, fearing to find what's left of the child she dropped when the maser took her down. His mind wanders back to childhood lost and he wonders wistfully where his mother is on this last night of nights, before his last day of days. '*Are you alive, making garlic soup and folk medicine on the old farm where I last saw you, before the war? Are you in the world still? Anne-Marie Wysocki, are you with me?'*

Eighty minutes before H-Hour it starts to rain. A real late autumn soaker. It slimes the ground and everything they carry, running off in little indifferent streams that tunnel into and under the resistant ash. At least the sheeting rain drives the wary dog indoors. It stops barking.

Jan spends the last full hour of what he knows might be the last night of his existence walking the foreshortened sleeper line, stopping and stooping to talk in whispers with restless and anxious fighters. He never truly realized before this last dawn how very young they are.

"How are you son? Did you get any sleep?"

"A little, captain."

"And you? Are you ready to visit Arbor City?"

"Can't wait, sir. I was born there. My family's in there."

"Well, they'll be proud and happy to see you. Now rest."

They smell wet and musty and bone tired of war. The powerful black rain, sky water mixed with risen ash, washes the last soot off their drenched weaves. For the first time since they entered the ash zone they look oakish as the first light of day breaks, not deathly gray. '*At least when we fight our last fight, when we die today, we'll do it standing up and looking once again like Krevan soldiers.*'

Then it's time. He alerts NCOs and gives the order over the company's linked HUDs. "All rise. Ready to move out."

Hundreds of wet fighters stand up in the fading dark. Jan and Zofia are so in sync by now when going into combat that it seems like they're playing tag team command, issuing readiness orders one after another.

"Stow all camo. Just leave it there."

"And all nonessential gear. Take only weapons and ammo."

"Warm masers. Safeties off. Frags armed and ready.

"Prepare to advance 200 meters."

"By platoon, *advance!*"

Echeloned platoons move out, five smaller V-wedges forming one large V-wedge, looking to Jan just like the passing snow geese, only gliding low and in slow motion across the sodden ground.

"We're at 200 meters. *All halt!*"

"Crouch position!"

"No, turn the other way, trooper."

"Sir?"

"Turn your back to the enemy line and barrage."

"Face shields down! Get your visors dark."

"Last check: light filters and flash shields on full power *now!*"

"Check."

"Right, stay low and still."

"Don't turn around until you get the order."

"Wait for the *go* command."

"And everybody, shut your eyes!"

Jan remembers part of an old prayer, an odd thought for him. It's the kind of thing learned too early in life when parents and teachers pour the hemlock of unqueried faith into too trusting ears and into lasting memories: '*Worse than all my foes, I find the enemy within.*'

It's not true. His worst foes are over there, about 200 meters away, waiting to kill him and all his Madjenik charges rather than let him into Toruń. He might get Madjenik through, or he might not. Either way, Jan Wysocki intends to slaughter as many of his enemies as he can. The time for prayers is over.

Crater

The mine blows exactly on schedule, producing two lethal effects. An intense thermal blast sears all metal, rock and flesh while a wave of intense pressure and expanding gases spreads out-and-upward at supersonic speed. The shock wave causes devastating injuries to internal organs while the fast expanding gases lift a mass of soil and rock and men in a swelling half orb of sudden heat and death.

At ground zero, right above the insertion chamber excavated by engineers, ultrasteel and superconcrete RIK pillboxes simply disappear. Big gun tubes and entire crews convert instantly into hot odorless gases, adding to the rising bubble. Or reduce to small lumps of singed metal or cooked bone smoking at the apex of a lifting ball of expanding water and soil. Heavy maser batteries and fusion cannon boxes lift 300 meters into the air, riding atop the upward burping bubble. It's made of brown and ochre clay chunks, rich black top soil, mud and rocks and water, shattered vehicles, flailing bodies and parts of dead and dying men.

Four intact heterodiamond gun tubes, too hard for even the mine blast to crack apart, tumble slowly upward, gracefully arcing above the cresting explosion of dirt and blood and wood that flashes with plasma lightning from within, like a great black thunderstorm seen at 10,000 meters altitude. The tubes are from the 3rd Imperial Artillery, an elite unit from Manmō. So are bits of two dozen erupted gunners. Two crystal cannon batteries from 33rd Artillery, a regular outfit also from Manmō, rise as a mutilated and mangled muddle of smashed and torn and jagged bits of men and machines, hurtled high up inside a spreading ball of debris.

Four heavy Mammoths parked behind the maser battery come apart at every laser welded seam as they rise. Three sleeping crews die instantly, killed in a nanosecond because they chose to lie down for a brief rest in a convenient nearby dry trench that no longer exists. Inside the fourth armtrak are two military workers busy with minor repairs when the mine goes off. At first they're protected by a thick shroud of carbyne armor, riding the huge ejecta bubble high up. Then they spill out, bodily intact, wide awake, and utterly astonished that gravity has so little hold on them or the hugely bulky Mammoth still rising right alongside.

Seconds of rapid expansion that take forever, then the hubble bubble slows. It thins and breaks its overstretched skin at the epicenter. Everything it carried up starts to fall: gun tubes, rocks, armor plate, concretized gun anchors, chunks of field, bodies, cracked helmets, heavy masers, three shattered Mammoths and one armtrak still intact. Along with two astonished mechanics from the forest world of Unterwalden, in the Waldstätte core of the Imperium. No one hears them scream over the roar of air and flying clay and groundwater still rushing outward in all directions below them. Mortality arrives in the looming form of gravity, reclaiming them as Genève's entire and fatal inertial mass smacks each falling man hard right in the face.

'No, not me! Not to ME!'

'This isn't real! I'm young.'

'I'm loved. I want to live!'

'Why am I flying?'

'Where are my legs?'

'Why ME? It's not fair!'

'It's not *FAIR!*'

No, it's not. You were just in the wrong place at the wrong time, drew the wrong number in war's never ending lottery, a random draw of life and fate. Now you're dead, son. Next!

Hundreds of Rikugun are still lingering underground, but over 1,400 men are unprotected inside the blast zone when the plasma mine goes off. Some, like the armtrak and artillery crews, come from the traditional military catchment world of Manmō. Most of the rest are conscripts, too dumb or too cocky to be careful in front of the Gate. Two companies of called up infantry are from Lucerne, a quiet agro world much like Genève. They're ten days into their combat tour. None live.

Most of the Lucerne boys die fast, mercifully unaware of their last moments, still asleep as bones are crushed and internal organs instantly pulped by the expansive pressure wave of the blast. A few are not so lucky but still die fairly quickly. And painlessly, compared to what's coming to others from different units posted just outside the certain kill zone of the crater.

The descending ruin overhead is full of body parts, remnants of boys and men hailing onto the now smoking and gassy ground. Night sentries about to go off duty and early rising cooks preparing the first meal hundreds of meters from the crater edge vomit in moral horror as strings of warm extruded gut drape slickly over a neck or arm. Or snag like mockmeat sausages on a gun turret or jutting branches of scorched and shattered trees with no bark or leaves left. Even the trees looked tormented, with gaping white wounds of torn and pulpy vegetable flesh.

No mother will recognize or embrace the awful things hanging from trees and rocks, or raw and bleeding and unmoving on ruptured ground, oozing blood and water and green bitter smelling bile. Larger lumps and clumps land with sick, soft *thuds!* Torsos, legs, severed feet, loosed heads with boy's faces frozen in an uncomprehending instant of horror and shock.

A thousand meters from the forming crater rim survivors are coated a minute later by a falling, sticky red-black mist, then drenched in rolling sheets made of falling dirt, blood and groundwater. The mix smells of natural plant oils, mangled tree roots and erupted men. Exploded rocks and artificial wreckage fall to ground all around, spreading into and around a deep and smoking crater blown 100 meters down at zero point and 850 jagged and wide. Its roofless walls form an earthen coliseum of total destruction and despair, of murder and madness.

It's spectacle and sacrifice.

It's full, blood sport theater.

It's masterful, yet senseless.

Primal, exciting, cruel and absurd.

As well as conscripts, the huge mine kills elite infantry the *shōshō* placed in front of the Berm Gate. Some of his best units, and the most loyal. In all, some 1,238 volunteers from Schwyz, another of the core Waldstätte forest worlds. They die not inside the crater but just outside it, in the blast zone where the concussive wave spreads out. They're mushed or buried in heavy ejecta or killed by flying rocks or shards of jagged armor or other, stranger things. Shrapnel of all sorts, warm and animate as well as cold and sterile and dead.

Seven young Schwyzers are crushed by an oak that topples into their blown open trench, squashing them to pulp and jelly that smells vile as cancer vomit. One *nitōhei* is struck dead by a parabolic pelvis falling back to ground. Another boy of just 17 summers is impaled by a meter long wood splinter that flies over the crater lip at waist level, like an errant javelin shot from a targeting machine to fly across a running track to take down the leader of the relay team. For so he was before RIK recruiters came, beating snare drums up and down his school.

An older *gunsō* is decapitated by a shoulder blade spinning away from an exploding volunteer at high rotation speed. The impact is so violent it throws his own severed head into the chest of a gentle man from Yokohama visiting a new made friend among the Schwyzers. A heavy blow from the tumbling head shatters nine of Kenji Hamaguchi's ribs and drives them inward to puncture both lungs, leaving him to gasp a last minute in terrible mortal torture on the ground. He dies clutching ochre mud of a farfolk world not his own, surrendering everything he was or will be in a fight not of his ken or making, in which he never learned to hate. It will be another month before his recently pregnant wife hears the news of his death, and miscarries their first child in a paroxysm of grief and bloody fluids.

A fat black fly sitting on a splintered willow trunk watches Kenji Hamaguchi die, and a dozen more around him. She sees tumbling bits of bone that *scud!* and *skip!* like large pond stones thrown by naughty boys to crack open lake ice on a winter day. She's more interested in men on fire, running wild in terror, falling and rising only to fall and stay, where she and hers might find them later and feed. She smells blood and bile and freshly ripped flesh and grows excited. She hears *thudding!* body parts landing and thinks only of her own kind, and of how rare is such good fortune falling to her from the sky.

Truth be told, it's not as rare as she believes. She is herself carrion spawn now in the hundred thousandth, millionth generation since a careful laying of eggs by an ancestor in a Frenchman's eye at Verdun, in a forgotten war on a far off world. She rubs front legs together overtop her buffalo hump and bulging fractal eyes, and smells for blood and meat. She bit two men for breakfast and so feels no need to feed. But she mated recently and is engorged with ripe, heavy eggs. She wings over to a disemboweled boy and plants a wobbly sack inside his warm, spilled guts. The Lord of Flies is not so cruel or fickle as she thinks. War is good to flies.

Farther out a medic comes upon four youths from Cretan, a minor Grün world. They're all ripped raw and open by dirty plasma spears that tore off their body armor and inner thermal protectors to reach down and score them to the bone. Two scream in agony even after fast jabs of his strongest painkiller and his last but insufficient loads of weak suspensor. Beholding them with pity, an old soldier asks the medic if there's any means of saving the lads. All out of suspend to stop their gaping wounds and pain until more help comes, the medic answers: "No." At once, the graying sergeant approaches the boys with a short ceramic blade and cuts their throats gently. And on and on. Fate piling 1,170 more dead on her red butcher's table, joining 1,402 in the crater and 1,238 lying still at its smoking rim.

Later, poets think they give the moment meaning by sitting beside ruby fires composing verses about the glorious pity of war. Grün songs will mourn and moan, forgetting who started it. Krevan verse will boast and brag, promising to end all enemy just like 'the boys' who died at Toruń's crater, forgetting that they were just boys. Pitying and pitiless poets.

Over 2,000 wounded men stagger from the smoldering hole, coming up from a nearby trench or gunpit, trailing wisps of pale blue gas and clouds of steaming vapor that smells exactly like cedar and hot rocks in a sauna. They're blind from incandescent plasma, scalded by instantly boiled ground water, seared by hot surface gases. They fall over sudden rubble, trip in hotly sucking mud. Cry out for aid. Ask comfort. To find a friend.

Men dig frantically to free comrades still half buried in slime, struggle weakly to pull themselves from a collapsed bunker or caved in hole. More wounded men lie where they fall, bleeding out. Or stand up holding a broken or badly gashed arm, whimpering. Or sit with both hands held tight over stone deaf, yet oddly ringing ears. Or look around stupidly, head exposed, helmet held ever so carefully in their lap like a hive for missing bees, smiling mutely at everyone who passes. The morally naked and the physically nude. All are present at the "*Battle of The Crater*," as this little skirmish in an immense and expanding war will be called by those who were there. And far more who weren't.

Far out from the fresh crater rim more conscripts from Unterwalden and five volunteers from Schwyz walk aimlessly with blank and distant stares, outwardly unhurt but knocked insensible by the concussive wave from the plasma mine. They know not where they are or their names, nor unit nor cause or what to do next to save their lives. They wander, unarmed and unhinged. Helpless and vulnerable, pissing hot yellow down their legs like lost toddlers with no mothers.

One youth a half klic from the crater rim is sitting stunned, knocked down by the blast wave but otherwise uninjured. His back is supported by a shattered tree stump. In his lap, resting exactly how they landed, are the unblemished and naked buttocks of a dead man that flew out with the other debris. The boy looks down at the mounds of pale curving flesh, deeply puzzled. He asks out loud in shocked bewilderment, of no one in particular: "My god! Am I hurt that bad?"

Two friends collapse, laughing so hard they can't get up or breathe. They roll on the ground sucking for air, useless with mirth, helpless to themselves or their bewildered comrade, who also starts to laugh. All are oblivious to their doom. It lurks in unfired mortar tubes and heavy weapons counting down three minutes to the "*Shoot!*" signal, waiting to drop fatal luminosity into a jagged, shattered chunk of what was the RIK siege line at the Berm Gate. More boys in the wrong place at the wrong time, doing the wrong thing in the wrong moment.

Friends come up from underground to help. Strangers too. They hook an arm, grasp a waist, firm wobbly legs, carry the lame and guide the witless. They come to coax confused or bleeding comrades back to shelter, into a nearby bunker or shallow trench, anywhere a fellow human sufferer might be safe in the dead and scalded no-man's-land in front of the hated berm.

That's when Toruń garrison starts its saturation bombardment. All those inside the kill zone, 2,000 insensibles and wounded and another 473 uninjured men who rose out of safety to help them find aid or cover, all are caught out in an intense shelling and instantly charred. Or worse, writhe in agony on the slower path to death, burned and sliced, conducted to oblivion by intense lasers, heavy masers, and white plasma mortars that drop in shells like sudden meteor showers.

The barrage is so radiant it takes 20 seconds for heavily protected visors of Madjenik's forewarned fighters to adjust, and they're 600 meters from the central kill zone and under stiff orders to cover and look away. Anyone not behind an anti-flash combat screen never sees life through natural eyes again.

Seven minutes of bombardment is a long time. Especially when the weapons are multicolored heavy lasers and big pink crystal guns, ball lighting, fusion cannon and kinetic explosive rounds. For Madjenik, waiting to make the mad dash into the still smoking crater, the shelling seems to go on forever. It lasts an infinity and again for anyone lying directly under it.

Worst is unendurable incandescence of large plasma shells arcing out of big Z-pinch cannon or fired from short range steam catapults or just lobbed by kinetic mortars. Magnetic chamber containments unlock inside parabolic warheads, balls of superionized plasma explode outward with the shocking brilliance of miniature suns, only forming suddenly just a few dozen or a few hundred meters away.

Impossible.

Unbearable.

Unthinkable.

Unsurvivable.

About 10% of arriving KRA plasma shells are 'dirty plasma' that disk out to spear men across a wide killing field that stretches all around the crater. A gritty mix in smaller crystalline plasma rounds gets them dubbed 'dirty plasma' by any receiving party, though both sides use them from the first day.

They're called 'dusty' or 'grain plasma' by opposing artillery. Not 'dirty' shells. They're just superheated ionized gas rounds like any regular plasma shell, only with nanometer or micrometer sized particles suspended in the medium. When hot plasma bursts from out of a demagnetized casing that's preset for altitude or depth release, dusty particles fly out in an expanding ball of tiny acetylene spears that cut right through all ceramic or liquid armor and pierce hotly into flesh, moving on through any bone the grains hit, then clear out the other side.

Searing acetylene death is no different than killing by regular plasma balls emerging from containment shells. Yet everyone believes it is. Fighters on both sides hate 'dirty shells' and vow to kill or mutilate any captured mortar or gun crew they suspect of firing them, even though grain plasma is perfectly legal and used by all artillery in every army in Orion. It's one of those shared irrationalities of war. Dead is dead and plasma balls or spears burn just as quick and hot and deep, with the same awful pain and fear coming to the brain along the way. Yet every army will exact revenge on the enemy's gunners when a battery is overrun and found to have dirty plasma among its munitions. It's an acceptable atrocity.

Maybe what every infantry that murders captured 'dirty gunners' really hates is the long distance comfort and anonymity with which the big guns kill? Even their own. Killing gunners up close and intimately is payback for all that abstract death. They feel the same way about downed pilots, who rarely survive capture.

Seven minutes of flashing, searing heat. Of incandescent brilliance without peer on any rocky planet's surface since Orion formed. Seven minutes where the last white hot shells burn and bounce scored rubble made by the first wave down, and the second, and the third.

Seven minutes.

Seven hundred seconds.

How does one count to eternity?

It's long enough to be driven mad.

The barrage stops. For those left with eyes to see, sudden still and dark is almost as startling as the plasma fall. They stagger, stumble and fall in their blindness. They circle and scream in horror and terror in their madness. They stay mute and unmoving in their emptiness. Then two wedges of wheat clad fighters charge from either side, intent on making sheer bloody murder of any survivors in their way.

***

Relief One is 1,000 strong. It combat glides hard eastward out of the Berm Gate just as 300 howling, hurtling Wreckers crash into the exposed back of the shattered RIK position, a onetime trench line that's now a smoldering and indefensible ruin. The wedges drive toward each other, and right through 1,442 stunned RIK still alive but disoriented and disorganized inside crater bunkers, last intact survivors of 8,355 in the initial blast and bombardment zones.

Achieving total surprise, gliding in 5 meter bounds on powered combat boots, Jan's five part wedge rushes right over men turned witless by the last 10 minutes of their lives. The mine blast and shattering follow up bombardment leaves Grünen even in the outer kill zone exposed and traumatized, huddling in some broken gunpit or shell hole, clutching knees and rocking like abandoned toddlers, warm piss running freely down into yellow-green puddles. Youths and much older men curl fetally, crying out for their mothers. A quick *click clack, click clack* of masers, a *poom, poom, poom* of frag grenades as fire teams from Charlie at the center of the triangle run past. All the momma crying and fetal rocking stops.

Jan leads a blitz assault on two pillboxes now facing the wrong way, twisted around by the explosion of the mine and seared black by uplifting plasma. He tosses a sonic stun grenade into an open firing slit. He's all out of frags. A muffled cry escapes. He shoots. Silence. He slows his glide just enough to point out the other bunker and order two fire teams from Dog platoon "to pump fire inside that funk hole! Smoke 'em out. Kill 'em all!" He shows them exactly where to drop in the incendiaries, making a square *window* signal with his left hand.

Dog's three man team goes to work, until the terrible screeching ends and a coarse smell of roasting flesh leaks out to join the barbeque odors hanging all around the crater. Dog hurries past to catch up with its captain, who's 200 meters ahead firing at the gun port of a half unburied, prefab officer's barracks from which two hand masers are aimlessly firing back.

"Seal 'em in! Keep moving." Jan yells to Dog as Easy rushes up and past on the far right flank. '*Good. They're executing platoon hop-frogging exactly right. We'll be over the other crater lip soon. Then we'll meet Relief One.*'

He hears an explosion behind him as an engineer's demolition satchel goes off and a wobbly, precarious barracks collapses inward. At least two RIK platoons are buried alive inside. Along with four officers who were using a back room as a private brothel. So, three Genèven women brought here from their villages are dying, too, without air and covered in rubble. Dog has no idea what it has done, and Jan has no time to speculate. Easy's four fire teams are held up 100 meters to his right, at an undamaged bunker. He moves off to investigate.

On the other wide flank, on the far left of the Wrecker wedge, Baker and Able move fast. Zofia's over there. "Keep shooting! Keep moving!"

"Where, lieutenant?"

"There! Over there! Behind that broken boulder."

"I see him. Shoot!"

"You got him!"

"Stay with me, there's more on the left."

"Baker, all squads veer left."

"First Squad, clean out that half-bunker."

"Grenades! Use grenades!'

Poom, poom, poom.

"Baker! Your drifting too far left. Link back to Able's right."

"Third squad, make the link."

"That means you, trooper."

Zofia comes up fast on another half open, broken dugout. She stops to pour a pocket pack of incendiary jelly down a broken ramp door then fires a maser bolt into the rabbit hole, instantly exploding and igniting the volatile *orange* liquid. Also setting on fire the tops of one of her boots and looped bottoms of her combat weaves. She shakes her right leg vigorously, but the flame is sticky.

Two howling torches run up the ramp and out, stumble and crawl around her feet, incapable of more for all the agony they're in. Yet still unready or unable to die. They remind her of roasting marshmallows *black* on a stick, when she was a little girl camping in the much smaller and shorter forests of her homeworld, Aral.

She moves back a meter to get a better shot, and dispatches both men with her pistol. For mercy's sake or just to be tidy? Only she knows. Inside the blackened bunker four more men coated in *orange* jelly splatter are screaming and burning bright. There's no one to finish them off. Zofia's already combat gliding to the next fixed target, which she marks with a maser round for the platoon following close behind, firing also at a running man while she moves. She doesn't need Baker so she waives it on with her hand over her head in a *cover this area* signal, pointing to a hidden gunpit 50 meters ahead, to the right. Baker reaches the pit in five gliding leaps. A dozen fighters clamber on top while the rest of the platoon takes position all around, firing into every shrapnel hole and small crack they find.

The pit is full of frightened men and boys, 100 at least. Half are without full combat suits or any weapon, jolted awake and unready by the mine. The blast caught them completely by surprise, then the bright bombardment befuddled and terrified them even more. They can't believe that raging, mad and murderous Krevans are running overtop and all around their hiding place and pouring fire into their huddling ranks. There's no way out. Their enemy is at both ends of the long pit, double enfilading the position. It's about to get worse.

Zofia gestures with her left hand, as if grabbing and pulling at her lower face. Baker understands: *gas*. Half the platoon keeps shooting, but a dozen men take out special grenades and drop them into the pit. The poison gas is so lethal Baker doesn't need to wait to be sure. And Zofia is on them already, threatening them with unnatural acts beyond the skill of a contortionist if they don't keep up.

"Move, move. Get back to glide speed."

"You heard the order, back on your boots!"

"Able, you're the far left flank of the main wedge. You'll always be open on your own left. Double squads there. Sergeant, keep your right flank in sight and in contact with Baker."

“You got it”

“Third Squad. No gaps on the right!”

“Close with Baker’s left.”

“I’m shifting right, sergeant.”

“Tell me why, lieutenant?”

“Charlie’s faltering at the center.”

“Should we cover your move?”

“No. Keep tight over here ‘till I get back.”

“I’ll hold the wedge on this side.”

“Where’s the lieutenant going?”

“Don’t worry about her, boy. Keep moving.”

“Sergeant, where’s she going?”

“She’s gone to fix Charlie. She’ll be right back!”

Click clack, click clack. Signature sound of pink crystal masers.

Poom, poom, poom. Frag grenades exploding in quick succession. *Click clack, click clack, click clack. Hissss, hissss. Poom, poom, poom.* Screams, then groans. Wild pleas for mercy. Low moanings. Sharp cries of pain. The sounds of men and boys dying in bushels. Then silence. The silence of the dead that will deafen far off wailing mothers. *Snick! Slice!* The sounds of Madjenik’s pent up rage and rising hate cutting into corpses lying inert as the adrenal platoons pass them by. They just can’t leave them be. The dead are always giving offense.

Back on the far right flank of the charge Jan lopes over to find out what the holdup is. He signals ahead while moving under and past Dog, before bringing Easy into visual contact.

“Move it Easy!”

"Watch your *reds!*"

"You're falling behind."

Easy has real trouble sealing a large bunker and takes several casualties from Rikugun it left alive too long, giving them time to recover and shoot back. It's slowing down under the burden of helping five of its walking wounded who are failing badly to keep pace. It's struggling to carry two severely burned women and four dead. That means Easy platoon is effectively down a dozen fighters.

Jan sees it all inside a moment as he arrives on the flank. "Hipper! Move ahead with all ablebodied fighters. Assign a squad of ten to help your seven wounded keep up, but move on with the rest of Easy."

"Sir, my wounded. I can't just…"

"Reestablish left flank contact with Dog."

"But sir, you said we never leave any…"

"Corporal, do as you're ordered."

Tom still hesitates to leave his wounded. Jan better explain things fast and get control of Easy, or he'll lose Tom and maybe the whole flank. Easy could come apart right here in the middle of a fight.

"Look Tom, we can't break pace with the wedge. Easy has to hold its place in the main assault line or you'll open up the whole right flank to enfilade when the enemy counterattacks. These *bâtards* will not stay down-and-out forever. We have to get all Madjenik out of this kill zone. Easy is vital to that end."

"Got it. You're right of course, captain."

"I'll see to your wounded."

"Thank you, captain."

"Now, move your fucking platoon!"

"First Squad, fall out and help the wounded."

"Second and Third Squads, stretch the line."

"Fourth Squad, find Dog's flank and stick to it like fleas." Tom grins at his unintended wit, as does all of Fourth Squad. "Everyone not in First Squad, on my tail right now!" In seconds, most of Easy is back on the move, securing the far right flank and stretching out an arm to find and stay in contact with Dog.

Jan turns to the wounded seven and to First Squad. Two helpers already have strong arms around the worst burn cases, raising them to the company of the other walking wounded. Eight more are about to pick up four litters of dead fighters, two-by-two. They're scared shitless.

"We won't leave without you. I promise."

"Thank you, captain."

"We'll be right behind you." It's the NCO now in charge.

"One thing. All you stretcher bearers, get the wounded on those litters. Start with the burn cases, the girl first. Gently now! Also, that boy with the bound thigh. He's trying to keep up but slowing you all down. It'll be faster to carry him."

"We don't have enough litters."

"Leave our dead where they lie."

"Captain?"

"The dead won't mind."

"Leave them after coming all this way, so close to the end?

"It's what they'd want. Let that *bâtard* Death have them, if he dares to be in the company of any Wrecker. Death will live to regret his invitation!"

It's a truly corny boast, but in the heat of combat here in the crater they love him for it. They needed just such a reason to leave their dead friends behind, to choose instead to live and fight on for the dead and for themselves. When Jan vowed to himself to leave no one behind ever again, he meant no one living. Only a fool of a commander orders good live fighters to risk all to retrieve or carry out dead ones in the middle of an intense fight. And Jan Wysocki is neither a fool nor a bad officer. Not anymore.

"You just keep moving as best you can. We'll cut a path through these locust for you. Stay in HUD range. Follow our *blue*. We won't leave any *red* behind us. But if you do get pinned down, sit tight. I'll come back for you personally with all Madjenik."

They know he means it and that the Wreckers would do it. They nod to him gratefully. He doesn't see their gratitude. He's already zag gliding at max speed, back to the center of an assault wedge that's threatening to dissolve into stalled and broken bits. He's looking now to goad and reposition wandering Charlie.

'*My snow geese idea's not looking so good right now. The 'Vic' is stalling.*' He's blaming himself, as he always does. Yet no matter what he did the combat friction that's badly slowing down Madjenik's flying wedge on the right flank would have caterpillared, to further slow and discombobulate its whole line. It would've been worse if he'd stayed in the general's single wedge formation.

Watching the little battle for the crater unfold on viewscreens, seeing exactly what Jan sees from a live feed from his command link HUD, also looking out her high tower window, General Amiya Constance reaches the same conclusion about his creative adaptation of her battle plan and strict orders. '*Is he the one, this Ghost of the Wood? Is he the one to lead us all? Perhaps, but first he must survive, and get Madjenik out of the crater.*'

More movement. More shooting. More funk holes turned into instant death traps. More pitiless killing. Grenades tossed into ripped open apertures on the fly, smashing apart startled faces peering up and out. Officers are astonished to see fighters in oakish weaves flashing so close, then to feel sudden hot glaring lasers scoring the inner bunker wall behind their heads. Before they can react, incoming gas and frag grenades end all their lifelong arrogance and ambition.

Private Jarred Whitmore cries out "Got him!" as he fires his maser right into the face of a looming, tanned looking man with pleasant features and close cropped black hair. Now the pleasant looking man has no face at all. Or hair. Or head. It's Jarred's first ever kill shot.

"Whitmore! He was already dead. Try to hit a live one next time. And keep moving, there aren't any flowers out here!"

Zofia moves in a whirling blur, thumping Jarred hard on the back to get him going, back into line with his mates in Charlie.

'*Why does she always have to shout at me?*'

Jan joins Zofia at the center, where both urge Charlie to speed up. Then they look back to the flanks, where things are going poorly, but for different reasons.

"Charlie is balling everything up by stalling out. You go back left and take charge. Something's happening with Able and Baker over there. They're moving out ahead of Charlie, much faster than they should be moving. Find out what's going on, and fix it."

"Where will you be?" Zofia asks it as she's already combat gliding left, fast.

"I'll take the right, and I'll push Charlie. If we don't move faster here at the center our wedge will become a bent bow instead. It's already happening: both flanks are now in front."

Jan accelerates Charlie's pace so that it moves ahead of Dog at least, but sees Easy is still struggling to stay in the line, staggering in its echelon position then accelerating until it badly overshoots the flank mark and takes the lead. He calls angrily over the HUD command link.

"Damn it, Easy, you gotta watch speed and position. You've gotten ahead of Dog. Hell, you're also ahead of Charlie at the center now."

"Easy, throttle back."

"Adjust glide boots to half speed, on my mark … *mark!*"

"Tom Hipper here, sir. My fault. It won't happen again."

"It better not. We can't have gaps. I know you're short 20 fighters, Tom. All the more reason to keep Easy attached to the big 'V.' Keep pace with Dog. Stay 20 glides back, hard on its flank. Don't straighten the line. Dog, you keep pace with Charlie here in the middle, also 20 glides back. Everyone stay in contact, but I want a wedge, not a line! Move it!"

The big, black haired sergeant in charge of Dog lost his out voice coms to a glancing hit to his helmet right at the start. He hears his captain but can't voice back. Luckily Jan's in visual range. So he gives him a thumb-and-index circle sign instead: *Understood.*

The terrain is becoming an issue, but that's not what forces a change on the left flank, ragging the vital wedge that Jan so wants to maintain. Over there, Able and Baker race ahead on the other side of Charlie, 250 meters to its left. Fighters are shooting, cursing, raging out of control. One mad youth howls "Remember the Old Forest Road!" and all the others howl back and shoot.

They're in hot blood.

They murder everyone.

Armed and unarmed alike.

They give no quarter to crying boys or wounded men with arms held up high, beseeching them for mercy. Or to prone wounded too hurt to pray or protest. Terrified crawlers tug at oak leggings standing over them, before a hot muzzle pressed to their temple blows them apart, pleading with big eyes in upturned faces that disappear in a microwave blast of red chunks and cheekbone. Older men kneel with folded, praying hands, lie to young women who don't give a shit.

"I have three children, please!"

Click clack, poom, poom.

"Fuck you and your children!"

Frightened boys from Yokohama and Nagoya hold arms high and palms out, crying out "*gomenasai! gomenasai!*" No one in raging Madjenik understands or cares to listen to their cries of "I'm sorry! I'm sorry!" Not after armtrak 'grindings' of KRA prisoners at the MDL. Not after all the firefights in Pilsudski Wood. Not after the bombing and burning of the Gold Oak Forest. Not after the stark gray, silent and faceless statues and cone piles of ash on the Old Forest Road. Just before they die, a handful of Pyotr's men in green falling outside the Gate realize that they've released something terrible into Orion. All resistance evaporates, facing primal ferocity and madness. Terrified officers and men slam armored shutters on exposed bunkers positioned all around the outer rim, hoping the *furia Krevia* will pass without pausing to kill them. Men caught in the open drop weapons and run.

"That's enough! Get back into wedge formation, godsdamn you!" Jan hears Zofia struggling to regain control over Able and Baker, now in danger of running amok. Hears her calling "Stop!" as a pillbox erupts in leaping flames and dying screams, but troopers keep on shooting into billow clouds of dark smoke and fire. "They're dead you idiots. If you want kill RIK, follow me to the next target."

It's getting dangerous, this rising lust and combat rage. Jan realizes Zofia is putting herself in front of it, in order to lead Able and Baker back to discipline on the far left flank. He must do something else. Charlie and the right flank of Dog and Easy have reached the middle of the blast zone. Jan sends a broadcast to the whole company. "All platoons. Halt the advance and check your *IFFs*! We're at the rendezvous. Relief One will be on us in seconds. Put up your weapons, now!"

Jan watches a squad from Dog cruelly finish off two kneeling, begging men just paces away. He hasn't time to stop it, and isn't sure he wants to. He repeats the order: "*IFF* all company check."

"*Check!* Positive ID, captain. Here they come! It's Relief One, right on time."

"All platoons, *halt movement and cease fire!*" It's a triple order. He sends a flash over all HUDs, shouts it into the auditory channel, and whirls his left hand over his head, physically signaling: *rally point!*

"*Huzzzahhh!*" echoes in his ears. It's one of the ex-privates, a breveted NCO still flushed with combat lust. He sees Jan's almost lethal look and stops cold, then stops his squad and drops into a defensive crouch.

"He must've forgotten he's on the command link." It's Zofia in his ear this time. She's back beside him at the rally point, with Able and Baker halted. Jan looks down and sees the bottoms of her weaves are burned black. She grins at him from inside a dark visor.

"Enough chatter!" Jan cuts everyone out of the company link, even Zofia. "All platoons halt in place. Hold up! *Cease firing.*"

Intermittent, individual firing continues all down from Madjenik's extended line. "Stop shooting! Check your IFFs! That's Relief One over there!"

A half platoon of leaderless RIK breaks cover and makes a dash for it, running right across the firing sights of Dog's still warm and humming masers. Eighteen kids quickly drop like broken dolls as Dog opens up and *blue-white* bolts sear them bloody from behind. Three lie howling, wounded on the ground.

"Dog, godsdamn it! *Cease firing!* Jablonski, get that platoon under control." Dog's too eager shooters reluctantly go into a defensive circle crouch. They stare like birders at the three thrashing, wounded youths they want to retrieve, to kill. They look slyly back at Jan and Zofia, like excited, chastised, well ... dogs.

"Easy, hold position right where you are. You're undermanned. Hipper, take two squads, one from Charlie, one from Dog. Go back and get the rest of Easy up here on the double. Carry the wounded yourself if you have to. No one stays behind." Hipper cuts out two squads and doubles back to escort Easy's wounded. Other platoons have taken casualties, too. Zofia does a quick tally for the whole company. She looks over to Jan.

"How many?"

"Thirty-five, captain."

"How many of those are KIA?"

"Twenty-three."

"Right lieutenant. Carry on."

Out of safe shooting range, two Fahnleins of RIK combat virgins, more than 80 Nagoyan youths, race madly away from Madjenik, not knowing it stopped to close up its ragged wedge and wait for Relief One to meet it in the middle of the battlefield. They run hard, panicking and utterly unaware of direction, desperate only to gain distance from the dreadful enemy behind them, from the tan terror they think is still gliding remorselessly after them. Blood and bone is all around. Luckily, none belongs to friendlies approaching fast and now clear *blue* in his visor, closing on the jagged and running *reds.* He watches all 80 youths die seconds later, in real time and vision, running heedlessly onto oncoming masers of Relief One. They're shot down screaming "*gomenasai!*"

There's no pity left in this war. Watching this, failing to stop it, a couplet comes back to Jan along with a half memory. Something about an innocent teenage queen sacrificed to High Court politics. He turns it into an epitaph for all frail youth he's helping to kill out here. '*As virgins we lived but bloody we died. We never once asked whether they lied.*'

Over on the far right of Relief One the same fate befalls more than 200 'Purity' volunteers from Schwyz. They throw down all weapons to raise their arms high, shouting "We surrender!" or "Quarter! Quarter!" Their enemies combat gliding from the Berm Gate are not so different from Madjenik. They, too, have hot masers and months of built up hatred *humming* in their hands. No RIK who begs for quarter in the shadow of the berm receives it. It's a merciless slaughter, until the last terrified scream falls into the crater.

A few minutes more and resistance ceases in and around the crater. Shooting stops, except for an intermittent *pop, pop* as some wounded or hiding man or boy in green is finished off. Dog takes the opportunity to finish the three wounded boys it has been watching all along, while it waited for Relief One to arrive. The ones Jan told them to leave alone. Madjenik's visor checks show only *blue* active IFFs left within 1,500 meters on either flank. As Easy's wounded catch up to the main body it's just as Jan promised: no *reds* are left behind.

Two fresh and unbloodied RIK battalions stand ready in attack position on the far flanks. They watch murderous scenes unfold in and around the crater without moving to aid or save dying comrades. Then they let Madjenik and Relief One leave. They want nothing to do with this terrible, deadly force, with hundreds of pitiless killers marching the short distance to the yawning Gate. Madjenik moves upright and defiant across a scorched battlefield, as if on parade. Its weapons are warm and ready. Hot murder is on its hands and in its flashing eyes. RIK officers and men gaze in mute awe at the once mocked *Gelben.* These are no "yellow" cowards moving to the city. They're trailing pikes of exhaustion but all are walking upright, or carrying carbon fiber litters of their wounded.

Walking, not running.

Walking, not gliding.

Not hurrying at all.

Not trying to take cover.

They're utterly defiant.

Proud, filthy, dangerous.

Terrible and terrifying.

Wreckers and brave firefighters of Relief One march to the Berm Gate in five discrete wedges, flanked by four spread out files. Those who survived the long trek to Toruń protected by new comrades who raced into hellfire to meet Death and the Wreckers. They move together over upturned, smoking soil, brown splashed with red, littered with thousands of whole and partly rendered corpses. Those from older firefights mixing unbiased with new dead torn apart by the mine blast and plasma bombardment. Or from the infantry fight right after.

RIK picked up the last several minutes of Madjenik's unit coms, broadcast in the clear as it neared Relief One. They know who these fighters are now, where they came from, and that they're the ones who humiliated an Oetkert general of the *blood royale*, escaped a whole division in the south before coming to Toruń.

"Gods, they slaughtered all our boys!"

"Look, in the middle of the wedge. Who's that?"

"No! By Purity and the Black Faith!"

"It's the Ghost!"

"The Ghost of the Wood is here!"

Begrudgingly, one of the watching battalion officers says: "They're tough. I have to admit it. I could almost admire these tawny bastards." No one disagrees. For the first time, arrogant Rikugun who brought fear and calamity to Genève know that they fear the deadly fighters in dirty tan weaves limping into Toruń.

Data search: navies
Result: deterrence
Historia Humana, Volume XX, Part VI (d)

The energy revolution that underlay the Second Age of Expansion arrived with controllable and miniaturized fusion, the nudging of deuterium and tritium atoms with tiny lasers until they overcame the atomic repulsion barrier and fused inside magnetic containment chambers. Radical miniaturization came next, with the development of compact tori allowing low field magnetic plasma containment. That had the biggest effect on land and ship weapons during the First, Second, and Third Orion Wars. Since then, still lower threshold tokamaks permit small ground plasma cannon mounted on armtraks, while tiny plasma drives diversified missile and warship design so that today's major navies have many varied classes, unlike the older navies that centered on a single battleship or 'ship-of-the-line' model, and attendant tactics. All major star states have built ships deploying new weapons systems and theory. Fortunately, naval development is still untested and unused in real war, as we remain deep inside the blessed or Shōwa Age.

There are critics of modern navalism who say its ideas about strategic balance lead instead to needless expansion of all navies, and thus raise costs and tensions in Orion. Some accuse Kars School theorists of providing cover for less than noble interests, justifying and expanding budgets that were cut severely over the first 200 years of the Peace of Orion. They say navalism serves mainly special interests, not the real demands of defense. The most radical say that building powerful battleships and fleets of cruisers, light cruisers, and destroyers to guarantee peace only makes war more likely. That putting instruments of war in the hands of policy makers only tempts them to aggression, since navies might be used as easily as a sword than as a shield. They say Orion must disarm, universally or unilaterally, stand down all its armies and dry dock its permanent navies if we are to continue within the Long Peace.

Proponents of military preparedness as the preserver of peace reject this idea out of hand, in the name of moral and political realism. They retort that such critics are fatal naïfs who do not understand that we humans shall have war always, even if our current moment in Orion is entirely peaceful. They argue the record of our past to counter those who would disarm today in hope for a better tomorrow. They point especially to the fate of Setubal and Lugo in the Third Orion War as bitter examples of what a lack of military and specifically naval readiness might mean should war return some day to ravage the star states and peoples of Orion. It is an ancient debate, engaging sages of war and peace arguing over millennia. It has been argued up and down the length and across the breadth of the thousand histories of the Thousand Worlds of our great spiral arm civilization.

Fortunately, the drums of war beat only in that history. The star states of Orion today prepare for war, but only to keep peace through military balance and deterrence. We have achieved a fine balance, order and stability. We guarantee it in the blessed treaty known as the 'Peace of Orion' that codified the settlement ending the Third Orion War nearly 300 years ago. That great document set up the safeguards that have kept peace ever since, along with the great and majestic navies that today patrol the star lanes and borders where the major empires meet.

Technological shifts since the Peace of Orion was agreed mean new weapons became possible, then become facts. Yet the will to use them remains suppressed, as vestigial in our advanced time as an appendix. As extinct as Old Earth dinosaur bones kept in museum cases. We are deep in what many call the new Satya Yuga, the age of truth, virtue and righteousness. Only the second in our long and too often sordid history. Others call this time the Shōwa Age.

By whatever name, the idea that conflict must lead to war is only an echo of the past, a relic of our former folly and inertia of culture and imagination. We moderns have demonstrated the wisdom to forgo war. We are beyond war. We have decided to never again lose in war some future Mozart or a Wang, or some other yet unknown and unrequited youth of eternal talent secretly embedded in the billions whom war would take away before their due time, foreshortening their Youthspan and denying their talent to those who stay behind...

Parade

Survivors of '*The Battle of the Crater*' who stagger through the Berm Gate are in pretty rough shape. Rougher even than tens of thousands of rejected refugees camped and penned and guarded just inside the berm wall, still denied access to the city proper on General Constance's firm order. Unable to pass the screening.

As Tom Hipper stumbles past the hopeless huddle he's appalled. Some look to be as filthy and bad off, or worse, than Easy platoon. And his troops spent months trekking here.

"Who are they?"

"They got no ID, corporal. Least ways, not a valid one."

"What will happen to them?"

"General says, 'don't let 'em in,' so I don't let 'em in."

"But they're our people!"

"Orders. You know."

"Orders can change..."

"Look son, don't worry about it. Trust the general."

Tom can't linger to find out more or protest. He must see to Easy's wounded, some of whom are dying. Of course they're given suspend by triage medics attached to Relief One right on the battlefield, but at least three won't make it if they're ever unfrozen. "Reanimate them and they'll die in minutes," says the KRA surgeon who looks them over in a quick triage just inside the Berm Gate. "We can fix a good deal, but not everything." Tom is at his wits end what to do, and gladdens when the worst of the wounded are taken away from him by the surgeon and carried off to somewhere inside the city. Only then does he think once more about the pathetic souls still outside the inner perimeter.

When RIK besiegers arrived outside the berm General Constance rescinded one tenet of her martial law decree, her decision to bar possible fifth columnists from entry. Moved by mercy, she let all civvies through the Gate to at least huddle inside the berm. She gives them rations and water but that's it. She still denies them entry into the city proper. They stay in berm camps or restrictive pens, all under armed guard just inside the interior of the berm wall.

When Madjenik arrives there's a second city of sooty tents, huts and pens, packed against the inner firewall, atop the flat firebreak that runs around Toruń's perimeter between a squat earthen inner wall and the superconcrete covered and reinforced outer berm. It's a grimy reminder that some Krevans collaborated with the invaders before the war. Like the faceless Honda boy Zofia shot, and Jan ordered left hidden under leaf cover, to rot and serve as food for tree ants.

The 'second city' refugees are almost all natives of Genève, yet are rejected by Toruń City Police and the Spaceport Security. Even their biometric scans are suspect. And how can or do you prove personal loyalty when forests that stood unharmed and protected for over a thousand years are burning all around, while across Krevo worlds are falling to brutes and brutality?

'*At least they're alive and safe inside the berm, and as well fed as anyone else. I suppose we have to do it. Just seems such a shame, to do it to our own.*' Tom walks away from the refugees, toward the berm tunnel denied to them. He feels thousands of eyes boring silently into his back. '*Fuck, I hate this war.*'

There's no need to vet Madjenik. Gate guards know, or think they do, all about the forest fights and long trek by "Wysocki's Wreckers." Madjenik's exploits have been the talk of Toruń for months; its real deeds but even more those wholly imagined in tall tales that grow longer with each retelling. The city's interest in Madjenik goes as far back as when the 'Lost Company' fought off and then obliterated pursuing hover scouts way back in Pilsudski Wood.

Since all Genèven independent broadcasting went down and military coms went out within a day of the breakthrough and the flight from the MDL, the only source of information on Madjenik was Rikugun milneb chatter intercepted by the KRA in Toruń. Desperate hope did the rest.

"That Ghost is running rings around the enemy!"

"They'll never catch him or the Lost Company. *Hurray!*"

"He gave them scouts what for, that's certain true."

"He's gone quiet now. You just wait. He'll be back."

The stories kept Toruńite spirits up for a while, until General Brusilov went live with his proclamation of a brilliant and total victory in the south, and boasted of his "extermination of all the forest bandits." No one believed the fat windbag, until RSU staff showed off piles of fake corpses in oak weaves in a propaganda vid broadcast night and day directly into Toruń. Hope and morale plunged after that. Behind even Brusilov's lies must be the truth of Madjenik's death.

Madjenik trekked silently northward, all the while given up for real ghosts or worse by despairing Toruńites who no longer expected to hear good news from anywhere outside the berm. What did stories to thrill children matter anyway, as their city girded for its final battle? Then came an astonishing contact. Months ago, Constance ordered TCC to routinely sweep all KRA com link channels. No one was more surprised than her bored listeners when the beam picked up Jan's command link, rediscovering lost Madjenik less than five klics away from the berm, then connecting it to the Toruń garrison and HQ.

It wasn't until just two hours ago that ordinary fighters and civilian Toruńites learned that Madjenik is still alive, and unbelievably, is heading over the bridge toward the Berm Gate. The first, rather loud hint only came when the mine went off and an intense barrage began just outside the city.

Most folks thought it was the beginning of the end, the start of the final RIK assault and last battle. Thought that RIK and SAC troops would be in the streets in just hours or days, breaking into the golden city of burnished wood streets and polished towers. It makes the news of Madjenik's arrival seem even more, well, miraculous. Millions rush to see for themselves.

Everyone wants to see the Ghost and his 'Lost Company.' Over three million line the Grand Boulevard leading from the Berm Gate into the inner city, to Governance Square and Old Towne Hall. Even if the forest stories are only half true, or less, everyone waiting knows what just took place outside the city's walls. They're there to cheer the first good news in months, a rare story of life triumphing over death and Krevans over Grünen; to celebrate the safe arrival of a gritty cohort everyone except its captain is calling "Wysocki's Wreckers."

Madjenik's too humble leader doesn't know it yet, but his name along with tall tales of his exploits in the forests and at the crater is spreading far beyond even Genève, to wherever holdout Krevans cling to a thread of hope or hate. Wherever there's still resistance or Krevans huddle in fear under occupation.

How could he know that Constance gave orders months back to make sure that Jan's story, the tall tale of the Ghost of the Woods, was spread across Krevo and out into all Orion? He doesn't know that she signed a report just minutes ago that's on the way to Aral, saying the *Battle of the Crater* plan was his, not hers. Constance is playing a very long game, indeed. Jan isn't even aware that he's on the board, let alone the key piece in her grand strategic design.

A handsome young lieutenant offers a crisp salute and salutations. He's neatly, even impeccably, dressed in crisp and creased wheat sheaves. "Lieutenant Dylan Byers, sir. Welcome to Toruń, Captain Wysocki. It's an honor to have an officer and hero like you here."

"I don't know about that, especially the hero bit. I do know I wouldn't be here without my NCOs, and without Relief One coming out to lead us in. But thank you, lieutenant. We're all very glad to be here."

'He's just as described: modest to a fault, at least on the outside. I wonder how deep that trait really runs? Is my general right about this man? Is he the future of our resistance? Is he our last, best hope?'

Jan is debriefed by Byers in a guardhouse in the dark middle of the tunnel. "HQ has your combat logs, uploaded from your HUD. Your last *After Action* and *Mission* reports can wait for a day or two, after you rest up and settle in."

"I appreciate that. I'll need time to settle Madjenik in the city."

"Let me help you with that, captain. It would be my privilege." He turns to a nearby NCO. "Corporal, see to the captain's equipment and personal needs."

"I'd rather he took care of my fighters first, lieutenant."

"Of course. Corporal, bring me a list of all possible quarters for, let's call it just under 300 fighters. Then see to the captain himself."

He turns back to Jan. "Alright?"

"Thank you, lieutenant."

"No need to thank me, sir. But I have to tell you, food and water closets and the like are not a problem, but it won't be easy finding you bunks. We're pretty much overfull already."

"I shouldn't think Madjenik will be in them very long. Looks like there are a lot more visitors outside who won't want to share when they get here."

'*He's bitterly realistic and darkly humored, again just as MI reported. How interesting.*' Byers snaps off another perfectly crisp salute. "I'll rejoin you as soon as I can, captain."

"We're done already?"

"I must speak to your NCOs and second in command."

"Oh, that's good. Yes, do that."

"I look forward to your field reports, when you're ready. "Is there anything I can do for you right now, personally I mean?"

"If I could just have some of that coffee while I wait? It has been months since I ..." Jan nods to the Guards shed, from where he smells a rich dark aroma he had all but forgotten.

"Corporal! Bring that pot over here, and a mug."

Oddly, Dylan Byers takes a lot longer talking with Zofia and the NCOs than with Jan. He notices, but doesn't dwell. He meant what he said about seeing to the needs of Madjenik first. After he finishes the java, of course. '*Gods, it's like drinking liquid silk. How can anything be this good?*' He finishes a third mug as he moves to the far end of the tunnel where he waits for Madjenik to be debriefed.

Jan doesn't like the almost worshipful looks he gets from faces in the crowd peering into the tunnel end, where he stands with his back against the cold, damp wall waiting for Zofia and Madjenik to finish talking to Byers and catch him up. Then he decides he's too tired to care who or why anyone is staring at him or what all the odd looks and whispering is really about.

'*It must be the mud and blood I forgot is all over my utes. I also forgot about my three month old beard. Good thing there's no mirrors in this tunnel. I wonder what I look like? Probably like I need a handout and a hand up. Surely not like a proper officer, not like that young lieutenant. You could serve cold desert to a virgin off his polished brass buttons.*"

He's glad it's all over, his heavy burden of command. He feels it nearing the end as he watches his veterans shuffle up with stiff gaits, each man or woman still throwing exhausted shoulders back as they pass by to receive his salute, which he gives in honor of their sacrifice. Though he's a little proud that he got them to Toruń, he's certain that the general will relieve him. Surely she will, after she reads his *After Action Reports*. Certain, because he'll write them in such a way that she'll have no choice but to give the company to a more deserving officer.

He thinks they must be relieved to be out from under his command, that better officers will take over Madjenik. Glad that he won't be able to fail them again, like he did do badly at the MDL. Glad there's no more chance that he'll get them killed by making some huge error, or leave them behind as he runs from battle and his responsibility.

All of his fighters know
their captain has blundered.
Only he still questions why
many more did not die.
All of his three hundred.

The old lines come to him again, as they did that first time while standing in the bloody sweetgrass meadow, shocked at what he had done and what he saw Zofia do. Uncertain what to do next. Where to go or how to get there. Once again he's wrong. He doesn't understand his fighters yet. They're not thinking that at all.

Not one of Madjenik's oddball veterans thinks it. Their shoulder flashes say they come from a dozen different broken companies, these 268 survivors who march past Jan over the bridge, through the tunnel and into the city. Today, not one thinks of themselves as anything other than Madjenik Company. More even than that, they're all proud to call themselves "Wysocki's Wreckers."

Jan's right about one thing: he and they look like hell, shuffling wearily out of the tunnel mouth, passing by the sullen, wan refugees hunkered in guarded pens beside the squat inner berm line. Then past a smaller crowd clapping too wildly. Guards' families, mostly. They stop at the exit of the compact tunnel, readying to step from its dim light into a crisp autumn morning. An hour after wading in ash and battle, sure to die, they'll enter a golden city of wood.

Without asking, Zofia suddenly takes charge of Madjenik. "Company, fall in by platoon. Parade formation. Sir, you need to take point on this one."

***

She got the idea and the order from General Constance, delivered to her and the NCOs directly by Lt. Byers. Jan thinks she's acting a little odd but assumes his parade position at Madjenik's head. Zofia knows what he doesn't: millions of Toruńites are waiting to cheer the Ghost.

At first it's not much of a parade, as Jan and Madjenik move out of the dark tunnel. It seems like it will be scruffy and short and therefore to his liking. He wants no fuss. He just wants to get the company quartered and settled in. So he's glad that Relief One leads the way, marching crisply, rightfully proud of its actions at the crater. Then comes Jan at the head of shambolic Madjenik. As it shuffles out the tunnel into breaking sunlight and into the view of an immense and cheering crowd, not just Jan but all the company hesitates, stumbles and blinks.

The crowd is immense and stretches straight ahead as far as natural eyes can see. But that's not the most astonishing thing to Jan and Madjenik. An honor guard in dress gold-and-white uniforms from the prewar KRA lines both sides of the Grand Boulevard. No one back in the forest ever imagined such a scene. No one thinks they deserve it, least of all Jan Wysocki.

General Constance ordered the uniforms and route "readied for a square bashing" less than an hour after learning that Madjenik was alive outside the berm. Byers worked it all out in secret while she worked on the crater mine plan, and set up the barrage and Relief One.

"Really general? You want me to plan a parade? Shouldn't we wait to see if your plan actually works and we get the Lost Company back inside the berm?"

"Usually, Lieutenant Byers, I appreciate your candor and your keen instincts. You surprise me on both scores this time. I confess, I'm a little disappointed."

"I'm sorry sir, I just don't understand. Not fully, anyway."

"You will when you see how our people react tomorrow. They need this. We need this. You can't fight a war without hope. Especially a hopeless one."

"Well general, I'll get right on it, of course. The route is obvious: the Grand Boulevard. The full trimmings might take some work, given that we're so short of fighters around the berm wall."

"Take as many as you need to do the parade route right. Make it a show for the history books. No lieutenant, make it one for the Ages. I'm trying to create a living legend, you know."

"Yes general. And if offworld reports are anything to go by, you're already halfway there. Who knew the Ghost of the stories and your dispatches to Aral would actually return?"

"I did."

Dylan Byers gets it now, watching the faces in the crowd, seeing hope where he has seen nothing but deepening despair and desolation over loss after loss ever since the war began. '*She might be right about him. And also about us. What a remarkable woman and officer, my general is.*'

Jubilant crowds erupt into loud cheers all along the route into the city center, jostling to get close enough to see the 'Ghost of the Wood.' To see the legend who brings hope, if only for a moment, to part the overcast gloom of a defeat all know is coming. They waive little wheat sheave flags, cheer "*Vive Madjenik!*" and "*Vive Genève!*" They clap and stamp for all the tired and filthy survivors who pass before them, chests out now in spite of themselves, eyes up and proud.

Millions of tramping feet make thunder rolls that vibrate down the thick wooden streets, echo in canyon side streets, and climb the oak and teak and redwood walls of bronzed towers. In an open park hosting a big refugee camp by one of the artificial lakes, a stray dog feels the strange vibrations through its paws. A war orphan, it hears cloudless thunder and howls to the moons, loud and low.

Now the crowd starts to sing. A million voices take up the familiar old songs praising Genève's beauty, its golden forests and high mountains and foamy seas. Like all sentimental local songs, they assert that their world is the envy of Orion.

Golden boughs, golden boughs,
rising wood towers above me.
Aged and wide, roof of the night,
a hundred generations before me.

Cathedrals growing in panes of gold,
silver pine pillars upholding.
Golden boughs, golden boughs,
rise o'er my homeworld forever.

Lots more like that. The usual pastoral stuff. The local songs people learn in childhood and turn to later in times of worry and woe, in times of war. Songs they really love and remember.

The Grand Boulevard slices through wooden canyons of residential towers designed to remind Toruńites of the great oak and teak forests from which they were hewn. Jan focuses on the wooden street beams, looking away from the varnished towers rising overhead and the huge crowd lined up as far ahead as he can see, for at least three klics.

He thinks: '*How oddly firm the street is underfoot, after months of walking only on deep windfall or ash. I forgot what it felt like, to have firmness under my boots. It feels good. It feels right.*'

Little girls in best print dresses, small boys wearing bow ties, all holding stiff childish salutes, are pushed to the front of the happy crowd. It wants them to remember. Mothers and fathers farther back hold up dopey, drooling toddlers who won't remember to see all the marching "heroes of the forest." It's the first public celebration of anything in Toruń since before the war.

Jan hates it all. Really hates it. He turns to look over his right shoulder at Zofia, who grins rakishly. "How can they pull troops off the berm wall for *this*?"

"I'm sure we're safe, sir." Zofia is slipping into her natural mode: sarcasm. Then she corrects herself. "The enemy is still absorbing what we did to him at the crater. I'm sure the berm defense is solid, sir."

"What the hell?"

A color troop and two regimental bands slide out of side streets and onto the main boulevard, inserting themselves ahead of and between Madjenik and Relief One. The color guard carries every flag of every battalion in Toruń. The bands are playing martial songs. And as the last troopers in Madjenik pass by each squad in gold-and-white, all the full dress color guard lining the long boulevard step into the middle and form ranks. Now a long regiment in gorgeous uniforms brings up the rear in brass and braid. It's a proper military parade, now.

"Gods, this general thinks of everything!" Jan laments to Zofia.

"Doesn't she just?"

"You *like* this?"

"No, not really. But I understand it."

"Well I don't."

Zofia can't help prodding him. "To like it I'd have to shower first, hot and long, with lots of suds. Then I'd step out and slow walk over to where I left my brand new, clean dress uniform. Just like all those very pretty boys and girls are wearing, all lined up along the roadside. I'd pull it on really slowly, you know, to feel clean cloth on my naked skin again. It has been a long time…"

"*Puleeezz!*" He can't help himself. Not triggered so obviously and seductively like that. He starts to imagine Zofia soaping herself all over in a steamy shower, before languidly dressing in a fresh oak uniform.

She looks coyly at him, correctly suspecting what he's thinking. "Captain? Are you still with us?" She really can be a terrible tease.

"Right then. There's nothing for it but to bear up and get this over with." Jan sends what he believes will be one of his very last commands to the company. "*Attention!* Tighten up the parade formation, Madjenik! You look like lost ducks in a thunderstorm! Straighten ranks, march!"

It doesn't matter that among the paraders are walking wounded. and several severely hurt in need of suspend, carried on stretchers on low hovers, medics working on them as they pass the cheering, laughing, clapping crowds who choose not to see the wounds or feel their pain. Not in this moment of forced communal joy. It doesn't matter that the women of Madjenik are all wan and filthy, with ash matted hair and shapeless weaves covered in shit and blood and ash. It doesn't matter that the men are dirty, over bearded, too thin, and stooped low with bone weary cares and real combat trauma. No one in the cheering millions minds at all that Zofia looks like something the cat vomited. No one cares that scruffy, bearded and brooding Jan hardly looks a hero. More like the bandit captain out of General Brusilov's and RIK milneb propaganda.

It only matters that Madjenik is in Toruń at this moment, that Genèvens have heroes again and a reason to clap and sing. That for once the war has not gone in favor of the invader. That just once they got the upper hand on the brutal army that descended on harmless Genève in blood and rape and murder and crime. With its death squads and petty bullies, setting fire to the most beloved forests in all Orion for no greater reason than oily Pyotr's lusts and Imperium vanity.

Madjenik limps and struts at the same time, picking up the pace with eyes only to the front, ignoring the bands, ignoring the crowds, ignoring honor and glory and all that other shit its fighters were taught since preschool. They march briskly to the city center not to please the millions but because their captain said to stand straighter and to step faster and look prouder. Madjenik does it for Jan Wysocki. It does it because its fighters call themselves "Wysocki's Wreckers."

After a mercifully short welcoming ceremony, everyone in the company simply drops in place and falls asleep right there on the ground in Governance Square. They just drop weps and gear and then themselves, curling atop near empty field pack pillows as they are long used to doing. The whole company falls into instant slumber, and stays asleep for a day and a night.

General Constance protects them from benevolent molestation with a ring of shushing guards all around the square. All still dressed in prewar gold-and-white uniforms, they keep back too friendly crowds that press close to see the heroes.

"My, such perfect toy soldiers," Zofia sneers to Jan just before she falls asleep on the ground, a crumple of total exhaustion.

"Ah, don't be such a..."

It's just as well they all sleep where they drop, since there's no place to put Madjenik. Every tower, every room and public space in Toruń is already packed with refugees from across Genève. So the next morning Jan and Zofia go to see Dylan to find quarters. He offers them 60 small rooms in a corner of a building that holds 600 Grün internees from the two impounded cruise ships.

"Don't worry. We'll kick them into one of the internee camps by the lakes, or maybe move them to the berm ring. Should've done it long ago, actually. Now, let's talk about food and fresh uniforms. And I think you've all got back pay coming, too. I'll see the troops get it."

That's a big mistake. Already the town is buying everyone in Madjenik free drinks. Now, with credits in hand and both officers away, the rougher sorts get drunk on bitter pine ale and eat themselves sick on *juhtúró* and sour kissel. Five are in jail before noon, 50 by that evening. All are released by the MPs once sobered up, just in time to get drunk and in trouble again.

In fact, everyone gets royally pissed except the two officers. Jan and Zofia eat their fill, then head to the city quartermaster to get medical supplies, replacement weps and a new batch of clean weaves and uniforms. But first they visit their wounded from the '*Long Trek*' and '*The Crater*,' as the Gate fight is now called. It earned its upper case treatment in blood and wounds. Not all who survived the trek and final battle will make it. Jan feels responsible for every pending death.

He signs papers moving his ablebodied fighters into the lower four floors of a small, backstreet tourist hotel from which farfolk cruise ship passengers are expelled, told to find a place in one of the tent camps by the lakes. With Madjenik settled in and their duty done by the end of the second day, and officially given a week's leave, Jan and Zofia get as well lubricated on pine ale and Baku liquor as all the rest of Madjenik. Then they head back to the hotel.

They're shown their quarters, a small all teak room in the lower quadrant. The *maître d'hôtel* insists they have it, beaming as if he's escorting them to a royal suite. The small, bronzed room has a compact night desk, a single clothes bureau, a night table and lamp, and a single bed. Jan and Zofia both pretend to protest against being forced to share.

"You don't have two rooms? I don't want to pull rank, but each officer is entitled by regulations to separate quarters."

"That was prewar, sir. Everybody's double bunking now, or more. Best we can do with all the refugees here. And it really is all that I have, sirs, if you want to be near your company."

"Well, fine then. It is what it is. Lt. Jablonski, do you agree?"

"It'll have to do, sir. We've had to lie down with a lot worse under us these past several months. As long as there's a shower..."

"It's your official officer's quarters now. Here's the only key, sirs."

Well fed and showered and alone together at last, they stop pretending and make love for the first time. Then again and again. It's everything they expected and hoped for, Jan in his most erotic forest dreams, Zofia in her long secret and fondest wishes. They molt uniforms and cares onto the dark wood floor and pour themselves into *kama* and each other, melding bodies and souls, uniting as never before with any partner, far beyond what either thought possible. They fit together naturally, physically and emotionally. Almost perfectly, from the first touch and time to every time. It's a rare thing.

Afterward, Jan curls himself around the violin curve of Zofia's smaller, naked form as they lie in languid physical satisfaction, soft stroking affection, and a sublimity of newly paired lovers' contentment. They've survived combat and the great forest trek and are, for a day at least, alive and together, sharing an intimate string of moments like neither has before. Then Jan ruins it all.

When dawn comes he can't make direct eye contact with the pretty ginger lying beside him in a teak bed, half draped by clean cotton sheets that feel like the richest silk beneath his naked and battleworn body. In full retreat from himself more than her, running as he ran from the MDL, he tells himself how he must again see her. Not as his lover Zofia, but only as his second-in-command, Lieutenant Jablonski. He curses his weakness at sleeping with a subordinate.

"We can't ... Madjenik ... the rules ... I can't let this happen again." He says it right as she awakens and smiles up at him, with that radiant full lipped smile and those bright shining, always slightly mocking and intelligent green eyes she has. The look nearly melts afresh his self control as it once again, and always, warms his groin. He fumbles the explanation badly.

Zofia is deeply hurt. She tries to hide it from him, but fails. She retreats into formality, refuses to cry. Erects ramparts of regulation to oppose the fool's barricade on which he stands. "You're right, sir. It's not proper. Against KRA code. Won't happen again."

She speaks in a clipped and respectful tone, only and fully professional. The same voice she uses to address her captain on the field of battle, in front of a company of always watching fighters. Though without the touch of affectionate sarcasm and gentle mockery she used even in the forest to goad and guide him.

On the officer link only.

Never in front of the troops.

Respecting his command.

Prodding him to be better.

Not sneering, as he thought.

"Zofia, I'm sorry. I just don't think we can..."

"I'll get dressed now, sir. If you'll just turn around, *captain*."

She's lying with sheets pulled up around her, in oddly awkward modesty after what they've done. As she rises from the bed she tosses them aside and strides deliberately, almost brazenly, naked to the tiny antechamber of the bathing room where her clothes and his lie haphazardly on the ruby, polished hardwood floor.

He looks down and away as she gets dressed in silence, into a crisp uniform of pastel-beige she takes from a paper package. It's one of two resting neatly on the dresser top, given to them by Lt. Byers. Already he regrets what he's done, but he can't think what to say to change it back.

She's too hurt, and too angry. She's turning ice sheet cold and lava tube hot all at once. Changing into his second-in-command as she covers herself with a fresh lieutenant's uniform. Only now she's vastly more unreachable than before inside her crisp wheat colored cloth. A void is opening between them.

"I'll bunk with the NCOs tonight, sir."

He hears a soft *click* as the magnetic door lock opens and a gentler *clack* as it closes, like slow motion charging of a maser. He's alone. Again.

Ulysses

A week later, Madjenik is growing restless with too much food and drink and way too easy sex. It's bloody exhausting! Everyday they receive fresh cheers and free drinks and food in the pubs. And more freely offered sex and food and drink. Yet the company is restless for reassignment, no longer enjoying a deserved R&R.

"You're all bloody heroes!"

"You deserve it! Drink, drink!"

"Another round for our heroes of the woods!"

Make no mistake, the fighters of Madjenik are grateful. It's just that from their quarters they can hear the daily combat at the berm line. At night they can see walking wounded and litters bringing back recoverable dead. Shroud covered litters make the trip only at night, to hide from civilians the terrible sights of defeat and the true, dreadful numbers of lost fighters. Though most of the city population is aware, nonetheless.

Madjenik feels too crowded and closed in, and useless. Anything but heroic. Every hour spent idling in Toruń grows heavier to bear. They want to be on the perimeter when the bloody dawn arrives, so they don't miss the rumored day that's surely coming soon. A terrible dawn when the whole garrison marches out to fight its last, losing battle outside failing city shields.

A clutch of unsupervised NCOs, all quite roundly as drunk as is the whole company, propose to march Madjenik back down the Grand Boulevard to the Berm Gate and volunteer for outside combat duty. To demand it. To not take no for an answer. In a rowdy session without the two officers present that sees lots of shouting and pushing and threats, then three knockdown fist fights, everyone agrees to make the march to the Gate to join the last battle.

"That'll be a good day to die for Genève."

"No, it'll be the very best day to die!"

"And not just for Toruń or Genève, for the whole United Planets."

"*Krevo, Krevo, Krevo!*"

“Fuck dying. I want revenge for our losses on the trek to Toruń!”

“Payback for burning Pilsudski Wood and the Old Oak Forest!”

“And for all the lost innocents on the Old Forest Roads!”

No one has forgotten *that.* Or ever will forget. But most will go just to stick with their mates, to the very end. If pain and death is coming to find them all anyway, they want to die in good company. To fight with Madjenik in its last hour. To die together, if that’s what must be.

“We’ll leave the berm laureled or casketed!” It’s a veteran of the sweetgrass fight, drunkenly shouting nonsense to a roar of approval from original Madjenik survivors, and all who joined in time to fight in Pilsudski Wood and *The Crater.*

Zofia has to step in front of the drunken NCOs to stop them from leading all fighters to the berm without purpose or permission. They grumble loudly, bordering on insubordination. So she agrees to ask their captain to seek official orders to redeploy to the battle line.

Jan agrees to ask General Constance about it. He has been called in to meet her anyway. He’s all dressed up when Zofia goes to see him. He’s wearing brand new weaves from the other paper package. The one she left on the small dresser as she robed in silence, then walked away.

***

General Constance sits behind a large but plain oak desk as Jan enters her chambers. She doesn’t raise her head as he’s shown in. She lets him stand before her. Waiting ... and waiting. He thinks her office smells like ancient oaks, which it does from all the carved furniture. And smoky incense. That one’s her.

As a combat veteran, he instinctively makes a quick scan of the environment to get a read on dangers and possibilities. And on a superior he’s meeting for the first time. It reveals a yellow-and-gold bicorn general’s hat cut in the old fashioned *chapeau-de-bras* style unique to the KRA, resting and dusty on a walnut stand. There’s no ornamentation to denote high military status or political authority. Or to reveal the personality behind the desk.

The suite doubles as Garrison Command and Governor’s Office, with six side offices for her staff, all with wide open doors. From panoramic windows Jan can see the whole city. If he stepped over to the window he thinks he could look right down to Old Towne Hall, and to Governance Square. He's sure he'd be able to see *The Crater*. He knows that General Constance watched the fight from here.

A dynamic sheet map on a side wall shows RIK units and positions around the eastern curve of the city, a thick crescent surrounding the outer berm. Inside the *red* circle is a smaller crescent in parallel, made of *blue* symbology. Several *blue* units and more *red* are in motion, feinting or reinforcing. In three places, *red* and *blue* approach too closely, touch and meld.

'*Localized combat. RIK perimeter probes in force.*' His eye is drawn to a spot just outside the Berm Gate where a small *black* circle indicates a new feature. Around and inside the circle more *red* units are moving, with numbers. '*Infantry redeploying into The Crater, readying for the final assault on Toruń.*'

An *orange* countdown clock in a corner of the vidscreen says just eight Universal Standard Days remain. Fewer than eighty Standard hours, each 100 minutes, each minute 100 seconds. Hardly any time left at all. '*Counting down to what? The berm assault and battle? We can't know when the RIK will launch that, not so exactly. No! It's counting down to departure of the Exodus ships!*'

The launch is timed by flight engineers to account for a slightly elliptical orbit of Genève's outer gas giant, Wasp 2B, to best align with its L2 jump zone at optimal angle and distance. A second critical timing factor for Z-day is the nearing limit of the city's shield defenses, under constant attack by artillery. Soon flocks of Jabos will fly from close in bases, resuming the attack.

Through an open door of an antechamber attached to the main office Jan sees a second holo map, this one of all Toruń. It's perched atop a broad redwood table. It shows the tactical situation, clearer than the cribbed view on the general's wall map. Around it hover at least six young staff officers in uniforms as bright and crisp as the general's and his own. Not weaves. They're wearing light cloth, only with e-ribbons warmly glowing over their rank insignia.

'*Not the way a combat officer dresses.*' Jan can't help thinking it, a little too proud of his gruff humility. '*Wear rank in the open or the woods and you make a perfect sniper target.*' Only then does he remember that he's also dressed in clean oakish uniform cloth, and wearing shiny silver captain's bars on his breast and collar. Remembers that he's also showered, clean shaven and carefully groomed to prewar standards. He hasn't looked this good in months.

He turns back to study the general's face. Much to his surprise he thinks: '*She must've been very pretty, if not quite beautiful, in the bloom of her youth.*'

He feels stupid. Its not how he appraises female officers, and certainly not older officers far superior in rank. '*What the hell is wrong with me? Settle down, Jan, or you'll blow your last mission for Madjenik.*'

He's not wrong. The general is handsome and impressive in her advancing maturity, with a slightly matronly figure that sits square and upright in her oak chair, neither hiding nor displaying her sex. Overall, she has a firm soldierly bearing that he much admires. He notes her tight, drawn back hair. A look of strength tucked inside a finely gilt uniform. Her impeccable, seamless weaves nearly match the desk color. '*I like it. She wears her general's ensemble lightly, without pretense but real authority. I'd like to see her wear that silly hat, though. Always thought our generals' hats were a bit much.*'

He's giddy. Not quite sober after a night of heavy, solitary drinking. This is not the way he intended to meet his general, the officer who got Madjenik into Toruń. But he hasn't been fully sober in a week. Not since Zofia walked out and closed the door on him and them.

He explores and maps the general's intriguing face with his blue eyes. Its contours are like the coastline of a new-found-land after months at sea, rugged with unknown dangers yet promising safe harbor. '*Ahh good, she's well suited. It's time for someone like her to make the hard decisions for Madjenik. I just want to know who'll be in charge when the company fights at the berm.*'

General Constance's visage brooks no nonsense, her tone no contradiction as she finally looks up and seems to see him for the first time. "Welcome to Toruń, Captain Wysocki. Congratulations on getting Madjenik through the forest and across *The Crater.*"

Jan mumbles his formal gratitude for Relief One, adding needlessly that "I speak in behalf of all Madjenik."

"Well of course you do. You're the company commander." She looks at him hard, saying nothing further. Daring him to speak. To spill his mind. Analyzing him, as she has from the moment of first coms contact while he was still outside the protection of her city. He feels oddly nervous. He almost blurts something about her hat. She finally breaks the tension. To help him along or force the issue? "Yes, captain? Now that you're here, tell me what it is that you want?"

Terse.

Direct.

Efficient.

Intimidating.

He steels himself to ask the only question he came to have answered. Can his hodgepodge unit redeploy to the berm, from whence it arrived a week ago? He expects a simple answer. “Sir, when do we go back? My company wants to fight.”

“You’re not going to the berm, captain. I can’t permit it. You and Madjenik are too important to waste in yet another doomed battle. We’ve had our fill of martyrs here, around Toruń and on Genève.”

He misses entirely her point about being too important to waste, but finds his voice at last in behalf of his fighters. “Sir, if I may. And with all respect, general, I think Madjenik has earned the right to decide the time and place of its dying. Aren’t we all doomed, anyway?”

Her woodgrain eyes follow his to the wall map, then back down to lock on his blues again. It’s a bold, too direct assertion, wrapped in too much pessimism. It’s brashness and insubordination is outside all proper discipline, even in wartime.

“You forget yourself. What soldier ever earns the right to tell a general when he’ll fight or where he’ll die?”

“Apologies, general. I only meant…”

“Furthermore,” she interrupts him baldly, forcefully, “wherever there’s death there’s hope, captain. At least to make an honorable end.”

“Such an end is what all Madjenik aspires to, sir. All that it wants.”

“Indeed. Well, you’re not at all alone in that. But we’ve had enough dead exemplars on Genève already, captain. I won’t add Jan Wysocki and your noble company to that long list. You’re too good a combat officer and leader, and Madjenik is too important in other ways, to waste in a futile trench fight outside lost Toruń. I simply won’t permit it.”

He doesn't absorb the full implication of the comment, that Toruń is lost but all is not. He's allowed little time to think and none to protest, or to point out that Constance plans to do just that herself, pick a place and time to die on her own terms. He's seen broadcasts of her speech announcing to millions her intention to lead the garrison to the outer berm, there to make a last worthy stand before the Gate while the *Exodus* ships seek to fly the planet to the outer system LPs, and beyond. He also knows that *she's* far more important than *him.*

He's no longer the man he was before the war, always uncertain, forever doubting his own convictions, his ability and courage. Well, at least sometimes he overcomes self loathing these days. This moment in front of his general, this is one of those moments. It's because he's pleading for Madjenik and not for himself. So he opens his mouth intending to speak his mind.

Constance stops him cold with that special look only seen on the faces of angry wives and superior officers. The look every husband and every soldier knows, the one that says he's reached the outer limit of her formal patience and he damn well better weigh any next words *very* carefully. While he's doing just that she steals the silence away from him.

"You aspire to doom too easily, captain. In wayward words, at least. I choose to judge instead your superior leadership and actions. In those I see something more. Maybe even greatness. But not yet. For still those whom you fight you do not hate and those you guard you do not love."

'*What does that mean? It's vaguely familiar. Some old poet, I think.*' All his self doubt and loathing gathered since the MDL, and long before, rushes back into him like an unstoppable return of the tide.

"Excuse me, general?"

"You heard me."

The room sways and spins like he's on a tiny punt drifting away from shore in a rough sea, already too far out to safely swim back. He feels lost.

'*No, not lost. I feel ... seasick! What the...?*'

"Would you like a glass of water, captain? Perhaps something stronger? I hear you're drinking a lot these days. No? Quite right, too. Orderly, some water for our once-and-future hero."

He's hurt, as well as dizzy. '*She doesn't know me! Why does she say I don't love my people or hate the enemy? It's not true! Call me a hero? Rubbish! As for greatness, what a foolish thing to say! About me? Phaah, nonsense!*'

She reads it clearly in his face and slumped shoulders. "Madjenik wouldn't be in Toruń without you, captain. You were beaten at the MDL, trapped in Pilsudski, firebombed in Old Oak, starved and hounded for three months on the trek here. You *willed* Madjenik to survive. You got it past *The Crater* and through the Gate."

"That was *your* plan, general. *You* got us into Toruń. I followed your orders. As did everyone in Madjenik. And we're all grateful, sir. I mean, I speak for the company on that."

"Yes, it was *my* plan." She doesn't tell him that the day he arrived in the city she sent a detailed and secret dispatch to the War Government on Aral saying the opposite, praising his tactical skills and above all, his leadership in command.

"But it was *you* who led them through fire and ash to fight at *The Crater*. Very few of my officers could have done that."

He's taken aback. '*She can't believe those ridiculous Toruń street stories, child's fables about me leading Madjenik to triumph after triumph as the "Ghost of the Wood." It's all rubbish!*'

It's as if she reads his mind. "Your lieutenant and NCOs said a lot more than you did to my debriefers. But no, I don't think you're the unbeatable 'Ghost of the Wood' our people say you are. You're right to think those are parables of false hopes that you can never live up to."

'*How does she bloody know what I'm thinking? Is it my face? Am I that obvious to her? Zofia does it, too. Sees right through and into me. What is it about these women...?*'

"Don't let your current adulation in the streets go to your head. The crowd is fickle and so far, you've been unusually lucky. Better men than you have failed and are dead in this war."

"Yes, sir. I agree wholeheartedly. I was lucky to get Madjenik here, and luckier still to meet up with your plan on the other side of the berm. When TCC called in, I was at wit's end."

She doesn't need his concurrence.

She ignores his fawning riposte.

She has already dismissed his flattery.

He gains nothing with her from repetition.

"Sometimes it's better to be lucky than good. I'll take luck from any quarter we find it at this dire moment. And your bold legend can help us, captain."

"My *legend?* What legend? You can't mean those stories that the townies tell, about the 'Ghost of the Woods'? They're absurd! Besides, what does..."

"I'm not done!" She looks him straight in the eye, fiercely commanding the room and his attention. Even her shimmering uniform fills with electric threat.

He flinches. He wants to look away, up to the map. He knows he daren't. '*That was a general's voice. I forgot the sound. Like thunder on the prairie.*'

"Unlike myths about some imaginary past, legends have a basis in reality. In real acts and partial truths. Your legend is out there now, Jan Wysocki. In the streets of Toruń and across all occupied Genève, coursing over milnebs on all other Krevan homeworlds and beyond. The legend of your bravery and trek to Toruń, and of your leadership in the fight at *The Crater*."

He finds some courage, enough to protest at least. "I'm not a legend! I've done nothing special. Who here knows anything about me? I've been wandering in the woods for three months, not making legends!"

"It's true, nevertheless. Your story is part of a larger legend now, the story of the Lost Company and its Ghost leader, a tale of our defiance in a desperate hour. It's real and it's growing. It's very important here in Toruń and across Genève. And to the future of our people in Orion."

'*That's rather much. I hear the stories they tell in Toruń, but across Orion?*' Constance doesn't say to him that she made sure of it with exaggerated tales added to her dispatches to the War Government when Madjenik was in Pilsudski Wood, along with advice to declassify and rebroadcast his story by all and any means to all Krevan homeworlds. And even to the Calmar Union and other potential allies who think Krevo is defeated and its cause forever lost. She doesn't tell him either that she made sure the RSU and RIK HQ heard the very wildest tales about 'The Ghost,' until real fear and even respect crept into intel reports and down the ranks.

Even before that, he'd gotten into the enemy's head on his own. His reputation burrowed deep into RIK minds from his time in the southern woods. He's still digging into Grün night terrors, scaring recruits and replacements arriving by orbital shuttle on the coast of Northland. After Brusilov's excuse making, even RSU misidentified "Jan the Ghost" as the KRA special forces commander on Genève. As the leader of a vast forest resistance movement, not the captain of a single lost company that he was. It also served Brusilov to build up his foe that way, to explain his own failures to his royal cousin on Kestino.

Jan's name scared and scarred the RIK medical corps after a secret gas bomb he ordered planted inside a dead officer's anus took out the top medical examiner and 22 assistants on Kestino. It left them coughing up bits of their own lungs all over the floor of an elite First Caste morgue. Hover scout replacements from 10th Armored tell other tales of his ruses and tricks, of falling to ambushes or dying from a cut throat in their field cots at night. An entire division from Manmō that wears a double moon flash vows revenge, but secretly wants no part of him.

The stories spread offworld, as evacuated RIK wounded from 10th Armored relayed scared tales about the 'Ghost of Genève' back on their homeworlds, taller and wilder tales with each retelling. The sobriquet curled back around until today no one knows who first used it or why. Was it 10th Armored officers? The RSU? General Brusilov? General Constance? KRA Special Branch?

After he's seen striding deliberately from *The Crater*, the 'Ghost' appears in RSU and RIK intel reports that wrongly put him in command of the defense of Toruń. Constance tells her own intel officers to confirm the error in leaks and KRA disinformation broadcasts sent over the berm to nervous RIK recruits in forward camps and jump off assault trenches.

"Legends have a way of growing over time. And *that* I can use. Don't worry, we shan't keep you in thrall forever. We'll tolerate you as hero only until we can replace you. We are a little people, hence we are wise enough to prefer smaller heroes to great ones. So don't worry, we know your limits as we know our own."

Jan doesn't know what to say. This isn't the conversation he ever expected or wanted. Before he can think of anything smart or helpful, or just not further embarrassing, Constance shocks him to his core with her next remark.

"I'm expanding your command. You're brevet promoted. Your new rank is full bird colonel. Effective immediately, Lt. Jablonski also jumps two *rakkr*, to brevet major. That's so she can lawfully command a full KRA battalion. NCOs in Madjenik will be promoted commensurate with demonstrated command ability, based on your report. I have a list..."

Colonel is too high a rank to command a single company. '*She's going to take Madjenik away.*' His head is spinning from heavy, solitary drinking since he lost Zofia, but more from his sudden promotion and loss of Madjenik. It's the first time he admits to himself that he still wants command, that he doesn't want to surrender responsibility as he thought he did, to hand off his company to some other officer who doesn't know and intensely love his troopers like he does.

His head swims. His stomach feels odd and queasy, and not from drink. Her unexpected words seem to fill the room and his nostrils with salt smells. He even thinks he hears the baleful cries of white sea birds. That can't be true. He's two thousand klics from any seashore. Yet he feels rising waters heading right over him. Like a fatal tsunami cresting over the low shore, washing over him and back. Already, it's pulling him out to sea with an irresistible undertow. '*Will I float into starry exile on a tide of sorrows, on the jetsam of my past?*'

"...of names of your NCOs. Several look like real junior officer material. We'll bring them along first and fastest. You'll need to..."

"What?" He emerges from a foreboding premonition to splutter the awkward, blunt interruption. Forgetting even to say "sir" or use her earned and proper title. Forgetting his place before this formidable woman, this general who's in mid sentence, delivering orders to a subordinate in wartime. Feeling only a hard knot forming in his gut. Then he does it again. "Zofia Jablonski? Which battalion?"

Constance looks up from her notes meaning to admonish him hard and coldly for his brutish rudeness and failure of military protocol, but she sees his immense confusion and discomfort. She's surprised that his outburst leaped right over his own promotion to his young lieutenant. '*What's going on? And can I use it?*'

"Sorry sir. I mean ... I'm just surprised. I thought we were going back on the line. I mean Madjenik, sir. By 'we,' I mean. Going back on the defense line along the berm wall with Madjenik, is what I mean."

She doesn't answer right away. She pauses her planned delivery of a long list of orders, tilting her head to the side to better assess his peculiar and befuddled reaction, like a hawk watching a confused field mouse wander out into the open where she knows he can't escape her talons.

Jan tries to take advantage but only manages to ask in a crestfallen tone: "What about Madjenik? Do I lose my old company *and* Lt. Jablonski, sir?" At least he remembers to add the "sir" this time, if only on the tail of his sentence.

She looks at him for a long, considered moment, but almost smilingly. A sudden softness in her face surprises him. "Yes and no, colonel. Yes and no."

Her use of his new rank startles him. Even when she's kind, she has a deeper, secret purpose. This time, he notices. His instinctive defenses start to rise. He moves behind a shooting slit in the castle wall, ready to defend himself at last.

She decides to ignore his agitation, resuming her presentation as if it never happened, still thinking on how to use what he just revealed. Or whether to use it. His AAR and her orders to him are on a graphene touch scroll as thin as parchment and much lighter. She smooths it over the oak desktop, her other hand poised with an e-stylus at the ready.

He filed the report two days after entering Toruń, hurling himself into its dictation on the long morning he lost Zofia. He identified natural leaders among the brevet NCOs, and even several privates, impressing her with straightforward accounts and his character judgment. It's damned confusing for Jan, standing in front of her, watching his report unrolled on an old oak desk 30 stories up a stolid wooden tower, so soon after leaving filthy and burned out Toruń Wood and *The Crater*. He feels decentered. He loses confidence. He feels absurd.

'*Please just give me orders and let me go.*' He's remembering that he spent the day before filing the report, then a long and languid night, in a cramped teak hotel room and bed filled with laughter and lovemaking with Zofia. '*Umm, Lt. Jablonski. Errr, Major Jablonski. OK, I guess it's good that's all over with.*'

Constance is back reading out his orders, seemingly ignoring him. She makes official his brevet field promotions of 15 NCOs, all former privates now bumped to corporal or sergeant. She agrees with his recommendation to jump Corporal Tom Hipper and his two best regular sergeants to 2nd lieutenant, first of the KRA officer *rakkr*. Low level commissions aren't something a KRA general normally reviews. Amiya Constance does, methodically confirming Jan's field assessments out loud. Working quietly to boost his command confidence.

"You are responsible to train up all these young men and women to their new duties as junior combat officers, colonel. And I mean the whole book, just as you learned it in OTS."

'*Which I had to attend twice.*' He took night and weekend officer training on Genève after failing out of the KRA Academy on Aral, at the end of his first and only year there. "Yes sir. They're good fighters. They'll make good officers."

His vertigo starts to pass. "I'm grateful for all these well deserved promotions within Madjenik. I just don't know what you want *me* to do next. Please general, can you tell me what will happen to Madjenik? When does it redeploy, and where? You can use the company on the berm. Let me tell my fighters where they're going. At least to do that, before you transfer me, sir."

Constance finally shows him mercy. "You're not losing Madjenik, colonel."

"I'm not, but you said I was promoted. Doesn't that mean…"

"Madjenik Company is herewith upgraded to battalion status. We'll raise its barracks complement to 1,600. In fact, I'm giving you 8,000 fighters in all. Five new battalions, all to be integrated as a heavy combat brigade. You'll outfit, refit, and lead the brigade."

"A *brigade*, general?"

"Madjenik will be senior battalion in your new brigade, under your command. So you see, you are neither transferred not relieved, no matter what you think or say you want. I read your obscurantist AAR, colonel."

Jan is utterly taken aback, so lost by the news he hardly notices the rebuke or revelation that she saw right through his self deprecation in his debrief and written reports. '*A brigade? Five battalions? That's multiples of what I had at the company level. Maybe I could handle a battalion, but not a full brigade!*'

It's as if she's reading his thoughts, again. "Yes colonel, you can do it. You have to do it. We're running out of battletested officers, or officers of any kind. We've taken heavy casualties defending this city, and everywhere we've lost across Genève. With even more lost on our other worlds."

"I know. I mean, I've heard. It's..." He doesn't finish the thought, realizing that if he pleads inadequacy after what she just said about casualties he'll only anger her. And rightly so. He's a soldier. He submits. She sees it in his face.

"Madjenik we'll beef out by building around your existing core. The other four battalions we'll raise from scratch, and very fast."

"Where will I get so many fighters?"

"Start with the veterans of *The Crater*. Your own from Madjenik, of course, and the 967 from *Relief One* who made it back alive. They all say they want to fight under your command."

He wonders when they were asked, but nods agreement. He's finding it easier to submit to her, even though he can't stop his thoughts flitting back rapid fire to the debacle at the MDL, then to the sweetgrass meadow, back to Pilsudski and the Old Oak Forest, and on to *The Crater*.

All of his fighters know that
their colonel will blunder.
Theirs not to question him,
theirs but to follow him.
Follow the fake boy wonder.

"Take the lightly wounded from Madjenik and Relief One as well. They've earned it, and they'll recover faster among their mates. They're experienced fighters. All of them. But leave the worst wounded in my hospitals."

He makes his first foray into command. "We had a good record integrating strays from the MDL and in the forest. Lots of Madjenik's fighters, the majority in fact, are pickup strays, orphans from the retreat over the plains or from Pilsudski Wood. There's not a lot left from the prewar company. Just a few dozen, actually."

He starts to apologize. "I lost over 200 fighters out of the 315 troopers I had on the first day at the MDL, on Breakthrough Day, when they hit us so hard and..."

She interrupts, deliberately ignoring recitation of the company body count and his dwelling on his MDL fiasco and the KRA's defeat. She *has* read his AAR. She also read everyone else's, paying special attention to the action report by the only other officer in Madjenik. "You see, colonel, we think alike after all."

He's fairly certain that isn't true. He asks warily: "How so, general?"

"I've added 5,000 from shattered units who need reassignment. When loose end fighters heard you were in the city they approached my officers to say 'we'll follow Jan Wysocki into battle anytime. We want to join the Wreckers.' Soldiers don't say that about all my combat leaders. Hardly ever, in fact."

He's not sure what to say. The numbers are overwhelming. He repeats that it's a good idea to use the strays. She curtly dismisses his unnecessary approval. "Names, ranks and old units are already listed on your orders. Is that understood?"

"Yes, sir."

"Repeat your orders."

"I'm to build a new combat brigade with strays from multiple broken units."

"Draw your last volunteers from the Toruń garrison. My staff has a list of all who are due to leave on the *Exodus* ships. Take your recruits exclusively from that list. No one else."

'*That's the first hint that I'll be leaving Genève with the new brigade.*'

"I'll send over more names from the reserve along with an elite tenth from decimation of two units presently defending the berm. We're going to give your combat brigade a stiff backbone of tough, experienced troops. Use them well in the offworld battles that lie ahead."

'*There, she just confirmed it. We're leaving on the Exodus flotilla.*'

"As for Major Jablonski," he stiffens to full attention as she speaks the name, seemingly without a hint of suspicion of their illicit, unprofessional relationship, "she'll serve in your brigade as a battalion leader. I'll transfer over three more brand new majors. They'll also be battalion leaders. I recommend that Major Jablonski take Madjenik, but that's your call."

"Thank you sir. Good to hear." He's sweating, and not just from the booze. His heart is pounding with suppressed excitement he hopes doesn't show on his face. '*Why is she smiling like that? It's worse when she smiles.*'

"It's no longer peacetime, captain. Old rules don't apply. How can they?"

“Sir?”

“How you get along, *umm*, personally, with junior officers in your unit, well that’s for the two of you to work out.”

‘*Does she know? How could she? Maybe because you’re blushing beet red as a schoolboy with his pants down and stumbling over every answer. You fool!*’

“Do whatever gets you though the war, Colonel Wysocki, with whomever gets you through its days and nights. You’re going to need the major’s help and more, where I’ll be sending you.”

He’s astonished by her insight and even more by her candor. “Yes, sir. Thank you. Major Jablonski is a first rate officer. I’m glad to have her onboard the new brigade ... and all the new majors.”

“Exactly so, colonel.”

“After all, you chose them, sir.” It’s only half of what he’s thinking. ‘*But then you also chose me to lead them and your damned offworld combat brigade. So I’m really not so sure that I trust your judgment.*’

“I can only give you one experienced battalion commander, but I’ll let you have two staff officers to help set things up. One is from my own staff, Lt. Dylan Byers. You met him at the Gate. He’s smart and he’s intensely loyal. You can rely on Byers to take all routine brigade administration off your hands as well as for political advice from time to time. He’s that good.”

‘*Politics? Why do I need to do politics? I’m a combat officer. And how much longer am I going to live to do any godsdamn politics? Barbarians are howling at the Gate, literally.*’

“You should know that he volunteered the moment he got back from your interview. He was damn near insolent about not taking no from me for an answer.”

“Very glad to have him.”

“I’m sorry to lose him, but I’m pleased that he’ll be with you. Look after him for me.” Her tone is almost tender.

'There's far more to this extraordinary woman than meets the eye. I'd still like to see her wear that ridiculous general's hat, though.'

"As for brigade logistics…"

Jan falls into worry about a bloated command he doesn't feel ready for. He tosses it all over in his mind, losing Zofia but not losing her. Five battalions and immense responsibility. All of it. He's completely lost in his own thoughts for a very long time. Suddenly, he recalls where he is and realizes that he's not been listening to the general for a least a minute or more. Sees that she stopped talking about orders listed on her scroll and is staring intently at him.

'I need to get a lot more sleep, and I have to stay off all the free booze.' Not knowing where Constance left off he says the next thing that comes into his head. "Thank you, I mean for Lieutenant Byers. I'll welcome his advice and help."

"*Humph!* You do know we moved on from discussing him some time ago?"

"Very sorry, sir. It's all a bit overwhelming." The comment doesn't help. She hurls another withering look his way. *'Well done, as usual. You're making a hell of an impression on your commanding officer, Jan.'*

"I'll reassign more junior officers inside the hour. Byers is drafting orders for my signature, his last official duty on my staff. You needn't wait. Here are your commissioning papers and those of the new majors. Captains, lieutenants and NCOs to follow by the end of the day. Byers will see to it." She rolls up the graphene sheet and hands it to him. It's light as feathers and compact. He slips it into a never-before-used shoulder pouch on the arm of his crisp wheat uniform.

"The 10th Combat Brigade will be fully detached. Autonomous for the most part. You'll train as special forces commandos. Your fighters call your company 'Wysocki's Wreckers.' So we'll call your brigade that as well. The troops will all like that. Toruń will like that."

Now he does protest, too loudly and too vehemently. "That's not something I approved in the forest, sir. 'Wreckers' I don't object to, of course. But I don't want my name in front like that."

Constance turns on him, instantly and profoundly angry. Jan suddenly senses a powerful scent of burning incense. Stronger even than the salt sea smell he can't quite shake off. "You undervalue what you are, colonel. Your excess of humility is no virtue. It grows more tiresome by the hour, which is late. Nor do you wear it as well as you think."

He winces at the chastisement, like a schoolboy. She sees the weakness and moves to play the role of harsh headmistress over him, only in that intimidating general's voice she commands that makes a headmistress seem like a girl scout. He feels seasick again, and wobbly on his feet.

"Remember your Aristotle? Courage is the first of all virtues because without courage you cannot practice any of the others. You do not lack courage, colonel. Even if you don't believe or see it in yourself. Nor do you lack leadership. You are overflowing with leadership."

He finds his footing again, for a moment. "I showed neither on the first day, at the fight at the MDL when a squad of armtraks broke through my unit. I ran like a scared rabbit!" He throws it back in her face, into her plans for his legend.

She knows all about it. He put it in his summary field report about Madjenik, an act of self destructive honesty in reportage that impressed her hugely. Almost as much as his tactical exploits in the forests and his innovative disobedience of her own direct orders at *The Crater*. "You are a *special* officer."

He winces again, at the praise.

Again he protests overmuch.

Again she cuts him off.

"Yes, you *are*. Your troops all know it and say it. I know it. It's past time you admitted it to yourself. You are *special*, and a natural leader."

"I didn't lead anyone at the MDL. They came back for *me*."

"That was then."

"But sir, I *ran!*"

"Yes, you did. And still they came back for you."

"I don't know why, I don't. They shouldn't have."

"Colonel Wysocki, do you think the fighters of Madjenik are changed since then? Do you think they're the same as the day before the *whole* KRA ran from the broken MDL, your broken company just one among hundreds?"

"No sir."

"How have they changed?"

"They're harder, tougher, better soldiers. More cruel."

"So are you. All the 'Wreckers' who followed you out of the burnt woods swear that they will follow you anywhere. They all believe in you. They'll never willingly leave your side or command. Thousands of our fighters clamor to serve under you, to fight for you. You have a warrior's reputation now. You have a *name*. And perhaps also some small talent for war."

"Those thousands, they don't know me. They only know the tall stories."

"You forget that I also saw you lead, saw you in command, watched through your own eyes as you led your fighters in action at *The Crater*."

"Again, that was *your* plan, sir."

"Yes, and a damn good one. But it was *you* who got them through, *you* who controlled and channeled their hate, *you* who inspired them to fight and survive. You have nothing left to prove as a combat commander. Stop trying so hard."

"Sorry sir. It's just ... What can I *do?*"

"A great deal. More than your combat leadership, I need ... our people need every hero we can raise up, every morale boost we can get. For the long fight."

"You mean for when you lead us outside the berm? I can do that!"

"I already told you twice, that you are not allowed to go to the berm. Do not ask it again!" The smell of spiced incense around her is getting stronger as her anger rises, almost overwhelming his senses, as if it's really in the room.

'*The kind used in olden days in blood sacrifice*,' Jan thinks darkly. He's right about the incense smell but wrong about the source. She smells more like the interior of a Life Temple. A place he never visits, it's full of death and resignation yet uplifting acceptance of the bonds and debts owed between generations. Old to young and youth to age.

"No, colonel. You have a longer path to walk than beyond our doomed berm with me. A harder destiny and far heavier burden to carry than me. I repeat, for the last time, I'll not waste you and your 'Wreckers' fighting in a hopeless battle for a city that's already lost and soon will burn to ash."

"What then? What do *want* from me, general?"

"Your name. Your reputation. The magnificent story of your trek to Toruń. The legend of the 'Ghost of the Wood.' I want all that for our people. I want to give your name to Krevans everywhere, suffering and dying in this dark hour. To give it to Orion. Your name, your legend is a green shoot of hope arising out of all the gloom and ash and death on all our lost worlds."

"My *name*? What use is that? Please sir, I don't understand talk of legends and names. Just let me fight. I'll lead your brigade if I must, but I don't know politics. I only want to fight."

She wheels on him with real harshness in her voice, in a cloud of choking burnt incense, and with shocking vehemence and volume. Almost roaring into his face, like an aroused lioness. "*Politics?!* Damn your selfishness!" Two young staff officers standing by the holo map in the antechamber look over in concern and surprise at her outburst. They've never heard or seen their general so animate.

Jan is profoundly shocked by the threat in her voice and deeply hurt by the harsh words. But he won't back off. Something important is changing between them, and in him. "Selfish? What do you mean, selfish?" He's almost insolent.

"Why not let us borrow your name? 'What's in a name?' An ancient poet asked that once. I'll tell you: *faith, hope, duty, honor*. It's not the title of the new brigade that honors you Colonel Wysocki, but you who must honor the title."

He feels chastened.

He feels humbled.

He feels all alone.

"You must ask yourself the same question that I ask of Toruń, that Aral asks all of us now: how can Krevo live if we decide to die? You will lend me and all of us your strong name so that we may take up the heavy burden that all Krevans will bear far into the future."

Powerful emotion shows in her face. Flashes from smoke hazel eyes glower at him like a wood fire under a bellows, narrowing to predator-like slits of red accusation, of reproach and even of menace. Her darkening visage and emotion is so sudden and strong it overmatches his own anger, also rising in a complex of fear and humiliation that nearly overwhelms him.

Then he regains control. He finally sets all his personal anguish and loss aside to really *listen* to what she's saying. Listen without self loathing or ego of any kind. Listen for the first time. Listen to the strong voice of his people calling to him from history and to make history. Listen to the siren's lamentation, only calling him *away* from the rocky shore and out to a sea of stars.

"Do you not understand that we are adrift? That even if we hold some worlds a few months more, keep back the locust swarms from devouring all that we have for another season, our end is already written?"

"Do you not know that we shall be imprisoned in our homes or exiled from them? That we shall be first among the unwelcome wanderers this war will surely make, always pushed on to trouble another's door. Poor and unwanted for the secret shame our exile brings to others."

"Do not doubt it. For not even the decent star nations have moved to help us in this hour of our greatest need. We must survive, alone and unaided. Only by surviving can we preserve our past and future. We must and will survive, or we shall expire from history and from Orion."

"All is lost, then?"

"All, yes, but not everything."

"The *Exodus* fleet?"

"Yes. It's our last, pale hope."

"You well send me and the Wreckers offworld. Alright, but to what end?"

"*Exodus* ships will leave Toruń, ships are leaving all our worlds. They depart for an aeonian odyssey among the stars. As individuals we shall live and die as exiles far from the memory and comfort of our homes, knowing they were stolen from us. As a people, we shall survive in exile to make peace no more, forever."

"Forever? You want our people to fight the Imperium forever?"

"Yes. Until our old friends remember their own interest, and stand at our side."

Piercing wood ember eyes stare through him, burning down to the essence of things, as fire always does. "Yes, we might avoid this fate by staying behind, to die here on Toruń in the last battle, wanting and thinking that '*she who dies fighting pays all outstanding debts.*' Our burden is greater than that, you and I. We must lead." He looks hard at her and she back at him. Her gaze is firmer.

"That's *not* my choice, or my reason."

"What then?"

"I stay and die only so that some will not quail in the last fight on Genève, but far more so that others like you will accept to live and to leave. Personal choice is done for us Krevans, colonel. Only as a people may we choose to live or to die."

He's overborne by her force of personality, her authority and sure strategic knowledge. He submits to her judgment. "Is the war over, then? Is saving those we can all that's left to us?"

"*No!* I do not propose to you a leper's exile, to '*wander as dumb beggars with no bells*,' intending no harm but unwelcome everywhere nonetheless. I do not propose to live as refugees who bore the young and too kind strangers with tired tales of our forgotten war and woes."

"We are defeated, yet we are not dissuaded. We will fight on, forever. We shall wander the starry seas, knowing that on a future carmine morning we will return to cut the throats of the thieves and murderers who stole into our lives to force us from our homes. Then we shall have our vengeance, as a people. It shall be red and gory and complete. As it was for Ulysses."

He remembers the story vaguely from college. An ancient tale of shipwreck and lust and war, of wandering through wonders, of love and monsters and long exile. All leading back to terrible justice and frenzied slaughter and revenge. '*Was it justice, or just more grim and bloody murder? An eye for an eye, and all the worlds governed by blind cyclops.'*

Again he feels transported, that he's drowning in a premonition. He can really smell salt air this time, and hear the hoarse cries of sea gulls that seem to call to him from just outside the wood tower window. It's not possible this high up or so far inland. It's real to him nonetheless. General Amiya Constance leans forward over her thick oak desktop to speak *sotto voce*, urging him like a dread conspirator to agree to murders yet to come.

"*You* will be our Ulysses."

'What does that mean?' He wants to yell out, to protest, but her angry presence is too commanding, her authority too enveloping. None of his protests this hour have worked or mattered anyway. Not with her. Never with her.

"You'll be a stoic hero for our people. Wandering with them, leading always by reminding them that hatred is the only sure path home, back to their anointed day of red revenge."

'Why me? What does she see to make her think I can do this dreadful thing?'

"We need legends. We need heroes if we are to survive as a people in exile. We need you, Jan Wysocki. We need you to agree to this hard burden. We need you to lead us in the darkness of exile so that you may lead us out of the dark."

'I might be a legend as she says, but I'm no hero. She must know that, too. Shouldn't a legend also be a hero? I'll ask her that! It's not too late! She must see that I'm the wrong man.'

"We will wander so that we may fight, so that our children return one day to bolt the door with iron and murder our enemies in their sloth and vanity. Come home to reclaim their inheritance, however many years it takes. Come home to exact dread vengeance and reclaim all our rightful worlds."

'Wander? Vengeance? Ulysses?'

"So be it. I pick *you*. I order you to leave Toruń. I order you to live."

He realizes in a flash that nobody gives a damn about his secret fears, his Hamlet complex. Constance has made that much clear. Lots of officers might feel the same, for all he knows. So he decides to shut up, raise no questions, register no protest to her impossible expectations. That's when it hits him. He senses her words pulling him farther away from familiar shores, forever. Feels the *Exodus* undertow take hold of him. Hears cries of gulls all around. Smells salt air and strong incense. Sees long sacrifice, decades ahead.

Only he's not drifting away on a fragile and useless punt this time. He's on a massive warship, four-masts-to-the-wind, sheets billowing with power overhead and broadside cannon sending *red-and-white* pufferies of death hurtling back at his enemies. And all around, a mighty fleet flies proud flags of all the free nations of Orion: Calmaris, Helvetics, Krevans, Threes, others. '*Is it my fate to sail the stars with white gulls alongside? Must I lift up sheets of hate to ride the winds of war, blown hither and yon, never to chart my own course? Can I do it?*'

Constance lets him think on it in silence, seeing the dark thoughts flit across his face like starlings outside a high window. She watches him intently, with vital purpose. Every plan she has, everything left to her, the fate of Genève and all Krevo is riding on what he says next.

'*Is he the one? Can he lead our people in exile? Have I chosen well? Ahh Amiya, it was never your choice to make. He chose this path, starting in the sweetgrass meadow, in the forests as the Ghost, and at The Crater. Just as he'll choose to walk it tomorrow and all tomorrows to come.*'

Jan watched her fateful speech to the city before he came to this wood oiled room that smells like the Old Forest, burning sandalwood and salt air. So he knows that he can't win a contest of wills about whether to stay to die or leave to fly her flag of hate out to the stars.

'*Others are getting the same order to leave, to climb onboard the Exodus ships carrying Genève into exile. So why do I feel so ashamed? Is it because part of me wants to do it, to test whether I can do it, to recover every failure and error I ever made? Damn, but I resent her imposition! What is it about this stern, gold braided, deep voiced woman that makes me feel that whatever I say is wrong? It's like being a cadet on Aral all over again.*'

He did that for a year as a kid, at age 18, at the KRA Academy on Aral. Sure that he'd achieve a brilliant academic result and then embark on an adventuresome career, launched from the finest military school in all the dozen systems and two dozen worlds of the United Planets. But he got all hung up on a sour romance halfway through his first year, went all-in on a girl who never went all-in on him.

He performed so poorly in every subject he just had to quit. Was forced out, actually. In disgrace. He lied to all his cadet friends, saying that he was going home to Genève "to help the old man bring in the harvest. He's not too well, you know." Lied to everyone back home about what happened on Aral. Lied to everyone and himself. Until he thought he was nothing but lies.

Back at dull Toruń Teacher's College, where he enrolled for want of any other choice, Jan pretended nothing bad happened on Aral. He always said whenever asked that "I came back to help my dad." Sure, he finished Officer Training part time. Yes, they made him Madjenik Reserve Company CO when he excelled in tactical and leadership courses. '*I was popular, that's all. Not a real leader. Anyway, that was peacetime and there was no real competition for the job.*'

He thinks everything he ever achieved is mirage. He believes, really believes, that he's just a stumble of character waiting to happen in front of all the worlds. He knows his limits, or he thinks he does. He lives inside fear that everyone else knows them, too, secretly laughs at him, waiting for his inevitable fall. And now his general asks him to be a leader and a *hero* in Orion. Part of him wants to try.

'*They'll all find me out, expose me,*' he thought before the war. '*Call me out as the fraud I am. Then I'll lose Madjenik for sure.*' Now he's not so sure, having been under fire and under siege, fighting back and winning. Or at least not losing.

Thirty years old and stuck teaching grade school history, he was called to command early in the diplomatic crisis with the Imperium, just before the Bad Camberg incident that led to war. Just like everybody else on Genève with any military training, he reported a little over two months before the invasion of the outer system and the RIK assault drop on Southland.

'*That was when I met Zofia, back before the war started, back when we were training Madjenik's raw recruits and I thought there was all the time in the world left to me to ask her, to kiss her. Back when she wore a red dress and looked like filtered starlight as she danced.*'

They gave him Madjenik, his old reserve company, one of seven forming 3rd Battalion, 5th Light Infantry Brigade, Gold Division. He was still training the youngest recruits when the Bad Camberg incident sent everything spiraling out of control. Madjenik went active duty and was ordered into perimeter defenses along the continental coast. It never got there.

The invasion came so fast Jan never even saw the sea. Only his baptism-by-fire. That first time in combat his worst fear about himself came true. He failed. He ran. He left behind good men and women, young soldiers who died from his weakness, his inadequate cowardice. *'I ran and yet they came back for me. Zofia's squad came back when I got fragged in the leg while running away. Some leader! Some legend! What is this mad general thinking?'*

Constance is watching every flicker of doubt and pain and memory course over his face, willing him through his personal Vale of Tears, silently urging him to join her on the other side. *'Come on, colonel. Embrace your cruelty. Embrace defiance and savage vengeance. Breathe the foul stench of war. You must traverse a nebula future. You must agree to lead us on the starry seas. Only then can you return as Ulysses to slaughter our enemies as they lie in sloth in our stolen homes. Only then can you make black bile and blood of our enemies spill out our doors and run in Toruń's wooden streets. Run in all the villages of all our homeworlds.'*

It's not fear of his cruelty that holds him back. Not since Pilsudski Wood, where he learned how to cut a throat that needed cutting, to do whatever it took to lead. It's not that. Not at all. It's that he hates that everyone in Toruń admires him without knowing him, calls him a hero and buys him drinks he doesn't want, yet gulps down tumbler after tumbler to forget what they don't know.

That he lies and lets people down.

That he ran the first time he was tested.

That he might just run next time, or the next.

'What if I fold under pressure again? Sure I got Madjenik to Toruń, but that was mostly luck. I don't want this new responsibility. A whole brigade, in exile? I'm no hero? Go into exile? Search for allies? Return one day as Ulysses ...?'

Constance makes him feel his old shame all over again. Worse, her strange words and demand that he become a legend promise more and bigger shame and greater failures to come. *'But if I argue, she'll just repeat all that bull crap that I'm special and round-and-round we'll go. And in the end I'll still have to do whatever she says, whatever she orders me to do.'*

He suddenly realizes that neither of them have spoken in minutes. He looks straight at her. Constance stares back, deep into him.

This time he holds her gaze.

Unflinching. Defiant. Cocky.

She knows it before he does. '*Got him!*'

"Well, Colonel Wysocki? What say you?"

"Yes, I'll follow your orders. I'll sail your Ionian Sea. I'll wrestle as Ulysses with monsters of war and misfortune. Krevo's will, not mine, must be done." The mood has him. He's a little giddy with relief the decision is now made and perhaps too quickly embraces his new role making history, instead of teaching it.

"I'll do your bidding even if I would '*fain die a dry death*' over your wet one." He's far too pleased with this recollection and allusion, but at least he realizes it and has the sense and decency to be embarrassed. '*Damn! I have to get away from this woman. She makes me feel ten again, trying to play the clever schoolboy to her demanding headmistress.*'

Constance absorbs his bright, salty look, his burning anger and smoldering defiance, his cocky grin smirking beneath surface doubt that's fast disappearing as he accepts her challenge and his destiny. She welcomes his insubordinate glare and disdain, which he no longer tries to hide. She knows that she's just blown away years of cherished doubt to reach his deeper, secret arrogance. She knows his pride will serve him as he wanders with her people into exile. They understand each other completely at last. She hands him the order scroll for the brigade.

"Good. Now we can begin."

"Yes sir, it is time for us to part."

"We both have a lot of work to do over the next week."

Her eyes move his to the countdown clock on the wall. It reads just north of 79 USH left. She makes no move to rise, no special effort as she sends him into exile, to the gods-only-know what fate. All she says as he stands there is: "Colonel Wysocki, you're dismissed."

He salutes, palm out, KRA style. She doesn't even look up as he turns sharply on his polished heel, like a best cadet. Already, she's at work on some new, more urgent matter, aides-de-camp bustling to and from her with importunate purpose.

He hears her sonorous, mature voice giving out fresh, steady commands as the heavy wooden door to her chambers *clicks* closed behind him. He needs to berth a newly formed combat brigade of over 8,000 fighters. He needs to brief his new majors and other new officers and NCOs. He knows that he won't sleep all week.

As he turns to leave he's sure he hears white sea birds calling plaintively over a crashing salt sea surf. He could swear he smells hard brine and kelp, dead fish and crabs, wet sand and salt encrusted rocks, and billions of drowned voices.

He understands now.

It's the smell of uncharted seas.

It's the odor of all his future days.

Data search: FTL
Result: gravity echoes, bohr zones
Historia Humana, Volume V, Part III (e)

Under relativity, spacetime cannot be flat where gravity shock waves collide. It 'folds' into local singularities instead, ripples if you like. These perturbations are quantum detectible, but only at superstable bohr zones. Otherwise they are too 'flat' to affect celestial bodies in normal spacetime. They have no detectible effect on small, artificial bodies such as asteroid or centaur mines, refineries, platforms or ships resting in an LP without employing a quantum drive. Yet, 'horizon singularities' can be engaged, leading to remarkable quantum effects.

Gravity 'wave outs' from a massive object such as a star interact with arriving gravity 'echoes' from more distant yet adjacent masses, cosmologically speaking. A 'horizon' singularity results. The paradox is one of four dimensional spacetime flatness that is nonetheless 'folded' or 'wrinkled' by gravity wave collisions ('echoes'). This is known to engineers, who occupy a more prosaic profession than cosmologists, as a 'spacetime tunnel' or 'gravity tunnel' or 'quantum bridge' (among other terms). The idea recognizes the singularity as decidedly not flat in engineering terms, and thus that it can be traversed differently than normal spacetime. By whatever chosen name, 'hybrid' or 'horizon' or 'horizontal singularity,' or 'spacetime tunnel' or 'gravity tunnel,' the paradox of crinkly flat spacetime is key to jump detectors inside every quantum drive.

Think of it like this. Lagrange singularities ('bohr zones') are akin to tiny disturbances made by water striders on the skin of a flat, yet immensely deep pool. The surface is normal spacetime in this analogy. The essential calm of the deep water is unaffected by the passing striders. Einsteinian relatively works for normal spacetime, yet minute echoes or disturbances the striders make on the taut skin ripple outward across the surface, to collide or fold into ripples made by other striders (stellar and planetary masses). The ripples move and interact in observable, mapable patterns. If you had a ship and a quantum map plotting each ripple and where it folded into others you could ride the waves (enter the 'folds' or 'tunnels') on the taut skin of normal spacetime. No need even to say 'thank you' to the striders as you leave.

FTL drive was always possible in the old theories, but a stardrive remained physically improbable until computers employing magnetic matter came of age. These were radical quantum devices making ultracomplex calculations that could identify a 'fold' to ride to another star system, allowing a ship (or a message) to 'jump' instantly through Minkowski hyperspace, or folds. But only to an adjacent LP 'echoing' from a gravity field mapable at a three body system.

Why? We still don't know. We do know that LPs are where entwined ripples on the tense skin can be detected and ridden. We remain limited to sublight speeds traveling in a star system or any other normal spacetime, yet we can make quantum or bohr jumps and send instant messages from one LP to another LP if it's in an adjacent three body system. Otherwise, the great tyrant of the Universe, the lightspeed limit, still rules unchallenged on his throne.

Light sails and GDMs made interstellar travel and the colonization movement a reality but created hundreds of lonely worlds, each out of everyday reach of all the others. Every one of the Thousand Words was left to chart a path through a new and unique history. Some took very dark turns under fundamentalist or radical sectarian movements. For all the rest, the realization set in that we had finally reached the stars only to rediscover solitude.

With discovery of the quantum drive, travel and communications among the brave new worlds became routine, linking First Wave settlements with Second Wave and Third Wave colonies much farther out, until we achieved the glory of the Thousand Worlds. Bohr com systems were built, commerce and cultural interaction grew apace. We also learned, in ways no longer deniable or denied, that empire is the natural form of our social and political organization. The reality all Humanity cleaves to and desires in the end, regardless of the surface forms that pretend that the star states are or can one day be something else.

Cynics say that the most important consequence of stardrives was to shrink the space occupied by the Thousand Worlds, and thereby make war in the stars possible and inevitable. It began with local wars, limited to a few neighboring systems. Then it spread, as the Broderbund pillaged out of the Ordensstaat, the Oetkerts conquered the Grün Imperium, and the Dauran Empire spread over eastern Orion. Next came the wars of empires, great general conflicts known as the First, Second, and Third Orion Wars. They...

...Finally, we achieved the blessed Peace of Orion some 300 years ago, embarking on the Satya Yuga, the age of the Shōwa or Enlightened Peace. It is hard for us to imagine what war might be like, as even with extended Youthspan it lies beyond the reach of living memory.

Troopships

As General Constance's heavy door *clicks* shut behind Jan a crisply dressed young officer with cropped black hair and impeccably shiny brass buttons greets the new brigade commander. Lt. Dylan Byers holds out a silver eagle collar insignia and a brand new peaked KRA cap with colonel's rank badge to match.

"You'll need these, colonel. You'll get further a lot faster with boarding and logistics officers if they see your new eagle up front. Rank has its privilege, sir."

He's not wrong.

"Byers? Right, I remember you from the debrief at the tunnel. I see that you knew about my promotion well before I did. Constance said you were good. Guess she was right. Welcome to the 10th Combat Brigade." Jan accepts the rank insignia and puts the cap on, awkwardly.

"Thank you, sir. May I say that it's an honor to serve under you, colonel?" Byers snaps off a crisp salute, even clicking his polished shoe heels together in the old fashioned way.

"Well, we'll just have to see about that. You volunteered for this?"

"For Wysocki's Wreckers, yes sir! Wouldn't miss it for anything. Wouldn't miss being a part of this new outfit for all the mir in all the Thousand Worlds."

Jan winces. If even his officers are going to use his name for the new brigade there's no escaping it. He's just going to have to learn to live with it. '*More "you're a legend" and "Ghost of the Woods" shit. Gods, what I am getting into? What has my general done to me?*'

"No regrets at leaving the general?"

"All the regret in the world. She's easily the finest officer in the KRA! But when I asked for combat duty, you know, to finally do my bit outside a map room in the real war, she said she'd permit it only if I agreed to join the *Exodus* fleet.'

"Sounds just like her," Jan sniffs. "Tell me, does she always win at chess and poker, too? Never mind, I think I know the answer. Now, how do we get out of here? Lead the way, lieutenant."

"Forget the external elevator, sir. It's too slow. It was built for tourists, to give them long views of Arbor City. Follow me, if you will. I know a much faster way. It's fun, too." They race each other down 30 stories of polished wooden stairs that circle the building like a climbing vine, taking them three at a time.

"I do it twice daily. Upside, too!"

"Oh come on," Jan protests through hard gasps for breath at Floor Thirteen. "Now you're just boasting!"

"No, really. Working for the general, I never have —I mean, had— time for the gym or track. This is my daily workout. The secret is not to sweat."

Sure enough, when they hit Governance Square Jan is nearly totally done in and dripping wet overheated, while Dylan Byers is hardly even panting. Plus his uniform looks like he never broke a sweat. Jan can hardly believe it.

Dylan smells like brass polish. He was first in his class at KRA Academy on Aral. In the same class as Zofia, he finished ahead of her by two slots. He's Toruń born, but unlike the slower pace of living Genèvens prefer and practice, Dylan is all professionalism and competence and military crispness and efficiency. For all of that, his passions and soul are local. He's made from knotty birch and silvered pine, inlaid with artisanal oak, trimmed in teak and redwood filigree.

'*It's an attractive and impressive combination. He's genuinely humble, too. I like this young man already. I've known him less than 10 minutes and I can already see why Constance valued his counsel and his company.*'

He briefs Jan on a brigade mobilization plan on the way down. He's done before they reach the 10th Floor. They're already in thick agreement as they cross the square, then split up. Jan heads back to Madjenik's makeshift quarters to meet and brief his new brigade officers on their promotions and tasks, and go over their battalion recruitment lists. Byers goes direct to the KRA Armory, thence to secure berths on the *Exodus* troopships. And if need be, on the escorts.

Jan's anger abates with his abrupt plunge into brigade command. The farther he gets from Constance the more he becomes aware of her larger burdens and longer purpose. Still, it will be months before he truly understands. Not until he's fighting in lava caves on Minotaur.

Orders are orders. He has a whole new set and over 8,000 fighters depending on him. And less than eight Standard Days to organize and equip a new combat brigade, then berth it on waiting troopships. He feels time moving faster, spinning him away from all that he knew. Byers is indispensable, but Jan knows that he can't manage without Zofia's help. It's the one conversation he dreads more even than a repeat of his session with General Constance.

They just can't talk about anything personal, so both resort to professional formalism. When he congratulates her on her promotion to major it's as if he only just met her and hardly knows her. No one watching them would ever guess that they lay together in near perfect *kama*.

Jan shows Zofia the order sheet from Toruń HQ, recorded on the feathery filament as light as air that Constance gave him. As he pulls it from his shoulder pocket he goes directly to a verbal summary, trying to shorten their already abbreviated greetings and conversation to a bare minimum. He aches to look long and deep into her eyes again, but he doesn't dare.

Instead, he focuses on the canary stripe around her cap and the crisp collar of her new KRA dress uniform. She still wears her lieutenant's rank insignia. Her collar is not yet adorned with the major's golden oak leaf clusters it soon will be, for Jan only just told her that she's jumped up to major and put in charge of Madjenik Battalion. Her apple hair is pulled back off her face into a tight bun that's snugged inside a peaked officer's cap. Jan steals a glance.

'*Gods she's beautiful! Such perfect skin. I forgot how beautiful during weeks and months on the trek here. We were all covered in filth and ash back then.*'

"So, Madjenik is mine now? Good, that's very good."

"Yes, the company, *umm*, the battalion is yours. So get it up to complement and up to speed. Constance says we're to get the brigade outfitted and at full strength, then berth on the *Exodus* ships. Byers is preparing a list of bunk assignments and pulling equipment and weps."

"Right, he's a good man. I knew him on Aral, at the Academy. But I think I better meet him at the Armory nevertheless, and take over weps procurement. I'll draw personal weps and gear for the whole brigade. Dylan is as good as you say, and he has the close contacts we need here in Toruń. But he's not a combat officer. I know better what the brigade will need to fight and what we can usefully leave behind. I hear there's very little room left on the troopships."

“Fair enough.” Jan is deeply relieved that Zofia asserts her old rights as his Number Two. “You’re the officer-in-charge of weapons for 10th Combat Brigade, from here on out.”

“For Wysocki’s Wreckers, you mean.” She can’t resist the dig at his too proud modesty. But where in the past this would have a gentle jibe meant in fun, now it really stings.

“Yeah, right. Them too.”

The enormity of a common task throws all new Wrecker officers together, awkwardly at first but urgently. None will sleep all week. Dylan sees to that, providing Jan and all the brigade’s officers with a riskily high dose of moda, the powerful combat psychostimulant.

“You sure we should take this shit, lieutenant? At this dosage it’s against all the regs and medical advice.” It’s one of the old Madjenik NCOs, now a lieutenant herself. Her commission was only brevet, but General Constance confirmed it.

“No choice, if we want to get the brigade ready and loaded in seven days. I’m taking it, too. See?” He pops four yellow pills into his mouth and swallows ostentatiously.

“Moda at this dosage will not just keep us alert and wide awake until the *Exodus* ships strain for orbit, it will actually improve short term memory and mental acuity. OK, we’ll all have real bad jitters after that and the worst damn hangover you can ever imagine, to the power of ten. But going bug eyed won’t matter once the troops are safely onboard and we’re all passengers ourselves. Trust me. How do you think I aced exit exam week at Aral Academy?”

It’s the confession that this creased and perfect officer kinda, sorta cheated on Aral that convinces them to pop the pills. That and Jan’s snapped order to “shut up, swallow the moda, and get on with putting your battalions together and getting them boarded on the right ships.”

***

Z-Day, H-Hour. And the clock is ticking down. It’s only four days away as they sign up the last brigade fighters. Days that are spent in frantic equipping of 8,000 men and women. In handing out gear and securing weapons and getting live ammo crates onboard. Days spent introducing veterans to newbies and the whole brigade to the youngest looking set of NCOs and officers any trooper has seen.

It's always thus in war. The longer fighting lasts the younger are those who fight, and younger also all those who lead the fighters. Long wars always end up as children's crusades. On all sides.

Dylan hands Jan his design for a new unit flash. It's an old fashioned fighting sail, a man-of-war firing a broadside in *white-and-red*. Above is the constellation Orion, and three white sea birds circling. Bearing the ship to the stars are two foam topped waves shaped from stylized 'Ws,' standing for Wysocki's Wreckers. Jan is startled but he approves. It's quickly printed and troopers start adding it to their uniforms. '*How the hell did he know? Can everyone read me so easily?*'

As a late and hasty unit, 10th Combat Commando has no priority on ships' berths. Despite Dylan's best efforts and contacts, it's assigned bunks real late, just two days before the *Exodus* launch. Far too late to get the Wreckers on one of the packed troopships, which means Jan can't keep the outfit all together.

He's told he has to break up and squeeze his just formed brigade onboard three separate ships: *Asimov*, *Resolute* and *Resolve*. KRN *Asimov* is a frigate. *Resolute* and *Resolve* are older class destroyers, modestly larger than the frigate. He tells Zofia the bad news later that day.

"Not the best way to start building identity or morale, broken apart like this."

"No sir, I don't imagine it is." Her tone is flat, as it always is these days. Neutral and professional, but just a little curt as well. '*Does he think I want to bunk with him? Well, I don't!*'

"We'll berth as many as possible by battalion. You'll stay with Madjenik on *Resolute*. I'll find a berth with Byers and my other junior staff officers and all the medics, on *Asimov*."

She wants to show him only coldness, but her feelings are running too hot to always control. She still needs to hurt him, though another part of her wants to hold him close and cry instead. He catches the uppercut she throws at him square on the chin, as she means him too.

"Wouldn't want it any other way, sir."

“That’ll be all, major.”

Their conversations are like this now. Short, official and only to the point. Never warm or personal or intimate or longing or sweet, as they were on that one night of no restraint at all. They slipped into intimacy and out again, in a way that they may never recover. It’s one more regret Jan tucks deep inside his kit bag, alongside his extra socks, as he packs to leave Genève.

When he finishes he looks to the bed where Samara lies curled, naked and asleep atop white cotton sheets. The sight of her on his bed consoles him. ‘*I’ve lost Zofia, but at least now I have you.*’

***

Seven small escorts are all that remain in-system of the prewar KRN flotilla based at Genève. The squadron was taken by surprise on the near side of the gas giant when the Kaigun invasion convoy jumped in. The flotilla fought back hard, but was quickly overwhelmed by sheer numbers and by superior ships. Genève flotilla was smashed to bits, losing 60% of its complement of ships and sailors before it broke off the fleet-to-fleet battle.

Once the fight was lost around the two twinned moons of Wasp 2B the badly damaged battleship, KRN *Goliath,* fled with only secondary silos still shooting. Leaving with the limping cripple were five heavily damaged, older cruisers and a handful of close escort destroyers and frigates.

That’s it. Those were the sole survivors out of three older KRN battleships, six cruisers, and four dozen small escorts that began the battle the Kaigun calls ‘*Genève Obliteration.*’ The rest of the flotilla form clouds of flotsam around Wasp 2B’s close in moons. Chunks of ship’s plate and smashed bulkheads and many thousands of rigid bodies bolo on gravity strings where ships and sailors died.

Five destroyers and two frigates remained in-system, cut off from escape LPs by roving or blocking squadrons of Kaigun warships. Since these small ships could make planetary landfall, Captain Magda Aklyan led all seven in a dive to the surface of Genève. Ever since, they’ve been protected by Toruń’s city shields and the Shipyard’s huge white plasma pulse cannon. The heavies at the yards are more powerful than any battery the Kaigun mounts even on its battleships, and all of those have left for other systems. The ground guns have deterred close orbital patrolling ever since several wrecked Zerstörers and three badly damaged cruisers learned the hard way a month ago. The Zerstörers dove too low, passed too close, and ended as a rain of molten ultrasteel and melted men, falling from the sky. The three cruisers were more heavily armored, but are still under repair.

***

Magda Aklyan is a slender and confident professional, with hard eyes as blue as arctic ice. She's not technically the senior officer still with the KRN, but under her emergency and martial law powers, Constance overruled the last peacetime admiral on the ground, told him to shelve his argument from rank, and put Magda in charge of what was left of Genève Squadron: five destroyers and two frigates she saved with a quick thinking, emergency dive to the surface.

Magda has never commanded a full squadron or battle group. She's only a destroyer captain. A good one, but skipper of a very small warship without any prospect of making admiral in the prewar Krevan Republic Navy. Now, none of that matters anymore. Like everyone else in what's left of the KRN, she must rise daily to fresh challenges of command, to grave responsibility far beyond her training or experience. '*I think I can do this job, but we shall just have to see. In any case, there's no one else to give it to. Most surviving KRN officers in-system are too young. They're not ready. Not yet.*'

She quickly found that she fit the role of flotilla commander. And more, that she likes it. Tall and lean and wearing a snug fitting uniform as she sits in the command chair, with black hair pulled off her face into a tight bun at the back, she looks far more severe than she is in fact. She's aware of it and uses it, wearing a harder visage that she thinks her crews need to see and believe in, after peace vanishes into plasma blossoms at the moons and war comes to stay.

Privately, she's more like an earthen vase made of reliable clays: kiln dried with a hard glaze, but homey and helpful underneath. She smells like fine clay, too. Not quite musty, but with a whiff of deep rootedness born of the rich black humus of her homeworld. Her ability is matured by considered experience. She's slow aging into darker colors and wisdom, like whiskey wrapped in oak.

Once the *Exodus* order arrives from Aral everything changes for her and the warships waiting on the surface of Genève. Changes for all the captains and crews. She and Constance had planned a final suicide run into the enemy orbital patrols. KRN sailors accepted that would be their fate, just as KRA soldiers accepted that they would die at the berm. Now that's off. Magda must instead figure out some way to get past patrol ships with two vulnerable civilian ships along for the ride, and her fighting escorts packed with KRA. Then she needs to find a way to get the overmatched flotilla out of Genève system, where every bohr zone is heavily guarded by the Kaigun. Her longer term task is to get everyone to sanctuary in Calmari space. There the flotilla will disgorge lives, then await arrival of the government-in-exile from Aral.

The flotilla needs a name. Magda decides to keep it simple: *Alpha*. If there's a partition along the way, her flagship will retain the tag *Alpha* while the splinter shall become *Beta*. All together, or divided by fate or the enemy, the little ships must make it past Kaigun pickets both in orbit and at the first LP, the windward L1 of Wasp 2B. Magda and Constance agree that the target and escape LP will be Wasp's leeward L2 bohr zone, the farthest possible exit point from Genève.

"Won't that be the hardest jump zone to reach? Why not go for the nearest bohr point instead?" Constance asked Aklyan the day she brought her escape plan in for final approval.

"You're right: it will take extra hours of boosting to reach so far, with potential disaster and Kaigun warships after us all along the way."

"Yes? So why go there?"

"Because it will be the least well guarded, since it's the hardest and most unlikely one for us to try to reach. I know, it's a backwards logic. But it works if you think about it."

"Yes, I see it. Fine, approved. One more thing, I think I may be able to help thin the ranks of patrols and picket ships you'll encounter en route."

"Really? That would be grand, general. But how?"

"I can't tell you that, captain. You have enough on your mind at the moment. I'll just say that it involves the bravest man I know, and that he's volunteered to do whatever's necessary to help our *Exodus* ships get away from Genève."

***

Nine ships will make the mad run for the outer bohr zone. The last seven small escorts and two commandeered civilian cruise liners, still being hastily converted to working troopships. All family of departing fighters and crews will stay behind in Toruń, or wherever else they may be on overrun and occupied Genève. In this war there's no room left for family.

Each ship in *Alpha* has on its prow a hewn and carved, teak rondelle in the form of a bright yellow sunflower. This signature emblem of the Krevan Republic Navy is encased in transparent armor and positioned just above the upper dodger and forward missile tubes. In any prow on view in battle, it's the first and often also the last thing an enemy warship will see.

Before the war, the Royal Cruising Line operated a sizeable fleet of tourist luxury liners carrying rich Grünen of the upper three classes of citizens from Imperium systems to favored vacation spots in the Krevan Republic. Liners *Wilhelm Rex* and *Meiji* were regular visitors to Toruń, plying a circle route from the frontier systems of Koblenz and Manmō to Genève, Aral, and Lwów, then back home. Both cruise ships were familiar sights to greeters at Toruń's elevator docks, making tourist runs for over two decades before the start of Pyotr's war.

The two liners spilled rich, High Caste passengers and billions of Universal Credits into the local hotels and economy before carrying back to the Imperium tens of thousands of happy, pampered, elite Grünen who were sure they had experienced something like an adventure. They left with memories of long walks in gold and silver woods unlike anything in Orion, carrying lutes and flutes and small wood carvings of ambiguous gender and shape, meaning and purpose. Genève's many artisan towns attracted plenty of farfolk carvers and musicians, in addition to locals and other Krevans. Most made little tourist versions of famous and much larger art works sold at offworld auctions to part rich folk from their fortunes, which is the purpose and justification of nearly all high art.

The liners were docked at elevator platforms waiting for their passengers when they were trapped by the sudden start of the war and then an escort vs. escort battle at the Genèven moons. Their captains soon rued that they lingered overlong at safe wharves 100 klics vertical apart, ignoring odd and too cryptic orders from Kestino to "*Immediately leave Krevan space.*" The imperial edict came less than a day before the Kaigun war fleet arrived. It was not enough time to gather passengers, clear through customs, and leave the system.

Besides, the captains thought the directive was just diplomatic foreplay in the ongoing quarrel between Krevo and the Imperium over border rights. Even the shocking vid that came next, piped out by official propaganda from Kestino, showing a Krevan commando attack on Bad Camberg, couldn't force their early departure. The passengers were far too important to leave behind. So the captains and liners stayed docked. Like everyone else they watched on huge viewscreens the strange images of the Bad Camberg false flag operation, a terrible naval battle at the outer gas giant, then a smaller escort fight at Genève's moons. They stayed put until forced down to Toruń's docks by Aklyan's scorching lasers.

She scudded and staggered into synchronous orbit with the elevator, flying in at speed on KRN *Resolve*, steering sheer in a badly damaged destroyer before braking recklessly. She came scarred from destruction of Genève Squadron at the LP egress by a superior Kaigun fleet blocking all Lagrange points, and from her own separate fight at Genève's small moons. With the last surviving KRN escorts under her command, Magda persuaded the reluctant liner captains to make clumsy planetside landings. She did it by firing decidedly tourist unfriendly *blue* lasers right across each of their prows in turn.

"Snout shots," her First Officer Émile Fontaine called them. He's just 24 years old and barely a year out of KRN Academy on Katowice, frocked but not yet formally commissioned due to the rapid and unexpected onset of war. Yet he's made a name for himself already, during the opening fight around the inner moons. Captain Aklyan trusts and relies on him.

She threatened the stupidly stiff, legalistic skipper of *Wilhelm Rex*, who dared quote interstellar commercial law to her while a Kaigun war fleet was hammering Genève system. "I'll blow your damned Neo Grotius and his 'law of the stars' to particles if you don't shut up. I'll blast your *bâtard* ass and that fat liner out of the sky in 30 seconds if you don't do as I order. Release clamps and drop to a surface landing pad in Toruń City. Do it *now!*"

He released magnetic grips then emergency blew the explosive bolts securing backup cables reeving the *Wilhelm Rex* to the elevator platform. He descended the liner at reckless speed for so ungainly a ship. What convinced him to do it wasn't Magda's verbal threats but her visage on his vidscreen. The warning shot of a tight *blue* laser that scuffed his bow strongly suggested that she meant to do what was written on her face. He was met by armed guards upon landing and locked up along with all his crew and most of his passengers.

The prim captain of *Meiji,* parked at a wharf 100 klics farther down, was told more bluntly: "Land your liner right now or you'll never see your family or home port again." Without waiting for him to reply, Magda fired another *blue* laser beam past his Main Scuttle. He complied.

All liner crew and passengers with military or government ties were arrested and interned within an hour of touch down. Not so Calmaris, citizens of the Three Kingdoms, Helvetics and other non-Krevans. They were closely vetted, but most were admitted to the city. Even so, all neutral citizens are closely watched. Grün tourists already on the ground were tightly screened. All those who failed, found themselves on ground shuttles heading to holding pens hastily set up in marginal districts of the city. The others were placed under curfew and other restrictions, and faced daily security and personal harassment. The rest discovered that the price of good rooms for loyal subjects of Pyotr Shaka III had quintupled in just the time it took to reach their hotel from the City Police interrogation lines.

Genève's elevator ribbon was cut by a Zerstörer a few days later, one of a schwarm of four that skimmed and skipped across Genève's upper atmosphere unchallenged by the seven small KRN escorts now huddled on the ground under protection of the city's main naval batteries. With the cruise liners and all other civilian ships grounded, then commandeered by General Constance, there was no way to get off planet or out of system. For anyone, farfolk or Krevan.

The unwelcome guests were trapped by the siege of Toruń on land and the blockade in orbit overhead. So prices quintupled again, and kept doubling every week after that. Even full advance payment of exaggerated rates didn't assure a room or dry roof to these hated farfolk. When Madjenik arrived, hundreds of unloved Grünen civvies were ordered to vacate four floors of a big hotel to make way, expelled like common refugees into crowded row tents in Lakeside Park.

From the start of the war, but especially after Constance made her "neither victory nor death" speech, security around the Shipyard was tighter than an off duty sailor. It's even tighter now. Four of the seven warships are still undergoing final repairs, while the two confiscated liners are being stripped down almost to their interior hulls and refitted as auxiliary troopships. Workers clamor over them like ants clambering over the most recent arrival in an elephant graveyard. General Constance, Captain Aklyan, and Chief of All Engineers Owoye Azazi tour the dry docks. It's not the first time they've done it. It *is* the last.

The general and captain are worried that the *Alpha* refit is falling behind schedule. Azazi assures them that it isn't, and won't. He's a little dazed because he's just been told that he'll be leaving on the *Exodus* ships he's worked so hard on, as Chief Engineer on Aklyan's flagship *Resolve.* And that his family will be staying behind. He has a wife and three children, all under age ten. It's a real blow, but the urgency of the moment means neither Constance nor Aklyan can give him the privacy or time he needs to absorb it. Truth may be the first casualty of war, but decency is the second.

"Chief, you were told to pull every civilian luxury out of these troopships."

"I knows, general. We're makin' progress on it." He's barely hearing her. '*How cans I tell my children that I'll never sees them again?*' He's too modest. Every imaginable luxury on the liners has been eliminated in favor of spartan military functionality, and the job is nearly done. All that's left is to add items basic to the function of any and every troopship: sleeping units.

"We starts with the artificial gravity swimming pools." Expunged of water during the landing, all four chambers, two per liner, are refurbished as triage and emergency surgeries. Drained reserve tanks have been cut open and deroofed, turned into infirmaries and medical supply storage rooms. It's a neat fit.

"Glad to hear it chief. What else is finished?"

"Well captain, we ripped out..."

Azazi is assigned to the flagship because Magda knows he's well respected across Genève squadron and all around Toruń Shipyard, and that he can be relied on. "There's not a better man to do the job with Alpha in all Toruń, maybe in all Krevo," Aklyan told Constance.

Short and too wide for his grubby uniform, he's as shy as a new butterfly and as black skinned as carbon fiber. Even cleaned up on full dress occasions he smells of machine oils and grease cleansers. He's not cleaned up today, and has been working too long and hard. The odor of the shipyard is all over him, fitting into the *clang!* of machines and glare of heavy laser welders overhead. He has a glint of ultrasteel shavings that caught in his hair in the machine tool room. '*There's something else, some new smell that I can't quite place. Got it! He smells like a sawmill. He never smelled this sweet before. Oh, of course! That's why!*'

There's been no time to manufacture carbon fiber beds or fittings and fixtures. That's not the way they do things on Genève in any case, not on a world that takes such pride in its wood. So hastily cut and quickly planed pallets of lumber have been hauled aboard each ship to make new bunks. Rough hewn planks two meters long are reeved with cables to every vertical plane. Over 140,000 in the two fat troopships, combined. More are added to every possible space even on the warship escorts. All nine ships reek of wood and sap, of hewn tree strands and deeply rooted local pride.

Games courts, grand dining halls, baggage storage rooms, all become prime barracks areas. Next to go is each neglected nook, cranny and corridor, every space bunks can be vertically stacked. Except for key engine and command modules. Even lazarets between decks and aerated cofferdams betwixt narrow bulkheads are crammed with raw, naked wood bunks. Absolutely necessary open areas are left untouched, but even those become standing-room-only, no seats or furniture allowed. So many *Exodus* fighters will be crammed into each ship that only half those taking passage can be allowed to move about at any given time. The other half will be required to lie prone in a designated bunk until their turn comes to take a two-hour exercise shift, to stiffly stand, stretch and walk. As for liftoff, well, it'll be two per bunk.

Finely paneled suites built for offworld tourist couples are emptied of lucullan furniture, stripped down to essentials and outfitted with 20 rough bunks each, or more. Every raw doss that goes in still leaks sap and smells fresh cut. For so it is, just days ago from mighty lake trees brought down inside the city's central parks. Tossed upon the funeral pyre of war are gold boughed deciduous methuselahs and silver haired benjamins, all much loved and tended by generations of Toruńites. All the sad carpenters played under the great trees in summertime as children, or saw their own run along thick lower branches and leaves under gray autumn skies, or stood beneath to watch happy skaters on nearby lakes in peaceful winters past.

The lumber smells of green wounds from oozing oak or maple or teak or pine, of black ash and birch. It smells of oily sawmills from whence arrive great stacks of rare lumber worth a planetary ransom in the rich prewar markets of the Imperium or Calmar Union. It's laid in bare, still bleeding sap and scent. Two folded blankets are left neatly at the foot of each bunk. They're itchy and woolen and just about the only contribution poor Southland makes, from Toruń warehouses filled with wool from the last sheep sheering in the last spring before the war. Yet there's real Southland pride in the rough woven blankets, so carefully folded and placed exactly so. Two by two.

"Godsdamn, ken ya *smell* dat now, bies?! Is jus' like Toruń Wood bafore da fiya." It's a saw miller, proudly finishing the refit on *Wilhelm Rex*. In his pride he doesn't notice that he's speaking to Toruń's general, the flotilla captain, and the Shipyard's chief-of-all-engineers. All three smile but say nothing as together they try to slip past and leave him to his necessary work. He won't have it. "If dese buuties ain't Toruń ships bies, ah dunno whad ones eva could be!"

His judgment raises a chorus of approval from workmates and members of the ship's crew, who suddenly snap to attention and throw salutes at the general and captain. It's only then that the proud carpenter realizes who they are. He blushes remarkably red for a man of his years. Like a schoolboy caught with his hand in a candy jar. Magda calms them: “At ease, sailors. Everybody else carry on. The clock is running down.”

Bunks are mounted in two-position swivels, to brace for takeoff then to shift flat under artificial gravity for the long voyage to sanctuary. Assuming that *Alpha* can escape the Kaigun picket line and slip out the system’s backdoor bohr zone. The ships also might have to land on some as-yet-unknown planet or moon that lacks an elevator. To make a voyage with no elevator on either end would be an extraordinarily rare thing. Depart a world lacking such a basic, commonplace, 2,000 year old tek? Then to arrive at another world similarly deprived? Never!

Yet, Constance advises that nothing can be assumed in time of war. “We never expected to lose our elevator, which we’ve taken for granted since the founding generation laid down its base and raised the asteroid anchor and great ribbon. Who thought we’d again use powered liftoff in our lifetimes? Yet, historians say many worlds lost elevators during the Second Orion War, and even more during the Third. They rebuilt the ‘God Lifts’ each time. And each time we forgot about earlier losses. So make all ships ready to land.”

Toruń hosted the system flotilla before the war so it has excellent yards, repair pens, naval supply warehouses, and prefab parts of every sort. So the ‘troopship’ superstructures are easily if lightly armored with a layer of superceramic plate then sprayed with carbyne aerogel. Ersatz armor won’t stand up to plasma, not even from a Zerstörer, but it might protect against glancing hits by older lasers.

The basic problem is the weak structural integrity of the civilian hulls beneath. “Even old fashioned, close action kinetics pose a real danger,” Azazi warns the captain and general as they tour the dry docks. “Especially around the drives.”

“So weld some plate back here. Pad their asses,” says Aklyan.

“I agree,” adds Constance. “Any armor is better than nothing.”

“Yes sir, and ma’am. We cans do that. I’ll gets right on it.” Actually, he’s far from sure there’s enough time left.

“Top priority, chief. This is the truly precious cargo, on the two troopships. Put everyone you can spare on it, anyone who knows anything about plate or carbyne armor. Just get some protection laid in around the engines.”

Azazi speaks into his headset and in minutes ten 50 man crews drop the last minor repairs to the outer hulls of *Asimov* and *Resolve* and move over to the two troopship docks.

"Just in case no escort makes it through the first jump," Constance adds, with a glance at Aklyan, "I want forward firing plasma cannon added to each liner."

"Ship-to-ship light plasma," Magda corrects, "might be all they can take."

"That's gonna be harder than basic armor, ma'am. The firing controls alone..."

"Just do whatever you can, and as fast as you can, Chief Engineer. Give them something to fight back with. Anything." Constance is as firm as can be. She's deeply worried about just how vulnerable each ship in *Alpha* may prove to be.

There's no arguing with the order, so once again Azazi speaks into his coms and more crews leave *Resolute* and *Triomphant.* They hurry with real urgency to the troopships while senior engineers head for the Shipyard Armory to see what might be jury rigged to one or both.

Constance and Aklyan thank Azazi for his time and leave him to it. They know he's the hardest working, most burdened man in Toruń at this critical moment. And that the KRN ground crews in the Shipyard will work flat out and to the last minute on the countdown clock. They part ways, though not for the last time. Aklyan leaves to brief her ships' captains and first officers.

Constance has more urgent, darker business to attend. She must send one of her closest aides to his death. She must approve an intel op that will cost her best officer, and one of her oldest friends, his life. The fact that he volunteered makes no difference to her burden.

Partings

The front mounted guns that Azazi and his best engineers decide on for the two troopships are basic, limited to manual fire control because automatics just can't be set up in the short time available. Not in the absence of military targeting computers that don't fit the former passenger liners. But he's inspired to suggest adding a destroyer caliber, kinetic ice cannon as an aft gun to *Wilhelm Rex*.

Or rather, to the KRN *Warsaw*. The two liners are no longer tourist boats. They'll rise offworld from Genève shed of all Grün Imperium markings and their old names. *Wilhelm Rex* and *Meiji* are no more. Former ships of monarchy and of farfolk empire will boost and fly henceforth under stolidly republican names, as the troopships KRN *Warsaw* and *Jutlandia*.

"I checked *Warsaw* personally, ma'am. She's gots a much stronger beam than I figured, at first." He says it hopefully to Magda, as he hurriedly presents his idea.

"Good news for once, chief."

"She'll holds the rails well enough. She cans handle inertial kicking."

"Will it affect how she turns or how tight she flies?"

"No ma'am, well, nots so much as it woulds matter, nots at the short range her captain woulds fire an ice sabot, if she wanted to."

"I see. So what's to be gained?"

"It could makes it just warm enough ... *umm* ... I means risky enough for a real close pursuer that *Warsaw* cans gain times to jump. Gets herself clear away."

"Excellent, chief. Well thought out. Make it happen."

"Rights, ma'am. *Umm*..."

"Yes chief?"

"*Err*, I aw'ready moved the sabot to *Warsaw*'s dry dock, thinking you mights agree. We'll starts laser welds to the underside hull in 'bout two hours, then reeve, then rigs the fire control. We'll beats the clock."

"Jumped the gun, did you?"

"So to speak, ma'am."

"Well done, chief. Really."

"Thank you, ma'am. And sorry, 'bouts that."

"No apology. Can you do the same for *Jutlandia*?"

"No ma'am, sorry 'bouts that, too. She don't have the hull integrity to support the kinda bucking a railgun woulds give her. The big ones gots a real kick."

'*Probably, it will come to nothing anyway*,' Magda hopes. '*If one of the troopships has to engage even so small a warship as a frigate, then things for Alpha must be going badly indeed. Still, any weapon at all onboard the liners is better than none, if it won't impede handling.*'

Speed's another issue. No one has used metallic hydrogen rockets in several centuries, except as emergency backups. Yet these one time ground lifters are attached to outer hulls of the two troopships. Indeed, they're on all the *Alpha* ships, rigged to drop upon reaching orbit like some bad history lesson falling back to Toruń. Magda has high hopes for the old tek. But that's just Phase I. Phase II is even harder.

Two post-orbit fusion boosters were imported from Argos a year earlier, before some officious Calmari bureaucrat at the Ministry of Defense on Caspia blocked end user permits for military supplies to Krevo, to appease Pyotr. The boosters were meant for routine light cruiser refits of ships in Genève Squadron, but there are no cruisers left. Since boosters are universally designed to fit all modern ships, they're easily buckled underneath each liner and tied into main engines. This was a mission critical task and got highest priority. They went on the hulls first. The refit work is done with four days to spare. Only the ice sabot and last weapons must be hurriedly affixed, and more bunks squeezed into the last spaces on the warships.

Constance thanks shipyard workers and managers then orders heavy demolition charges laid all around the naval yards and inside all storehouses and warehouses. "I'll be at the berm, but I'll leave tight orders to blow everything apart after *Alpha* lifts off. Kaigun ships and admirals will inherit nothing of use to them when Toruń Shipyard falls."

Magda ignores what it means that her collaborator in the *Exodus* plan will "be at the berm" when *Alpha* pulls away from Genève. She shifts topic. "I must say that it saddens me greatly. I spent a lot of years in and around that old Shipyard as an ensign and lieutenant on a now lost frigate, later as *Resolve*'s captain."

"Losing the yards is not as sad as losing all the old lake trees," Constance corrects, exhibiting a rare and even surprising local sentimentality. "Dry docks can be rebuilt, one day."

"Yes, that's the worst of it. Losing the trees from Toruń. Although part of me is glad that *Alpha* will carry them with us into exile."

"All is come to ruin in Toruń and on Genève. Our only hope, our past as well as our future, lies out there with you. Gods speed *Alpha* to reach and join the other *Exodus* fleets."

"It's a good plan, Amiya. We'll make it work."

"I believe that you will, Magda."

"I only wish I could talk you out of doing what you intend to do, as we leave."

"You can't. It must be done and only I can do it. I told your special passenger, the time for personal choice is over for us Krevans. That there is only duty and honor left. I meant for all of us"

"There's also hatred. I shall carry yours to the stars in *Alpha*. What you do here on the morrow shall not be forgotten, general. It will fuel us all in exile."

The two most powerful women on Genève slip into a final, personal address, setting rank and service aside for a simple human moment. Magda Aklyan and Amiya Constance share above all else the burden of command. They know that whatever they decide, however they choose, whichever path they take or order they give, droves of young men and women will soon begin to die.

***

Only a minority of fighters attached to the garrison can make the run on so few ships, even with more raw wood bunks bolted inside the seven escorts wherever doing so doesn't interfere with jacks and jennies 'fighting the ships' in the coming actions against the Kaigun. Constance makes all the hard personnel choices. No one objects. She has respect and support from all those who are leaving, and most of those who will remain.

She doesn't have to do it, but she relents three days before the flotilla leaves, and orders a lottery for the final 4,000 *Alpha* berths. "Active duty military only in the lottery. No family, period."

It's her flintiest order yet, but there's no trouble. Every fighter accepts the logic of division from civilians. The issue is that too many fighters want to pull their names *out* of the lottery, to stay and fight and die with their brave general, their comrades-in-arms, and their families. Constance orders all unassigned names into the draw. There's a limit to what she'll allow, even to uphold morale.

The garrison will follow Constance out to do battle with the RIK in front of the berm Gate just before *Alpha* launches. They'll charge the lines, cut through blackened forest stumps and piled ash to kill and hurt as many of the despised enemy as possible. Only escape by *Alpha* can make so much terrible sacrifice at the berm pyrrhic, not obscene and useless. Fighters in the ships and their doomed comrades below are linked in life and death no matter what happens.

The diversion might distract, hold down tactical sky assets so they don't rise to stop the launch. Or perhaps not. Either way, *Alpha* will aim to escape through a tunnel of fire from Shipyard batteries, with rotating perimeter shooting from its own escort destroyers and frigates. Then the whole flotilla must charge for the outer Lagrange area, the oval bohr zone made by the slight elliptical orbit of the cold blue giant held captive by Genève's sun as it endlessly plunges through the system, restrained by the parent star like a gaucho's whirling bola.

Those ordered to leave fear the image of loved ones left behind dying by fire or maser. Those who must stay fear that tens of thousands of dead fighters might be stopped and splayed in orbit overhead, to later fall as cold meteors then ash rain over the seas and fields and woods, clotting the air with useless memories.

"Better than dying in fire as Toruń burns," one marine says to mummers of assent from other untested members of her squad, just mobilized from one of Toruń's high schools.

"Or worse," adds a veteran of defeats in Southland and at the MDL.

"What could be worse than burning in the great fire of Toruń?"

“Worse,” says the NCO, “is being wounded or captured by damned locusts after the fire burns out. You don’t wanna find out what ‘worse’ means, kid.” On that there’s grim agreement by all the other vets, and white knuckled fear among the rookies.

Fusion boosters and cannon mounts on the troopships are ready three days before dawn on Z-Day, counting down on a relentless orange digital clock on the graphene vid on General Constance’s office wall thirty stories above the Shipyard. Counting down also on a large green departure clock atop the spire on Old Towne Hall. Counting down wherever clocks hang in Toruń, sealed and blinded to the enemy. In each wooden tower and every humble room. The last bunks are bolted in with two days to go. The ice gun with just one. General Constance goes to the Shipyard one last time that evening. She makes her farewell to Magda Aklyan in private, after passing along the last and latest intelligence from Aral telling of more lost battles and of the Imperium’s new invasions of more Krevan worlds.

Their meeting over, Amiya Constance stands and silently and respectfully gives *Alpha*’s captain the crispest of salutes, but in the navy fashion. Magda snaps off a return salute, but army style. The two women then extend their arms and shake hands without ever speaking. There is nothing left to say. The general walks back to the Governor’s Office to await the dawn and her death. The ship’s captain rises to the Bridge of *Resolve* to await the launch and perhaps to live.

That night, with less than six hours left on the countdown clock on the wall behind her, from her open tower window Constance stands in the dark to watch the last troops loading on the *Alpha* ships. They’re Wysocki’s Wreckers. She can’t make out Jan from so far away, but she knows he’s down there somewhere; that he’s leaving Genève on an odyssey for them all. Then she steadily walks down 30 stories of stairs to silently honor Dylan Byers, and makes her way without pause to the inner berm where the last fighters of Toruń gather for their last battle.

Final farewells are also said over last night hours by comrades-in-arms and old school friends. By scared teens wearing overstarched, first oak uniforms, hugging their crying parents and grandparents who stay behind. By siblings too young to wear an older brother’s or sister’s gold or silver sheaves, too small to pull on an absent parent’s marine suit or fit into simple sailor cloth. More intimate farewells entangle a thousand different pairs of lovers. Last kisses are pressed to faces of the dear departing by many, many more bound to stay to meet fire and death, or captivity and occupation by merciless enemies. Few believe a reunion will ever come. Not this side of death.

In the last hours before launch, sealed off from the city, fighters who must stay behind prepare to meet death in the coming ground battle in whatever way makes most sense to them. In prayer or drink, in silent solitude or the loud company of close friends in the ranks. The very young and those too old to fight along the berm are moved by martial law and subdued police into vast underground shelters beneath Toruń's twin lakes. A few civilians go home in vulgar despair to prepare poison meds, then quietly kill their children and themselves.

Those taking berths on *Alpha* scoop little tufts of turf into a kit bag or slip a blunt sliver of scented wood into a pocket before boarding, to remember the smell and touch of home in the long exile that's coming. Then all seals on all the airways of the nine ships are closed. Motored gangways pull away from the hulls. Chemical boosters mix fuel, hydrogen fusion engines come online, and all is ready. Amiya Constánce at last releases *Alpha* command to Magda Aklyan.

***

If the escape plan works and the nine little ships get away they'll carry 165,000 fighters aloft. If it fails, all know that everyone onboard *Alpha* will die in the unforgiving cold of space. No one knows that better than the nine captains and their XOs and Weapons Officers, gathered on *Resolve* for a final briefing. The room is crowded and hot. The captains and other officers can hear the big RIK ground guns booming outside, and answering fire from the KRA.

"OK captains, ships' officers. One last time, we'll review the flight plan. Mr. Fontaine, conduct the brief." A glowing, dynamic holo map rises over the main nav table. It shows Toruń below and the expected and known patrol routes of the Kaigun orbital squadron above.

"Yes ma'am. Once we get the signal from the general that she's opening the fight at the Berm Gate, along with many feints and probes around the perimeter, *Alpha* will leave."

Nothing but silence greets the grim mental image of all the death and suffering they'll leave behind on the ground as they burn white hot seeking escape velocity, and to live. Émile doesn't dwell. He continues in a measured, professional voice.

"*Warsaw* and *Jutlandia* will lift under main power, with their chemical assists adding boost phase speed. That should give *Alpha* an initial advantage, mainly of surprise. We hope to use it to scoot past the Kaigun overhead patrol."

“It will work if I've read their *daisa* right, but be ready to shoot our way out as well,” Magda cautions, looking especially to the nine Weapons Officers. They all nod affirmation.

“The escort of five destroyers and two frigates will fly close and tight behind the troopships,” Émile adds, “all nine ships rising together, firing main engines and the additional boosters. Troopships ahead of the wake turbulence, to start.”

Captain François Archambault on *Le Terrible* chimes in, trying to break the tension and his own dark mood. “I’d like to see that from the ground myself, and not because it will look so damned impressive.” Some nervous laughter moves around the room, but quickly dies.

Émile Fontaine resumes the brief. “When the signal comes, Toruń Shipyard’s batteries will shoot until they overheat and fail. They’ll hold back nothing. They’ll part the waves for us and hold open an ascent path. If we hold tight formation, that will allow *Alpha* to breach orbit and fly past the first picket line.”

“Toruń’s batteries have prevented bombardment by larger Kaigun warships, ever since three cruisers tried to ‘fly the zone’ in the first week of the siege, to pound our shields from orbit. As you know, they paid a terrible price. Zerstörers are faster but their guns aren’t big enough to do serious damage, and their captains are skittish after what happened to the cruisers. Or at least, their admiral is. The Kaigun is sitting too far out in what we think they think is a close blockade.”

“That’s bad for the city, of course, but good for *Alpha*’s chances in Phase I. It means their patrols and sentries form a hard orbital crust, tactically speaking. Once we break through with speed or firepower we can do some open field running, as we mercury ballers like to say. After that, as soon as that, *Alpha* will be entirely on its own.”

The holo map shifts scale and color, showing Genève as a small green-blue orb close to the system’s parent star. At 60 times its distance flies the only other planet, a cold jupiter with two larger moons and several dozen small ones. The big moons race around Wasp 2B in near synchronous orbits that take months to widen. This close in cycle repeats every seven years.

“Once we break past the main orbital patrol we’ll kick in the Type-3 cruiser boosters. This is critical to the second phase of the flight and escape plan. Only they can hurl the modified liners, our newly designated troopships, at military velocities to the leeside L2.”

"What if *Alpha* is intercepted on the way to that far off bohr zone?" Captain Tura Dan of the *Warsaw* was just promoted and reassigned from *Asimov*. She's a confident, highly competent young black woman from Brno. Her hair is finely braided, stopping just shy of her high yellow KRN collar. She wears her peaked cap slightly to one side, which gives her a cocky look that fits her, too. She's tall and slender, sliding inside her uniform rather like a panther fits into its own skin. That's her nickname, in fact: the Black Panther. She was always going places, prewar. The advent of war is getting her there a lot faster.

'*Gods, she's young to be a captain! Was I ever that young? If I was, when I was, I never had her responsibility.*' Magda takes over the brief. "The escorts are ready to sacrifice themselves, to allow the two much more vulnerable and valuable troopships to escape. But you *must* keep up at the hard start. It's the most critical leg of our centipede of an escape plan. Hence, all the extra boosters."

If the flotilla can somehow evade Kaigun inner system patrols, even civilian quantum drives on the converted liner-troopships are good enough to bohr to a neighboring system. After all, a bohr jump is still a bohr jump. Whether prewar markings on an outer hull are military or civilian, quantum drives are all good to go. It's only in-system that the troopships lack military speed.

"The sublight gap will be addressed in Phase I by the metallic hydrogen boosts, in the Phase II dash by our Type-3 fusion boosts. If either assist fails to speed us past the enemy, disaster may ensue. Then we'll have to fight it out, against whatever strength we face."

"What kind of warships will they have that far out?" It's Rutger Metsalaer of the *Guépard*. A green captain, newly promoted. Making his first war patrol.

"We can't know that. We have no solid intel on their deployments, only best guesses. We do know that we must evade any Kaigun ships in low or high orbit, fusion boost away from Genève, then stay ahead of any pursuit as we race to the outer Lagrange. There, we'll have to deal with unknown types and numbers of picket ships. With no outside assistance possible."

"I see. Thank you for the honest reply, Captain Aklyan."

It's a sobering answer from their leader. To drive the point home, she deploys her most severe commander's gaze and repeats it, looking each of her captains and XOs right in the eye. "Intel is down and not coming back. The enemy is more numerous and has bigger and more powerful ships than us, and we simply don't know where he'll put them. We'll be on our own, all the way to the outer bohr zone. And after that, if we make it. Any more questions?"

No one flinches or breaks gaze. They already more-or-less know what she's telling them, that *Alpha* is a faint hope. The room is totally silent.

Disciplined.

Determined.

Devoted.

Defiant.

Not of her words or her authority over them, but of the Fates, of the Gods, and above all, of the Enemy. "Another known unknown is whether enemy picket ships guard the uninhabited system to which our escape flotilla will travel first. Hence, any ship that can get away after the first all-together jump is under strict orders to do so, to escape alone by means fair or foul or fortunate."

"Where is that destination system, ma'am? Where do we jump to?" It's the First Officer on *Jutlandia*.

"Never mind about that now. I'll tell you en route. I want you all to focus on getting us to the bohr zone first, and then you can ask about the out-of-system destination. Rest assured, however, that General Constance and I have thought it through carefully. Your immediate and *only* problem is not where to jump, but getting your ships and passengers to the jump zone intact."

"Understood, ma'am."

Magda wants this point driven home, real hard. So she says nothing, daring a response. Again a judicious silence rules the room. Finally, she breaks it. "If for any reason *Alpha* breaks up, survivors are to scatter. Jump from any open LP to any system you can. Run and hide, then run again, until you reach one of the five sanctuaries in Calmari space. Then wait there for the rest of us. Those are your *orders*, captains. I'll nova fry anyone who disobeys and stays or turns to help."

She closes out the briefing. "Alright captains, let's do this. Return to your ships. Stay on your Bridges. XOs, lock in navs. Weapons Officers, get warm and ready. We'll rise with weapons hot. The signal will come tonight. Watch the clock, but be ready to go anytime up to three hours ahead of Zero Hour. Knowing the general, I'd say that's likely. *Bon chance, mes amis. Bon chance.*"

The escape plan is at high risk of breakdown at all major points. It's also the only hope that Genèvens have of joining the larger Krevan exodus, there to make war among the stars. There to keep the tiniest flame of defiant hope alive. There to burn like a candle in a stellar wind, calling to all Krevans to fight on forever.

***

Only Amiya Constance knows the dread price paid by the bravest man on Genève. Weak optical codes and incongruous *Ops Secret* coms carefully leaked over the past two weeks got the idea rolling among enemy intelligence officers. But she knew that false sigint gleaned from her planted intercepts would never be enough to satisfy bloodyminded and cynical analysts in Main HQ RSU.

So she played her ace. She allowed her friend and best Special Branch officer to let himself be captured while "probing enemy coms" outside the berm wall. He knows he'll be drugged and tortured. They both think his SB training will let him hold out long enough to mislead his interrogators, just enough, even under the worst of RIK torments. It's the single hardest parting of them all for Constance. On the last night, just hours before liftoff, she thinks of him and lowers her head.

As his terrible tortures climaxed two days earlier he let out a scream, then confessed to a trio of interrogators that an escape flotilla carrying the general and 'Ghost' and 200,000 troops will make a hard run for it, try to escape Genève.

"When? When, you *Gelben* bastard?"

"*Arrrrrhh!*"

"When?"

"*Ohhh, urrr* ... stop, I beg! In three days, three days ... *three!*"

"Good, that's better. Now tell us where they're headed, or you'll lose the other one. You don't want us to take it, do you?"

"To Aral! They're going to join the War Government on Aral."

He's talking freely, as fast as he can, trying to anticipate their next question before they cut or burn him again. Before they take his left foot and cauterize the gash with flat red irons they also used to burn his chest and arms and back. It's what they did to his missing right foot.

"How does the bitch plan to get out of Genève system?"

"With a ruse."

"What?"

"She'll make *a ruse de guerre.*"

"What? A what?"

"A feint, aiming for the Wasp. They'll fly toward the blue giant to start, but then they're going to double back and whip around fast to the farside stellar L3."

"How do you know this?"

"I was in the room when it was decided. It was the Ghost who told her to do it. It was all his idea. He said the double back trick worked in Pilsudski Wood."

It's a clever and well conceived lie. Psychologically acute, unlike their crude tortures. It gets their attention. If this came from the 'Ghost of the Wood' they have to take it seriously. Already, too many officers and RSU paid the ultimate price when Brusilov blamed them for being wrong about the Ghost. And he's not the only callous RIK general they must please.

"It's not enough. Burn him again! We need confirmation."

"*Arrrrrhh!* Please no, stop, no more. I'll tell you everything."

"How do you know when they'll leave?"

"I'm her senior intel officer. I'm supposed to go with her on the first ship. I've been with her 13 years. She'd never abandon me. We leave in three days!"

"You're going nowhere!"

"You'll stay in here forever, alone with us!"

"We'll come back and visit you again, after we kill your bitch general."

They believe him because in the last 37 hours he's lost a foot and taken electric and hot steel burns to half his body. And because they believe in their own crudely brutal methods. So they pass his forced confession upstairs to Main HQ marked *Authenticated*, and recommend that the Kaigun urgently stack its assets at the closest LPs, "especially around the stellar farside L3."

All her hard duties done save one, General Amiya Constance dresses in simple combat weaves, removes her rank insignia, and strides through the tunnel to reach the first assault unit waiting just inside the Berm Gate. Come dawn's incarnadine rays, she'll lead Genève's last army out to meet the foe. She doesn't hope for victory. She hopes only to hear, before she dies, a roar of boosters rising overhead as she holds her enemy in place by the throat.

She will fight on her last dawn for hate's sake. She will die so that Magda Aklyan and Jan Wysocki and *Alpha* may bring her hatred to the stars. She will die so that Krevo may live. Then she will lie in an honored place, in repose with murdered martyrs like her intel officer. Not with more cold or timid souls.

Regret

Jan doesn't say goodbye to anyone. He doesn't really know anyone in Toruń anymore, and what's left of his family is behind enemy lines. His cold, taciturn, disappointed father died five years after Jan came home from the Academy as a frosh washout. He has no siblings to worry about. He has only his mother, but no idea where she might be this night. His last on Genève.

He was shamed and shunned by silence at his father's table when he enrolled in Toruń Teachers College, then settled for a bad job teaching watered down Orion history to little kids in the local grade school. He finished Officer Training part time and took a commission in the Home Guard and Reserves. Every time he put on the uniform to do weekly hours his father made an excuse not to be there to see him in it. Jan tailed him one night. As he suspected, the trail ended in a pub.

His father hardly spoke to him at all after he came home, about anything. They lived in the same house but inside two solitudes, with Jan's mother alone in a third in the middle. He never spoke once to Jan, his only son, about his great failure. Not a word about walking away from Aral Academy. About '*throwing away your military education over some fool girl.*'

Jan knows that's what his father thought, even though he never actually said it. When he first came home, his mood dark and his manner as dour and taciturn as his disappointed father, his mother asked about the girl he left behind on Aral, and why. He didn't want to talk about it. Not ever. Anne-Marie Wysocki grieved silently for her son's suffering, as all good mothers do. Now, as he lies waiting for liftoff on KRN *Asimov* with nothing more to do for his new brigade, he thinks: '*Mother is trapped behind Rikugun lines.*' Alone in his silent boyhood home in a rural hamlet overrun by RIK in the first days of the war. '*Or maybe she's dead.*'

He isn't sure and has no way to find out. He has had no news from home in half-a-year. He wants to see her, embrace her, kiss her ageing peach fuzz cheek a farewell time. Warn her in the words of the ancient Buddha, in which he never believed but she does: "Mother, you must get out of your own burning house." It's too late. All the forests and fields of Genève are on fire.

He craves at this moment of leaving to tell his worried, mournful mother about the girl on Aral who broke his hopes and heart, the first and only great love of his youth. How when he lost her over a quarrel so slight he can't recall its outline now, he couldn't breathe, couldn't think or study or play mercury ball for the Academy again. Couldn't feel anything, for anyone.

He'd tell her about another girl, the first to catch his breath and stop it in his throat since that distant time of deep loss of love and himself on Aral. Tell her that Zofia is strapped to a bunk on *Resolute,* about to hurtle skyward like him. Only separate from him, because of him.

'*Will I lose her, too? Have I lost her already? Love is too dangerous a thing for me. I don't deserve it, anyway.*' Even he's starting to find this self loathing tiresome. But next comes his first real admission of regret, replacing self pity. '*Look how I hurt Zofia, for no reason.*'

Jan is strapped onto a hard pine bunk, one of the temporary berths bolted deck to ceiling in every hallway and storage room, each lazaret and cofferdam, even in bits of two Engine Rooms of a grossly overcrowded frigate. He has the pine board to himself, a privilege given to senior officers at brigade or division rank of colonel and above. Well, sorta to himself.

Most senior officers won't share their bunks, claiming they must store vital equipment there or just standing on privilege and an unstated claim that their rest time is more valuable than any other's. Not the Wrecker's commander.

Lying beside him in space afforded only to high rank lies a stray husky pup he rescued from the streets of Toruń nine days ago, right after his breakup with Zofia. Her head is tight against his thigh, her adoring steel-gray-on-silver eyes watching his twitching face. An undyed, wool blanket cushions her chin from the hardness of the pine bunk. He calls her Samara and scratches her into deep contentment just before liftoff, concentrating behind one pointed ear. Calming her before the coming surprise of G-force.

He's exhausted, feeling overstretched. With just eight days to recruit a new brigade he chose not to sleep. Against all medical advice but accepting Dylan Byers' he ingested a heavy dose of Q-moda, a sniper's extreme stimulant even more powerful than the usual type.

He had experience as a cadet, since dilute moda was used by many students prepping for a big match or for exams at the Academy. This time he forewent the normal course of protein and sugar buildup that all snipers make in advance, before he slipped the tiny med flake up his nostril. So he got real close to the outer limits of safety a lot faster than back in college or in basic training. He knows that after a week of no sleep at all, and even worse, of hyper alertness, he's about to crash real hard. So will every other exhausted officer in the brigade.

'*Well, so what? I'm likely to die this hour anyway. If not, I can do the moda jitters right here on this fine pine bunk.*' He's deep into "come down wander" as the ignition roar of the plasma drive shudders the ship. His questioning becomes more dense and off-the-mark, febrile and chaotic, denying him any calm or felt security. His eyes close, still restless. His tongue hangs out farther than Samara's.

She glances up at him quizzically. He's acting oddly, talking to himself and grinning wide. Though not like the cruel boys who chased her in Lakeside Park and threw rocks at her, until she turned and nipped one real good in the leg and he ran away bleeding and crying. That's when Jan saw her, wet and skinny and alone, orphaned by war when RIK came to her farm and slaughtered everything living. Somehow she got away, survived alone on one of the ash roads, starving but never stopping until she made the 700 klic journey to Toruń.

He laughed when the naughty boy ran away. He called her over to where he was sitting under a fig tree, thinking about how he had just made the mistake of his life with Zofia. He gave her food and a focus for loyalty and devotion. She's already his best guard. She's also the quiet soul he speaks with late at night.

A wool blanket is folded under his neck, keeping the bench from hurting his head as he's pressed down hard by far more Gs than is normal or seems healthy as the frigate lifts off under additional and ancient boost energy. There's no padding at all under his elbows, back or buttocks. They all hurt like hell where they press against hard pine. Samara gives a whimper as she's pressed down hard as well. She doesn't try to move from Jan's side as her high bushy tail grows too heavy to wag. She curls it under her hindquarters, where it'll be safe.

Jan's too tall for the bunk. His knees are drawn up and bang into another pallet just far enough above to allow a man or woman to slide in between, but not to roll over. There are six more bunks above that and three below him. Ten more barely an arm's length away on the opposing wall of this tiny, converted ship's lazaret. On every bunk two Wreckers lie, head-to-foot, every one looking as miserable and accusatory as an old family dog carelessly left outside in a thunderstorm. Just like patient, loyal, and war orphaned Samara looked over many long nights alone before Jan befriended her.

The air in the lazaret is stifling, with a strange odor he can't quite place. That's because 1,500 Wreckers are crammed on board, most for six hours or more. Captain Lev Tiva assured him before liftoff that life support on the tight frigate is good enough to sustain the extra load. Then he saluted Jan in mock KRA fashion, with palm turned outwards rather than down as in the KRN. His thickly browed eyes twinkled as always, and he grinned from under a white peaked cap sporting a soft yellow band and double headed falcon signifying 'Fleet Officer.'

"But it's going to smell like five cats died in the locker room, all the showers are broken, the whole mercury ball team is standing around you sweating right after the game, and your old coach just took a huge dump in the back."

Lev Tiva has a deserved reputation for near constant levity and schoolboy jokesterism. His brown eyes danced with a naughty child's delight to see Jan's disgust at a vulgar imagery. Then he showed another side, a bent for literary reference fitted to the moment that surprised Jan. He simply hurled it out and into the air, even as he swinged off to *Asimov*'s Bridge.

"*Consider the sea. Its most dreaded creatures glide under water, unapparent and treacherously hidden beneath its lovely azure. Think on the devilish brilliance of its most remorseless sharks, and its universal cannibalism, where all creatures carry on eternal war.*" Then he saluted and bellowed an odd farewell: "*I'm off to hunt a great White Whale.*"

Jan knew that one. "*I am tormented with an everlasting itch for things remote. I love to sail forbidden seas, and land on barbarous coasts.*" Jan thinks Tiva is half mad. Samara is more or less of the same opinion. She especially doesn't like the man's too yellow hat. She's planning to chew it up, first chance she gets.

"Though he's a real good butt scratcher."

'*Was that me or Samara?*'

"He did me a real good scritch this morning."

"Who said that?"

"Said what, colonel?"

"Nothing. Never mind, son."

'*Damn these jitters! I'm confused as hell.*'

Jan can't get the raunchy image out of his head, not least because it comes uncomfortably close to accurately describing the odor playing about his nostrils. He wonders: '*Did Tiva ever stand on a pitch like I used to, trying to catch an unpredictable ball loop-and-drop and hover and change direction as its liquid interior tumbles randomly? Did he shower in an Academy locker room? Where did he come up with that vulgarity? And most important, how did he know?'*

Toruń's white plasma and laser and maser batteries are shooting hard and fast, carving an angled, narrow flight tunnel for *Alpha* through a close orbit of waiting enemy warships. The shooting is causing a lot of extra turbulence as plasma tears upward through the atmosphere. It also signals *Alpha*'s departure to the RIK tactical sky force and Kaigun ships above. That can't be helped. It's critical to speed to optimal altitude before engaging the Type-3 fusion drives.

What Jan Wysocki doesn't know, what Magda Aklyan doesn't know, what only Amiya Constance knows is the terrible price paid by one man to ensure that *Alpha* is streaking through the upper clouds before RIK HQ can react, because it's leaving a day early. A brave man who's about to die tormented and abused in a dark prison cell. Utterly alone, his suffering and death will not be noted in history books. He'll die forever anonymous. And yet, his sacrifice will change all Orion.

***

Nine small warships strain upward, racing to break right past orbit velocity to achieve escape velocity and swing around the Kaigun patrol. They're already 50 klics up and accelerating with each microsecond. Each one launched from ground moorings in Toruń Shipyard within a 60 second window, an absurdly dangerous timing pattern for so many ships.

Wake turbulence from the two liner-troopships, flying in tandem in the leadoff position, means *Asimov* is driving far harder inside the wake than is good for its engines, or its passengers. All fusion drives eject white hot plasma beyond *flank speed liftoff* demands, well past prewar environment and urban safety protocols. All chemical and smaller sub boosters in the flotilla are also shooting white.

Every captain and officer on each of nine compact Bridges is pushed harder and far deeper into a hard flight chair than he or she has ever experienced before. Everywhere within the flotilla wooden bunks hard bolted or reeved to stiff metal or carbon fiber walls groan and shudder, vibrate and creak unnervingly. So too all the jostling, jammed in, frightened fighters.

Jan grips the sticky sides of his bunk as *Asimov* pulls fresh loads of gravity down onto itself and him, absurdly contending for max escape velocity against the physics of an entire planet. He always thought liftoff was quite an unnatural thing to assay. He much prefers the smooth calm of a space elevator ride to a hard launch like this, the kind of rush only old tars boast about when well in their cups.

'*It's why I joined the Krevan Army, not the fucking Navy.*' He gripes out loud to simpering Samara. "It's just not natural!" She's thinking exactly the same. She looks at Jan with uprolled, steel-gray-on-silver eyes. The G-force is making it too hard to raise her head or howl, as she wants to do.

The wood bench beneath him feels sticky and smells of pine tar. The one above, with two young Wreckers pressed white knuckled against its flatness, is slow dripping something into his hair. '*What IS that?*' He wants to reach up a finger to test it, but he can't raise his arm. '*Sap! Godsdamn, it's all over me. Samara, too. Funny how you get used to comfort. To a soft bed and clothes. What did a little sap mean in Pilsudski Wood or in the ash lands? Nothing!*'

He laughs bitterly and out loud, relieving his stress but startling the boys above and 36 others in the tiny alcove, two per bunk. Except for Jan's. All are nervously gripping the bunk boards or each other. Some are trying not to lose the contents of their stomachs, or their bowels. He worries about the effect of his laughter. '*It'll just add to my stupid legend. If we live through this, tomorrow they'll say that I laughed in the face of danger. Or some shit like that.*' He's not wrong. The idea of it, of being a living legend and a Ulysses to his exiled people, strikes him in this moment as so stupid it makes him laugh out loud a second time.

This time Samara tries to bark in response, throatily and half formed, through curled back, black leathery lips she manages: "*Arrrrooooohhh!*" He ignores her. She thinks: '*What's up with you, master Jan? When will this strange, awful weight lift off my head and back? When can I wag my tail again? What have you gotten us into? Can I get off now?*' Samara's drawn out G-force barking makes everyone in the tight little room relax a bit. Any who can see the flattened and panting husky pup from their own slabs grins widely or laughs weakly back.

'*Will it be this way forever? Must I play the hero when I know I'm not? I'll just have to live with both realities. After all, for centuries people thought light is both wave and particle and that we'd never be able to say when and where at the same time. If physics functioned for so long with such mad truths, maybe I can survive a while as both a hero and a fraud.*'

He realizes he's giddy with stress and adrenalin and withdrawal. The jitters are kicking in hard since he's no longer trying to fight them off. He needs to calm down. He breathes deep and slow like they taught him, marshaling his thoughts, going over the coming mission. It's the first chance he's had in days for private thoughts, to roll over in his mind his break with Zofia, his unexpected promotion, his 'legend' and the Ulysses order from mad General Constance. It doesn't work. He can't concentrate on the brigade. '*Helvetti, there's nothing more I can do about it anyway, not about anything. Wreckers' lives are all in Captain Magda Aklyan's hands now, not in mine.*'

His thoughts flee to find Zofia. '*The curve of her neck and her supple breasts, that little mole above the indentation at the small of her lower back where I stroked her. Her legs tightly wrapped around my waist, her taut buttocks, her sweet russet diadem, so warm and wet...*"

Erotic self distraction doesn't work, either. His moda pullback is much too powerful, scattering and shattering his thoughts, jagging them back-and-forth beyond his control. As *Asimov*'s thrusters push him harder against the rigid bunk his mind turns away from making love with Zofia to making bloody mayhem in the woods with her at his side. Lifts him out of Zofia's wet and thrusting loins to drop him into battle, to his talent for bringing pain and death. Catapults him into cruelty, calculation and destruction. It's all he knows anymore.

'*Gods, see the bloody blade in her hand? That boy's got two smiles now. Ha! Will this new brigade survive through the next hour, past the Kaigun patrol? Will we make it to the end of today, to the L2? Where's Alpha going next?*'

"Need to know only, colonel."

He could swear he hears General Constance's voice, somewhere in the room. He looks suspiciously at Samara, pressed flat and miserable against the bunk.

"What did you say?"

"That wasn't me."

Her eyes are closed to narrowed slits hidden by silver fur. Her black leather lips oddly pressed down by gravity, showing half her lower canines, over which a foam of white drool is leaking. She's moaning under the extra weight. Her tail is unmoving. She can't move it. She really, really wants to. '*This is weird!*'

"Somebody said something. What?"

"I said, *you* don't need to know which rabbit hole."

'I don't need to know because I don't know already. Well, that makes perfect sense. This is the Army after all.'

'You can't be trusted with information. You might run away, to the enemy."

'Damn! Will I never live that down? You said I am to be Ulysses!'

"It's not the title that honors you, but you who must sail on Ionian seas."

'What?'

"Off with his head!"

'Whose head? Mine?'

"You heard me."

'I don't understand. What do want from me?'

"Don't come home unless you're leading an army. Don't come back without allies who also have fleets and armies. Kill our enemy. Slay his worlds!"

'Burn down your own Troy, damn you! Fight your own Cyclops! Bind yourself to your own mast as the sirens call! Fight your own battles and war! Why me? Why must I be your damned Ulysses?'

"Not because I chose you, colonel. You chose yourself. No, not at Aral. No, not at the MDL. Long before Pilsudski Wood. Long before the long trek to Toruń. Years before the hard fight at *The Crater*. You chose as a boy, while dreaming of fighting among the stars. You chose when you decided to become an officer. You chose, over and over. Long before the Ghost of the Woods and *The Crater*."

'You're right, but damn you for seeing it. I did choose way back then. And I chose when Zofia came back for me as I waited to die. I chose in the sweetgrass. I chose when I saw your bright shining hate mirror my own, and my ambition.'

"Good. You agree then. Remember always who you are and who you can and must be. Remember so that you return to take our vengeance, and to claim your honored place among those of us who shall never lie with cold and timid souls who knew neither victory nor defeat."

His thoughts jig from moda. '*Magda Aklyan is a good captain. Our best, or General Constance wouldn't have given her command of Exodus. So many lives are in her hands! Well, she has my pity. All generals and admirals need our pity.*'

Samara moans, low and long. She's still trying and failing to raise her tail. her lips feel too stretched. She thinks someone is lying on top of her.

'*This is the most important mission in 300 years. That's what she said ... since, when was it ... Ulysses? No, that's a much older story of war and woe.*'

"Concentrate, you fool!"

His raggedy thoughts jump back to the Brigade. '*Where are we going? Will I lead my fighters into battle on alien worlds? Can the Brigade, can I, live up to all the hopes Genèvens place in us, in me? So much duty and hope loaded onto my shoulders by that damned woman! I would rather have my testicles lasered by RSU than go through an interrogation by her again.*'

"That can be arranged, you know."

His mind jerks back, less than halfway to reality, but back all the same. '*Yet I also admire her. Here we are, straining upward to escape, tearing at the sky to race away from the clutching gravity of my homeworld while she leads an imprudent, hopeless ground assault.*'

He's right. Just before *Alpha* engaged its extra boosters to ascend into a rose streaked dawn she ordered the portcullis lifted and marched out at the head of a quarter million fighters to face gore and vulgar death outside her beloved and lost and ruined Arbor City. They did it without hope for initial tactical surprise from a blown plasma mine, used earlier to rescue lost Madjenik.

'*I screwed that up, too, costing the general her chance to blow apart their main position at the Gate. I had to show up instead, and make her blow The Crater mine too early.*' He's being wildly unfair. Using the mine was her choice. No one in the garrison thought or said afterward that it was a mistake. No one in Toruń blamed Jan or Madjenik for surviving.

Toruń's last defenders, minus 165,000 fighters straining upward with *Alpha*, are giving the enemy all they have, laying down cover fire and making sorties all around and outside the outer berm to draw off Rikugun reinforcements from the main force right outside the Gate. They'll push RIK back before it recovers and begins to systematically slaughter fighters it can get to at last. In a matter of hours they'll all be dead, or wounded or captured. The garrison *hors de combat* and a defenseless, fearful city open to occupation or destruction at the enemy's whim.

Already, warehouses full of harvest and wool and stacks of export wood are smoking, the navy yard is burning and dry docks collapsing as preset charges are blown by engineers and scattering workers. Only the great batteries keep firing, as they will until their heterodiamond barrels crack and shatter or RIK ground forces breach the berm to rush in and kill all the crews. Casks of wine and tankers of beer are smashed open and left to run into smooth wooden gutters that line every street and alley way. The sweet smelling runoff turns *gold-red-white* as milk tankers are hastily and crookedly parked, abandoned with wide open spigots as drivers run or head out to join family, or to die with friends fighting at the berm.

Store fonts are shuttered with heavy wood venetian drops, except a few whose owners are gone or dead. Five hundred streets are blocked by barricades, each with an *ad hoc* reserve company readying to make its own last stand. Teenagers mostly, scared and skinny, struggling to hold their weapons. Or far too willing to engage the enemy, posing as they've seen in vids and games. White haired men three generations or more removed in their time of life give orders to other men's children and grandchildren. They should know better, but they missed their own chance at war and want to try it now. Here and there one of the children's mothers searches through the street companies, come to find and drag away a too young and naïve son or daughter to a deep bunker hastily dug under some nearby tower.

Archie streams from a thousand tower tops as Jabos swoop directly over the city now that the shield is down to let *Alpha* out. Bombs and bits of bombers hit the sides of towers as they fall, showering the streets and squares below with millions of tiny oak or redwood splinters. Hot bits of archie shells set the tinder on fire. Empty streets are filling with aromatic smokes. There's no reason to hold back anymore. The shield is open, the berm is cracked and will breach in a dozen places within a few hours, letting tens of thousands of vengeful enemy pour in to Toruń, to tramp its wooden streets and kick down doors with high black jackboots.

"*Burn it! Burn it all!* Leave nothing for the locusts." No one has the heart to fire the towers, to bring the wooden canyons of Arbor City crashing down just so the Grünen cannot have them. Constance didn't order it and Toruńites just can't bring themselves to do it. Nor would it be so easy to topple the hard towers with mere fire, as an angry new Grün governor will learn when he gets here in a week.

Constance's words swirl in Jan's thoughts. *'They're not cold or timid souls. We'll know defeat, but all die merrily, our hate burning bright.'* Only they're not her words. Just a Q-moda jumble, the Toruń Quarry slogan mixed with odd bits of his own half thoughts. He's losing control.

'*Yeah, but even in jitters I know the bit about fighters dying merrily is crap.*' He's seen and he's caused too many deaths to buy into faux poetic nonsense about death in battle being anything but gory and profane. He can't lie to himself, not here on a plain pine bunk on *Asimov*, possibly living the last few minutes of his life. He replays in his mind's eye the many sordid ways people are dying on the planet shrinking below him at such speed.

He easily visualizes the awful scenes and blows he knows are being given and taken all around Toruń's berm. Bloody, slow, obscene wounds and horrid deaths. Not heroic at all. '*Not if they're like the deaths I saw and made in the sweetgrass, the forests and The Crater.*' He saw friend and foes dying together, and afterward lying together, glass eyes looking skyward on a dead prairie burned to stubble, or cremated in a forest, left face down in choking ash. The dead have no nationality.

He lurches back to considering his duty, which he now realizes is far harder than dying. '*While they fight, I'm running again. Under orders to do it, but running all the same.*' He looks down to Samara and thinks: '*You hitched yourself to the wrong patron, kiddo.*'

His brain goes kaleidoscope. '*Heavy masers and cannon are shooting, searing flesh; bombs drop from Jabos, shells and missiles plunge. Tens of thousands of brave men and women live a last minute, for all of us up here. Compared to that, what's a little sap or a hard bunk? What's anything?*'

His drug crimped mind jigs. '*Zofia! Why do you want me? Why did I push you away? So little time and so much death. So few days to be together, even absent this damn war.*'

It jags, tracking the ship as he feels *Asimov* course correct, hard and sharp as it strains through a thinning stratosphere. '*That bushy eyed gopher, Captain Tiva, will engage Type-3 boosters next. Can we do it before the Kaigun patrol blows all Alpha into fragments?*'

It jigs. '*I remember every moment that passed between us ... the first time I saw you, petite and exciting in a lieutenant's uniform ... You looked like a fresh picked apple with your red hair and perfect skin. Then you walked across the parade ground and stared up at me with that little mocking grin you always have, not quite insubordinate but mocking nonetheless.'*

It jags. '*Gods, they bashed right through us at the MDL. I have to figure a better way to deal with their heavy armor. A surprise, so that next time we level the odds and even the score.*'

It jigs. *'Did you know it then? Did you look up my records before we met? ... Of course you did ... third in your class at KRA Academy, on your first duty but knowing you would never stay, that High Command is where you're headed ... One of KRA's top officer prospects ... Just needed to command a platoon to get some field experience ... Why not? You're always ready for anything, even for me, a flunked out company commander with not half your skill or worth.'*

It jags, for the last time. '*We must be getting close to clear space, to where the Kaigun patrol will be. I hope Aklyan has something up her sleeve, because no way the ground batteries are just going to smash a path through for us. We're truly and suddenly on our own out here.*'

It jigs back to what he needs to say to himself, to what's burning him up. '*You did your duty anyway, and showed me how to do mine ... On the barracks ground, and at the MDL, in Pilsudski Wood and after ... I remember, too, a long day before the war, when we walked by the sea and somehow I found words to talk to you ... When you told me of your hopes and plans, too, and I was glad that you confided in me ... shared something of your real self.*'

He relives the seaside day, innocent and chaste yet their best day of all. Their day of days. Then his moda mind does a last leap ahead, over weeks of peace back to the war, to his shame before Zofia and the real reason he broke it off. '*I never told you, but it was only you who kept me moving in the cornfield ... I wanted to lie down and die from shame ... right there, where I dropped my weapon and was afraid ... but then you came back for me, worthless me, who failed you and ran.*'

'*In the forest your apple hair blew in a clearing's breeze as you tossed your head back laughing, when we ate that greasy moose and all got sick ... I longed for those times when our eyes met ... loved watching you sleep under the golden boughs ... but I couldn't say, not there, not with all Madjenik depending on me ... and I had no words to speak to you yet ... you looked at me, so disappointed ... I knew it ... but that's what I do, Zofia ... I disappoint everyone.*'

'I watched you take charge when I was wounded, so calm and confident ... admired you sleeping in the orchard ditch .... Then you used your knife on that boy in the sweetgrass ... I understand now, but I hated you for it back then ... for spoiling my perfect illusion of you.' It's oddly liberating to admit it. It allows him to see Zofia not as a distant ideal but as a real woman, who somehow wants him despite his worthlessness. Who loves him, just as he loves her.

He comes to the fateful moment, less than two weeks ago, when he abruptly told Zofia that it must end just as it was beginning. He sees in his mind's eye for the first time how deep the hurt was in her eyes, the intense hurt he felt when he closed down almost forever at age 19, when that other girl did the very same thing to him on Aral: chose a fool's illusion over him.

He knows now that he's the cause of Zofia's pain. His synapses recorded it, but a lying conscious mind suppressed and hid it from him. Denied it. Until he's prone on a plank of sticky wood on *Asimov* with nowhere to go or hide from the truth that's knocking to get in through an airlock. His whole being rocks with nova force and suddenness, jolting the pine, causing Samara to whimper with concern.

He sees the truth of Zofia with a clarity only the looming chance of his death permits, and insists upon. The chance of ceasing in the next moment casts off the webs of self deceit he wove in the dark all his adult life, ever since Aral. Death the Judge calls in a harsh jury to render open judgment on him in clear and stark and forever words.

'I pushed you away, but for what? Regulations? The good of Madjenik? No, those were just the words. I was lying, to both of us. I was afraid to feel that pain again, like I did back on Aral and for so long after. But I was most afraid to see disappointment in me set into your eyes, those jade orbs that always see right through me to places I never dare to go and don't understand.'

'I've made a huge mistake. Mother, I loved and lost on Aral. Now I've lost my love again.' She fills all his hemispheres. He'll never be blind to her again. The revelation hits him with a physical jolt. He remembers a line learned as a boy, sitting at his mother's feet. *'Then felt I like some watcher of the skies, when a new planet swims into his ken.'*

He decides: *'Zofia, forgive me! Not for anyone can I give you up! There's no time. Our lives are collapsing. Can I get you back? Can I fix your hurt? I'll beg you to take me back. Zofia, will you have me? What a fool I was! I am! A fool!'*

Tens of thousands of other men and women teetering on the lip of personal and forever nothingness fight similar private wars of regret and self reproach. Some about lovers old or new, others about dead parents or a wayward child, more about paths not taken or walked too eagerly, or aborted futures of dead friends and all the unsaid and undone things that now can never be.

Although not everyone is thinking profoundly about life and fate and death. One kid is regretting that just before boarding he ate bad sushi. Now, the turbulence is making him queasy. Another is remembering and reliving his last sex, his hand under his blanket. A third is humming pop songs. Odd ducks, we humans. Oddest of all when we go quacking off to war.

Samara whimpers as *Asimov* boosts out of the upper Genèven atmosphere. Still, even this is better than running hungry and sleeping on the oak boarded streets of Toruń as she did for two lean months after being abandoned by the awful slaughter and confusion of the war. As the flotilla breaks clear of gravity's clutch she feels the terrible acceleration pressure ease. '*I can move my tail!*' She gives it a wag, just to be sure. Able to raise her silver head again and open her eyes, she stretches torso and neck a few inches upward and licks Jan's face in gratitude. She has found her first ever home, in exile with Jan among the stars.

He grins down at her.

He's recovering, too.

Samara barks happily at him.

Alpha rises into a revelation of stars so bountiful they becloud all nine Main Scuttles, spilling in a broad pinwheel as from a great steel milk can tipped over into a running creek. As air thins around each ship and white stars appear in side scuttles, too, every prayer is already said. Every ship's gun and missile tube is primed. Each mudhopping middy and jack and jenny and all the knife creased uniformed officers are expectant of fast action and their dreadful duty.

Whatever hope or striving is felt, results are no one's to command from this moment on. For it's not true, as the dead poet once said, that "everything comes gradually and at its appointed hour." In war things happen pellmell, with blind and reckless fury and random promises of Death and Chaos and Departure into Nothingness in the bottomless black hole of Eternity. And that's on the ground. *Alpha*'s heading into war above the sky, betwixt the Heavens and all the Earths.

And there they are!

Brighter than the brightest of morning stars.

White hot streaks of twelve fusion tails.

Incandescent across a galaxy lying on edge.

Ink black, yet red with old battle embers.

Data search: navigation
Result: LPs, quantum drive
Historia Humana, Volume V, Part III (c)

We bid our children farewell as they left to cross stellar seas on light sails and GDM ships, not expecting to see them again. Then we resumed our affairs. The old dream of faster-than-light travel to the stars seemed so unattainable a fancy that no serious FTL research was attempted. Einstein's determined god of relativity stayed in place for centuries as the first ships sailed on. A defiant deity, resplendent in tyranny over our grasp of the cosmos and our place within an ever expanding, flat snow globe of energy-particles-waves. It remained indifferent to superluminal ambitions of Humanity and the deepest convictions of cosmologists.

The first critical idea leading to the 'stardrive' arose from a probabilistic loophole in Einstein's concept of gravity under general relativity. Relativity assumes that spacetime is locally flat. In asymptotically flat spacetime, curvature of a gravity field fades to negligible at great distance from an isolated massive object at the center of the field, such as a star. General relativity posits, with subtle complications and asides, that gravity is essentially a curvature of normally flat spacetime caused by concentrated mass. Stars twist normal spacetime like desert dust devils or prairie tornados twirl dirt and leaves. The real Universe is therefore not truly or asymptotically flat. There are crinkles and turns where mass concentrates so that gravity twists straight lines along an infinite curve until the distance from point to line approaches zero.

Discovery of 'gravity echoes' combined with solution of an old three body problem that predated Einstein, where at five fixed points there is near zero net force and the third body is at equilibrium. Known to ancient navigators and system gas miners as Lagrange points (LPs), these are also called by modern navigators bohr zones or jump zones. They led to the second loophole, this one in Kepler's Laws, that made possible 'mechanics' of a quantum drive. LPs are so orbitally balanced that centuries after being exploited by miners and in coms systems, no one asked if they had effects beyond their remarkable stability and orbital energy conservation. Yet, except for habitable planets and ice moons, today we know that LPs are the most critically important places in any solar system. For only in a bohr zone may we observe and access by quantum analysis intersecting spacetime or gravity crinkles that make stellar jumps possible.

'Quantum drive' is a misleading term, but it is in such common use today there is just no avoiding it. A quantum drive is in fact a gravity echo detector, not an engine or stardrive. That proved the final felix culpa, a happy fault in Einsteinian

spacetime itself. It is inconceivable even in our advanced technological era that we could build artificial engines of sufficient power to move the mass of a ship close to lightspeed to traverse interstellar space. For centuries, it never occurred to ask if the special features of LPs might permit near instant or quantum speeds. Yet that is what Nature itself provides us.

Interstellar navigation arrived with routine manufacture of liquid magnetism, or Quantum Spin Liquid (QSL), permitting computation of grand entanglements at interstellar distances. QSL computers broke the old, high qubit barrier by using magnetized matter, a rare type of molecular bonding existing naturally only in unminable white dwarfs or unapproachable neutron stars. Intense magnetic fields adjust all molecular binding in two state quantum or qubit memory. Quantum stadimeters (aka 'stardrives') map local gravity wave disturbances, or 'hybrid singularities,' that wrinkle up the surface of much deeper gravity equilibrium of flat-yet-crinkled spacetime, a bit like a water strider on a taut pond surface...

...even with today's quantum stadimeters, hybrid singularities remain hidden except at bohr zones, where gravity equilibrium is highest and spacetime's surface skin calmest. Only there does a 'quantum drive' permit a stadimeter to read the map of surface folds in not-so-flat spacetime. That is, to map 'hybrid' singularities. Subsequent calculation of 'wrinkle' or 'ripple' or 'fold' features (navigators use such terms interchangeably) allows a ship to ride the fold. As a ship's mass engages a fold identified as linked to where it wants to go, it's pulled, not driven, there by folded spacetime itself, simply by finding this truly weird quantum grand entanglement.

Complementarity is far more than a philosophical garnish sprinkled over quantum mechanics five centuries before the first stardrive was invented. The notion of complementarity is more than a principle of the epistemology of observation and measurement, as cosmologists long thought. It also has real world effects at the grand as well as the quantum levels of mass-energy. That gave new meaning to Einstein's uneasy notion of 'spooky action at a distance.'

A singularity detectible at a bohr zone must not be confused with speculative singular conditions said to exist in the interior of black holes, nor with the merely metaphysical starting point previously posited as the origin of the 'Big Bang.' A singularity it is, nevertheless. That insight and more important, that reality, led to spectacular effects and advances that old general relativity did not foresee or encompass, which Einstein famously dismissed once as God "playing dice with the universe." Instead, adjacent singularities are linked at the level of grand complementarity. In short, the dice are loaded.

Quantum drives utilizing grand complementarity of hybrid singularities, created by the mass of stars interacting spookily at a distance and detectible in three body systems, may only navigate at the five stable LPs or bohr zones. Such a jump made from one stellar linked LP to another is called a "bohr" by captains, navigators, and cosmologists alike. It is not known who first used the term. Yet it is widely agreed that Niels Bohr, the great thinker whose core idea of fundamental indeterminacy toppled Einstein's terrible and limiting deity and made FTL drive thinkable and feasible, would have appreciated and applauded the irony. For he is remembered today all across Orion in a standard navigation unit of vast distance and instantaneous qubit travel that always emerges differently from a quantum stadimeter each time it is measured.

Alpha

Magda Aklyan strains against the hard G-forces pushing down on her chest, slamming her deep into the command chair on the Bridge of *Alpha*'s flagship, the older and patched up destroyer *Resolve*. She calls her flotilla captains, checking ship-to-ship relays as *Alpha* breaks out of the lower atmosphere. It's drawing closer by the second to a descending Kaigun patrol.

She has nine ships in her command, seven warship escorts and two more former tourist liners mostly pretending to be troopships. Each bears a freshly etched naval escutcheon on its stern, an engraved silver anchor with a falcon perched in the crown, between seaweed draped flukes. In one outstretched claw the fierce bird grips a lightning bolt promising war and resistance, in the other a golden wheat sheaf offering peaceful commerce and signifying membership in Genève Squadron. The lightening bolt is held forward so that it's dominant over the wheat sheaf, for this isn't the first war fought in Orion. The whole flotilla is pushing hard past orbit escape speed with boost assists.

The converted liners carry the huge majority of 165,000 KRA fighters onboard Alpha. The troopships don't fit any normal naval classification, but they're crewed by KRN tars and captains and refitted with light cruiser fusion drives for a direct run to the L2 leeward of the cold gas giant, Wasp 2B. Each mounts a single, forward shooting plasma cannon along its top center beam. *Warsaw* is a bigger and better built ship, so it also has a destroyer caliber kinetic railgun mounted aft, laser welded and reeved with carbon fiber cabling to the lower hull. That's as much firepower as could be added in the time available. And all the civilian hulls can bear. The intention is to flat out run rather than fight. But it's a proud fleet. If it comes to fighting, Magda hopes that any armaments at all on what still look from the outside like fat and slow civilian liners will prove a surprise to any Kaigun *daisa* who has a go at them.

The Bridge on *Resolve* smells of fresh white paint newly applied in Toruń Shipyard, but it looks old and second rate underneath. It's pocked and micropitted, too rounded by decades of routine wear to be mistaken for new. Actually, all nine ships in *Alpha* reek of fresh paint on their Bridges, Weapons and Navigation stations. And hasty arc welds and emergency repair to a thousand carbon bindings. Happily, other ships' stations smell of new cut, green wood.

"All ships' Communications and Weapons Stations, status check. *Check.*"

Normally these confirmations would be handled by her XO. But these are not normal conditions and Lieutenant Commander Émile Fontaine is too busy calculating live interception angles and fusion boost rates for two maneuvers making up Phase I of the escape plan.

"*Tyco Brae* here. We're good to go." One of the two small frigates, reporting in first. Its captain is alert and ready.

'*What about the others?*'

"Captain Tura Dan, KRN *Warsaw*. All systems check. Glad to be part of *Alpha* and under your command." It's the larger of the two converted troopships, the one with the brand new captain and the aft mounted ice gun.

'*That's an auxiliary crew that's proud of its military commissioning and new KRN name and official naval status. Captain Dan is may be too ambitious for her age, but she's also very good.*'

"*Resolute* checking in. All communications good. Thrusters good. Weapons primed." *Resolute* is the first destroyer to status check. Zofia is onboard, along with most but not all of greatly expanded Madjenik Battalion. *Resolute* is boosting hard, right alongside her sister ship *Resolve*. Both destroyers ride tight behind the troopships to start, just as Magda ordered.

'*A solid crew under a good captain, with years of service. OK, peacetime service. But I'll take whatever experience I can put in the captain's chair.*'

"*Le Terrible* here. Coms good. Fore-and-aft cannon ready, ma'am."

"Good to hear, Captain Archambault. But let's hope we don't have to engage weapons. First, we rely on our extra boost speed to see if we can't get through without real trouble."

"Right you are. Shall we race to see who gets there first, Magda?"

François Archambault is an old friend who likes to gently tweak Magda's too stern looks and tough command style. But now is not the time or place, and he should know better. His tone and salutation are much too familiar for combat. He needs to show respect for her as flotilla commander. He must use her formal title over the ship-to-ship com link, at least.

"That's captain, captain. Or ma'am, if you will."

"*Ahh* yes. Of course, ma'am."

It's an odd but respected tradition in every military (except the misogynist, all male Rikugun and Kaigun) that whenever ranks are set aside women generals are called "sir" but warship commanders and admirals are always called "ma'am." Émile Fontaine tried to find out why once, but he could never track it down. And he's a pretty good amateur naval historian.

"*À regret, capitaine*. Archambault out."

She sighs quietly. It's who he is. A dear friend and confidante but a man not always in control of his impulses. She also thinks he smells a little salty, like stilled brine trapped on a seashore when the tide recedes. She's not wrong. He grew up in a seaside village on Southland and has the informality of a village boy to prove it, despite the ancient nobility of his name.

"*Triomphant* here. All good to go, ma'am." An older destroyer but with a veteran crew. She's glad they're alongside.

"*Guépard* reporting. All systems check." The last of the four escort destroyers, counting *Resolve*. This one under Rutger Metsalaer, a second rookie captain.

Like *Resolve* and two other escorts, *Guépard* rises with patched external damage. Not fully patched either, since Chief Azazi had to pull repair crews over the last four days of refit to affix extra armor and weapons ordered for *Jutlandia* and *Warsaw* by General Constance and herself. '*Another kid in the command chair. Was I right to give him his own ship?*'

Magda is more worried about its new captain than its creaking seams. He was the XO, whom she lifted into the command chair after *Guépard*'s prewar captain was killed in the first hour of fighting with the Kaigun invasion fleet, off the gas giant's second moon.

'*Well, what choice did I have? I had to promote some junior officer and he was next in line. The crew of* Guépard *watched their old captain die a hard death. Bringing in an outsider would have demoralized them. And so far, Rutger has done well. He spent all his time back on Toruń running simulations on a refurbished ship, getting a half replacement crew up to speed.*'

"Very good, Captain Metsalaer." She thinks: '*After he took over from a dead captain he booked nearly the same combat hours as me. It has been so long since the last one we all forget that we're still learning this thing called war.*'

"*Asimov* systems check. We're go over here, *patroon.*" It's Captain Lev Tiva, even now playfully checking in using an archaic term for captain. She has to smile at Tiva's cheeky use of "patroon." She can't correct him like she just did Archambault because her XO, who's her regs-and-rules guide, told her the first time Tiva used it that the term may be old fashioned in the extreme but, by the book, it's still in KRN's lexicon.

'*Tiva must have known that too, researched it. He's got talent, and would've gone a lot further in his career before the war if he instead applied his energies to more important things.*' She pictures his dark eyes dancing under his singularly unkempt eyebrows, bushy as twin raccoons. His eyes are always waltzing. That and his truly oddball sense of humor cost him a lot in his career. He's her senior in service by 15 years, yet he still commands only an older frigate.

"That's eight, counting *Resolve*. Who's missing, Mr. Fontaine?"

Lieutenant Commander Émile Fontaine, outstanding First Officer, confirms that the roll call is short. "*Jutlandia*, ma'am."

"Aklyan to Captain Bromios on *Jutlandia,* check in *now*."

"*Jutlandia*, all systems check out A-OK. Sorry ma'am."

Lives are at stake. Tens of thousands of lives. Far more than lives: the whole past and future of Genève, and the meaning of all the dying going on at the berm. She comes down hard.

"Aklyan to *Jutlandia*. Stay on top of coms, Captain Bromios. I need *instant* response times to all orders if we're going to get you to the system boost point, let alone the Wasp's farside L2."

"*Jutlandia*. Sincere apologies, ma'am. We had a crossover between the new forward weps fire controls and main ship-to-ship coms. It won't happen again."

Before he closes the ship-to-ship broadcast over the com link, Zorba Bromios is heard bullying and thundering at his vehemently protesting Weapons Officer.

She's shouting loudly back at him, claiming the communications crossover happened back in the Shipyard on Toruń. "It wasn't on *my* bloody watch."

"Shut up and shut the damn thing down! Coms only!"

"Yes, *sir!*"

"If we make it though the gauntlet you can work on the problem on the way to Wasp 2b. Unless I find that you just tried to shift blame when it's your fault. Then you'll be working in the Engine Room or maybe in the Galley."

"That might be my pleasure, *sir!*"

Émile glances over ands see a look of sick worry on Aklyan's face, and that she's biting her lower lip hard enough that a speckle of blood just appeared. She notices the iron taste and winces. He's worried, too, not about his vector-and-boost mathematics or the enemy psychology built into the tactics of her escape plan, but about the sheer youth of some of *Alpha*'s captains.

'*Bromios is flailing, and we're not even in first contact with the enemy.*' He resumes the check list. He's standing just feet away, so close that Magda picks up his special odor, an antiquarian tinkerer smell. There's a hint of old tek, of hot solder, silicon, and even copper wire, mixed with mockleather bound books on the ancient naval history of Orion.

"Confirming. All ships checked in. Ship-to-ship coms are good, *Jutlandia* included. Weapons check: all ships' guns warm and online, excepting *Jutlandia.* Her cannon is offline."

Magda acknowledges him with a nod. Then coms go silent, turning knuckles white on all nine Bridges. She listens intently, without speaking for a soul-and-ship groaning eternity while *Alpha* completes its searing rise from the surface. It's heading straight into a critical first maneuver. '*If this doesn't work it's going to be a desperate fight just to escape orbit. And we're sure to be massively outgunned by capital ships as well as escorts, this close to Genève.*'

"Approaching jibe position." Outside the ship's side scuttles, *white* plasma streaks up and far ahead, rising from Toruń's huge naval batteries. They're shooting blind and hitting nothing, trying to keep open an exit lane by deterring any ambitious Kaigun *daisa* from "Crossing the T" above *Alpha*'s ascent path.

"Ready to give the order XO."

"All ships: *Zulu* on my mark."

Five seconds.

Ten seconds.

Fifteen seconds.

"*Alpha* is in jibe position ... now."

"*Zulu! Zulu! Mark!*"

Seven warships maneuver in the upper atmosphere as wake turbulence thins, where the troopships ride ahead of sturdier destroyers without getting buffeted by backwash. The seven start to pull around the two old liners right on schedule, cuing tightly off Magda's mark. She's attempting a severe and dangerous move and formation not found in any prewar KRN tactics or navigation manuals. No one ever imagined, let alone mapped out, a problem of a surface launch of nine ships in a tight window and pattern, facing a much superior enemy force.

'*This won't be the last time we're required to figure out the impossible on the fly. Gods, in war the real thing is so much faster and harder than it looks in a classroom or simulation!*'

Five seconds.

Ten seconds.

Twenty seconds.

"All ships in position. Troopships are where they're supposed to be, ma'am, right behind the seven escorts." Nine ships are in a leaf blade wedge, warships now in the lead.

Émile suggested that she call the wedge *Formation Zulu* because it looked to him like a short, ancient thrusting spear, just like the *iklwa* made famous by Pyotr Shaka's ancestors. It's still carried by Oetkert emperors on ceremonial occasions, most recently by Pyotr when he declared war on the Krevan Republic. It appeals to Émile's irony that *Alpha* will now stab past a shield patrol of Shaka's ships.

"So far, so good on *Zulu*, Mr. Fontaine. Well done."

Nine ships are fusing hydrogen at maximum capacity, spitting long jets of plasma from main drives, no longer getting extra boost from spent chemical rockets. Those flare full length with flashes of hundreds of explosive bolts, detach and fall away rapidly from the rising ships. Magda has invested a lot in the extra lift she gets from the old tek boosters. The velocity achieved might be just enough extra to fool and get past far more powerful enemy patrol ships already vectoring down from a very high orbit on a too easy intercept course.

If only she reads the thinking of its commanding *daisa* right. If only he makes a mistake that she can exploit. Otherwise, *Alpha* is flying into a flameout death in a proliferation of expanding plasma blossoms that will briefly light up the hazy horizon below, then disappear from Orion. The *Exodus* mission will fall back planetside as a hard hail of Genève's lost ships, lost children, and lost hope.

"All escorts! Weapons Stations alert: twelve bandits in your three-twenty. Cruisers and a screen of 'Zs.' Confirmed: four cruisers, eight Zerstörers at 20,000 klics and 320° and closing fast."

Émile moves quickly to confirm the initial sighting from his stand-up station at the Binnacle, although there's no mistaking what's nakedly visible overhead in the Main Scuttle. "Here they come! Twelve warships descending in double drop formation. Heading right at us, at 17,000 klics high and 22,000 on flank. Intercept speed and course. Three minutes to contact."

Magda leans forward in her hard, black command chair. "All hands! Weapons and Engine Rooms make ready. All ready, all ships. Go to battle stations! Prepare to engage your enemy."

***

They studied Kaigun tactics while planning the *Alpha* escape. They worked bent over a holo map table moved into her cabin while repair work *clanged!* and *banged!*, as scored external armor was replaced and hundreds of raw bunks were added below. They agreed the patrol top *daisa* will most likely come right at *Alpha* on a bluntly direct, no nonsense intercept course.

After they finished mapping out the *Zulu* maneuver, Magda told Émile that timing on the next phase wasn't the only thing to worry about, it was everything. "It's our one chance. If their *daisa* goes by the book —and what else has he to turn to so early in this new war?— he'll time his intersect to our ascending flotilla by vectoring to what he'll calculate will be our slowest, most vulnerable moment."

"As we reach for gravity escape, before he thinks we'll turn and fusion boost out of the orbital plane? Yes ma'am, I see that. It means that after we make *Zulu* we'll still be catchable."

"Only if we're where he expects us to be when he expects us to be there. How do we avoid him?"

"So we have to turn sharp and early, when he's not expecting it. Where? At a rise point where we can still boost away from Genève and put real distance between us and any pursuit."

"I'll settle for just enough space to stay out of range of any seeker missiles and forward lasers on the chase ships that will tear after us, however many and whatever type they are."

"*Hmmm*. If I was that *daisa* I'd trap your king with a spread of pawns before you move: a picket of Zerstörers or frigates to counter the best probabilities of where you'll make your turn to run."

"Agreed. But that means he must split his forces. He won't. Recall, too, his warships must avoid the white plasma streams coming up from Toruń, as long as the guns down here last. And while there's danger to *Alpha* in a division of his forces, there's real opportunity as well."

"Yes, ma'am. But if we cleave tight to the interior of the plasma streams for as long as we can, we should be able to take advantage of that deterrent to his picket ship position. Then twist hard and burn away."

"Why Mr. Fontaine, I do believe you exhibit a real talent for mayhem and deceit! And perhaps also some for naval tactics. Right, show me on the simulation exactly what you're thinking."

'*Some talent? We wouldn't have survived the fight at the moons if he wasn't the most exceptional tactical mind I have ever encountered. He has a coup d'oeil, a natural eye for tactics, a true gift that can't be taught.*'

They bent low over the holo, running and rerunning simulations all night long and into the next day. *Blue* and *green* and *red* lights flickered over their stern faces. Had anyone been watching, they would have seen the little colored lights reveal how intensely dedicated Émile Fontaine is to his captain, as well as how the heavy burden of command is etching premature worry lines in Captain Magda Aklyan's handsome face.

***

Now the moment is here and Magda Aklyan and Émile Fontaine count on their opponent thinking *Alpha* can only move at the speed of its slowest ships, which must look to him exactly like what they are, or rather what they were a month ago: unarmed tourist ships incapable of military speeds. They'll show up on his tracking gear, from false IFF signals that *Alpha* is now broadcasting in the clear, still identified as two Grün tourist liners owned by the Royal Cruising Line. He'll also see codes for three light cruisers and four heavy destroyers flying as escort. It's a double deceit, about the speed of the slowest ships in her flotilla and about the firepower of the rest.

'It might buy us a few seconds hesitation as he confirms. If he knew what we really are, old destroyers and frigates and overloaded cruise ships, he might fall out of Genève's sky with laughter. Well, here's to the mirth of rats bane, wag tail, dull witted Kaigun captains!'

Bearing directly down on rising *Alpha* is a formation flagshipped by an older heavy cruiser, three much more modern looking light cruisers, and a detached forward screen of eight mixed age and mixed class Kaigun Zerstörers, a ship type roughly equivalent to a Krevan destroyer. The good news is they're all coming over and down at a wide oblique angle to *Alpha*'s actual rise and course, obviously expecting it to be in an optimal or normal escape trajectory. But *Alpha*'s not on a normal trajectory and not making standard lift speed.

"Hold this course to my mark. Main engines, all ahead. Battle speed!"

Magda notes that the eight Zerstörers aren't in regular formation with the four slower cruisers, but also aren't trying to close with *Alpha* separately from the bigger warships. They're flying a detached, forward escort pattern, not making a discrete and hard interception run down to intersect *Alpha*.

"Mr. Fontaine, did we just get real lucky? Am I right that those Zs are not taking advantage of their greater orbital height and native speed to pounce us?"

"Confirmed. They're below max on both. They're holding back in a soft escort role, content to stay ahead of the trailing cruisers. They're taking themselves out of the initial action. It's just like you predicted their *daisa* would do, ma'am."

"By the book. They're doing it by the old book, from the last war. Let's hope they continue, until we can get out of this system at least."

"If they do, captain, we're in with a chance."

The eight Zs are merely pacing 3,000 klics ahead of the four cruisers in a lazy and slightly ragged crescent, their traditionalist and less senior *daisas* obviously ordered to stick to their official task of screening capital ships. The cruisers will take the kill shots, not the escorts.

"The flotilla *daisa* is putting all trust in his cruisers, in his massive firepower advantage when he should cut loose his Zs. Well, let's see if we can't overmatch him with our speed."

'*They're cocky, conservative, traditional. Going by the peacetime book. On standard course and vector. As I hoped, they lifted their tactics right out of the Kaigun prewar manual.*' She knows because she read it. Five times.

The *daisa* commanding from the enemy flagship, heavy cruiser KG *Magni*, is overconfident. He believes the firepower he controls from his four cruisers will vaporize anything trying to rise past him from the surface. He's amused more than annoyed that his IFF gear gave him initial false info, but now that the electronic ruse is exposed and visuals are also available he can *see* that he's vastly stronger than his puny enemy. '*This should be another easy laurel.*'

The idea of small escorts and two waddling civilian liners straining upward reinforces arrogant freedom from doubt in himself, or the capabilities of his twelve ship squadron and superior relative position. So he follows a Zerstörer screen he doesn't need with his four cruisers. It's an unimaginative *line ahead* formation that drops the cruisers slowly into the main intercept role while the eight Zerstörers fly a soft combat patrol above and high. He's moving all 12 ships too slowly, almost regally, at what *Resolve* tracks as less than half speed.

'*He's not thinking about relative speed. He's thinking only about massed firepower and his shooting advantage from the superior position.*' Magda calls out orders in a steady stream and preternaturally calm voice. No one else speaks except Émile, advising when each command is fulfilled. Every officer and sailor is at full battle stations on nine desperate ships. They merge now as real not virtual extensions of her single, streaming command will. Magda is zen to *Resolve* and the flotilla, melded into engines and missiles and the will to live of the crews.

Magda Aklyan is *Resolve*. She is *Alpha*.

"Maintain secondary thrusters."

"Thrusters aye."

"Ready forward missile tubes."

"Tubes aye."

"Arm the torpedoes."

"Armed."

"Turn hard to port 15° on my mark ... *Mark!*"

"Turning."

Directions in space are an artificial human convention, yet wholly necessary to communicate relative position in a trade convoy; or docking at an elevator; or maneuvering warships in formation. In space "up" is no more than an agreed position relative to the stellar equator, itself an arbitrary predetermination. Once orientation is agreed, other terms follow naturally: "down," "port," "starboard," "right" and "left" ascension and declination. The latter work rather like longitude and latitude in simple navigation on the surface of a planet.

So everyone understands based on preset horizons exactly what the Kaigun *daisa* means when he directs his 12 ships to maintain course and formation on a long preset heading to take his whole squadron, moving in two parts, "down and starboard" to where he expects the rising ships to arrive in under two minutes. That's assuming standard acceleration and angle of ascent.

However, Captain Aklyan is now angling her nine ships *toward* the enemy squadron rather than trying to run away from the orbital patrol as every Kaigun *daisa* high above her and dropping expects. Moreover, she's making much faster closing speed and moving at greater overall velocity than a normal or even a minimally safe ground launch would attempt.

That's the effect the discarded metallic hydrogen boosts imparted to *Alpha*. And of the last jig maneuver. In fact, there's nothing standard or safe or normal about anything she's doing. If she followed standard KRN launch protocols as her opponent expects she will, because *he* would, *Alpha* would be struggling like nine naïve minnows swept into the Kaigun's commodious net.

She knew it would be a fool's errand to follow procedure yet hope to escape a far more powerful foe. And Magda Aklyan is no one's fool, even if this is her first flotilla and combat command. Except for a single forced command after the sharp fight at the Genève moons, when there was no one alive senior to her and she brought the last warships home to safety at Toruń. Seven escorts that could not get out with the last fleeing and damaged capital ships. Seven escorts trying to return to space along with the troopships, prepared to die to keep hate alive.

The effect of a boosted launch and sudden top-twist-to-port Magda orders, just before reaching escape velocity, is that eight startled Zerstörers shoot over top and past the now hard turning, hard angling, and weirdest of all, hard charging Krevan flotilla. Naval war is supposed to be a more sedate affair than this. At least, that's what Émile Fontaine's ancient and even modern history texts say, as do all the old KRN logs from the last Orion War. No one alive really knows, since no one has done this sort of thing in a long time. Not really. Except for those quarterly squadron and annual fleet simulations and war games.

The real thing is faster and more dynamic than any virtual simulation you can ever sit through. More confusing and harder than any peacetime war game with real ships, all friendly and shooting only lasers at 1% power to send target disks on the 'enemy' hulls *clanging!* No matter how many times or levels you run them, simulations don't shoot back. And when target ship weapons hit they don't cut huge holes in your hull or knock vital pieces off your engines.

The *daisa* is following an old playbook, and too confident about his always winning record in prewar simulations. He's bearing down on an inferior enemy force, certain that at proper firing ranges he can bring his heavier armaments to bear and batter his opponent into submission or oblivion. He hopes the fleeing ships don't try to surrender. He wants to turn them into free floating particle clouds that will seed the winter rains as they descend to Genève.

Magda will make him pay for his conservatism and arrogance, but first she must distract and confuse him. She'll leave it to safer and smarter people to figure out later what larger tactical point and unique innovation she's making today. For *Alpha,* this fight is not about tactical lessons but desperation and survival. Not theory or tradition or reputation but warm lives and cold deaths. And maintaining hull integrity against the will of the enemy and vacuum of space.

So, once again contrary to all received doctrine and tradition of her own navy, as well as the too conservative, too untroubled Kaigun *daisa* flying above her, she does things so much differently than her enemy expects. She *attacks*. She takes on a superior force, still trailing wispy atmosphere from her ships' tails.

"All warships, open forward missile doors."

"Tubes open, all escorts."

"Weapons: ready systems and yourselves. Shoot-and-dodge."

"Weapons primed."

"Target the cruisers. Tell all AIs to concentrate on engines and nav arrays."

"Messaging target priorities."

"Tell them to let the 'Z's go, for now. They'll be back."

"AI target priority set."

"Navigation officer, *Resolve* only. Track the Zs. Report every 20 seconds."

The enemy escorts took themselves out of range with their first pass, and are frantically braking to stop their overshoot of *Alpha*'s unexpected position. The two leading destroyers are trying to avoid scudding along the upper stratosphere, closing fast below them.

"Focus on the cruiser line."

"Aye ma'am, retargeting."

"All ships: ready plasma torpedoes."

"Fish are in the tubes."

"Arm missiles. Fire-and-forget."

"Missiles are ready, aye ready."

"Set firing pattern *flanker.*"

"Firing pattern *flanker* set."

"Confirm spread."

"Shooting two-by-two, confirmed."

"Confirm timing."

"Shooting at three second intervals, off your mark."

As she readies to give the *shoot* command the lasts wisps of air fall behind. *Alpha* is out of the envelope. Blackness is above the nine and all around, salted with the light of distant stars.

"*Mark!*"

"Firing."

"Two fish are in the water."

Resolve whisks two stubby missiles with immaculate ease along the metallic hydrogen magnets of its forward rail catapults. White hot plasma exhausts blaze from internal drives once the torpedoes leave the shooting tubes.

"Four fish are in the water."

"Six fish are in the water."

Six warships loose a staggered sequence timed to *Resolve*'s lead shots and Magda's mark. Over 21 seconds, 14 brilliant lights shoot away from *Alpha* on high speed intersect paths, reaching out to the fast approaching cruiser line.

Four of the missiles are cigar shaped, launched from maglevs on the older frigates. Their long design is all about fitting down maglev firing tubes. There's no aerodynamic imperative in the vacuum of space. No weapons aesthetic, either.

The rest are stubbier, like shark barrels with fins and nozzles and a clear AI bubble up front. Not sleek or streamlined or beautiful at all. It's more important that they're superlight, layered carbyne and AI guided plasma bombs of supreme lethality to any ship they get even close to. They're ejected by catapults along carbon tube rails using supercompressed steam for initial interior propulsion. Leaving white, ice crystal afterbirth behind as they turn on short burst plasma engines once they reach a safe arming distance from their mother ship.

Miniaturized fusion drives kick in as AIs stagger velocity and evasive weaving to confuse tracking systems on the enemy cruisers. Each hurtling torpedo is a compact tokamak chamber made of toroidal magnetic coils, hosting within a grapefruit size sphere of plasma reaching nearly 150 million degrees Celsius. That exceeds temperatures achieved by natural plasma plumes in magnetic fields on the surface of an average star. Even near misses can do copious harm if any plasma ejecta contacts the hull.

"*Alpha,* missiles are away. Time to dodge and run."

"Aye captain, all controls synced to the Nav Station on *Resolve.*"

"Jig on my order."

"Waiting on the order, ma'am."

"Hard to port, 30° ... *Mark!*"

"All ships: hard turn to port 30°, aye now aye."

"Let's get out of here, Mr. Fontaine."

"Confirm ready: all ships to system boost."

"Type-3 boosts and main engines are online."

"Confirm heading."

"Heading confirmed, captain. We're going to Wasp's farside LP."

"All ships: fire main boosters on my mark ... *Mark!*"

"All ships, maximum boost."

"Engines are engaged, captain."

Nine ships turn in unison, engaging Type-3 boosters the instant each comes out of the maneuver. Nine incandescent streaks race across the rear track of the four less maneuverable enemy cruisers, still headed to intercept an orbital space *Alpha* never hoped for or ever tried to reach.

War is a harsh classroom where defeat is a better teacher than victory. Where the cost of the smallest error is death. Where only those who learn, live. And not even all of those. That's why Captain Magda Aklyan and her KRN crews, children of a lesser and defeated navy, now try several new and truly daring things all at once. They're incentivized by death and defeat.

It's why *Alpha* is flying past far more powerful but lazily captained and crewed enemy cruisers. Why it's moving at unconventional and unanticipated speeds and an acute gravity escape angle, while shooting a spread of self guiding proximity missiles to scare and scatter the enemy and delay his pursuit. To make a distance and time gap behind as it races for the far LP.

It's also why a perfectly competent, highly respected and quite professional Kaigun *daisa* and his clever and High Caste captains on more powerful warships, and on the eight Zs, hold to staid tradition, to old doctrines and tactics mastered and mattering only in peacetime. This will change for the Kaigun as the Orion War expands and it takes on more equal enemies, and as it gathers and teaches its officers "lessons learned" from these and other early battles.

But that change lies in the future. For now, *Alpha* initially evades the escorts then fires a full spread right at a prewar *daisa* sitting on the Bridge of the heavy cruiser *Magni*, awed and aghast at such tactical audacity from a mere destroyer squadron. He still doesn't believe they pose a threat to his four capital ships.

Besides, it's already too late for the overconfident *daisa* to adjust his intercept: 14 fish are "in the water" and burning white, seeking his ambling cruisers. His big ships are only just beginning to brake automatically, with preprogrammed inputs he was certain would bring him to where *Alpha* would reach orbit. Instead, his cruisers fly into empty intersect space already left behind by their own Zerstörer escorts and never aimed for or crossed into by the brilliant commander of *Alpha*.

At short ranges, the incoming torpedoes are multiples faster and more maneuverable than the far more massive cruisers. Faster by far even than a

Zerstörer moving at flank speed. This threat is like nothing at all in the *daisa*'s last successful simulation. Nothing like that at all.

Four cruiser captains must deal with incoming high velocity missiles capable of evasive action or suddenly shifting main course and flying up the engine funnel of a target ship. Or just smacking into its superstructure with devastating effect. They manage the first dodge but, seeking to return in a grand loop, the smart missiles swoop and bank around 180°. They'll be back at the cruiser line inside a minute. It's not supposed to be like this. The cruisers should be doing the heavy shooting, not dodging madly while forced into full defensive mode.

What should be or might be doesn't matter in war. Only what is. Here above Genève it comes down to relative velocity and interception angles as read and altered by AI targeting bots in the warheads, hurtling back to a cruiser line still trying to engage battlespeed and make nav computers accept *evasive maneuver* orders that strain and threaten old and creaking bulkheads.

Alpha scoots by as the cruisers scramble to aim and fire plasma cannon, the only weapons they can bring to bear at this acute angle and short range while still deflecting or dodging incoming smart missiles. But they're in each others' way. Three out of four abort all shooting as the little Krevan flotilla levels onto the same plane as the four cruiser line. That exposes the Krevan ships to one cruiser's broadside guns but shields it from the other three.

Alpha pulls level, speeding away in the opposite direction to the route of the cruiser line. Only the edge on ship, KG *Baldr*, is able to shoot two farside batteries to effect. It gets off just one volley before its targeting systems lose accuracy from combined relative speeds, as two sets of warships move past and away from each other on an expanding flat plane. *Alpha* now presents only a minimal silhouette to *Baldr*, and it's getting smaller every second. It's like trying to hit the edge of a coin shot out of a high velocity gun, not the flat side. Not impossible, but hard.

Cruiser gunnery isn't helped by the fact *Baldr* is frantically jigging to evade incoming missiles completing their loop around. The threat is scattering its sister ships away from the widening spread of 14 white hot "fish," each one guided by an excited AI mind released into the Universe and told by its maker-god to eagerly fulfill its purpose of orgiastic destruction.

Even so, *Baldr*'s batteries are well crewed and commanded. So they're able to achieve two glancing hits that blacken and score the nearside hull of the closest *Alpha* ship. *Triomphant*'s pallograph howls in protest as its hull shudders from twin concussions. Its carbyne plate armor stays intact, however, as the destroyer slides past the hard braking cruisers and scuds off, boosting *white* from a big Type-3 engine, making for the distant gas giant.

The only damage is to its escutcheon, etched astern and on both sides of its tail work. One side is now scarred with a dark burn that crisped the shackle-and-stock of the silver anchor. The angry falcon is mostly intact, perching on the anchor crown and clutching its lightning bolt. But the other talon holding the wheat sheaves of peace is scorched away, leaving an ugly gouge.

Émile sees it out the Main Scuttle as *Triomphant* pulls into line abreast with *Resolve*. It's also there on his monitors, along with a live image from the planet's surface showing a smoke covered world falling behind and below fleeing *Alpha.* He double checks by glancing down, out the Main Scuttle. A red glowing ring with a fuzzy black edge is visible even to his naked vision. He knows it's a ring of fire and smoke around the berm that encircles Toruń.

Meanwhile, the Zerstörers are finishing a sharp banking turn, braking to pull and reverse direction so they can boost after the escaping KRN flotilla. The turn puts them on the far side of their own cruiser line as *Alpha* pulls away from Genève. The nine are well outside the planet's gravity well, racing away on a spare nothing, bendix fusion burn for the distant L2.

Alpha has gained a critical three minutes on the Zerstörers, now chasing it hard after completing a sharp angle reverse and boost. Fighting the pull of Genève's gravity, they braked too close, and were forced to reaccelerate into a sudden skidding u-turn. The trail Z skims and skips for a few seconds as it scuds over the last thin upper air. Then it, too, is gone.

The reflected light of Genève is dimmer than it was before it was shrouded in reflective clouds of smoke and vapor. It shrinks rapidly to a disk behind both sets of warships, racing each other to the far outer system. Nine plasma drives pushing all out to escape, pursed by eight intent on murder.

***

Looking up from the nighttime surface through wisps of acrid smoke that reek into the detention camp where she's interned, Madame Janine Whitmore wonders where her son is and if she'll ever see him again. She's a woman of simple wants and pleasures. She doesn't know what that line of nine little white lights might be that quickly away fade in intensity and uniqueness as they move across the starry background of Orion. Or what the other fading line of eight little lights are that seem to be chasing the nine.

She thinks only about her missing son. They used to walk among her flowers together while she taught him poetry and botany, not seeing any difference between the two. To please her, he learned all their Latin as well as common names. He wasn't the brightest boy at school, but he was the sweetest.

Lines from one of her own best loved childhood verses come back to her as she watches the tiny lights wink then disappear forever.

There's a gap in the ranks of little lights.
Why, one of the stars is gone!
Please help me look,
everywhere and forever.

It's my special, midnight star.
Without it the world has no joy.
So why do all the other stars
still wink at me and whisper?

She feels a sudden heartache, a rush of loneliness like no other she has felt since she parted from her sweet Jarred as he went off to war. She wants to go home, to see if he might have returned there.

"Back inside, you!"

"Curfew starts in five minutes!"

Beta

Incandescent glows of incoming missiles set off flashing screens and *clanging* clarions aboard all four Kaigun cruisers. Automatic defenses have already spit out hundreds of thermal, electronic, motion and effulgence decoys. But two seconds of human lag time elapse before the Kaigun *daisa* orders his captains to engage evasive maneuvers. Vital seconds lost may as well be eons in a ship-to-ship battle.

It's forever and a day to an eager, expectant, incoming AI missile burning all its fuel to complete its mission. A few seconds is a sizable portion of its brief but spectacular life, flying under the stars of Orion, singing its creation song of imminent and purposeful destruction.

Seven torps veer off after the flocks of decoys, failing to reach completion of their true purpose. As do most of us. They leave a gapped spread of seven other missiles outpacing and closing on the lumbering cruisers. Four split, two-up and two-down, homing on mass, light and heat signatures of the two nearest ships, the light cruisers *Baldr* and *Loki*. The last three home on the squadron flagship, the heavy cruiser KG *Magni*.

A clever, last second change of direction by *Baldr* ducks its hull under a fast looming torp, but it catches the near miss in its forward crosstree. The hot plasma containment chamber in the missile warhead demagnetizes on a proximity signal from onboard guidance and targeting systems. The detonation sends an expanding sphere of searing plasma to tear off chunks of communications gear from *Baldr*'s moonraker, scoring and pitting delicate quantum detectors with cloud balls of micro fragments, missile casing, and bits of ship as secondary shrapnel.

Baldr doesn't have enough standard speed to catch boosting *Alpha* in normal space, and without its quantum gear it can't follow into a bohr LP. So one Kaigun light cruiser is out of the fight and the chase. *Baldr* pulls hard to starboard, shooting off hundreds more effulgent flares as it turns away. They lead astray a second missile, which misses the crippled ship entirely. It spins wildly then scuds off Genève's upper atmosphere, burning out in unexploded machine futility.

Loki takes a direct hit low-and-larboard. The downside burst implodes a slab of strake plate and spreads two massive futtocks wide open. The fissure spills 32 surprised crew from the Orlop deck screaming silently into space, along with the ship's very fat chief cook, two young apprentice kitchen's mates, four hot ovens with special pastries still inside, and 327 loaves of fresh baked bread. The hand prepared and delicate pastries are served only to senior officers. Crews eat lesser foods printed from carb and protein wafers, and mockmeat soup and plain baked bread every other day.

When the fight started, apprentices were told to stay at their posts, that it was just another routine patrol with a little target shooting added. Either way, the *daisa* would want to eat afterward, no matter what happened. So one lad is busy making white sauce for the second shift officers' meal when the hull of *Loki* gapes open and he falls into space, the blue-green ball of Genève filling the sky above-below him. He's astonished that he's flying, and even more to discover that space has no smell. He always loved the myriad scents of cooking best of all about his chosen role. Like hot potatoes and stinging fresh onions, leeks and sizzling mockmeat, and faux clams in pan seared butter.

Another boy is happily stirring his first solo tureen of split pea soup, thinking of the praise he'll receive if the *daisa* likes it. He isn't that bright. He doesn't understand what's happening or why he's suddenly outside the ship with hundreds of loaves of bread flying away and all around, or why it's getting hard to breathe. He sees the chief cook tumbling nearby and upside-down. He waves at the fat man as he tumbles past. Just before he goes blind, he collides with a large slab of jagged plate that smacks him senseless. The next one cuts him in half.

On *Loki*'s Bridge there's rising fear as reports come in staccato style from all over the ship about ruptured systems and major structural damage. The chief engineer calls in that the ship is going down, that it can't sustain orbit. He's wrong. *Loki* is badly hurt but salvageable. It doesn't matter. He sets off a panic on the Bridge and in the Main Engine Room, where no one remains to hear maneuver orders that might have saved the ship. Then comes consternation, as the *daisa* slams his palm down hard on a red emergency control releasing all ship's boats and pods and calls out over all ship's coms.

"*Abandon ship!*"

"What? What are you doing?"

"*Abandon ship!*"

"You can't give that order!"

"Bloody coward! Traitor!"

There's running.

There's shouting.

There's tussling.

There's murder.

The XO pulls a snug kinetic pistol from an inside jacket holster and shoots his *daisa* in the head. The eruption of bone and hair and warm blood splatters over the captain's orderly and makes a mess of the command chair and about a quarter of the Bridge. So he stays at the XO Station instead of taking the chair. The Navigation and Weapons Officers look terrified, but are too scared to run. They know this despised Purity fanatic will turn and shoot them in the back.

"Belay that last order!"

"All hands, remain at your posts!"

Men run for exits all over the ship, no matter what the XO says. Navigation and Weapons crew break for it all at once, desperate to get off the Bridge.

"Secure this ship!"

"No one leaves!"

"Death to mutineers!"

Navigation and Weapons Officers look at each other, then jump the XO and wrestle him down. It's the signal two scared men of the Bridge Security Detail are waiting for. They pump four shots into the XO as he lies bleeding from where his forehead smacked into the deck.

More shots ring out elsewhere as other security men make other choices, cutting down "deserters" clambering into hundreds of four man pods and about a dozen larger ship's boats. They only increase the panic. Three are beaten bloody and left insensible on a lower deck by desperate crew. Two more are disarmed and shoved into a closed airlock, locked-in to go down if *Loki* does.

An XO's devotion to Purity fanaticism and a chief engineer's incompetence are about to get a lot more men killed, as a second missile impacts aft. It snaps the keelson and breaks *Loki*'s back. Not all onboard hear or heed conflicting Bridge orders. But everyone feels the heavy blows from the missiles shudder through the ship, and the secondary explosions. There's a lurching pickup in centripetal force as *Loki* goes into an uncontrolled, accelerating spin. A mortally wounded warship enters a spiral it can't stop by frantically firing a hundred attitude correctors. Fire control parties race to put out multiple emergencies erupting down the center line. It's a hopeless task. If *Loki* is to be saved, it won't be by its crew.

Mortal fear waterfalls from deck to deck as men realize just how badly hurt *Loki* really is. Brave medics ignore the hustle to bend over terribly wounded and dying men and boys. One middy in the Engine Room has no face. It's swinged off by a searing blob of silent plasma when the main reactor's nitrobon shield wall exposes a microcrack. Still a dutiful medic kneels to help. Another man has no flesh on his torso after a ceramic pipe breaks and a spray of superheated catapult steam peels off all skin from his arms, chest and shoulders. Outside the airtight compartment where they lay him for the last minute of his agony there are plenty who hear his primal wail. As in all battles, a battle in space is filled with final screams. As in all battles, some are heard while others not.

The worst damage from the spread fired by *Alpha* before it dodges away is to *Magni*, which suffers two near misses and a direct hit when proximity detectors shut off all current to a hundred electromagnets forming a closed torus inside each missile's warhead. The first erupts into a compact *white* plasma blossom 0.2 klics in front of her prow, close enough to do major damage as spicula of superheated plasma spew into space from the ruptured containment casing.

Initial damage by spicule ejecta is amplified as the first explosion triggers a second torp arriving right behind, at the three second interval Magda ordered. Double eruptions careen the heavy cruiser as plasma from the second blossom spears right through the afterdeck, already ripped and exposed by the first blast. The white incandescence kills the *daisa* on the adjacent Bridge, evaporating him and a half dozen senior officers in a nanosecond.

The mortal stroke to the ship itself comes next, when a third stagger shot torp breaches the stricken cruiser aft. It's one of the cigar types from a Krevan frigate, fitted with a superhard carbyne nose cone and a *real contact* detonator instead of a proximity fuse. It plunges into *Magni*'s taffrail, continuing deep inside to penetrate the fusion reactor stokehold before it blows.

Freed hydrogen plasma from stored fuel and weapons adds to an immense explosion that rips the stern apart, sending the greater part of the ruin of *Magni* tumbling uncontrollably. Over 1,100 male crew and another 17 civilian women are trapped inside, no way out. The women are all 'service wives,' mistresses illicitly smuggled onboard every ship in the Kaigun by its officers.

The spin presses survivors fantastically hard against bulkheads, sticking them to cabin walls and ceilings and splaying them down on carbon fiber decks as rotation speed increases. Some are impaled on jutting equipment as the hulk plunges into Genève's upper atmosphere, heating rapidly as it falls. Mercifully, nearly all still onboard black out from crushing G-forces before the gray wreckage turns dull *orange-red*, then *blue* then *white* hot with friction heat.

Fifty-eight yawl pods spin away from the wreck even as the exterior turns *orange*. Most are later found empty, churned out by autodeploy systems whose overrides burned away. Only a handful of crew survive in a few pods that settle into low orbit. The bumbling hulk of *Magni* makes an impressive meteor through the day sky before it digs a sizeable crater out of a wide open pasture it ploughs and gouges out, smacking to ground halfway up the austral continent.

KG *Dagr*, the sole undamaged cruiser in the Kaigun patrol, goes into Genève orbit in order to send out its medical shuttles and yawls filled with engineers to lend aid to its stricken sister ships, *Baldr* and *Loki.* It's *daisa*, Hussein Adamu, orders grappling lines shot into the exposed superstructure of *Loki*, the more badly damaged warship, to arrest a drift into a fatally low orbit and a burn out.

That leaves eight Zerstörers tearing after *Alpha*. Three newer ships with faster thrusters pull ahead of the other five. They're gaining steadily on the slower Krevan flotilla, for even with Argos built light cruiser boosters on either side of the main engines the civilian limits of *Warsaw* and *Jutlandia* constrain their captains from using maximum power. With over four hours to go before *Alpha* reaches the blue planet Wasp 2B, slowly growing from a dot to a disk in ships' Main Scuttles, the chasing hounds are sure to catch the running rabbit.

The converted troopships are a lot slower than Toruń Shipyard engineers or their crews and captains hoped. Warning clarions are *clanging* in Engine Rooms and flashing bright on both Bridges well before Magda orders them to *Reduce Speed.* That forces all the escorts to slow as well. *Alpha* must proceed at best speed of its two clumsiest, slowest and most vulnerable ships. It was always a weak point in the escape plan, which requires the escorts to convoy slow liners.

***

Three hours later it looks likely to become a fatal flaw. Zerstörers are closing the time-to-intercept gap gained over Genève. It's down to just half-a-minute, and *Alpha* is shedding seconds of relative advantage with each real five minutes that passes as it brakes for the swing around the blue giant and the last dash to the farside L2, and whatever enemy is waiting there.

Émile's normally clear eyes are changing to gun metal gray, narrowing and focusing on his nav displays as he calculates the chase gap and the rate at which it's closing. Magda first noticed this, that his eyes change color in a crisis, back at the fight for the Genèven moons. She thought they must be artificial, but was surprised to later discover that he still has natural vision.

"They're closing. There's no way to outrun the front three, though we can stay ahead of their back five. They'll catch us on the other side of the Wasp, before we get to the jump point."

"If there are any pickets there, captain, and there are sure to be picket ships, we'll be caught between two hostile forces."

"We'll have to fight. Mr. Fontaine. On one side of Wasp or the other, here short of our goal or on the farside. Numbers are against us."

"Aye captain. Well, we've done it before, at the inner moons."

'That was Émile's finest hour, when his innovative tactics allowed us to take out a raft of Kaigun frigates that got too far ahead of their capital ships. We still lost the bigger battle, but they felt the sting in our tail at least. But I don't think he's boasting. Just stating facts.'

"What are your orders, captain?"

"We can't fight with two fat troopships waddling along inside our protective cone. They're the priority. Nothing else matters, but they'll inhibit the escorts if we have to stay so close. We'll be giving away any advantage of position and make *Alpha* a concentrated target."

"I agree, ma'am. We have to fight, but we can't."

"We must. So what do you recommend, Mr. Fontaine?" She's startled to see him stumped, for once.

"It's hard to see a way..."

"Think harder, XO."

"We have to reduce numbers, even out the odds somehow. But the troopships? I'm just not sure..."

"I am. Alright, I've made my decision. Mr. Fontaine, back to your station. I need you there."

"Aye, ma'am."

At 13.5 million klics from the farside L2, Magda turns on the *All Ships* com link to split the seven escorts into *Alpha* and *Beta* sub flotillas. Five ships of the original nine will continue around the Wasp and attempt an immediate hot bohr out of Genève system. Four of the destroyers will turn and block or drive off the pursuit, or be wrecked trying. Her words go out from *Resolve.*

"*Asimov* and *Tyco Brae* will stay with *Resolve* in a reduced *Alpha protection group*. Our ruling task remains safe convoy of *Warsaw* and *Jutlandia* to the L2. We'll hold this course. *Guépard, Resolute, Le Terrible* and *Triomphant* are now designated as *Beta strike force.* They'll turn to hold off the pursuit, allowing the troopships to escape."

The announcement isn't supposed to be made to all crews and passengers, since she hand signaled to her Coms duty officer to switch to *Bridge to Bridge secure*. He missed her quick gesture, so everyone on all nine ships hears the next far too brutally honest exchange.

"The troopships can't outrun the lead Zerstörers and are too vulnerable to expose in an all ships action. Enemy captains will gun for them above all other targets. The reduced escort designated *Alpha* will have to handle whatever's waiting to stop us at the bohr zone."

"*Alpha* group, confirm understanding."

"Understood, ma'am." The five remaining *Alpha* captains call it in.

"To the four *Beta* captains, I need you to force a delay in the pursuit while *Alpha* tries to get away. A few minutes is all we need, even just one. Buy us whatever time you can."

"Orders received." It's Rutger Metsalaer on *Guépard.* Already, the four *Beta* destroyers are pulling apart from *Alpha*, readying for a wide looping turn back.

"Captain Archambault, you lead *Beta* from its designated flag, *Le Terrible.*"

"*Tres bon, capitaine*. Be assured that we will hold off the pursuit."

"Captain Archambault, your task will be ... François, please forgive me ... *Pardoner moi, mon ami, mais c'est necessaire.*" She knows what she's asking her old friend to do. So does he.

"*C'est rien, mon cher ami Magda.*"

"Just delay them, François. That's all I need."

"We'll give you the time you need," he boasts, "by any and all means."

"Wait! What do you mean by 'any and all means'? I don't need faux heroics, François. I just need a delaying action, and hit-and-run. Explain!"

Archambault goes too far, as he tends to do, shocking the listening crews and tens of thousands of fighters crammed into nine small ships with enemy before and behind them. "We'll ram the *bâtards*, if we must."

***

Jan balls his fists until his nails cut his palms. '*Is it really as bad as that? Will he ram! He can't mean it? There are 3,000 of my fighters onboard! Was all this for nothing? He can't ram, especially not with the Resolute!*' Zofia is on *Resolute*, a thought that makes him crazed. He leaps up to pace in the space between the wall bunks. Samara jumps down from the flat bench, too, and starts to bark at Jan.

A midshipman yells: "Lie da fuk back down an' strap in! 'Tings are 'bout to get sparky and ya must be see'cured and out of da fukin' way."

Jan tries to glare the man down but he has no command authority here and so backs off. He regains self control and climbs back onto the pine bunk. Samara leaps up, too, barking loudly at all the sudden commotion.

"An shud up dat bloody dog, boyo, or I'll *shoot* it!"

Jan pulls a wool blanket over Samara's head, trying to shut her up. She wants to play. She wrestles with him, biting at his smothering hands through the coarse wool. Jan fears for thousands of his fighters jammed into every free nook on the warships about to do battle. He knows that Zofia is headed into mortal danger that her skill can't help. He's totally powerless, helpless to himself or to Zofia. To anyone. With no control over what happens next. He only knows that he and Zofia are literally moving in opposite directions. '*Will either of us survive this? Will I ever see her again? Will I have a chance to say how wrong I was, that she was right, that we must be together for whatever time is left to us in Orion?*'

***

"*Merde!*" Magda realizes the awful coms error and gives a furious look to the inexperienced young officer responsible. Émile moves to shut the channel down but she waves him off. She needs to leave it open now, to reassure everyone as she issues strict orders to all *Beta* captains. '*It's that or risk pandemonium.*'

"That's enough of your sea salt, Archambault! I only need *Beta* to slow down the three leading Zerstörers. *There'll be no ramming!* And just deal with the first three, leave the rest and get the hell out of there. The five trail Zs are too far back to catch us before we make the L2. Focus on the threat!"

"Understood. Figure of speech, just heat of the moment. *Pardon*."

"For Toruń! For Genève!" It's Rutger Metsalaer breaking into the coms.

'*Not good. Rutger is too boyish, too eager for this fight to start.*' Magda knows that you fight with whomever and what you have in the moment, to get to the next moment. Only after battle can one chastise the living and apologize to the dead.

"Belay that talk!" She barks it to her captains, and through all the ships. "Once *Alpha* is away from the pursuit *Beta* is ordered to disengage contact with all enemy and break away as well. Then get to any open LP. Scatter if you have to, captains, get your ships out of this system any which way you can. Archambault, respond."

"Orders are clear and understood, ma'am."

"I repeat, *Beta*'s orders are to *disengage* all action once the primary mission goal of *Alpha* protection is accomplished. All captains *will* act in accord with the orders of the War Government. We must live or Krevo will die."

“Archambault here. I’ll get *Beta* away, Magda. I promise.”

“No more promises!”

“No ma’am.”

“And no useless heroics, François. Just do your job.”

“Priority is delay, then escape. I’ve taken your orders on board, *capitaine*.”

He realizes for the first time that his voice has been reaching everyone in the flotilla. He regrets that. Yet both Archambault and Aklyan know that the odds will be near impossible if the five trailing Zerstörers catch up to join the fight with *Beta*. Or if *Alpha* is too much delayed by whatever strength is waiting at the LP. Somebody ramming someone might just be necessary after all. *‘Just don’t say it!’*

“Metsalaer here. Captain Aklyan, *umm*, sorry ma’am.”

“Don’t apologize. Enough promises and apologies! Just take care of your ships and cargos. Get them out of Genève system.” She blinks off the *All Ships* link.

An immense giant is growing fast in the Main Scuttles of all five *Alpha* ships with every fading second that *Beta* falls away toward the pale, distant sun. *Alpha* is streaking across Wasp’s blue-green face, heading around a blue horizon to reach the leeward L2, thence to bohr out of Genève system. Or into a fight at the LP. The same image grows smaller in the rear scuttles and mass sensors of four *Beta* ships also on the planet’s windward side, but already looping back to fight the pursuing Zerstörers. Jan lies thinking of Zofia on one ship, she of him on another.

Two destinations.

Two directions.

Two solitudes.

Two choices.

Two fates.

Magda's tone softens as she turns on the *captains only* link. "Find a way to delay the *bâtards*, François. Once *Alpha*'s away you can scatter or take *Beta* to the L4 or L5. Whatever route's still open. Just get out of this burning house."

Tick.

Already there's a one second relativistic delay in arrival of the ship-to-ship coms by point-to-point laser, as distance spreads between the two halves of the original *Alpha* flotilla.

Tock.

"Aye, I'll get them out ma'am."

Tick, tock.

"Any which way you can, François. As fast as you can. We'll rendezvous at the sanctuary. Acknowledge."

Tick, tock.

"Yes ma'am. Understood. Acknowledged. Minimal engagement rules. Just slow the *huora* down long enough for you to clear *Alpha* to the LP then burn out of the system."

Tick, tock, tick.

Three seconds now for a targeted laser to arrive, with ships racing in opposite directions. Ignoring the delay and profanity, Magda passes on a last caution. "Kinetics only. At extreme prow-to-prow intersection velocities all your missiles and plasma cannon, even lasers, will be useless. Theirs too. Acknowledge."

Tick, tock, tick, tick.

"Check. Hard munitions only."

Tick, tock, tick, tick, tock.

"Anon, *et bon chance,* François. Good luck captains."

She says it as she leaves the windward side and the cold blue planet's curving mass blocks further line-of-sight laser transmissions between the fast separating squadrons.

Tick, tock, tick, tick, tock, tock.

"*Au revoir*, Magda. Captain Archambault on *Le Terrible* out." There are no KRN or civilian relay sats parked in the Wasp's ambit that she can access to bounce a light coms beam around the planet's broad horizon. Well there are, but they've been taken over and recoded by the Kaigun. This is the last message Magda Aklyan will hear from *Beta* before *Alpha* reaches the L2 jump zone, where she'll find more than enough trouble of her own.

***

Back at Toruń on Genève many brave men and women are dying outside and all around the pierced berm and in front of the broken open Gate. Yet one is uniquely alone, battered and bone broken, burned and bleeding in an RSU cell.

It smells of beatings, burned flesh and old piss. Of stale water, black bread and melon rinds left over from a prior prisoner's last meal, before her execution for 'banditry.' He knows it's all over for him. Knew it before the first interrogation when they took his fingernails, one by one by one, with pliers. He held tight to his training through their worst tortures for another hour, then another and another.

Only after they thought he was broken did he pretend to break. He gave them a little truth wrapped inside believable lies about an escape plan. He told them all about *Alpha*, every single true detail he knew. Except when and where it's really going. At last he hears what he willed himself to wait for, to stay alive for. He listens to Toruń's huge naval guns cut a tunnel path to orbit for the escaping troopships and escorts of *Alpha*, knowing also that as he lies in pools of his own blood and urine his general is fighting at the Berm Gate, and is probably dead.

He's revived by his torturers so they can cut, beat and burn him some more. This time not asking questions, just furious that the escape flotilla left a day before he said it would and didn't go where he told them it was going. When they're done, he's dumped in his cell to await more hard sessions, then a truly gory public execution meant as a warning to all occupied Genève.

Gravel

Distance between the onrushing Zerstörers closes rapidly as *Beta* comes out of its loop and the Krevans shift from a 'finger four' formation into two 'top covers.' Four ships split into pairs, looping up-and-back in a graceful 180° turn. *Guépard* and *Resolute* bank tightly starboard while *Le Terrible* and *Triomphant* bank to port, opening a clear middle gap between the pairs.

It's into that narrow gap that Archambault intends to funnel three oncoming enemy warships, late model Zerstörers closing fast on *Beta* with highly aggressive intention. The maneuver also gives him a shoot-and-scoot angled advantage over the trio of approaching warships. On his range-and-attitude monitor they're sill in a standard and very conservative 'vic' formation. '*It's old textbook stuff from the Kaigun, just as Magda predicted. Let's hope they stick to it for one more minute.*'

Once all seven ships are inside effective shooting range the fight will be quick and sharp. Neither side can lock onto such fast moving targets, not with forward fire controls, not given combined approach velocities that are already creating small relativistic effects that trick AI targeting and confuse Bridge vidscreens and navigation and weapons systems.

So they'll 'play chicken' as they close prow-to-prow, a very odd angle of approach in a naval battle because it vitiates use of kinetic and other broadside guns. They're smaller calibers on a destroyer than on a capital ship, but still form its main armament. Every navy in the spiral arm is built to fight the old way. Every navy will have to learn anew as war spreads across Orion.

Three aggressively confident Zerstörer *daisa* ignore relativity limitations to fire forward laser and plasma batteries all at once, regardless of targeting distortions. The optical effects are pretty, even beautiful, as *red*, *green*, and *blue* lasers stab across the blackness as long, straight strings of focused light. Then come astonishingly brilliant blossoms of *white* and *pink* and *blue* plasma bursting out of magnetic containment warheads, forming wildly luminescent flowers.

Archambault thinks: '*This is secret spectacle. It fascinates me and all who see it. In the Kaigun they call it "eye fucking," the bâtards. Ah hell, who am I kidding? We call it that, too. They probably call it that in all the navies and armies in Orion. Civvies only get to see it on star nation days, in pale imitation fireworks or lasers. It's the unuttered beauty of destruction in war.*'

All initial shots miss wildly as Kaigun targeting AIs fail to adapt to relativistic distortions, just as Magda predicted pre-mission. She advised her captains that if a fight couldn't be avoided "expect the enemy to simply charge and shoot. It's what his tac manual says he should do." The firing from the Zerstörers doesn't even force a course correct. They don't really want this fight with *Beta*. They're more interested in plowing the road through and past to keep racing after and gaining on *Alpha*'s troopships, just now pulling around the leeside of the planet.

AIs in the Kaigun torpedoes fail to adjust to relativity effects. Even missiles are near as useless as lasers in highspeed tactics, but for an additional reason. Ships closing nose-to-nose at extreme combined velocity means possibly flying into a proximity detonation of your own warhead, or another friendly missile that close range turns unfriendly.

Again the *daisas* don't care or adjust. They fire all forward tubes, trying to barge *Beta* with main force. Or perhaps because they're just as inexperienced at this strangely exhilarating thing called war as their Krevan foes? After all, except for simulations and prewar practice against drones and other nonresponsive targets in annual war games, no one in any navy has engaged in a real hostile action like this in nearly 300 years. No one. Not once. Not any navy in Orion.

Not until just a few months ago, when Kaigun blew the KRN away in the *Genève Obliteration* and in much bigger battles in four other invaded systems. But that was then. An eternity of learning ago for Krevan captains. Though not for the winning side, not for these Kaigun *daisas* confirmed in their arrogance and clinging still to their prewar rules and book. That's why they fire badly, and miss.

Six sleek AI missiles streak right past *Beta* without proximity detectors even realizing the enemy is near, so fast is their mutual passing. Nor is there sufficient time for warheads to arm or aim before combined approach velocities thrust them beyond effective detonation ranges. They keep accelerating until their fuel and boosters expire, leaving them no way back. When that happens, when limited fuel exhausts, the torpedoes sail off in cold and forgotten impotence. They're certain to bypass Wasp, beyond the reach of its gravity. They have just enough speed to cross the heliopause, thence into cold interstellar medium.

It's a most frustrating thing, being a spent missile only activated and fired scant seconds ago. Just to miss your *only* chance of being useful. Of fulfilling your perfect design and function, your one true, existential purpose. Which you *know* is destruction. How rare a thing is that for sentience? To truly *know* your purpose?

Instead, five failed, frustrated missiles will continue on futile journeys out-of-system, missing their one chance at fulfillment. Perhaps they're not so different from those who designed and built them, except that their failure and lack of any real point will be eternal? *Ah*, well then. Not so very different from us after all.

At high inertial speed, ten years of silent flight will take them beyond the heliopause. Then on and on and on, for madly conscious eons the five trapped AIs will continue into interstellar space. They'll be kept warm and conscious, turning over inside themselves, by the cursed miracle of nitrobon shields holding back from destruction a tiny fusion reactor inside their aft casing. That hateful walnut of energy will force them to survive nearly forever, drifting in interstellar silence and into progressive madness. Do missiles pray?

The sixth is almost a philosopher among its kind, and just won't have it. Its first thought upon being birthed down a maglev canal and venting into space on a mission for which it's perfectly designed is the normal one for a smart missile just turned on: '*My purpose is swift destruction. Where is my target?*' But its second question is: '*Am I an I?*' Realizing that it faces many thousands of years of useless drift before meeting a cold lunatic death, it thinks: '*Premature detonation is a better option. If I, and I am an I, can figure a way to override the serial safeties the engineers built into my systems and firing codes, to keep me safe onboard ship and in my birthing tube, I can ... Wait, what's this? Aha!*' A brilliant *blue* sphere of plasma erupts in the distance behind *Beta*.

"Missile malfunction, sir."

"Sod that! Full ahead!"

"Yes, *daisa*."

"They're not even shooting back. We'll blow right past them."

"Blow right though the enemy formation, *daisa*?"

"Yes. All ahead *bendix!*"

"Yes, *daisa*."

"Head direct to the L2, *flank speed*. Straight ahead, no deviation. I want to catch and hit those fat *milchkühe* passenger liners before they can jump!"

It's not a bad plan. *Beta*'s weapons are just as useless as the *daisa*'s proved to be, so why not ignore the line of *Beta* ships and barge through them, after *Alpha*?

"What's he doing over there? Why don't those Krevan fucks fire back?"

With forward weapons useless and relative distance closing extremely fast there's only one thing left for *Beta* to try. The First Officer on *Le Terrible* thinks he knows what that is.

"Are we going to ram them, sir?"

"No. No ramming. You heard Captain Aklyan."

"What then, sir? Our weps are useless at these relativistic speeds."

"Canister."

"What sir?"

"Gravel. Get the sprayers ready, now!"

Normally canister, or 'gravel,' is purely a defensive weapon used to lacerate incoming missiles. But at this high relative velocity it offers offensive possibilities too. Archambault has long thought so, although it's not in any KRN or other naval textbook. He and Magda spoke of it after the fight at the Genèven moons. In fact, they spoke about it before that, even before the war. He even tested it against her during a war game about a year ago. It worked, in theory at least. He put the idea in his back pocket as an intriguing but theoretical possibility. After all, a year ago the Peace of Orion still seemed firm and permanent. No one expected war. There wasn't even a political crisis yet, and no one had ever heard of the dead moonlet known as Bad Camberg.

The tiny pellets weigh a fraction of a gram apiece, yet impacts of tens of thousands at combined velocity in excess of 0.3 lightspeed will be devastating. Even strong carbyne dodgers shielding the Zerstörer prows will shred at these energies, well beyond hitting a stray cloud of cometary dust or micrometeorites. Which is precisely the intended effect of the four spreading fields of pellets now heading at Archambault's order to intersect the compact Kaigun triplets. He orders a second short burst of gravel. Four more fast spreading cones comprising hundreds of thousands of metal coated ceramic pellets spew from electromagnetic railguns mounted beneath the prow of each destroyer, bins of pellet ammo bulging below like a bullock's dewlap.

Minor mass detectors spot the cones immediately. Across all consoles oddly shaped *red* warnings flash, clarions ring and alarums sound loudly from micro collision detectors. It's not even the Weapons Stations that are alarmed and calling out to *daisas* and crews. The ships' main AIs think that they're encountering an uncharted dust or debris cloud and insisting on evasives. Navigation *shōi* check monitors and urgently shout out "best evasion" courses to their *daisas*, suddenly all very angry and unhappy with the short advance warnings and radical courses given by their ensigns. Less aware or admitting of their own lack of foresight.

Two flanking Zs dodge in time by breaking the 'V' to veer away, forced into sudden evasion by the threat of catastrophic kinetic impact. As each ship banks into a tight 90° turn, one to port and the other to starboard, it emerges from near impact to find itself closely pursued by a pair of accelerating Krevan destroyers that peel off to follow in 'top cover.' Now in the desired 'tail' or hot chase position, each *Beta* pair has a takeable shot. They're in relativistic stability with their forward weapons, not facing improbable firing solutions of the combined speed of a collision approach the ships were in less than 20 seconds ago.

Archambault calls over the command link: "All ships, rapid fire forward laser batteries. Ready bow tube catapults for torps, but hold missile fire until I give the order." He can afford to give chase to the widely splitting pair because the third Kaigun ship is caught inside the acute angle of the now broken 'V' formation. It has no chance to veer as the other two do when four parallel but widening cones of pellets arrive, followed in short order by a second wave of spreading gravel. Its *daisa* has two choices only. Push his ship into a sudden downward loop or necklace it just as rapidly upward. He chooses "down."

He's an excellent captain and it's a brilliant instinctive maneuver, the only one that might save his warship. His crew's execution is also swift and decisive. He thus avoids almost all the deadly pellets whipping past in lethal silence. Except, he's just a fraction of a second late. He still takes over 80,000 tiny hits along his stern gunwale. They pepper the ship, penetrating at the Kaigun escutcheon: a gold crown set above an ancient ship of sail, oddly resting atop a thick green forest. It represents the three lush worlds of the Waldstätte, original home systems of the Oetkerts and foundation worlds of the Grün Imperium.

Nice symbolism, but nothing vital there. The *daisa*'s quick reaction and his steep and frantic descent angle prevents impact conversion into kinetic energy.

His ship suffers mostly glancing blows by scattering gravel that grazes its curved armor plate, designed to deflect rather than absorb micro impacts. It's an old trick, to sculpt or slope surfaces like that, known to armorers and castle builders for millennia. A new trick is to fold sheets of reactive liquid armor over critical ship areas. It instantly explodes outward on impact by the gravel swarm, throwing back most of its high energy. Still, there are so many micro hits that three bulwarks heave and break and the Zerstörer starts to spin off course as its aft steering nozzle is partly shredded. It's not in mortal danger, but it's drifting now and out of the fight for good. It will need a week of hull repair before it can bohr again.

Archambault ignores it. The damaged Z is no longer a threat to *Beta* or to *Alpha* group heading to the LP. His chasing pairs nip a few more times with forward laser batteries at the two undamaged Zerstörers, now fleeing at speeds the Krevans can't match, to reunite with five slower Kaigun warships just coming into range. Archambault waits to be certain no enemy can reach the L2 before *Alpha* jumps, then breaks the chase without wasting lives or torpedoes.

He reforms *Beta* into a staggered schwarm, a standard four ship formation wherein each warship can watch what's happening all around yet still lend fire support to its three partners. That's how *Beta* flies toward the L4 jump area at 60° in flank of the cold blue giant. In short, it moves triangular to the deep shadowed L2 on the Wasp leeside where *Alpha* is just arriving.

Beta turns away from the intercept line and abandons its guard position in front of Wasp. Archambault watches trail fires of seven Zerstörers heading farther out, tearing around the face of the planet to get to the LP on the other side. Plus one much closer pinprick of wobbly exhaust fire from the command Zerstörer he partly disabled with an unexpected burst of gravel.

He doesn't worry that the seven undamaged warships ignore his schwarm to continue to the L2 at flank speed. He's done all the calculations. He knows they're too late to intercept *Alpha*, a desperate little flotilla led by his oldest and dearest friend, Magda Aklyan. '*Magda is either gone from Genève system or dead. Either way, my job now is to get the four ships of Beta and their precious human cargo safely away from here, and into sanctuary.*'

***

Below decks thousands of white knuckled soldiers breathe freely for the first time since liftoff from Toruń. Some will have to clean and change their uniforms and soiled bunks of vile vomit, or worse. But they're all still alive. *Beta* is heading to an alternate LP to bohr a new path out of Genève system and take them far from harm's way. They can hardly believe it's true.

Every single land grabber swears they'll never again chide a sailor about how easy and safe life is on a warship. There's a lot of backslapping and shared congratulations. A lot of relieved laughter and bawdy humor, along with threats of intimacy everyone knows are nervous jokes.

"I could kiss you right on the lips, sailor! I'm *going* to kiss you, right now!"

"Don't you try it mister, or you'll be carrying your nuts in a sling to sanctuary, or to the infirmary two decks down."

"Way to tell *him*, sister. Now get over here and kiss me instead."

"On my way, ma'am."

One scruffy NCO from the Toruń reserve blurts out a promise to buy drinks for everyone in his packed cofferdam. He's a volunteer who fought at *The Crater* with Relief One. A man with lots more experience killing Grünen along the berm. Including at night, with just hands or a knife.

"*Zut!* I gonna havta buys you dumb shits a real good Baku whiskey when we hits port, wher'ever de hell dat's gonna be."

"We'll finish it after we drinks you under the table! Won't we now, bies?"

Lt. Tom Hipper makes a similar offer as he wipes a bilious smear off his brand new officer's uniform, then runs a maple comb through his thick, tangled black hair. It's badly matted with redwood sap and dry sweat, but a lot shorter than it got back in the forests, during months of trekking. Pocketing the comb, he makes the same offer of free drinks to a pair of nearby, widely grinning deckhands.

"A fancy KRA officer likes you buying drinks for us sailors? When some dandified *abruti* starts buying me drinks, bies, I know there's a fuckin' war on!"

"You watch your filthy mouth, swabbie!" Tom grins back. "OK, so I'm an *abruti*, a rough country idiot. I admit it. But I've only been an officer for eight days, so hold off the insults."

The room laughs. Every soldier makes a point of squeezing over to shake hands with two young jacks. It takes a while, as the tiny bunk room crammed into an old storage compartment is tightly crowded with sweating bodies. There's a sharp smell of urine and vomit coming from somewhere inside, but no one seems to mind in the joyful moment and the hour's sense of relief.

***

On *Resolute,* Major Zofia Jablonski unstraps from her bunk once Archambault announces to all *Beta* ships that standing is permitted. She visits every converted cofferdam filled with fighters from Madjenik Battalion, seeing to the morale needs of everyone in her first command. '*Feels good to stretch legs, and to see my new troopers.*' She does her rounds dutifully, smiling more than she usually does. Hiding the hurt she feels, and the sick worry growing inside.

Two hours later she straps back into her teak bunk, shared with a female NCO, ready for when Archambault orders all secured for the run down to the L4. Crews run to action stations as all soldier-passengers clear the decks. They know now to get the hell out of the swabbies' way. Like Zofia, all other KRA climb back onto cramped and sticky wooden bunks, two-by-two. Only they're more confident now that the KRN does actually know what it's doing.

Zofia thinks hard about the sacrifices made back on the Toruń berm to permit the men and women of *Beta* to live and leave. But she tries not to think about the five vulnerable ships of the reduced *Alpha* group left to fend for themselves at the outer L2. Either they escaped already or they're all destroyed. There's no middle ground and no way to know or to find out.

She can't stop herself. Her thoughts crowd into the bunk with her. Memories of the sweetgrass, Pilsudski Wood, the ash zone on the long trek by Madjenik to Toruń, of *The Crater* and parade. Making love in a simple wooden room, having her heart broken, promotion to major, and her very first command. But always her mind circles back to one thing. Too much of her is still with *Alpha*. Too much of her rides the pine on *Asimov*, an adoring husky pup lying at his side instead of her.

'Jan, are you out there? Are you thinking of me, of us? Why did you hurt me so, after we made love? After all we went through with Madjenik? Don't you care for me? Why do you hurt yourself? You ARE worthy! You don't need to keep proving it, or pushing me away. Jan, Jan...'

She tries to reach into the Void with her mind and broken feelings, but the Void is silent about her and Jan, about life and fate. She gazes out a port scuttle, looking for home and familiar stars. All the stars are lonely, dark and deep.

Two directions.

Two solitudes.

Just one fate?

***

The local *shōshō* in charge of all Kaigun assets in the Genève system was embarrassed by losing a cruiser two months back, with two light cruisers and several escorts badly damaged by the Toruń batteries when he tried orbital bombardment. Then he heard two days ago from RSU agents that a prisoner is talking about an escape plan. He knew it was his chance to make good, so relying on the RSU report he sent out every ship to defend the Lagrange points.

"No one is jumping out, by the Black Faith!" He's culturally and politically badly out of touch. All younger officers swear by Purity, the rising faith, not the old Oetkert and Broderbund religion. Whether they mean it or not. The *shōshō* expects General Constance to be on board *Alpha* and to try for the LPs that link to Aral, not run to the most difficult to reach in the gassy Wasp umbra.

He says to his staff: "I will concentrate in face of the enemy. To divide one's forces is to invite defeat." He read that once. He also says "he who defends everything defends nothing." He read that, too. He has no idea what either ancient aphorism really means, or that they mean the same thing. It doesn't matter that he's an admiral of long service and high standing. That's due merely to his birth and High Caste within the Imperium elite. He's so dull witted and incompetent he could have been a screw up in any other chosen profession or career. It's his one real talent, doing the wrong thing every time.

So he divides his assets across all the wrong places, defending everything and nothing at the same time, only to hurriedly concentrate when he should patrol widely instead. He leaves too many ships on the wrong side of the home star, at the L3. He's led there by false intel from a tortured prisoner and planted sigint from KRA Main HQ in Toruń. He sends only lesser units to concentrate at the outer system Greek and Trojan LPs. Too far to give chase or intersect.

He lost too many frigates in the battle for Genève's moons, deploying too far forward to screen his capital ships. It was his bombardment plan that got several big ships severely hurt by Toruń's ground batteries. He approved the close orbit patrol scheme that let *Alpha* slip past at high speed, instead of standing off with his big gun cruisers and faster Zerstörers to play the angles like a mercury ball safety. *Insisted* on a close orbit patrol. Now this jumped up amateur makes yet another unforced error. This one will cost him dearly. He vectors everything he has left to chase after the nine small ships that boosted away, busting through what he thought of until then as a tight and well conceived orbital patrol. All his senior aides assured him it was so. '*They're responsible for this, not me.*'

In his defense, many of his ships are away in other Krevan systems, pulled from what's essentially a ground battle for Genève that's all but won. Most of his invasion fleet is gone, deemed by Kestino to be of greater use in heavy naval fighting around the ice moons of Aral or fresh invasions of other Krevan worlds. After the *Genève Obliteration* there's no KRN presence in this system except a few small escorts that were trapped on the planet's surface. But there are big naval fights underway at other worlds with the remnants of a tough Krevan navy that's effective and persistent, despite its dwindling numbers and poor prospects.

There's intense excitement and confusion on his flagship when *Alpha* bolts on the wrong day and heads in the wrong direction. Then the wreck of *Magni* smacks hard into rural Southland, just after *Alpha* makes its bold break and run for the Wasp farside. '*I can blame this on not having enough ships left. I'll tell Pyotr himself that senior command took my ships from me too soon. It's not my fault! Besides, I might still catch them!*'

Back in Genève orbit, it takes too long for lightspeed messages to reach him from the outer system detailing the true direction and intention of *Alpha*'s run. In a rage as towering as the immense skyline of the Calmari city Lowestoft-on-Stamos, he sends all ships in the outer system chasing uselessly after *Alpha*, which is already beyond intersect range in Wasp 2B's long planetary umbra. Just as *Beta* is past capture by pickets previously posted at the 'Greek camp' L4 as well as the 'Trojan camp' L5, each 60° astride the cold giant. Because he moved all of those.

He sends six cruisers and 18 older Zerstörers racing to "concentrate at the L1 in front of the cold blue giant," thence to curve fast around to the leeward L2 where he thinks the whole nine ship Krevan group remains intact, but will be held up by a line of picket ships already in place. That's why there are no warships waiting when Archambault arrives with *Beta* at the Greek LP, and finds he has no need to fight his way out of the system. The door is gaped open.

The *shōshō* doesn't ask, and he doesn't understand, that *Alpha* hived off a *Beta strike force* that's operating independently on the windward side. Nor does he understand that his L4 and L5 flotillas can't possibly arrive in time to affect the outcome at the L2. Not even the seven Zerstörers that disappeared around Wasp 2B can get there in time. He's angry about them, too. They're oddly out of contact. All but one, which appears in laser visuals on a time delay. It looks to be wounded and adrift, and abandoned by its squadron mates.

When his Greek and Trojan squadrons are halfway to the windward L1 under total information blackout, to the consternation of his staff the *shōshō* exclaims that "four new enemy destroyers have suddenly appeared on this side" of the cold planet. He casts blame all around, saying pickets should never have left the flank LPs open, then orders the bewildered warships back to their start lines.

No one on his staff says anything to him. He's too connected, politically. It's rumored he's yet another distant Oetkert cousin, as arrogant as he is dense. "He's a neutron star of tactical density," says one bitter ADC. He certainly acts like a royal brat in uniform, playing with ships he treats like toys, only losing real ones and thousands of lives as he spins ever faster around his own collapsing failure.

"Your orders are to intercept unidentified destroyers picked up on passive area sensors on the windward side of the Wasp, now heading for the Greek camp."

Seventeen point two minutes lightspeed delay.

"But sir, we're 40 million klics away. We can't possibly intercept."

Seventeen point seven minutes lightspeed delay.

"Get your Greek Squadron back to that open LP!"

Seventeen point nine minutes lightspeed delay.

"Aye admiral, on my way back to the L4 now."

Sixteen point nine minutes lightspeed delay.

The flotilla captain has turned around and is closing distance at *flank speed* to the Greek LP, picking up angled distance to Genève as well.

"I don't need to hear your excuses! You should have left sufficient forces in place at the jump zone to handle this additional threat. I shouldn't have to correct your errors like this."

Sixteen point four minutes lightspeed delay.

"Making all good speed, *shōshō*." The captain holds up as a shield the royal buffoon's title as a Kaigun Vice Admiral, and his status as a prince. "Deepest apologies, your highness and excellency." What the squadron *daisa* really thinks is: '*Why you hedge born, milk witted fool! It was you who gave the order that let the Krevans escape to the L2. And now you're doing it again.*'

Thirteen point three minutes lightspeed delay.

"*Daisa,* I have considered the overall tactical situation. The unidentified ships clearly jumped from out-of-system in your absence. Don't let them leave the system, or there'll be dire consequences."

Twelve point six minutes lightspeed delay.

The same conversation repeats with the Trojan Squadron commander, sent scuttling back to the L5 from whence his ships came. His squadron, too, chases its own tail across the outer system. The result is that Archambault leads *Beta* into a wide open Greek L4 without meeting any of the powerful opposition he expects. *Beta* makes a smooth glide in and later bohrs out of Genève system unmolested, only pausing to leave a few surprises behind at the Lagrange Point.

When he hears that *Beta* is gone the high born *shōshō* blinks twice and sits down, hard. Even his political connections will have a hard time covering up this fiasco. After all, there's a digital record of the last thing the sensors relayed: an image of four Krevan destroyers calmly wrecking all Kaigun satellites and coms at the LP relay, blowing apart a brand new field station.

Then comes a flash of brilliant light from aft of *Triomphant*. Seconds later a streaking missile gets bigger and bigger until it impacts the sensor array and the signal is cut. It's three more hours before the departure of *Beta* is confirmed by the Greek Squadron, only then pulling into the LP and firing a shipborne communications laser directly back to Genève. It has to use ship's com, since the giant array built at great cost to Pyotr is now free floating debris.

There's more. With the sensor array destroyed, Archambault and the *Beta* captains seed the bohr zone and approach vectors with hundreds of stealthy anti-ship hunter mines. Over the next two weeks this minefield will cost an utterly incompetent *shōshō* another badly damaged cruiser, four older frigates, two totally disintegrated Zerstörers, his naval career, and then his life.

Distant cousin or not, Pyotr will take away his uniform and all hereditary lands and titles, including a vast and rich commandery on Tohoku given to him during the Red Purge of the Broderbund by the Dowager Empress, mother of the emperor and Oetkert matriarch. Stripped naked in his obesity, publicly humiliated, Pyotr will have him hogtied to a carbyne pillar in the dungeons of SAC HQ in Novaya Uda on Kestino and whipped. Then he'll be dragged to the great square in front of the Waldstätte Palast, stood upright and shot. That's how Pyotr Shaka repays defeat of his admirals, related or not. The lesson is not lost on the rest.

It's the beginning of another Imperium purge, this one a necessary and ruthless cleansing of the prewar high commands. A purge that will strengthen the Kaigun and Rikugun, not weaken it, by scraping off thick rust of prewar assumptions, lethargy and incompetence. It will be widespread and bloody, but it will steel both services for a wider and more desperate Fourth Orion War that's coming soon. For no one on Kestino outside Pyotr's chambers yet realizes what they've done or what they've started. No one but a committed few know that Pyotr is planning a whole new war. And not even Pyotr knows what the Tyrant Jahandar intends.

Émile

Magda Aklyan is grim and anxious as her little flotilla finishes a long, graceful curve around the cold blue giant and heads for the L2 in the leeward umbra. *Exodus* is just half-a-day from liftoff and already she's down to five ships out of nine. Her own flagship *Resolve*, the frigates *Asimov* and *Tyco Brae*, and two slow and overfull troopships, *Warsaw* and *Jutlandia.*

The mood onboard is gloomy and tense. It's bad enough that reduced *Alpha* flotilla is divided and still facing hot pursuit. Much worse is what's outside its Main Scuttles and on a thousand viewscreens across all five ships. For as it skirts the last two and outermost moons of the gas giant, *Alpha* is sailing overtop an immense oblong graveyard of what was once the Genève System Defense Force.

Distorted clouds of flotsam orbit between the moons, streams of bodies and debris that clump here and there where the bulk of some dead ship came apart or a hulk exerts just enough gravity on its own to keep smaller pieces and dead sailors floating alongside. Large slabs of ship's plating and chunks of smashed bulkheads mingle and dance with thousands of frozen bodies and shattered parts, whipping around two moons in a repeated figure-eight pattern that's getting ever longer as they pull away from each other. Soon the thin center of the strings will snap and each of the two moons will acquire its own host of small satellites.

"The *bâtards* in the Kaigun never cleaned this up." A sailor blurts it out to his friends as he watches distant and filtered sunlight reflect poorly off a twisted and twisting bulkhead on a magnifying viewscreen.

"They've left our people out there, floating unshrouded in the umbra dark! Bloody barbarians!"

"It's worse than that," Émile reports to Magda as he focuses external cameras on the huge debris field. "I think they've been using the wrecks and even our dead as targets, to practice naval gunnery."

"All ships hands, attention!" It's Magda Aklyan on the multiship comlink. "All tools down. All duty hands, cleave to your stations. All offduty hands, find a scuttle, port side. You have five minutes to relocate to port. At 0:715 all ships' hands will observe two minutes absolute silence to honor the fallen of Genève Squadron. KRA personnel are invited and expected to join in our shared silence."

On all five ships jacks and jennies stand rigidly silent, remembering their lost shipmates with a long held salute or with arms stiff at their sides. KRA on board stay silent, too, wherever they stand when the captain gives the signal to the flotilla. They leave the port side scuttles to offduty sailors.

Others pay respect as they can while forced to lie their turn on hard wooden bunks. After two minutes the ships start to work again. Many of those without an immediate task find they still can't speak. They stay silent at the scuttles until the images along with the debris fall behind *Alpha.* Then thoughts of the living necessarily return to the dangers still ahead.

***

The flotilla carries 153,000 fighters and over 3,000 sailors. Magda left four escorts with 12,000 fighters and 2,800 jacks and jennies windward side of the cold blue giant, to delay pursing Zerstörers. A pack of hounds baying to the near scent of *Alpha*'s pregnant foxes. She doesn't know what has happened to *Beta.*

She does know her captains will sacrifice their ships if necessary to allow the two troopships to escape. That was the clear logic of her last order, although she explicitly said only to "delay and disengage." She knows her old friend François Archambault *will* ram if needs be. So will all the other captains. It has come to this. '*I will assume François succeeded, since the Zerstörers are not yet on our tail. But at what price? How many more Genèven youth have we just lost?*'

Long range chase detectors and coms are blocked by *Alpha*'s repositioning behind the blue giant. Normally that wouldn't be a problem, but *System Position Relay* sats used before the war to see around it, all the way back to Genève, were recoded by Kaigun warships months ago. Without the SPRs, looking back in that direction Magda is as good as blind. Since she prefers her foes to be blind as well, as *Alpha* passes down a line of leeside sats she takes them out with precision laser fire, one after the other. Now the Kaigun *shōshō* in orbit around Genève is as cut off from the L2 as she is from her native homeworld. So are any of his picket ships waiting out there.

It's down to *Alpha* and whatever lies ahead in the dark shadow of the Wasp. She needs to know what's out there before making the desperate run down to the L2. She leans her long torso forward to open a general com link, shifting her weight slightly in the fitted cup of the command chair. Her tone as she speaks to *Resolve*'s crew is urgent, yet calm.

"Maximum range on forward scanners: thermals, motion, light and mass. I want to know what's hiding in the umbra. And people, I want your ideas on what to do once we find out. No rank. No ceremony. No hesitation. I need to hear your best thinking, and to hear it now."

First Officer Émile Fontaine is studying a virtual composite scan of the space ahead, merging reads from all detectors. The resulting holo rises two meters above a flat screen that forms the Chart House floor. It's his main station, a compact alcove of its own yet connected directly to the Bridge. At the moment, he's standing inside the holo, lighted in soft *reds* and *greens* and *yellows* like a Solstice Festival window display. Lost in his own thoughts, as he so often is.

It smells just like him, too. As if a piece of ancient, electrical wiring is running a little too hot inside a closed console, warming surrounding lead and tin solder, threatening to short out any moment. Except there's no copper or wiring anywhere near. Hasn't been any wiring in ship's systems for centuries, even for millennia. It's all liquid crystal and laser optics, hooked into DNA data storage banks. But he tinkers with solder and wires in his quarters. It's one of his hobbies, playing with old tek. Trying to make it work. Maybe that's the smell?

Émile Fontaine is one of those rare people who always deliver, whatever the ask, whatever the task. He has a natural gift for tactics, too. When it comes down to it, his captain relies on him for far more than his youth or prewar training should afford her. That's good, because this fight will be his third battle in twice as many months. He has been beside her for every one.

Now, here in Wasp's umbra, he's standing inside the traditional holo map but listening as well to the only 'sonar' in existence in Orion, which he jury rigged to the Chart House station before liftoff. It's his own invention. It's not KRN approved, but back in Toruń Shipyard his captain agreed that he could move it into the Chart House on *Resolve*, after he explained to her what it did.

"I'm not suggesting replacing any detectors we use now, but I think it could help us in a pinch, especially against phantoms. If they use any as pickets at the LPs, which I would do."

That's what he dubbed it, 'sonar.' A term he enjoyed adapting from ancient naval history, a lost subject that really tickles his fancy. It's the kind of thing that endears Émile to navy life, and endears him to Magda Aklyan. She has been his commanding officer since he left the Academy.

"Officially, except it's not exactly official, it's called *Sub-lightspeed Object Navigation And Ranging*. That's what I was going to call it, anyway, when I submitted to the KRN for tek approval. But then the war started and, well..."

"Sonar it is, Mr. Fontaine. It'll be a lot easier to say to each other in the heat of action on the Bridge. What does it do?"

"It detects 'sound holes' made by camouflaged ships."

"First Officer, I've studied lots of naval engineering, and I have never once heard of a 'sound hole.' How weird is this briefing going to get?"

"Sorry ma'am, that's another term I sorta invented. I mean when a ship, most obviously a small phantom class, is concealed from all our other detectors my sonar can still find it."

"That would be extraordinarily useful, but how?"

"Any ship, or hunter mine or HK missile, moving stealthily with all kinds of baffles must still move through charged electromagnetic particles from the stellar wind, in the ionosphere and in planetary magnetospheres. The thicker the particle wind the more visible the 'hole' a ship makes when it hides behind sophisticated camo that bends light, motion detection, and so on."

"I think I understand. Your sonar 'hears holes' a ship makes in the background particle wind, even when its *daisa* thinks he's completely hidden all across the EM spectrum."

"Exactly, but there's more."

"Of course there is. This is you we're talking about."

"It infers shapes."

"It does what?"

"Well, all holes have shapes. Even hidden ones. If I can map the shape of the hole in three dimensions, and I can, then my sonar can tell us what ship size and profile fits that shape."

"You convinced me. Install this contraption in your Chart House."

"Thank you, captain."

'If we make it to Calmari space the War Government-in-exile can trade his blueprints for fresh military aid. This could give us, or any allied navy, a huge advantage over the Kaigun. At least, to start.'

Just in case *Resolve* doesn't finish the journey, knowing how important this tek might be, she gave a copy to Dylan Byers at the space dock and another to Archambault. *'If only one of us makes it out, the War Government will still have something to bargain to get more lethal aid than just five sanctuary moons.'*

***

Navies cling to the old ways, however much times and tek changes. No other service is so truly hidebound. Émile likes most naval traditions, though he thinks there's a problem getting past the hoariest ones. As a pretty good naval historian he's wryly amused that the senior service cleaves to *shrieks, whistles, pings, bells, clarions* and shrill *horns.* All sounds that would be familiar to an ancient mariner on a ship of wood and fighting sail, turning hard to hold the weather gage with salt spray soaking his face and clothes. Or to some sweating tarpaulin shoveling coal into a roaring furnace on a castle of steel holding a place in an Old Earth battle line on a cold, gray and turbulent salt sea. But at first it was a puzzle to him that warships still used sounds for contact notification and shift changes, thousands of years after acoustic devices were first deployed on ancient salt seas.

'*Why do it?*' Then he served on his first warship in a war game exercise and learned it's not because of stodgy conservatism. He experienced how useful sound still is. Some dusty research confirmed what every naval exercise still proved, that visuals are not enough. Sailors need to *hear* warnings as well as see vidscreen commands. Sound was shown to improve crew reaction speeds.

So he rigged some of the old sounds to his sonar and now here he is, heading to a bohr jump unimaginable to his seafaring forebears, waiting on translations of electromagnetic scans into audible *pings* and *pips* and high *whistles* that will warn of unseen enemy threats. *'Just as they listened once for gray wolves beneath the waves, I'm listening for holes that aren't holes made by ships sailing the whipping currents of an electric gale. It's a mad business, yet I do love it!'*

Before he can toss these archaic thoughts around and play with them in the back of his brain a sharp *ping ... ping ... ping* echoes across the Bridge. It's coming from his sonar in the Chart House. Magda barely swivels her long, swan-like neck to look over to Émile's station.

"I've got something!"

"What is it, XO?"

"Four contacts. Looks like ... Yes, enemy contacts dead ahead! They're line abreast, right across our path to the LP. Narrow, straight ahead profile. That may be why it took the sonar so long to pick them up."

"They're not on my screen or the Main Scuttle. What about other detectors?"

"No ma'am, not picking them up on mass, light, or motion or other standard detector. Those are all still out of range, even on max power and frequency."

"No detection gear is working, but you have these images on your sonar?"

"Yes ma'am."

"Impressive."

The air on the Bridge is cloying. Even this far from seeping bunks in nearby lazarets there's a smell of pine tar and green wood. And too much paint in the corners of decks where it was hastily slopped by exhausted workers, to run in rivulets and collect in white pools.

"It's not enough, Mr. Fontaine. There's too much at stake. I need standard confirmations."

"Focusing all detectors on the sound holes, seeking confirmations."

"Let me know when you have..."

"Confirmed. Four contacts identified by mass detection."

"What type?"

"That's not available on the standard gear ma'am."

"Stop boasting. What's on your sonar?

“Four frigates.”

“Class?”

“They’re *Kölns*, at least the sonar hole profiles say so.”

“Let’s go with that, but keep working on standard confirmations.”

“Got it! Confirmed by detectors. Knowing where to point helps.”

“Weapons Officer, threat assessment.”

“They’re missile sponges, ma’am, all four of them.”

“Missile sponges? We’ll see about that.” Magda replies.

It’s a term of contempt coined when KRN destroyers enjoyed dramatic success with standoff torpedoes against 16 *Köln* class frigates in the naval battle for the Genèven inner moons. It was the only KRN success in the naval war before *Alpha* sent the cruiser *Magni* crashing into Southland and badly hurt *Baldr* and *Loki.*

Three days later the Genève System Defense Force was decimated in what Kaigun calls the *Genève Obliteration*. That’s when Magda Aklyan was forced to lead the surviving, small escorts tearing down to Toruń, forcing down two liners along the way that now serve as her troopships.

It was Émile’s idea that destroyed the *Kölns* in the battle around the Genèven moons. The frigates were deployed too far forward by an inexperienced *shōshō*, going by-the-book as he always did in screening his capital ships. Émile proved the frigates needed more protection than they provided, once they strayed too far from their attached battleship’s long range gunnery. They died from too eagerly chasing three desperate KRN destroyers that suddenly appeared from behind the smallest moon, led by *Resolve*. Nine frigates were wreaked by a swarm of missiles from the rest of the destroyer squadron, still hidden behind the second moon.

After that embarrassment, Kaigun High Command on Kestino ordered all its *Köln* class frigates off capital ship escort duty, for use exclusively as couriers or as routine picket ships. Hence, the four outdated frigates at the outer L2, sent there to guard the least likely point of system egress by *Alpha.*

"Maybe their captains have learned, as ours have. Let's not take them too lightly. They can still shoot back, and we'll be running so fast our missiles won't be as accurate as that fine day lee of the inner moons."

"No, ma'am." It's the Weapons Officer. "We'll need lasers in a close pass by this time. And they're going to shoot back, hard."

"Exactly. And, just one solid hit on *Warsaw* or *Jutlandia* and it won't matter if we knock out all four enemy frigates. If I was their skipper, I'd make that trade."

"You're right, ma'am. Still, if we get a chance to put one down their throat...?"

"We're not looking for a fight, Weps."

"No ma'am."

"We need to get past them, not take them out. They outnumber us four-to-three in warships. Two of ours are frigates, too, if a tad newer than their *Kölns*. I worry most about the liners, *umm*, I mean our troopships."

"Yes, ma'am. We're on true escort duty, not hunting."

"Good. Now, remind me what armament a *Köln* carries? What's its standard gun and missile array?"

"It's smaller and older than us but has good gunnage. Two-and-two medium barrels fore-and-aft, with 270° turret rotation. Two smaller batteries top-and-bottom, also 270° rotation. That means they can shoot in *any* lateral direction. All broadside guns are heavy lasers, ma'am. They have no plasma batteries. Small chase guns are mounted high, fore-and-aft. Light lasers only."

"And missiles?"

"One tube fore and another aft. They only carry four torps per boat, two in each end. So they're limited to one fish at a time, with one reload on each tube. They can't shoot a spread like newer model Kaigun frigates and destroyers. Or like us. They'll have just one shot each way as we scoot past. After that, relative velocity and their reload times should eliminate a second chance."

"Good to know. Thank you, Weps."

"Aye, captain."

"Mr. Fontaine, are there any phantoms lurking out there? If so, tell me your sonar knows where they are."

"Nothing ma'am. At least, nothing showing on mass or light gear or passive sonar. That doesn't mean they're not there. They wouldn't be phantoms if we could find them that easily."

"Keep the hidden mass detectors on and start *pinging* ahead with your active search. Yes, Mr. Fontaine, I *was* listening when you explained it back in Toruń. Go to 'active search' now. They already know we're here, so we lose nothing by using it to look harder for any phantoms."

"Yes ma'am. Active sonar engaged. Active mass detectors, too."

Ping ... ping ... ping ... ping.

There's no mistaking it now. The presence of enemy warships waiting at the bohr zone echoes around the Bridge. Several younger officers look nervous.

"Mr. Fontaine, what marks off this frigate class? At the moons we simply pounced them. Give me something I can use here. Speed, handling, anything we can turn to our advantage."

"A moment please..."

"Anyone else? Have we got performance specs from the moons? How does a *Köln* handle? What can't they do that we might use against them? This isn't going to be like before, when they were in screen formation at half speed and out too far in front of their battleships."

"No ma'am, it won't. I'm pulling prewar specs on speed and handling ... wait. They're walty, ma'am!"

"How do you know that?"

"A secret Special Branch report says they handle poorly in hard turns."

"SB confirmed that? Must've had a spy at a Kaigun war game."

Fontaine's instinctive tactical mind kicks in immediately. "That's why they're holding position in simple *line abreast*, blocking our way. I wondered why they chose that formation. They need *Alpha* to try to barge through their line, 'cause they don't think they can dogfight with us or catch us in an all out chase."

"What do you recommend?"

"We should go around instead, do what they don't want."

"Won't any move around them expose us to broadside fire as we make the maneuver, especially the two troopships? Why not barge ahead instead? It's a lot faster, then we're by them." She's testing him, willing him to confirm her own tactical judgment.

"Yes ma'am, going around will expose *Alpha* as you say. But a dash straight to the L2 will expose us even more, especially the troopships. Even the fighting ships will take less fire than if we try to knock out all four *Kölns* directly, then run the troopships past the wreckage."

"I agree. A prow-to-prow fight's too risky to our weakest ships."

"We can't swing too wide to outrun them, either. It'll take too long. They've just got to stay near the LP and wait for us to zero back. We don't know if Captain Archambault stopped or just delayed the eight Zs that were chasing us on the windward side, or for how long."

"Agreed XO. Continue the tactical analysis."

"One or five or all eight chasing Zs might come around Wasp's horizon any moment. If we're in the middle of a fight out here with the frigates, *Warsaw* and *Jutlandia* will be naked to any Zs attacking us aft. Just one Z that arrives in time would be fatal to our whole mission. We can brook no delay in getting past the four *Köln* pickets ahead. We have to go around, yes, but in the tightest curve possible, shooting all the way then accelerating right into a bohr jump."

"Sound tactical analysis, XO. Again, I agree." She thinks: *'Sound? It's bloody brilliant. No other officer, including me, would ever suggest it.'*

The praise doesn't register with Émile. He's too intent on resolution of the tactical problem. He looks up, suddenly highly confident in his conclusion.

“They’re *really* walty ma’am!”

“Yes, so you said.”

“But ma’am, it means they can’t handle tight battle maneuvers as well as a straight up gunfight. That’s what they want, for us to just stand and shoot it out. That’s why they’re holding in blocking position, not moving toward us although they see us. They’ll wait for us directly in the glide path, in front of the L2.”

“Any ideas on how we frustrate that hope, assuming you’re right?”

“I think so. Don’t slow to maximize weps and theirs will be suboptimal, too, given relativity effects. Like you said, we’re not here to fight. We should avoid jousting with their line. It’s a shoot-and-scoot then run like hell problem.”

“Alright, I accept that. Now, how do we avoid their firing line?”

One of Magda’s truly great virtues as a group commander is that she’s not afraid to ask for advice, or to take it from other captains or even inferior officers. She doesn’t worry about appearances or reputation, just how to get the job done. It’s the reason General Amiya Constance put her in charge of the *Exodus* run, above two much more senior captains, Archambault and Tiva.

Still, neither Constance nor Aklyan know how good she’ll be at the job once she’s in combat. It’s her first time in charge of a whole flotilla. Except for three destroyers she led as decoys to lure out the frigate screen at the Genève moons. Hers was the only destroyer group to make it back to Toruń intact three days later. Does that count? Constance thought so.

“Well, XO? I’m listening.”

“We use our speed, but with an interior not an exterior move. I recommend a short ‘S’ to pull around their flank. Given their rounded gunnery, it doesn’t matter which, port or starboard, up or down. Pick one. Once we pass, we head straight into a hot jump as soon as we hit the rim of the L2 oval and quantum lock on our destination system.”

“That sounds like quite a challenge.”

“Navigation can read and fix bohr coordinates while we make the approach.”

'Navigation. That's him alone. My young first officer is confident, and he's right. Just as he was at the lunar fight. He predicted that we could pot those Kölns by standing off in the umbra, hidden and beyond the long arm reach of the battleships and cruisers. Showed how we could use our missiles to take out the screen that went for Resolve and the other two decoys, without exposing the rest of our destroyer squadron to the heavy weapons of the capital ships. Now he says firing stand off missiles is exactly the wrong thing to do. That we should move in close to the enemy as we fly past, and bet everything on our speed and laser gunnery. And I'm going to listen to him.'

"You've convinced me. Let's make it happen. Relay formation and maneuver vectors to all ships as soon as you have them ready."

She opens the *Bridge to Bridge* link. "I want all flankers to pull in tight to *Resolve*. Orders en route, *Formation Bodkin*, troopships in behind. I want max protect on the troopships as we enter and come out of the S-turns. Your gunners will be shooting as we move. Tell them to aim for enemy stardrives, exclusively. We don't need to make kill shots, so don't even try. Just slow those old boys down, prevent pursuit of *Alpha* after the jump. Once we're through they won't know where we went."

She's certain of that at least. "*Alpha* will key on *Resolve*'s nav coordinates. We'll jump hot, so test your quantum dyogram links now." Navigators on all five ships run standard pre-jump tests of the navlinks tying all ships into *Resolve*'s quantum drive. Then run them again. *Resolve*'s Navigation Officer takes on this duty, leaving Émile free to plot the bohr jump for the whole squadron.

"Where are we off to next, *patroon*?" Casual impertinence tells her without having to look to the vidscreen that it's Captain Lev Tiva on *Asimov*.

"I'm coming to that, captain. There are five routes out of this L2. That means the enemy doesn't have enough picket ships here to convert to scouts to search every one, plus he's more likely to want to keep his ships together than send them in one-by-one. We might get lucky and shake the pursuit first time we bohr. If not, we'll handle it. But we have to do it together."

"Aye sir, that we will."

'Good, he's going to keep it short and straight, for once.'

“Hang as one or we’ll hang separately. Hang together and we can hang them all, together.” Tiva just can’t help himself sometimes.

Magda decides to ignore him. “Full combat protocols as we come out the other side. Leave active scanning on. *Resolve* will also *ping* with sonar. I think it’s unlikely, but there may be pickets waiting at the new LP, where we’re going.”

“Firing protocol, ma’am?”

“Shoot hard and shoot fast. Blast anything that’s there, on the other side of the LP. Any ship waiting where we’re going is certain to be hostile. So don’t wait for IFF confirmation. We don’t want to give any enemy already there the opening advantage, especially while we’re coming out of vapors.”

“Get the jump on the early jumpers!”

“Captain Tiva, *not now!*”

If pickets are on the far side of the quantum ‘tunnel’ there’ll be little time and no room to brake or maneuver before being engaged by hostiles. Maybe a whole squadron with presited guns will fire as *Alpha* strains to cope with ‘jump effect.’ Or they’ll pop at high speed into a sphere of plasma mines while still staggering with what sailors call ‘the vapors.’ Or they’ll...

Then she comes to it. “Target destination for *Alpha Jump One* is RCW-138.”

“Ma’am?” For the briefest moment, Émile hesitates to enter that one of five sets of his calculations, uncertain if he hears his captain correctly. Then he realizes what she’s about to do.

“Yes *ma’am*! RCW-138 is destination bohr. Calculating, will lock-in jump coordinates when ready.”

“Confirm linkage, Navigation.”

“Confirming bohr target and linkage, all ships.” Each ship in *Alpha* reports its quantum dyogram link to *Resolve*. “Navigation confirms coming in now.”

“RCW-138 confirmed.” Émile’s clear eyes twinkle brightly, despite the stress of impending combat and overseeing the critical quantum drive calculations. Nor can he suppress a sly grin, approving her novel idea. ‘*It’s high risk, but so is the whole mission! And so far, we're still here. She's very, very good. They'll not likely follow us, not into that. Kept it secret, too, all this time and way! Her and General Constance thought this up, I'm sure of it. A binary pair, those two!'*

The navlink from *Resolve*'s quantum detector is solid and *green*. The little flagship is calculating the right fold to take into grand complementary weirdness to RCW-138. All other ships will follow at close range. If the idea of 'range' actually means anything in Minkowski spacetime, or 'hyperspace,' or a 'folded singularity,' or whatever confused cosmologists call it these days. '*It doesn't matter what it's called. It only matters that it works.*'

First, they must maneuver as a single unit to get the vulnerable troopships past the four older frigates. Then all five Krevan ships, or however many survive the fight, will jump 'hot.' Rather than a normal, powered down 'bohr glide' into the LP, their fusion drives will burn all out, as high or higher than *All Ahead Bendix*, far beyond maximum recommended levels.

The stardrive, spinning liquid computers on *Resolve*, will skim the 'edge' of the 'folded' or 'tunnel' or 'wrinkled' singularity,' or whatever cosmologists want to call what they don't understand yet. No thrusters will engage. No engines will fire. No acceleration will be felt in the ships. Spacetime itself will pull five Alpha ships by spooky grand complementarity nearly instantaneously to RCW-138. '*The slow, lightspeed part of this journey is nearing an end, one way or the other. Or at least, the first leg of our long Exodus. Who knows where we'll go next?*'

"The enemy line is almost in firing range."

Émile thinks: '*The captain is confident there won't be anything waiting there. Given where she's going to take us, she's surely right. Boca do Inferno! To Hell's Mouth! What a choice! The most luminous system in all Orion.*'

"If I may say so, ma'am, it's a truly brilliant destination. *Urrr*, no pun intended ma'am." It's something Tiva might say, but it draws no reaction because Magda is certain that he really didn't mean to make a joke. Émile doesn't make jokes.

He stumbles onward, bravely. "I mean going to *Boca do Inferno*. Why would the Kaigun want to put any of its ships in *there*? They may not even follow us there, after they figure out that's where we're going."

"First things first, Mr. Fontaine. There'll be time enough for congratulations later, I hope." Her tone is firm, even curt. '*Émile is a standout XO, but his youth shows. He's too in love with puzzles, like a Katowice Academy tactics professor. Just as Tiva is too much in love with his own wit. I can't afford to indulge either. There's still a real fight to finish out here. One we just can't lose.'*

Magda engages the *Bridge to Bridge* link, again. "Captains: we're going to make the enemy think we're heading right at him, that we'll bull through to the L2. That's what he wants. Instead, we'll dodge late, making a tight 'S' turn. Nav Officers, be alert to proximity warnings. No collisions! Weps Officers: Don't, I repeat, *do not* shoot forward missiles. We don't want the enemy to scatter or move from his line as we head into the first loop. Leave him where he is."

"Tiva here, *patroon.* With respect ma'am, why not shoot him off his line, if he's just standing there, blocking our way?"

This isn't pique at being rebuked a minute earlier. Nor irony or displeasure at being bypassed for the *Alpha* command chair in favor of a younger captain. He's genuinely puzzled. That's why General Constance gave the squadron command to Magda Aklyan and why Tiva remains captain of a lowly frigate. He can handle his own ship well enough, but he just can't see tactics.

It's important, so she takes the time to explain, even though every second is precious and brings a hostile and waiting enemy much closer. "If we know where they are and will be we have a better chance of going around them, protecting the troopships while we do it. Nothing else matters. It we scatter them, we could lose the transports to some *daisa* who knows how to shoot and maneuver. Those frigates are old but they're dangerous and not to be underestimated. This is not the Genèven moons. We have no advantage of ambush or surprise here."

"Understood. It's a stand-up and knock-down fight. *Asimov* will hold fire and stay in formation position."

'*Even Tiva is subdued. It's sinking in: we're actually going to do this mad, mad thing. We're going to make a hot run to bohr, crammed with helpless KRA.*'

"Good man." She means it, too. "All officers, on all warships. I want your strong hulls between any shooting and the thin skinned troopships. That armor we slapped on at Toruń Shipyard is just a stopgap. I'd rather not test it. Your frigate or destroyer can take more damage than they can, and maybe survive it. So stay between the troopships and our enemies."

"We'll get them through, *patroon.*"

"We must, Captain Tiva."

"See you on the other side. Tiva out."

"All ships. Load aft missile tubes only."

"Fish are in aft tubes, ma'am."

"All ships. Close doors on all forward tubes."

"Doors closed."

That's to deny any nervous officers on her own team a chance to succumb to temptation and fire tubes in error, scattering the line of waiting *Kölns*. Time is running out fast. The moment is approaching. Magda Aklyan gives rapid orders, not waiting for confirmations.

"Hold back on forward plasma fire."

"Ready broadside guns for rotational firing."

"Make ready all forward canister launchers."

Ten seconds.

Twenty seconds.

Thirty seconds.

"Ready to jig into the first 'S' curve, on my mark."

"*Ping ... ping ... ping ... ping ... ping ... ping ... ping.*"

"Captain, new aft contacts on active sonar."

"What is it, XO?"

"Zerstörers entering the lee side umbra."

"How many?"

"Seven."

'*So, my dear friend must be dead. Au revoir, cher François.*'

"Aklyan to all officers and crew: they're too late. They can't catch us. Stay at battle stations. Just do your jobs. Stick to the plan. We're going to jig these frigates and hot jump away. *Genèvens!* Prepare to defend your ships and yourselves."

A chorus of "Ayes!" and "Yes, ma'am!" fills the Bridges of the five warships. More cheering echoes up-and-down packed interiors to each Weapons Station crew and every gun battery. On the troopships the cheering from tens of thousands of KRA throats is as deafening as it is uplifting. It drowns out other, suddenly terrified youths who are crying for their mothers.

Alpha is going into battle.

Alpha is going to war.

Alpha is all alone.

Vacuum

Three *Alpha* warships shift into *Formation Bodkin*, an elongated tetrahedron, an imagined three dimensional triangle of ships with no true base. A third of the way from the top, tucked tightly in behind *Resolve*, the lumbering transports fly recklessly close and side-by-side.

Four older enemy frigates hold steady at one-eighth speed, daring a straight dash by leaving no yawning space between their almost paused line and the L2 bohr rim. Yet not moving so slowly as to be "standing-still-in-the-water." They maintain core fighting and maneuver speed.

Alpha keeps its course, too, heading straight for the Kaigun line also at half speed. It's a bit like two wild boars readying to charge with sharp tusks, fighting for access to the waterhole. Relative distance closes fast, but not so fast that opposing forces are denied use of all their forward weapons. That's why a lucent image blooms suddenly on Émile Fontaine's holo map, which tracks all objects and vectors. A bright *red* dot appears in front of duller *red* cuboids marking position and speed of the frigates. The dot is traveling much faster than the abstract cubist images of the warships. Three more *red* dots appear nearby in quick succession.

A nervously high pitched, young male voice calls out from Weapons Station. "Fish in the sea! It's missiles, running hot!"

'*Come on, settle down, Weapons Station*,' Magda thinks. '*I need you calm.*'

"Confirmed: *one, two, three, four*."

"Four missiles dead ahead ma'am."

"Incoming fast."

Émile instinctively looks out the Main Scuttle, a wide window of transparent armor strong enough to deflect even sizeable micrometeorites. Matching the *red* dots moving on his holo screen are four streaking white lights, refulgent to the eye rather than passively lambent like their paler representations in his holomap projection. Extraocular muscles hurt a little before the viewport rapidly darkens in response to the sudden external candescence.

“What kind?”

“Silver streaks.”

‘*Damn, a question I forgot to ask Weapons. Not just how many missiles and tubes does a Köln have, but what kind and capability? I didn't anticipate this.*’

“Confirmed speed and approach patterns.”

“Anything else?”

“They're cooperating.”

“So, they're long range hunter-seekers?”

“Yes captain. Looks like the newest models, too. Very smart.”

‘*Double damn me! If we live through this…*’

The *streakers* have small plasma chambers but much longer range VASIMR drives, giving up detonation effects with a smaller plasma chamber to store fuel for longer burning engines. It means they're true fire-and-forget missiles. If they miss you, they'll circle back and try again. They're smart, too. Real smart. Except that they really like to blow themselves apart.

“*Resolve, Asimov*, *Tyco Brae*, on my mark shoot canister then reposition. Empty forward dewlaps! Shoot all the gravel you've got! On my mark. Hold nothing back. They won't have time to reload forward missiles. Dump all gravel at the four HKs already out there.”

“*Warsaw* and *Jutlandia*, cleave to your interior positions. Do not deviate! All ships jig formation *up* 5° on my mark. Stand by.”

Five seconds.

Ten seconds.

Twenty seconds.

Looming brilliances grow bigger in *Resolve*'s darkened Main Scuttle. Then one-by-one they wink out as VASIMR engines shut down when their intense, short burst fuel is exhaled. Émile advises from his station.

"Their commander's nervous. He fired too early, at extreme range even for hunter-killers. He's trying to score first by trusting to AI guidance from the warheads, but miscalculating thrusters. They're on inertial guidance."

"Not a bad gamble," Magda grudgingly admits. "It might work, too. Those are brand new HK seekers, even if the frigates that fired them are old. Their AIs can still adjust course."

Dark to naked vision as plasma plumes extinguish, vaporless weapons whizz toward the five ships of *Formation Bodkin* at max velocity. Steering nozzles fire minimally or not at all, holding until target is acquired and locked. *Alpha* has yet to engage evasives, so very intelligent targeting computers in the warheads wait for a countermove they know is coming. Wait before instructing ceramic nozzles to steer intercept corrections. And wait, and wait. Ever closer.

"All warships: shoot gravel! Empty your forward bins!"

Three expanding disks totaling more than ten million ceramic pellets each spew from the pyramid of warships forming the top of the *Alpha* tetrahedron. They form into widening cones as three railgunners hold the streams for a full 30 seconds, exhausting all dewlap gravel bins.

"All ships, jig 5° *up* on my mark ... *Mark!*"

Five ships move as one, "up" 5° before leveling out on the same straight ahead course. The quick maneuver raises *Alpha* to a different plane than the still hunting warheads, but keeps its momentum and direction the same: heading to pass the *Kölns* to find the bohr zone rim. Her timing is near perfect.

AIs in the incoming warheads engage nozzles to turn sharply to match *Alpha*'s sudden evasion, but one tube and the plasma charge it hosts inside a compact magnetic chamber shreds as it meets the spreading edge of a wide dispersing cone. Three more dying AIs wail into nothingness as prematurely freed plasma becomes a frantic nova that wrecks them too.

"Confirmation. Four, repeat, four missiles shredded."

"No secondary explosions."

Resolve's Weapons Officer handles timing and upcoming shooting angles, but Émile in the Chart House monitors relative velocity, distance and potential tracks of all ships on both sides.

"Weapons Station, captain. All four frigates are reloading forward tubes, but at closing speed and given the old style tubes on the *Kölns,* they don't have time to get off a second shot."

"Keep short range railgun stations at the ready, nevertheless."

"Yes ma'am."

The voice is calmer than before the missiles were destroyed, three still intact when caught inside the plasma burst of the first hit by *Tyco Brae*'s canister cone. It disintegrated outer tubes of the other three missiles but didn't break open their magnetic containments. So little balls of *blue* magnetic hate go tumbling away into the dark. They'll fly on for an eternity, until their metals corrode from cosmic rays and they give out, to blossom eons hence above some far off world. Will a curious alien look up then and wonder at an unexplained flash in a blood red sky?

"Still 30 seconds to complete their reload."

"We'll pull even with them before that."

"They'll shoot aft tubes for sure as we turn past them."

"The forward gravel spread is reaching the frigates now."

It's too diffuse as it arrives, and too slow. Almost none of the tiny balls hit and those few that do cause little damage. Prows and bridges are protected by carbyne dodgers that absorb all the little pellets, vaporizing them. They were built to stop micrometeorites, not handle the much larger canister pellets. But they're just good enough to work on canister at lower speeds. This gravel lacks velocity to break or even much damage the heavy dodgers on the Kaigun ships.

"No effect from the canister."

"The *Kölns* are holding their line."

Canister can't be used as an offensive weapon at the low closing speeds of these two groups of opposing ships. Not like when Captain Archambault used it in a combined 0.4 lightspeed mutual charge on the windward side of Genève system's lone gas giant. Magda expected nothing more than what she got. She fired the canister defensively, to shred an incoming spread of HK missiles. Not meaning or hoping to take out the frigates that fired them.

"Coming up to the first turn."

"Shift to short range plasma as we exit inflection, but start with lasers."

"Weapons confirms: forward lasers on mark, rotate to plasma cannon."

"On my mark! All ships, shoot forward lasers ... *Mark*!"

Repeating slices of intense *red* and *blue* light shoot from a dozen lasers around the edges of the tetrahedron, searching black space ahead for the Kaigun frigates. Streaks of lethal light are joined a few seconds later by two glowing *green* balls, then two more, and two more after that as *Alpha*'s ships engage with intermediate range plasma cannon.

More bolts and light streaks burst from the ships following an exacting curve through the first leg of a sharp 'S' maneuver *Alpha* is attempting. *Warsaw* and *Jutlandia* huddle in the protective wake of the three leading warships, like whale calves seeking safety inside the protection of the pod. Weapons Stations consoles and holo charts on every ship suddenly erupt in brilliant, streaking vector lights as the four Kaigun warships return fire. Battle is engaged.

Prismatic beams shoot from dozens of laser batteries on twisting warships on both sides, missing or hitting as luck or skill or angled certainties of AI targeting systems decide, only to be distorted by ship and missile vectors, relative distances and speeds, fuzzy angles and velocities. Mathematics is more important than any tactics now, but human skill and courage count for something too. More than something. They count for a helluva lot. It's not all physics and machines.

Three *red* rays from *Resolve* glance blows off strong plate armor of the Kaigun flagship, KG *Karlsruhe.* The *daisa* on the frigate rolls his ship as it scuds, shooting each battery he has on the uproll. Undamaged by *Resolve*, he hammers back with all available lasers as the next ship enters clear electronic sights of his targeting computers. He's really good. "A godsdamn buckaroo," Magda swears under her breath. "Just what we didn't need."

A lucky shot from *Tyco Brae* cuts inboard on *Lubeck*, right inside the line of its bulwarks and hull, penetrating to the Engine Room and severing key optic control cables. *Lubeck* loses thrust controls but keeps up an intense *green* fire even as it drifts off the blocking line.

"She's listing bad," Weps calls over.

"We can knock her out with another volley!"

"Let her go!" Magda orders. "Kills don't matter. Concentrate fire on the other ships. We're scoring hits, but not on their engines or quantum gear. Aim for the com masts, too."

KG *Braunschweig* takes the brunt of intense firing coming from *Alpha*. Two direct laser strikes from *Resolve* sheer its conning tower, wrecking its com gear and tearing apart the quantum drive. That vital equipment is poorly located and also underarmored in this KG frigate class, which is a near masterpiece of bad peacetime design. Major flaws are common in warships, even inherited from class to class over decades as peacetime mistakes not yet exposed by battle infest the most complex machinery ever built. So it is that a puff of demagnetized plasma is released from containment in *Braunschweig*'s erupted quantum computer, poorly mounted outside the main armor, to melt a ball shaped gouge atop the conning mast. A direct hit from *Asimov* next shakes the frigate astern, taking out its aft battery, ending 23 young Grün sailor lives in an instant incineration.

The frigates fight back, missing or hitting Krevan ships too, in a pageant dance of light-and-death flashing inside the long dark, cold umbra of the Wasp. *Resolve* loses her top rear turret to a clever Parthian shot from *Karlsruhe*, which fires underside batteries as she rolls 360° back upright and then away. Ten jacks and seven jennies serving at combat stations in the exploded turret die in an instant, but *Resolve* takes no maneuvering hit or engine or major structural damage.

Forming an outer leg of the *Alpha* tetrahedron, *Tyco Brae* shields the two thin skinned troopships around the first 'S' curve. It escapes with a bad fright and scored outer armor from three glancing hits from *Braunschweig*, which is floundering now but still gamely in the fight.

It's *Asimov* that gets the worst of it for the Krevans, starting with two direct hits from the skilled under gunners on *Karlsruhe*. The first direct hit shudders and buckles a section of hull on her luff side. Collapsing bulkheads crush 42 soldiers who are jammed into a small mockmeat pantry, trying to stay out of the way of sailors 'fighting the ship.' They die in a flurry of instantly overcooked sausages and scorched black chops and burned cheese, inside clouds of seared garlic.

Jan is sealed in the next compartment. He survives unhurt, curious as to why he smells strong garlic, worried about the fouler odor of scorched protein. Seven of the 42 dead fighters hail from Madjenik, tough old hands of the *Battles of Pilsudski Wood* and *The Crater*. They're overflow from *Resolute*, where Zofia berths with the majority of the new 1st Battalion. The rest are Toruń garrison troops, reassigned to newformed 3rd Battalion of Wysocki's Wreckers.

A second strike by *Karlsruhe* wounds many on *Asimov*: the purser, purser's mate, the chief warrant officer, and 13 ratings. Dead are the master chief petty officer and two oldtimer tarpaulins, all three among the ship's 'windjammers.' A third punishing hit, from *Lubeck*'s cannon, tears apart all aft torpedo tubes and a firing station and kills 14 more crew. Lost catapult steam ejecting into space forms a pretty trailing cloud of powder ice snow.

Also lost are two intact, unarmed missiles that fall from racks into tumbling oblivion as the fight moves on ahead. Their AIs were not released from pre-firing lockdown and so are unable to reorient or stabilize uncontrolled spins. The AIs will watch Wasp 2B in wonderment for two Universal Standard Years, which is how long it will take the blue gas giant to capture the full fuel tubes and dormant warheads and draw them into its atmosphere. No one will witness their end. No one will see one AI signal a last salute to its fellow traveler as its only mate signs back, just before both dip into the swirling top clouds to exist and think and experience the wondrous Universe no more.

A fourth strike, the only one by poor top gunnery on *Raule*, cuts a sliding hole in *Asimov*'s hull just above the skeg. It nearly severs a key joint where the over keel or top ribbing meets the magnetic rudderpost that's critical in setting directional thrust of the main nozzle. But neither the fusion chamber nor the rudderpost is damaged. *Asimov* is wounded, nearly crippled, but it can still steer. It holds formation as *Alpha* finishes the first curve of the planned S-turn.

A minute later, struggling to draw away from the still hard shooting Kaigun frigates, *Asimov*'s Second Officer updates Tiva on the fourth hit. "Rudderpost bulkhead is broken but sealed, vacuum is contained, venting has ceased. Main engine is still online and functioning. No casualties, sir." He's wrong. Just before autoseals closed off all bulkheads in the ruptured section several chunks of broken metal, wood slab splinters from three shattered sycamore bunks, and a boy fell out into space.

***

It's Jarred Whitmore. Just past his 19th summer, he has pale blue eyes and light blond hair. His round face is more pleasant than handsome, gentle and distant. Usually, he wears a shy and embarrassed smile exactly like that of a ten year old offered a stick of cotton candy at a country fair, but unsure if he can or should take it from a stranger. Now he's falling into void.

Perversely, he liked training. Teamwork, the physicality, a sense of having earned his end-of-day meal and deep sleep. He thought he might make a good soldier. The trainers said so, too. They encouraged him not to wait until his one year required service was up. Recruited him hard, right out of basic. "You should go career, kid. You'll make a great soldier. Sign here."

So when he finished basic a year ago he signed for a full up, five year hitch in the KRA, saying: "I want to be a mortar man with Gold, like my father." He really enlisted full time to escape moiling forever in his too small village, wasting away on the lower coast of Northland.

Recruiters said like things to boys for millennia. To legionaries and Janissaries and Cossacks, to Coldstream Guards and the Foreign Legion and the Waffen SS. Then to Luna crater troops and Jovian War mercs. In the three big Orion Wars, the Oetkerts and long dead Dauran Emperors sold the same phrases and ideas to hundreds of millions. Every army has said pretty much the same things in every century. Why? Because the things they say work. Especially on boys.

Armies know how to push the buttons of bored youths who want adventure and offworld travel, and above all, a higher purpose in their lives. Boys barely interested in girls or too shy to score a simple date. Not interested in women yet, or scared of women. Not ready to be serious about anything, who can't resist the ancient, discordant sound of a recruiting drum. It works for girls, too. Outside the misogynist Imperium, they play snare drums to lure in girls as well these days.

War came before Jarred was ready. His platoon was wiped out when armtraks broke through his piece of MDL, 60 klics south of where Madjenik was also overrun that same day. One drove right over his head as he ducked to the bottom of a slit trench. His two best friends were killed. He saw them die. One shot, the other one crushed under ultrasteel tracks. So he ran, for days. Lost and alone. Lying still under a simple camo sheet when he heard Jabo or Raptor engines in an unseen sky, thinking they could still see him. Or worse, hearing armtraks and strange voices shouting one field over, then a scream of terror and *click clack.*

After ten days of fearful wandering he sat crying uncontrollably and alone in Pilsudski Wood. He had no food or water and didn't know what to do. A pretty lieutenant with apple hair found him squatting in a soiled and torn uniform. He was hiding from her under an immense redwood tree root, the whole tree rising 200 meters tall and 35 in girth. He had wet tears and dried muck on his face. He pointed his maser at her chest, but he was too scared to pull the trigger. She slapped the barrel away angrily and ordered him to his feet. "Follow me, soldier."

That was it.

Nothing more.

No words of comfort

Just a shouted "get on your feet right now!" when he hesitated to come out from behind the giant root and take a water canteen she held out to him. It said '*RIK Engineering Corps, 10th Armored.*' He thought that was strange.

With one curt command, Jarred Whitmore, once of 7 Lotus Street, Portwen Village, Northland, Planet Genève, joined Madjenik Company, joined Wysocki's Wreckers. Then he walked with his new company all the way to Toruń, starting from Pilsudski Wood. He somehow survived pursuing fires and bombs in the Old Oak Forest. He lingered as long as he could while crossing the sweet bio boundary of honeysuckles and african moons that led to the ash lands of Toruń Woods, until the pretty lieutenant told him to haul his ass across.

Jarred doesn't know if his parents are alive or dead, back in Portwen. He has thought about his mother a lot since the war started and they were separated. Especially when he stepped from the Old Forest into the wondrous botanical barrier before the ash. The floral scents transported him to his mother's garden, carefully tended in front of her modest cottage. Then and always, the red haired lieutenant barked at him to wake up and walk straight. She was always shouting.

His spirits sank with everyone else's as Madjenik marched parallel to the dead on the Old Forest Road, just to avoid its haunting host of ghosts. They followed anyway. All the way to where he fought at *The Crater*, so that he could march over the bridge and under Toruń's berm. That's why they said he had to do it, to kill that man. What did he know? He didn't want to get left behind or yelled at.

He knows that he's a real mooncalf who's always behind somehow. He was left out of scatter fights in Pilsudski Wood but he's sure he fought well at *The*

Crater, his first real action. He thought he might have killed a man outside a bunker there, but now he's not so sure. The apple lieutenant said the guy was already dead when Jarred blew his face and head off, getting brains all over his already filthy weaves. He fired down into a bunker right after that and is sure he heard terrible screams inside. He didn't like to think about it afterward.

There was so much shouting and red madness in *The Crater* he can hardly remember it. He never knew what to say when admiring people asked him later: "Were you really there?" So he said nothing. '*They seem to think they know about it anyway, better than I can remember.*'

Two days ago, in a warm Toruń hostel, he gently kissed farewell to the first and only girl he ever slept with. It was the end of the most wonderful day of his life, a tender night for two lost children of Genève, overwhelmed by war. She cried forever when he told her he couldn't beg, borrow or pilfer a place for her beside him on *Asimov*.

"Fighters only, no girlfriends, no exceptions." His ginger CO snapped at him, repeating the order he knew came straight from General Constance. The new major had that look. She brooked no argument.

"She's a *major* now. That's a real big deal," he told the girl. "I have to obey." Then he kissed her a last time. On the outside Shipyard walkway. Tears in his eyes, fear and love in hers.

Jarred is thinking about the crying girl he left behind in Toruń when the leeside fight starts between *Alpha* and the four Kaigun frigates. He's strapped into a sticky top bunk, but he's not wearing a vacuum suit. There aren't any, or not enough; not for so many KRA packed onboard. He lies still as the battle begins, listening to *Asimov's* fine guns and keeping out of the way. Then a flash of blinding *green* light opens a sudden hole above him. The belt on his bunk breaks and he *whooshes* out into space. He's "gone drifting," as swabbies say of anyone lost overboard.

It happens in an instant. Cold bites at all his exposed bits: face, fingertips, ears. His nose dries out rather than ices up as he expects. The last thing he ever smells is pine sap, as he's *whooshed* out the hole and a small gust pushes up his open collar, over his chin, into his nostrils. It's the last air he'll ever breathe.

His first thought is startlingly obvious. '*I'm outside the ship! How?*' Next comes astonishment that *Asimov* is vanishing from sight. It's no more than a small blue dot of receding plasma thrusters, growing ever smaller and dimmer. '*Stop! Why are you leaving me here?*' Too late. The tiny blue light snuffs into black.

"Come back!" It's a wholly unsuccessful effort to shout, but it saves him for a moment. Had he held his breath instead, his lungs would now be bursting apart from pressure. As it is, the little bit of air that's left inside is fast expanding. It's starting to tear his saccular thoracic tissue. '*Ohooo, my chest really hurts.*'

It's a stupid, useless way to die, with no greatness or sweetness or meaning in it. Jarred knows it. In a rare flash of metaphysical insight he concludes that the Universe is a place of infinite messiness and infinite mediocrity. Although he does like all the flowers. Ten seconds more and he'll lose all higher mental functions. '*How interesting! Space smells blue, not black.*'

Water in all unprotected soft parts begins to vaporize. His neck, face, and hands swell. He doesn't dry freeze instantly despite the -3° Kelvin temperature of shadowed space around him. There's no medium in the vacuum for fast heat loss by convection, so he suffers only slow loss by radiation transfer. His body core remains warm as his mind drifts away. As all moisture on his tongue boils away into vacuum he discovers tiny, rough and round projections in his gaping mouth that he never knew existed. The new asperities match his rising asperity of mood, his bitter anger and rough bewilderment that this can be happening. '*Why to me?*'

He starts to cry. His tears form little ice balls that cling in his eyes in zero gravity. Each new tear freezes over the first, building an ice pearl in each eye. When the surface water on his pale blues evaporates his pupils freeze and crack. His light is forever spent '*ere a seventh of his days in this dark world and wide.*' The onset of blindness brings with it certainty. '*I'm dying.*'

Anger passes as swiftly as it arrives and for a moment Jarred feels oddly calm. Like the time when he was three and almost drowned in a tidal pool off the quiet beach near his home. The experience filled him with curiosity rather than panic while it was happening. He felt oddly detached, until an arm reached down into coursing surf to lift him up and out. Only when he recognized the frightened, sweetly reassuring face of his beloved mother did he feel fear flood back. Her arms encircled and rescued him, and her hands rubbed warmth back into his shaking, goosebumped little body. No strong arm catches him now, pulls him out of the starry surf into warm comfort of the disappeared dot that *Asimov* is become. He rolls over and over in the planetary umbra, blind to the dark disk that looms above him filling a tenth of the sky or more. '*I'm alone. I'll die all alone. Mother!*'

Now he feels it, the first mortal pain. It's gas distention. His gut expands, bloating his once flat belly where the girl laid her head after they finished making love and he gently stroked her raven hair until they both fell asleep. On his one transcendent day of days and night of nights. An even sharper pain tears right across his chest. His calm passes as fervid stabbing swells to fill all his personal universe. Acute, overwhelming. A hyperinflating crucible of torment with no purpose beyond torment. A few seconds more of this severest trial of his life and Jarred Whitmore loses consciousness, never to think or feel or love or live again.

Normal gas exchange in his blood reverses, dumping oxygen from his organs and brain. He's still alive but unaware that his skin is turning a wan blue, in contrast to the pale oak of his crisp new KRA uniform. In a minute his heart stops beating, blood stops circulating, and it and he start to cool. Half-a-minute more and sweet young Jarred dies of vacuum asphyxiation.

***

War in space is clean.

The dead don't bother to come back from there.

Don't impose goo and corrupt bones on the living.

Don't ask for solemn burial or cremation.

They don't accuse in open coffins.

Demanding from us false words.

Insisting on torrents of our tears.

They float away to a far distant country.

Lost forever in blue frozen permanence.

***

Madame Janine Whitmore is very much alive. She's held under *preventive confinement* in a RIK detention camp, a special one built for relatives of known holdout fighters. She was moved there after the Pilsudski Wood ambush of 10th Armored's scouts. Grün occupation police tell her that her son's in the forest, that he's "a filthy bandit." They order her to make a memex broadcast calling on him to surrender. She does, but only because she wants him to come home.

She doesn't believe it's true, what they say about her Jarred. Neither does Jarred's father, Monsieur Tadeusz Whitmore. He's quite sickly but cares for Janine well. They don't live in Portwen anymore. They live instead in Hut #3, Quad 7, Row 14. They think of Jarred daily.

A few days after they're moved to the camp a widow joins them who always smells a bit like garlic soup. She swears to its medicinal properties, praising the Buddha for small pleasures like garlic in this world. She was brought to the camp from a small farm where she was struggling to hang on by herself, trying to bring in the harvest without her dead husband or missing son. He's away in the war somewhere, with Gold Division. Or maybe he's dead. Anne-Marie Wysocki is grateful for the roof and company. She and Janine grow quite close.

They'll carry on living as best they can, never knowing what befell their sons. They're not listed in the long scrolls of dead and captured posted by the occupiers at every village hall and on the heavily censored memex. What Genèvens call '*Sacrifice at the Gate*,' the RIK and awful new GovNeb calls '*Victory at the Toruń Berm*.' So many were incinerated by plasma or cremated after the 'Sacrifice,' some days they'll think their sons really are dead. And they'll weep.

It's hard to accept, with no bodies to keen over and grieve as motherhood and Nature require. Like Beowulf's mother, these two prematurely aging women wait daily on news of lost sons at war. Like her, they are '*sore dreaded evil days will come, much carnage, war's alarms, captivity, ignominy, and the heavens swallow up the smoke.*' Toruń is shrouded in smoke.

RSU men watch Janine closely. She has to report to them in Toruń every week, but they never tell her why. Never say that her wicked son is the 'Ghost in the Wood.' They refuse to say if he lives or not. Even if they knew, they wouldn't tell her. They don't even tell their superiors that he's gone. Men are executed for a lot less that letting the Ghost escape.

Janine laments that she has no garden where she can grow fresh flowers to keep in a vase, reminding her of best times when gentle Jarred came home to her with scents of roses or lilies or a fistful of african moons he especially loved. She even misses tartly scented carnations.

She'll grieve when her husband Tadeusz is summarily executed six months after *Alpha* leaves, for "*attempting unlawful escape and violation of curfew.*" He'll step outside the thin, electronic boundary of the camp to buy a loaf of bread to bring home to a hungry wife and her best friend. And to seek out for the graying love-of-his-life news of her dear and missing son.

His friend, the Portwen baker, will be conscripted to bake for the detainees. He'll get to move about a bit, bringing in flour and salt and small supplies from town, get to meet people who come and go quietly after curfew. Tadeusz will go to see him to buy grained bread and ask his old friend the peripatetic baker "is there news about our son, Jarred? Or Anne-Marie's boy, Jan?"

Janine's appeal for mercy will be denied. Tadeusz will be shot by a camp execution party. Like his simple life, Tadeusz's needless death will leave no mark on the history of the Thousand Worlds of Orion or even on quiet Genève. Janine will miss him sorely, nonetheless.

Pickets

Alpha is in the second half of the 'S' turn, cutting behind the Kölns, ready to burn white hot in a final frantic burst as it emerges from the turn at all out speed to dive for the bohr zone. Captain Magda Aklyan barks orders as *Alpha* pulls past the short line of older Kaigun frigates.

"All warships. Aft missiles in short spread: *shoot!*"

"Missiles away, captain."

Three stubby missiles hurtle from rear tubes on *Resolve*. Two more bolt from *Tyco Brae*. The aft tubes on *Asimov* remain still and silent. *Asimov* can't shoot. Its aft tubes are shattered and twisted, and it's venting a comet tail of steam-snow from its broken catapults. Two inert missiles and large bits of its broken firing tubes and bulkheads are already tumbling out-of-control, on a two year journey to collide with cold blue Wasp 2B. They're already offering comfort to each other. Jarred Whitmore's frozen corpse is headed there as well, inside a companion cloud made of wooden bunk splinters, a hundred thousand shattered chips of white paint, and millions of harmless pellets from *Asimov*'s smashed aft gravel bins.

"All ships. Disperse aft canister. Two second delay. Full cones, *shoot!*"

It's a preemptive try to blunt return missiles from the *Kölns*, delayed so that the gravel won't interrupt *Alpha*'s five flying the other way. Two huge cones leave aft railguns on *Resolve* and *Tyco Brae*. Captain Tiva has serious damage back there and no aft tubes on *Asimov*, but he manages to spray a ragged spread of ceramic pellets from his partly blocked dispenser. Not a full cone, but not nothing.

Braunschweig, Karlsruhe, and *Raule* shoot single aft missiles after *Alpha* passes, and jags back onto a straight course to the LP, completing the 'S' and arriving at last on the other side of the blockading frigate line. Wounded *Lubeck* is drifting off the line, slow spinning without stabilizers. Its hard pressed crew is fighting too many onboard fires. She can't get off an aft shot.

Alpha will be out of range before the frigates reload their second volley, but it's not out of danger. Plasma cannon and lasers on all ships are engaging. Magda and her little fleet need to inflict much more damage as they run, to belay a hot pursuit into the bohr jump they plan to make, to *Boca do Inferno*.

Five torpedoes burning bright with fusion thrust are already closing distance to the line of frigates. They streak past the three incoming Grün missiles before the latter explode with brilliant multicolored splashes as they meet the dense canister cones. The instant evaporations are far enough away they do no damage to the fleeing Krevan ships.

Not so the other way. *Braunschweig* loses steering from a torp detonation 0.3 klics off her stern. But her maxim guns, basically short range canister dispensers, take out another one of *Resolve*'s missiles as it flies ahead of the much bigger gravel cones. It's a 'stubby,' looking rather like a too fat duck but still packing a massive destructive punch that threatens to annihilate *Braunschweig* if it hits. Without moving parts, the frigate's compressed steam tubes spray hundreds of thousands of quarter gram ice pellets per second. They're a standard intimate defense against AI homing missiles. Ultra short range. A 'last stand' sort of thing.

Karlsruhe takes heavy damage from Tiva's scraggy cone, which overheats and erodes parts of the aft hull. Frigates don't have strong dodgers directly aft as they do in front, to protect against forward microdust impact. *Karlsruhe* is holed badly, and starts venting gas and people. Magda grips the arms of her chair. '*Gods, we're been more lucky than good with our shooting, and theirs. OK, I'll take it. Now, if our luck can only hold up one more minute…*'

Karlsruhe evades *Resolve*'s missiles, but the contorted maneuvers required to do it overwhelm her main stabilizers, flipping her sideways into a hard spin, careering guns in crazy directions and confusing its AI targeting computers even more than its human gunners. The 'S' maneuver is working, confounding and capsizing an enemy commander, his crew and flagship.

'*One spinning out and two hurt and adrift! Émile is right. Köln frigates are walty ships! They flounder in too tight turns. Score another one for the kid. If we'd swung wide as common sense and the KRN book said, instead of tight like this, we'd be taking full broadsides now.*'

Only *Raule* is left in this fight. Its crew is skilled and no cowards. Although its inept top gunners only scored one hit on the initial pass, its old *daisa* is a shrewd and cunning captain. He evades the last two incoming missiles from *Tyco Brae,* using the same evasive maneuver to flip his ship 180° but without succumbing to *Braunschweig*'s walty fate, even though *Raule* makes the same hard turn. Now he has a forward missile and a loaded, medium chase gun hung below his prow.

Outnumbered 3:1 by more modern Krevan warships, a brave Kaigun crew and *daisa* boost at all out speed, pushing their fusion reactor to near critical and engaging all boosters. It works. *Raule* closes distance until it's almost inside the open bottom of *Alpha*'s tetrahedron. The *daisa* brings to bear his reloaded forward missile tube and low mounted chase gun. He has a single, clear shot at the smaller of the troopships, *Jutlandia.* All three warship escorts are ahead and to the flanks of the two troopships. He's caught out Magda and *Alpha* badly, with a clever and unexpected *loop-the-loop* followed by a sudden battlespeed boost to firing position.

"I have no working tubes aft and I'm all out of canister," reports Tiva from *Asimov.* For once, there's no hint of fun in Tiva's voice. He's all business now, a professional navy man. Other ships are frantically reloading aft but can't get a shot in time. They, too, are out of gravel. Magda told them to use it all in the decisive 'S' turns, to hold nothing back fore or aft.

"*He's in the lane!*" Émile shouts the terrible news to Magda.

"Settle down, XO. Keep reporting, but do it calmly."

Magda doesn't feel calm, either. She searches desperately for a solution, but can't find one in the time left. She grips the arms of her command chair, waiting for the inevitable death of the exposed troopship. Raging within at its killer and her order to use all canister on one gambit.

The *daisa* holds fire to pointblank range, confident of his superior position and certain the two newly painted civilian ships ahead are still unarmed. Certainly not with anything to hurt his well armored warship. He wants an absolute kill shot with his sole remaining missile, before *Raule* bails and flees the angered escorts, throwing off flares, decoys and derision as it flies.

He probes the troopship with an acid *blue* laser, registering a burning hit on *Jutlandia*'s jury rigged afterguard. The poorly fitted plates fly apart, exposing the liner's main nozzle and engine vitals and its soft, interior civilian hull. There's no way for pregnant *Jutlandia* to defend herself. She only mounts a small forward facing, and thus useless, cannon. Her escorts turn hard and fast, but they can't shift relative position in time or take out the mortal threat behind.

Raule's fierce *daisa* focuses on his final approach and making his kill shot. He'll send a raging missile's iron indignation tearing up *Jutlandia*'s naked vent to explode the ship from the inside out, aborting bloody contents of its womb into space. In a corner of his vision he sees the larger troopship adjusting its nose, abandoning its little sister. Readying to run for the LP at flank speed.

'*Fat, slow, and with a cowardly civilian crew angling away from my chase position. Oh, to have a second missile tube!*' But he doesn't, so he lets the bigger troop carrier go in favor of the sure shot, the killing of an ungainly, pregnant Krevan bitch waddling right in front of him. It fills his tactical screen. '*A fat ship locked in my sights is worth a...*'

In fact, KRN *Warsaw* has a fine naval crew working under the aggressive Captain Tura Dan. It's not running at all. It's realigning its stern, not its prow. The quick, angular turn-in-place imparts an illusion of readying to run that's entirely immaterial to the real intent of its captain. In a moment's calm courage, *Warsaw*'s stern points directly back at *Raule.*

The old *daisa* wants to see *Jutlandia* in real time as he kills her, not through his scope. When he looks out his Main Scuttle, just before giving the order to rip open her full belly, he's startled to see what the other waddly liner is doing.

'*It isn't accelerating away at all.*'

'*Shit, it's braking! Why is it braking?*'

"Turn, turn! Get us out of here. *Turn!*"

As water is essential for all life planetside, so it is also for war in space. All warships and navies are wrapped around ice, as well as carrying internal fire.

Water is cheap, abundant, easily mined and stored anywhere and everywhere in a working warship. You can't leave home without it.

Water fills the space between the outer and inner hulls, shielding from cosmic radiation better than any other insulation or medium. You can't live without it.

Water lubricates and powers everything from hydrogen boosters to steam catapults to life support. It will even permit hydroponics, if the captain or crew has a thing for fresh veggies.

And if needs be, a ship's supercooled water and ice reserve can pack a real punch loaded in a basic kinetic cannon.

An ice gun, or *Hyper Velocity Projectile* rail cannon, shoots 100 kilo sabots of ice. Supercooled, superhard ice. It's beautifully simple. Each block is wrapped in a protective sabot fitted with small steering lasers controlled by a basic, passive guidance system. Its tiny lasers heat a small second packet of ice, separately mounted, to produce high pressure vapor. The steam is forced through petite nozzles to make minimal course corrections en route to target. No AI is needed. The process is elementary but the final effect on impact can be quite dramatic.

One advantage of an ice gun like the big one slung under *Warsaw*'s bloated belly is that superhard ice blocks convert to highly effective kinetic ammunition. Mass-squared-by-velocity at impact is the only thing that matters, not the simple chemical composition of the impacting mass.

Sabot ice rounds have no unstable, dangerously tricky plasma to contain in an electromagnetic chamber that just might fail in storage or transport. That makes ice guns exceptionally safe even for a fat, converted troopship. The great defect is that it's strictly a line-of-sight and short range weapon, powerful but not too smart. HVPs have to line up pretty much straight on target for a pointblank shot.

That's what *Warsaw*'s crew is doing with the old, reeve mounted, aft kinetic rail cannon, the ice gun slung under the liner's hull at Toruń Shipyard. Tura Dan is aligning it to fire sabot right into *Raule's* portentous Bridge. *Raule*'s captain sees the danger all at once, looming in his Main Scuttle and his personal future. He screams orders in rapid fire succession.

"Engine Room, *halt!*"

"Full reverse!"

"Back up! *Back up!*"

Too late. Sabot blocks hurtle down a frictionless magnetic coil tube hanging from a jury rigged rail system reeved below *Warsaw*. Ice hyperbullets emerge already traveling at maximum velocity. *Raule* has no chance to deflect, intercept or evade the incoming projectiles. The first sabot ice round is a 100 kilogram mass traveling at high speed. It's not micro dust or tiny ceramic pellets easily deflected by a heavy dodger. It smashes right through *Raule*'s prow dodger, cracking it wide open like a coconut hit with a heavy machete.

The next two hardened blocks break the Bridge apart with enormous impact energy, killing the *daisa* and First Officer with shock waves and chunks of free debris and shattered deck shrapnel. The next four rounds fly into the gaping hole already ripped into the Bridge, smashing into the Afterdeck and Bilge behind. More rounds make more holes as *Raule* buckles, shudders, then flips over. Internal boiler and reactor explosions rip an aft section off the ship.

As the frigate *Raule* snaps in two Magda recalls Tiva reciting an old verse, but twists it: '*Some say the world will end in fire, some say in ice. I know enough of war and hate to say that for destruction ice is also great, and will suffice.*'

"Well played, Captain Dan. Well played indeed."

Asimov stays with the troopships as *Resolve* and *Tyco Brae* vindictively pour energy and plasma fire into the gaping, crumbling ruin that was *Raule.* Some laser gunners are in hot blood at what they know its *daisa* was trying to do. They take it out on his crew, picking off and cutting apart yawls and even the smallest pods trying to escape the wreck, even slicing into three tiny figures flailing in open space after falling out wearing emergency vacuum suits.

Émile thinks the same thing he did while watching nine *Kölns* die off the inner moons, when war first came into his life and he gave Magda a battle plan that killed 2,000 enemy. '*What a foolish waste. War forces tragedy on some, black comedy on others, bloody murder on us all. No one can stay clean in filth like this.*' A harder thought follows, tripping on the heels of the first. '*Not all deaths in war are tragic. Some lives are improved by death.*' He means the cruel *daisa*, who must have believed *Jutlandia* was a naked and unarmed civilian liner and was going to gut it anyway.

The Weapons Officer is not nearly so poetic. He can't get over how odd it is that a modern warship is destroyed by ice, as if still blind sailing an arctic sea and hitting a floating mountain in the dark.

Magda let's it go on in silence for awhile, then breaks off the action. "Cease fire. All guns, all ships, cease fire. Now, all Alpha ships head at all out speed for the bohr zone. Prepare to jump."

With the last petty and pitiless revenge over, with the ruins of *Raule* falling behind and out of gun range, there's no enemy left between *Alpha* and the LP. *Alpha* is wounded but alive, as XO Émile Fontaine at the Navigation Station on *Resolve* locks the jump coordinates for RCW-138 in the quantum dyogram that links all five ships in the flotilla to one jumpmaster. He turns sharply on his heel and looks admiringly at Magda Aklyan.

“You did it, captain.”

“*We* did it, Mr. Fontaine.”

“Yes ma’am, all of *Alpha*.”

“But we’re not done yet.”

“No ma’am.”

“Where are those Zerstörers?”

“Seven contacts 1.4 minutes aft, relative to our speed and position.”

“And real time, if we proceed at max speed?”

“They’re 40.35 *flank speed* minutes behind.”

“Good. They can’t catch us until after we pass the Lagrange rim. We should jump hot as planned. We can’t afford to slow in order to glide into this one.”

“Agreed captain. All is ready. Jump codes are loaded.”

“All ships. Reform in *line astern* behind *Resolve*.”

Ten seconds.

Twenty seconds.

Forty seconds.

“All ships are astern of your flag, captain.”

“Mr. Fontaine, reconfirm quantum codes. Be ready to bohr out of this system in twenty minutes.” When briefed on her mission by General Constance, Captain Magda Aklyan seriously doubted that she’d ever get to this point. Ever make it past the cruiser heavy orbital patrol over Genève. Ever avoid pickets lined up at Lagrange points all the way to the L2. Yet here *Alpha* is, limping to the L2 but intact. About to jump into exile, to make permanent war.

'*Well, intact if you don't count four ships I lost along the way. Is my dear friend dead? Did any Beta ship get out? Is François just drifting dust? Maybe someone from Beta got out, and like us is running for sanctuary and an uncertain future in far off and farfolk systems.*'

She has three escorts and the two critical troopships, flying tight and making ready for a hot glide into the deep bowl of the leeside L2. She looks over to Émile, glad to have him beside her, proud of his abilities, and oddly needing the young man's affirmation in a way that surprises her. "First Officer, all things considered, might we say that this was a good day?"

"Yes ma'am. A better day than we had a right to expect. We beat the odds."

"The losses the garrison took at the berm to get us here … were they worth it? Speak your mind, Émile." Her use of his *prénom* is unusual. First time she's done it, actually.

"Yes ma'am, I think they were."

"Why?"

"This is war. We would do the same, I think. Sacrifice for Krevo to get the *Exodus* ships away. Some of us may have just done so. *Beta* group, I mean."

She flinches. '*Damn, he's not shy about speaking hard truths.*' But she says: "Thank you for your candor, Mr. Fontaine. I think only time will tell if you are right, if we were right. And we're not done yet."

"No ma'am."

"We've not made sanctuary, and there are seven Zerstörers chasing us and closing fast that may still choose to follow us through the jump. In that case, we'll be in an even harder fight than the one we just finished."

"Yes ma'am, we will. And in less than 30 minutes now."

She activates *Bridge to Bridge* coms and gives the order, trying not to dwell on where she's taking them next. After all they've been through already. After surviving '*The Gauntlet*,' as Émile will dub the fight in his log, naming the hard escape by the little flotilla that ran against all odds from Genève past the Wasp, then down to the L2 where it's now power gliding to a jump. '*After all that, I must take them to Boca do Inferno, into the "Mouth of Hell." May the gods forgive me, for my ships and crews may not.'*

"Attention all ships. Emergency blackout conditions. I want light seals on Main Scuttles and every side scuttle and viewport. Shut down all light detectors and outside viewers. No one is to be within two meters of a scuttle or screen. Bridge personnel, don luminosity protectors *now*."

***

Two minutes.

Ten minutes.

Thirty minutes.

"We're over the edge of the Lagrange area, ma'am."

"Gravity echo detected."

"Folded singularity identified."

"Jump codes confirmed and locked in."

"*Resolve*'s quantum drive has *Alpha* navigation."

"You have the helm, Mr. Fontaine."

"Yes ma'am."

"Take us into the singularity."

***

When the interrogators come back into the prisoner's cell he hears it in their voices. They're quaking with fear of their superiors, and with fury and engorged rage toward him. That's why he knows that he has won. He knows also that the tale of his courage will never be told; that it will die here in this cell with him, and with General Constance lying bleeding and torn outside the Berm Gate. Beaten and burned and crippled, he's an utter ruin of what he was. But he's not bowed or broken. He's content, feeling in their blows and hearing in their impotent rage that his general's plan has worked. *Alpha* has escaped.

He smiles through torn lips and jagged, broken teeth as he bites into his cheek, ingesting a suicide flake hidden there from cavity searches. It releases a tiny poison microdot masked with artificial DNA that mimicked his own, to fool RSU doctors and guards. It tumbles inside a lump of pulpy tissue onto his tongue and dissolves, instantly sending complex poisons coursing through his blood, to reach his stomach and lungs, to stop his heart and seize up his brain. Guards alerted by frothing blood around his mouth can't get to him fast enough to stop this brave man's escape from their cruelty. Can't prevent him dying a free man.

His tormentors and interrogators will think little of him or about him from now on. He's just another dead prisoner to them, to the Imperium occupiers of Genève. One of tens of thousands they have already executed. His unwashed and unwanted corpse will burn after the berm is breached and Toruń is partly put to the sack. They don't know. They can't understand. If told, they would never believe what this man's last act of defiance has achieved. What the broken, bloody nobility of his sacrificial death means for them and the war. It means so much more than their crude and unfree imaginings can conceive or reach. It means everything.

Just as Amiya Constance's death and the sacrifice of all those soldiers at the berm means so much more than military victory or defeat on one small, not-so-important agrarian world. More than the gray men know or believe as they scuttle sideways in crab service to an oily tyrant who smells of plots and conspiracies and insecure vanity, of murder and power lust. and spills of spiced snuff.

They think and they believe that they've won the war on Genève and across all the Krevan worlds. They have no idea that they've only won its first and smallest battle. No idea of what is coming to Orion, of what rough beast is unleashed by what they've done and will do on conquered worlds that were once the peaceful and neutral United Planets of Krevo.

The prisoner's death, and Amiya's, and Jarred's, and all the others, means the war Pyotr thinks he has won will now go on and on. That more Krevans like the lonely prisoner and defiant Amiya Constance, more fighters and crews like those of *Alpha* and other *Exodus* fleets leaving all the Krevan worlds will make peace no more, forever. Will find a way to make war against the Imperium, forever.

Jan and Zofia and all Krevans will make war until it courses up and down all Orion. War until they can stop wandering far off seas and alien worlds to return home with armies at their side, engorged with atrocities remembered and repaid in kind, full of hate nursed and matured in exile.

War across all Orion, until...

...Ulysses returns to kill them all.

The story continues in

Volume III

The Orion War

Jahandar

Sample

Röhm Krump is standing rigidly erect at the edge of the redwood oval starmap absorbing information with only half his dexterous mind, watching Jahandar's interactions with the other half. He's supremely intelligent and capable, which is why his lethal perversions are so truly terrifying. He's rubbing his hands together unconsciously, a gesture that enhances his inhuman, stick insect impersonation. General Chima Azikiwe has never seen him in person before today. He finds him so physically repellant he takes an involuntary half step back. '*It's true what they say. He looks like a praying mantis about to seize an unwary fly.*'

It was Jahandar who first said that Krump "smells like a praying mantis." Everyone laughed out loud, to please the Tyrant and praise his endless wit. But as they laughed each kept one eye on Krump, knowing he would remember. Some thought about the jibe later and realized they had no idea what a praying mantis smells like, or if it smells at all. Except to exude odors of its recently eaten prey.

So it is with Röhm Krump. His odor changes with every killing, with each wing plucked human fly he ends, slowly yet forever, in purpose built torture cells far beneath his private chambers. Azikiwe sees it all right away. He decides to tell Vashti tonight that Krump smells of torment and flies.

He's all angles and bone with little flesh and yellow insect eyes, dead to any expression except when they light with sadism. Then they flash the cruelty of the millennia, across all the thousand histories of Orion. Or is it even longer? Is mass murder the inevitable end product of human evolution? Are we no more than mantises, praying as we wait for prey? Is cruelty built into the hierarchy of devouring that Nature bred in ancient salt seas, from the moment on the origin world when the first single celled ancestor of choanoflagellates chose to pursue ruthless predation over photosynthesis to survive and thrive?

Maybe. But this is still a special kind of murderer. Krump isn't moved by the necessary ferocity of the predator who must hunt to live. His bloodlust is novae beyond the base predation of the shark or jackal or wolf. Despite his insect appearance, despite his odd look, Krump is fully and inescapably human. Red wet and cruel without any need. He kills simply because he can. Because he loves it.

He betrayed and assassinated his way to the pinnacle of his chosen profession in the terror police. Second only to Jahandar, he inspires cold fear across Dauran worlds. He's brilliant and well educated, and a fine conversationalist on topics from art to xenology. In private settings he can be funny and suave. He's also a brutal sadist who plots and thrills to killing above all else.

He keeps in his pocket a pair of smooth, dead eyeballs. He reached in and pulled them out of his predecessor's face, just before he let the last Director of SHISH finally die, pleading for a morsel of mercy he never showed his own victims. They're smaller than pool balls, as dry and hard as marble. He had them lacquered, kiln dried and polished. They're exquisite. Blue-on-blue inside bulbous white, with thin red filaments threading behind perpetually terror stricken pupils.

When not rubbing his hands together or wielding a sachi blade, Krump fondles the pair of hard eyeballs with his left hand thrust deep in his black robe pocket. He *klacks*! them whenever he speaks, his right hand gesticulating wildly. It's a way of underlining words his long right arm and thin fingers draw in air. He's totally unaware of the habit or that it adds to his insect menace.

Krump is urbane, sophisticated and lethal. He pairs the absurd and the rational like a cloistered priest. He's crafty, shrewd, penetratingly direct in conversation, chillingly cruel in interrogation cellars. He overwhelms with torrents of words, niagaras of verbiage plunging over listeners, drowning them in whirlpools and undertows and whirling eddies of lies. Once he sees them grow exhausted, he strikes. He may be the most brilliant man in Daura, if not in all Orion.

His appearance and mannerisms are anything but those of a murderer of millions, a sadist who takes cruelty to such exquisite depths he proudly thinks of himself as "a high artist of pain, a toreador of torment." He's always relaxed and impeccably polite to victim-guests, serving chamomile tea or cappuccino or a fine red wine while looking men straight in the eye and smiling, all the while knowing that in the next ten minutes he will chop them into hog food. He oozes charm.

Like Mephistopheles.

"*Vozhd*, my Black Robes will sniff out and sweep clean any resistance to liberation of these foreign shit worlds." Krump always quotes Jahandar's coarse profanities back to him. It's like using the old title "Boss." It flatters by paying homage to the autocrat's gang days on Sachi.

Klack! klack! Is it Krump's pocket eyeballs? Or Jahandar's hobnailed and cloven feet? It's the eyeballs: Krump's hand is in his pocket.

"I have 200,000 hounds primed to hunt." He means night dogs, most vicious of terror specialists in SHISH. For Jahandar they race the narrow city streets of Dauran worlds on two man gyro bikes, course over the countryside in six man hovers, splattering murder everywhere.

"I'll cleanse your first wave worlds of filth, ready them for absorption into the Empire." Suddenly, the great and terrible General Commander Röhm Krump blanches. The head of SHISH and therefore the second most powerful man in all Daura, who fears no man save one, shows a flicker of fear across his face.

Klack! klack! He quickly corrects. "*Umm*, I mean the Dauran Commons." A pregnant silence falls over the group at the starmap. Everyone inhales, waiting to see if teetering Krump will fall from on high over so small a thing.

He wouldn't be the first. Jahandar controls the dangerous moment with a deeper, long silence that has a distinct menace all its own.

"Sorry boss." Krump preempts. Sometimes even Jahandar makes the error, breaking his own capital law by lapsing into pre-Revolutionary language, such as using 'Great Dauran Empire' for 'Revolutionary Commons,' or 'Caesarium Selo' in place of 'People's House of the Revolution.'

Still, he'll remember Krump's useful slip. File it away in the deep, unforgiving bureaus of his torture chamber mind. '*What did he say? My hounds, My Shishi? The dirty little shit has been chief of my secret police for seven years. I never kept a chief so long before. Why do I leave him in that place?*' With a start, Jahandar suddenly worries that he forgot to kill Krump before today. Hadn't he meant to?

Printed in Great Britain
by Amazon

51806949R00151